High Country Nocturne

Books by Jon Talton

The David Mapstone Mysteries
Concrete Desert
Cactus Heart
Camelback Falls
Dry Heat
Arizona Dreams
South Phoenix Rules
The Night Detectives
High Country Nocturne

The Cincinnati Casebooks
The Pain Nurse
Powers of Arrest

Other Novels
Deadline Man

Short Story
"Bull" in Phoenix Noir

High Country Nocturne

A David Mapstone Mystery

Jon Talton

Poisoned Pen Press

Copyright © 2015 by Jon Talton

First Edition 2015

10 9 8 7 6 5 4 3 2 1

Library of Congress Catalog Card Number: 2014958039

ISBN: 9781464203985   Hardcover
        978146420 4005   Trade Paperback

Poisoned Pen Press
6962 E. First Ave., Ste. 103
Scottsdale, AZ 85251
www.poisonedpenpress.com
info@poisonedpenpress.com

Printed in the United States of America

For Susan

Chapter One

In the end, the truth was almost beside the point.

Chapter Two

Ten o'clock. Two o'clock. I knew the drill.

It had been many years since I had been pulled over by the police, almost as many years since I was a young deputy sheriff doing traffic stops myself. When I did, I wanted to see the driver's hands right where mine rested now.

Ten o'clock and two o'clock on the steering wheel. Left hand at ten. Right hand at two. Where I could be sure he wasn't concealing a gun.

Extra points if he had shut down the engine and held his driver's license and vehicle registration.

Unless the driver was being extra careful because he was a bad guy.

Then I would be on extra guard.

Traffic stops were scary, especially if they were on lonely roads after midnight. It was you and the driver and anybody else in the car and the darkness. Backup might be miles away.

You might think you were pulling over a driver to tell him his taillight was out. Unless the driver had killed his girlfriend or robbed a Circle K five minutes before and didn't know you were only being Deputy Helpful.

When I was a rookie, these stops were the only part of the job that scared me.

Now I was the driver and Sharon Peralta, my partner's wife, sat beside me.

My hands rested at ten and two, and the digital clock read one o'clock in the morning.

I had taken a chance roaring north out of Phoenix on Interstate 17 in her silver Lexus IS 250C convertible.

I took a chance doing ninety-five when the posted speed limit was twenty miles-per-hour lower. With budget cuts, traffic stops by the Department of Public Safety—the highway patrol—had plummeted so low that people started calling it the "shadow patrol."

But the shadow patrol nailed me as I climbed out of Camp Verde. Red lights and blue lights followed me as I took an exit that led down a cut to a crossroads. I pulled off the pavement onto the dirt ten yards before a stop sign.

A spotlight swept the inside of the car, then focused on our rearview mirror. That was standard procedure to keep the occupants of the stopped vehicle from seeing into the police car behind them.

I had already used the button to roll down the window when I heard the officer's voice.

"Do you know why I stopped you, sir?"

A Southern accent washed through my ear canal.

"I was speeding."

A flashlight beam flashed across the interior, lingering on our laps and our feet. She asked for my driver's license and registration. I handed them over.

She stood to the rear of the door so I couldn't see her. Her tactics were sound.

"Please stay inside your vehicle, sir. And please shut off your lights."

One didn't hear many Southern accents in Arizona today, even though many of Phoenix's early settlers were ex-Confederates. That accent had two broad and mutually exclusive presentations, hick and high-class magnolia. She was definitely the latter.

I said, "I'm sorry, Sharon."

As if she hadn't been through enough already.

All the lights on the DPS cruiser shut down.

Just a few years ago, we would have been left in profound darkness, with only the highway, miraculously blasted through the rugged country, as a reminder of modernity. This was the exit to Montezuma's Castle National Monument, seven-hundred-year-old cliff dwellings. At night, nobody would be here. The darkness would be primeval.

Now a tribal casino sat on a bluff to the east, polluting the high desert sky. If you asked me, it was a monstrosity. But nobody asked me. Nobody had asked me about adding five million people to the state since I was a child. I shook my head.

"Who is Sharon Peralta?" The cop had returned, stepping lightly.

"I am." Sharon leaned forward and squinted into the flashlight beam. Her eyes were tired.

"Is this your vehicle, ma'am?"

She said that it was.

"Do you know this man?"

"Yes, he's a friend."

"Sir, please step out of the car. Ma'am, you stay here."

I had been afraid this might happen, so I came out with it.

"I'm armed."

"Why is that, sir?" The magnolia debutante voice didn't seem stressed. And it was not as if she could ask to see my permit. Not in Arizona, which had some of the most liberal gun laws in the country.

"I'm a private investigator."

She asked me where the gun was and I told her it was in a holster on my belt. Then she told me to place it slowly on the dash and I did, carefully, barrel forward, hand away from the trigger. My familiar Colt Python .357 magnum revolver. But with the four-inch ribbed barrel, it was a mean-looking firearm. Her flashlight beam lingered on it.

"Anything else?"

Be respectful. That was another part of the drill. "No, ma'am."

It was even the truth. I didn't take time to bring Speedloaders with extra ammunition or a backup piece after the phone call woke me at nine minutes after midnight Saturday morning. I was sleepy and in a hurry and on the drive up into the High Country, I thought this had been a rash move. Now, I was glad to have only one firearm to explain.

The flashlight clicked off.

"Please step out of the car." Now her voice had lost its lilt. Or maybe I was being nervous. One thing was sure; I was wide-awake.

I opened the door and slid out, dropping my feet onto the hard-packed dirt and getting my first look at the DPS cop.

She was more than a head shorter than me, dressed in the standard uniform: tan slacks, tan long-sleeved shirt, shoulder patch in the shape of the state and colors of the state flag, seven-point gold star above her left pocket.

Thanks to the casino's neon, I could see that her hair was strawberry blond, tied back in a bun. Her features seemed attractive, even the slightly weak chin. Her expression was camouflaged by shadows. Age? Around thirty.

"Walk to the back of the car and put your hands on the trunk, please, palms down."

I did as she asked. The cold made me shiver. We were three thousand feet higher than Phoenix, where it was resort weather and the wrecking ball of summer only a bad memory. That was why Lindsey had given me my leather jacket. But it was in the back seat and I only had on a T-shirt, jeans, and athletic shoes.

The metal of the trunk conducted the cold through my hands, adding to the discomfort. It must have been a quiet night for her to take this much time. Or she recognized Sharon's last name. That might be problematic. I wished she would write the ticket, give me the lecture, and send me away with a "drive safely, sir."

Instead, I heard a discomfiting snap and she told me to turn around.

Her gun was out, aimed at me.

It was pointed at my face.

In the academy, they call this aiming at "the lethal T" or the "fatal T." The T consisted of the eyes and nose, a shot guaranteed to kill instantly.

Officers are usually trained to shoot at a suspect's "body of mass," the torso. That is an easier, surer target. But more criminals are wearing body armor.

She was not in a combat shooting stance, with both hands on the weapon for stability. Instead, she held it confidently in one hand, her right. That was unusual.

Seeing her finger on the trigger heightened my concern.

This was something definitely not taught at the academy.

Officers learn to keep the trigger finger aligned with the side of the gun's lower receiver and slide—"ready to engage," as the instructors put it. This prevents an accidental discharge.

But there it was, the pistol staring me in the eyes, the officer's finger on the trigger.

This situation left me one cough or involuntary nerve spasm away from being shot and I wouldn't live more than a few seconds. No time for last words. Words like, "Tell my wife I love her." Or, "Why did you shoot me? I was unarmed."

It is impossible to speak after your face has been torn apart and a bullet acts out the laws of physics inside your skull. Impossible, when you are already dead.

This is your brain, Mapstone. This is your brain blown out of the back of your head all over the bumper of Sharon's fancy convertible.

"I'm not armed," I said, forcing my voice to remain calm, its cadence slow, as I raised my hands. "I am not posing any threat to you. Please take your finger off the trigger."

She didn't do as I suggested.

I studied the gun. It was a semi-automatic, black with intimidating lines. I couldn't identify the maker. It wasn't the Glock that was standard with police.

A tractor-trailer rig approached on the Interstate, grinding uphill toward Flagstaff. If only the truck driver needed to pull off and came down the cut and somehow broke the spell that had this officer in its grasp. But then the semi was gone and the world around us was quiet. Not a single gambler came or went from the casino.

The nation's sixth-largest city was only ninety miles south but it might as well have been on a different planet.

I had the tactical solutions of a can of cat food.

When I went through the academy too many years ago, I had learned how to disarm a shooter without having a gun myself. This involved stepping close inside her reach and doing a hard, straight-arm bar to dislodge the weapon. But she was too far away and I had never tried this desperate move in real life.

She seemed to read this thought and took one more step back, then crooked her arm close to her side, the gun still perfectly aimed. If the barrel were an eye, it could have winked at me. I raised my empty hands higher, feeling the slick between the T-shirt and my skin.

"Why are you doing this?" My mouth was so dry it had trouble forming the words.

She cocked her head as if about to answer, then thought better of it.

"I used to be a cop," I said. "I know how stressful a traffic stop can be."

The strawberry blond Sphinx stared at me.

"Maybe you read about me. David Mapstone. I solved cold cases for the Maricopa County Sheriff's Office."

She said, "I know who you are."

The way she said it told me she meant more than a name she'd read on my driver's license.

And my self-possession started to crack.

"Do we know each other? What's your name?" I couldn't make out her nametag or badge number.

Then she lowered pistol in the direction of my groin and smiled.

"Where...?" That was as far as she got.

A pair of headlights on high beams. A car coming off the Interstate, headed toward us. I squinted and turned my head aside as the glare grew more intense. The car stopped behind her cruiser and kept its lights on.

More than a few beats passed in silence, her hair a halo in

the backlights. I prayed it was another DPS unit and that an officer would talk her down.

She continued to face me. "Friends of yours?"

Now it was my turn to say nothing.

She slipped the gun back into its holster with one clean move and snapped it in place.

The pleasant drawl returned to her voice, as if the past five minutes had never happened. She handed back my license and registration.

"You drive safely, sir."

Within thirty seconds, she was gone, spewing dirt and rocks. My savior behind the high beams remained.

My tongue tasted dust as wobbly legs conveyed me to the car and I put the Python back in its holster.

One last time, I turned and stared at the headlights.

After a few minutes, once we were back on the highway, I found the same headlights following us a quarter mile behind. I didn't know who was inside, although I had a good guess. But I was certain they had saved my life.

Sharon looked me over. Sweat was coming through the T-shirt.

"Are you all right, David?"

"Sure."

"Really?"

"She let me off with a warning."

And how. I set the cruise control at seventy-five as the Interstate climbed and climbed toward Flagstaff.

Sharon stared at her lap, dark hair curtaining off her face, and said nothing more. This was unusual. Sharon was a master conversationalist. Weren't all shrinks talkers? And they wanted you to talk. We had much to discuss, in fact. But I didn't speak either, about what had happened minutes before at the traffic stop, about the telephone call that had brought us here, or everything that had come at us in the previous day. The silence was so profound that my breathing sounded like screams.

I silently replayed the scene by the side of the road. It was late. I had been awakened and forced to drive after a stressful day. The mind plays tricks.

But the finger on the trigger was no illusion.

And I replayed the angry metal click of the woman's holster. It bothered me for more reasons than the gun in my face.

The old Galco High-Ride holster that held my Python had a strip of leather that wrapped around the frame of the gun. It is called a retention strap, meant to keep an attacker from grabbing the gun and using it on you. I could get to the revolver easily by grasping the handle and moving my hand against the place the retention strap connected to the rest of the holster. It would come loose with a snap and I'd be ready to rock.

But that was old school.

I cursed aloud.

"What it is, David?"

"It's some inside baseball cop stuff. Probably nothing."

She didn't push it. It wasn't inside baseball. Inside cop world.

Snap.

No.

Most law-enforcement officers didn't use those retention straps now.

Manufacturers had advanced the security of holsters substantially so that it was much more difficult for the weapon to be taken in a struggle. It helped that the semiautomatic pistols cops carried had smooth butts, no exposed hammer like the Python's to accommodate.

I stared into the red lights of a truck several car-lengths ahead, then signaled and moved to pass.

Now cops carried holsters classified as Level 2, Level 3, and even Level 4, based on the degree of protection they provided. But almost all had one element in common—to unholster the gun, the officer moved the strap forward. In the more advanced holsters, the pistol must be properly gripped and a lever switched.

None of these regulation holsters made a snap.

"She wasn't..." I absently let the car slow down against the gravity of the mountain it needed to climb.

"What?" Sharon asked.

I pushed down the accelerator and we surged forward. "I was thinking. Always a surprising thing when I do it."

She laughed and I kept silent.

I was thinking that perhaps the DPS officer was old school like me and refused to adopt a new holster.

Thinking perhaps she was not a police officer.

She pointed the gun at my crotch and said, "Where…?" Where, what? Where were we going? Where was Peralta?

As the cold sweat stayed with me, another thought came. If I saw her again, it would once more be in darkness and I wouldn't get a second chance.

Sharon said, "Do you still get panic attacks, David?"

I ignored her and held my iPhone against the steering wheel, shakily texting Lindsey one character, an asterisk. I watched the iPhone screen as the message was delivered.

After a few tense seconds, Lindsey texted back. Another asterisk.

In our personal code, it meant one thing: leave the house immediately. Go.

Chapter Three

The blue and red police lights were visible even before I took the Ash Fork exit off Interstate 40—the vision of Dwight David Eisenhower flowing from Barstow, California, to Wilmington, North Carolina.

We descended onto a two-lane road, crossed a wash, and I pulled the car into a broad, flat lot surrounding what had once been a gas station. All that was left was a rectangular streamline moderne building, long-abandoned, with an office on one end and two garage doors on the other, with a single yellow streetlight burning above.

I pulled in behind a Yavapai County Sheriff's Department cruiser with its light bar flashing. Nobody seemed to notice us. The cops were on the other side of yellow crime-scene tape, milling around a pickup truck illuminated by multiple spotlights.

It was a new Ford F-150, extended cab.

Mike Peralta's truck.

"David." Sharon touched my hand. The poor lighting couldn't conceal the agony in her eyes. "If he's…"

She stopped, squeezed my hand hard.

"It's going to be fine." I gently disentangled her hand, took off my gun, slid on my leather jacket, and stepped out into the chill. The wind was coming hard from the west and the air smelled of pines.

My stomach was tight, but after the encounter with the woman in the DPS uniform, I was focused and calm. Thanks to some fluke of brain chemistry, I usually excel in these situations. Panic only hits me later, when I am safe and alone.

But I had no confidence that it would be fine, as I had assured Sharon. He might have come up here and blown his brains out. He might have been murdered. His body might be in the truck awaiting me.

Another black SUV rolled past us down the street, turned around, and came back to a halt at the far end of the lot. It didn't take a Ph.D. to guess this had been the vehicle tailing us, which had chosen to come down the off-ramp at the right moment to save our lives. The SUV's lights went out, but no one got out.

As I drew close, gusts caused the yellow tape to make a snapping sound. A voice ordered me to stop. Two burly deputies and a woman wearing an FBI windbreaker came toward me, hands on their weapons.

Everybody was gun-happy tonight.

I said who I was. They told me to wait.

The woman walked toward the truck and I studied the deputies. Both wore Level 2 holsters. They saw me looking at their guns and both changed their stances as if in a dance move. I looked away.

You could tell who was from Phoenix. A dozen feds were in dark windbreakers with yellow "FBI" emblazoned front and back, and they all looked uncomfortable and cold, hands in pockets, some stamping their feet like old beat cops. The Yavapai County deputies wore heavier jackets. A DPS officer looked me over and I looked away.

A man wearing only a suit, crisp white shirt, and burgundy tie approached me. He looked perfectly at ease in the thirty-degree weather and steady wind. He was substantial, not an ounce of flab, all muscles and sinews and teeth. His face was most striking, long and heavy jawed, milk-chocolate skin with a shading of fine gray. It was a face to carve into a monument.

"You're David Mapstone?"

I said that I was, and he thrust his credentials directly in my face, waiting for me to read them. Federal Bureau of Investigation. They were issued to Horace Mann.

He was the namesake of the nineteenth-century father of universal public education in America. This Mann immediately began to school me.

"I'm the special agent in charge in Phoenix."

My breath came out as white mist. "Eric Pham is the SAC."

"Not anymore." He lifted the crime-scene tape and nodded for me to follow him.

I wasn't going to argue. It was two a.m. and I was surrounded by suspicious minds. I wasn't here to plead Peralta's case or change anybody's mind about what should have been the unthinkable.

Our feet crunched on the old concrete of the gas station pad. Mann stared ahead. "We called over a locksmith from Flagstaff and we used pry bars. We tried to drill into it. Nothing can open it, short of explosives."

I took a long breath when I saw that the inside of the F-150 contained no body of my friend, no blood.

The FBI agent who called had told the truth. The reason they wanted me was for the key to the truck's weapons locker.

And perhaps to see if I made any suspicious stops on the way that might lead them to Peralta.

Behind the front seats, rising from the floor of the cab extension, was the steel case that held Peralta's armory for the road. I handed Mann the key.

"Stand here." He placed me ten feet away from the action, but I could see him reach inside, turn the key, and raise the lid. He spoke quietly to other agents standing nearby but the frustration cutting into his expression was easy to read.

"Come here."

I obeyed. The gun cabinet was completely empty. Closer up, I inspected the cab. It looked showroom new. Peralta always had at least a stainless-steel coffee mug in the console cup holder. That was gone, too.

"This is Peralta's truck, correct?"

"Didn't you run the tag and VIN?"

He threw me an acid look.

"Yes," I said, "it's Peralta's truck. Who reported that it was here?"

He ignored my question. "What did he usually have in this thing?" He tapped the heavy edge of the gun compartment with a boxy finger.

It depended on the case we were working—and on Peralta's mood. I ran down a few of the essentials: a Remington pump-action 12-gauge shotgun, at least one assault rifle, usually an M4, and a Kel-Tec RFB Bullpup rifle—short, homely and highly effective. Plenty of ammunition. One of the FBI minions took notes.

"Why would a private citizen carry that much firepower?"

"This is Arizona."

"Are you trying to be clever?"

Behind me, someone muttered, "Can't fuckin' believe it. We've been all over it and not a goddamned thing..."

I tucked that information away.

Mann nodded at an agent. "Put him in my unit."

That wasn't good. At least I wasn't in handcuffs...yet.

This agent was wearing a parka, same FBI emblems. Somebody from the Flagstaff field office, prepared for the cold. He walked me over to a black SUV and I climbed in the passenger side. The engine was running and it was warm inside. The door closed and I resisted the temptation to examine Mann's paperwork. That was another thing missing from the cab of Peralta's truck: the files and other job-related documents he always toted around.

Peralta was a techno-Luddite and proud of it. I could barely get him to use a laptop. He did use a dictaphone. Without a secretary, I was left to transcribe his words to the computer and print them out for him.

The driver's door opened, Mann slid in with surprising grace for his size, shut the door, and faced me.

"I'll share a little dirty laundry," he said. "Since your friend did his thing, Eric Pham is on his way to a new posting in Anchorage. You ask me? He should have been fired."

That was fast retribution. Very fast.

Eric Pham and Peralta went back a number of years. Each respected the other and they had collaborated without the friction common between local law enforcement and the feds. After we opened our private detective business, Pham had tossed some cases our way. Who was I kidding? Tossed them Peralta's way. As I had spent hours on Friday being interviewed by the FBI, I kept wondering if Peralta was working a new case. If he had gone undercover without even telling me.

On the other hand, the bureau was very conscious of its image. If Peralta had really gone rogue, of course Pham would be shipped out as punishment.

"Dave." Mann rubbed his heavy hands together and rested them on the steering wheel. "We know all about you. Ph.D. in history. You were a professor at Miami University and San Diego State. Then you came back to Phoenix and went to work for the Sheriff's Office, clearing cold cases."

That was the shorthand, yes.

"We know you are Mike Peralta's partner as a private investigator and his best friend."

He stared out at a tow truck that had arrived and was loudly snagging the F-150. I let the words settle on me. Peralta was so self-contained, controlled, formidable, and often so maddening that he didn't make friends. He didn't need friends. He had been my training officer and then my boss. Even now, I hesitated to use the word "partner" to describe our business arrangement.

But, yes, aside from Sharon, I supposed that I was his best friend.

I watched a strand of crime-scene tape break loose and fly off toward Williams. A deputy watched it, too, wondering whether to chase the debris, and deciding to let it go.

"I wasn't always a fed." Mann's voice was low and friendly. "I started out at Chicago PD. My brother-in-law got me in. We were really close."

He paused and I nodded, turning in my seat to face him. His eyes now appraised me as companionable orbs.

"Trouble was, he was a drunk. A mean drunk. He beat his wife, a saintly woman. And you know what I did? Nothing. Not a damned thing. I let him off once when I stopped him for DUI. The guys and me didn't arrest him when we were called to their apartment and he was being abusive. It was the code. So I understand where you're coming from."

"Peralta isn't a drunk and doesn't beat his wife."

He watched me attentively, gave a few sympathetic nods of the head.

"You want to have your friend's back, Dave. I totally get it. I respect that. But Oscar, that was my brother-in-law, he never had my back. See where I'm going?"

Having been on the other side of countless interrogations, I did.

"You seem kind of nervous, Dave."

I realized that I had unzipped my jacket, then I had rezipped it. It wasn't much, but this was how it worked. If I seemed nervous, it was because a woman had come close to killing me forty-five minutes before, but he didn't know that and I wasn't saying anything about it. If I seemed nervous, it was also irritation. I was not a "Dave." Only Lindsey got to call me that. Otherwise, I suspected my body language was neutral and he was fishing.

"Things aren't too far out of hand yet," Mann said. "You can help yourself. All you have to do is tell the truth. What really went down?"

I ran my fingers through my hair and picked at some imaginary lint on my jacket. I turned away and shook my right leg. Now I had his attention, although he did a good job of concealing it. Then I smiled at him.

"The Reid technique has been debunked as junk psychology, Horace. It produces false confessions. It won't produce a confession here because I have nothing to confess. I got to our office after Peralta had left for the diamond run. It was routine. He's been on six or seven of them since we became PIs. I didn't know anything else until your people showed up with a search warrant."

His hands came off the steering wheel. "You think you're smart. Doctorate in history, all that. You're playing it really stupid. But that's the way you want it. I can't help you." He let the quiet fill in, and then, "This truck being dumped up here, that surprises you?"

I nodded.

"How do I know you didn't drive the truck up here yourself and then slip back to Phoenix."

"I was at home all night."

"With your wife, Lindsey?"

I didn't like him bringing her name into the conversation. I nodded.

"Let's say you're telling the truth. Why would Peralta abandon his truck up here? What does he have going here?"

Nothing, as far as I knew. We had never worked a case in or near Ash Fork. I told Mann that.

"Dave, you know Mike Peralta better than anyone."

"That's why I know that he's innocent. He's the most by-the-book cop I ever knew. He may be under duress. Or he's working a case that is above your pay grade and your bosses haven't clued you in."

"Dave..." he started again.

"David."

"Dave, we have witnesses and video footage showing Mike Peralta shoot a guard at Chandler Fashion Center, then carry away a million dollars in diamonds."

I shrugged.

"He was on duty, Horace. He was one of the two guards protecting the diamond shipment."

"He told you he was going to do this?" Ask the same question, again and again, try to find an inconsistency in the answer.

"Guard the shipment, yes. It was routine."

"The diamonds are gone," Mann said. "Peralta took them."

"Your people keep telling me that."

"It's all on the video. You've seen it."

I shrugged.

He looked over at the Lexus convertible. "Who's that with you?"

"My girlfriend." The last thing Sharon needed was more harassment from the FBI.

He snorted. "Does Lindsey know about that?"

"She's open-minded."

"Considering that vehicle is registered to Sharon Peralta, I'd guess that's who is in the car. Is she your girlfriend?"

"Why don't you give her a break? She was interrogated for hours. She doesn't know anything."

"But she came up here with you."

"That's because she was afraid her husband was dead in that truck."

He slipped a hand into his suit jacket and held out an evidence envelope. It contained a small rectangular piece of paper.

"Recognize this?"

He flipped on the dome light. Inside the plastic wrapper was my business card:

Peralta & Mapstone P.C.
David Mapstone
Private Investigator

I asked him where he got it.

"That was sitting on the dashboard of the truck, Dave, right in front of the steering wheel."

I reached for the bag and he pulled it back. Let's play keep-away. I didn't want to play.

"Why would that card be in the truck?"

"Why would I know that, Horace?"

His mouth tightened. He didn't like the familiarity, either.

"What about this?" He turned the bag so I could read handwriting on the back of the card.

MAPSTONE HAD NOTHING TO DO WITH THIS.
TELL HIM NOT TO TRY TO FIND ME.

"Is that your buddy's handwriting?"

It was. Peralta wrote in an old-school draftsman's capital letters. I had received countless notes and memos in that same script, when he was Maricopa County Sheriff and later, when he lost the election and we set up our private detective business.

Mann folded the evidence envelope, slipped it back in his coat, and breathed out a sigh. "We are going to find him. He's only been on the run for less than twenty-four hours. And sooner than you think, you are going to be charged as an accessory. Don't think that writing on the card lets you off. If I were you, I'd get a lawyer."

Peralta's pickup left the lot hooked to the tow truck, headed back to the Interstate. A deputy took down the yellow tape.

I faced Mann.

"Did you have somebody follow me up here?"

He looked through me. Classic fed move. "You should consider yourself under surveillance. I won't say more."

"What about a blond woman in a DPS uniform? Was that part of your game, Horace?"

He stabbed a finger into my chest. "Don't push me. I don't know anything about blondes, Dave. You're going to be lucky if you don't leave here in handcuffs."

I tamped down my anger. He could probably rendition my ass to Saudi Arabia for "enhanced interrogation," if I wasn't careful.

"Look, I'm as shocked as anybody about what happened. You know everything I do. Probably more. Am I free to go?"

He stared hard at me, that stone face trying to turn me into a pillar of salt. It wasn't working.

He snapped off the dome light.

"For now."

I opened the door, stepped out, and turned back to face him. "Peralta didn't do this."

He raised his voice against the wind. "He shot a man."

"How's he doing?"

Mann looked surprised by the question. "The hospital sent him home. It was a flesh wound."

I said, "That proves my point."

"What point?"

"If Mike Peralta had really intended to do damage, that man would be dead."

Chapter Four

Horace Mann let me go and the last cruisers and black FBI Sub-urbans left. Soon, the lot was empty, the old gas station stood yellow and forlorn under the cone of the single streetlight. It had been stripped of everything from its signs to the gas pumps. Plywood covered the windows and doors.

I took a moment to imagine the station in its glory along Route 66 in the fifties. Uniformed attendants, cars with fins, signs advertising clean restrooms and Ethyl gas, the bell-ding of the comings and goings. Now it was a dead zone presided over by the whoosh of passing trucks and cars on Interstate 40 that looped south around the village.

I walked back to the car, opened the driver's door, and leaned in.

"He's not there, Sharon. But there's no sign of foul play."

Her shoulders drooped. "Thank goodness for that, at least."

Then her eyes widened.

I turned and a shape emerged from the darkness.

I gave a visible start. That's me, the cool PI.

"Didn't mean to scare you."

He stood about six feet tall and wore a frayed Stetson, sheep-skin coat, and blue jeans. His face was not lean or rawboned from sun and wind. This was not the Marlboro Man. Instead, he had fat merry cheeks, a rosy complexion, fleshy broad nose, and a white beard that had never encountered clippers. Santa Claus. He might have been anywhere from sixty to ninety years old.

"Are you a cop?"

I said, "Not anymore."

"You drive up from Phoenix?"

I said that I had.

His fulsome cheeks worked silently before he spoke. "Lot of action for my little town, huh?"

I nodded, wishing for the second time that night that I had my revolver at the ready.

"I was watching from down the street. This used to be a hell of a town, ya know. We had a movie house, a good whorehouse." He spat a long stream of chewing tobacco. "Right on Route 66."

He aimed a thumb over his shoulder at a black-and-white sign that read, "Historic Route 66."

Get your kicks.

It had been many years since I had been to Ash Fork. My grandmother and I came through on the train, when Phoenix still had passenger trains, on the way to the Grand Canyon. The canyon was about sixty miles north of here. Otherwise, I had driven through Ash Fork a couple of times since.

My memory was that the town sat in a gentle bowl of grassland high on the Coconino Plateau between Flagstaff and Kingman, with piñon pines on the ridges and mountains in the distance. Millions of years before, it had been part of the volcanic eruptions and lava flows that created northern Arizona. It lacked the spectacular San Francisco Peaks and ponderosa pine forest of Flagstaff. Somebody had capitalized on Ash Fork's Route 66 past by putting a vintage car on the roof of a hair salon. I wondered if it was still here.

"The Interstate killed it?" I made conversation, wanting to get back in the car.

"Didn't help."

When that was all he said, I turned to leave but his voice stopped me.

"The world was different when we drove on two lanes, when people actually had to come down the main street of every town. When we traveled by train. Y'see, the Santa Fe Railway built this town and then murdered it. Ash Fork used to be on the main line. We got all the streamliners come through."

I named the major passenger trains: the Super Chief, Chief, San Francisco Chief, El Capitan, and the Grand Canyon. This seemed to please him.

Santa Claus smiled. "You know your railroad history. My God, they were something to behold. We had a beautiful depot and Harvey House. The Escalante. Then the railroad relocated the main line north in 1960 and we were only a spot in the Peavine."

"The branch down to Phoenix."

"That's right," he said. "It killed the town. We lost all the railroad jobs. They tore down the depot in the seventies."

He swept his arm.

"Now look at it. Nothing. This used to be Highway 66. Used to come right down Lewis Avenue and Park, each was a one-way. In seventy-seven, had the big fire in town. Another one happened ten years later. Now this is all that's left."

He stepped out into the middle of the road.

"C'mon, son. This is the safest place to be. If a car came by in the next three hours, I'd eat this Stetson."

I followed him onto the painted line and we stood there like two gunfighters in an old Western, waiting for the outlaws to come riding down the street. A tumbleweed obligingly rolled across, half a block ahead.

He shrugged in resignation. "Four hundred people now, give or take. Doesn't stop the break-ins. We got three registered sex offenders, too. Hell, I went to high school with two of 'em."

He walked west toward the little collection of one-story buildings. It was hard to imagine this had once been a thriving town center. I had to quickstep to match his long stride.

"Used to snow up here more often, too." He looked around, shook his head.

"It's a shame," I said. "Do you work on a ranch?"

He let loose another shot of brown liquid. "Hell, there ain't any ranching any more. None to speak of up here. I cowboyed most of my life."

"What happened?"

"All the ranches have been bought up as tax deductions or for subdivisions. You wouldn't understand. You're from Phoenix."

"I'm a fourth-generation Arizonan." I felt the need to establish my bona fides in a state where almost everyone was from somewhere else, and most either came to die or came and went.

He appraised me more closely now. He held out a rough-skinned hand and we shook.

"Orville Grainer."

"David Mapstone."

"You related to Philip Mapstone, the dentist?"

"He was my grandfather."

"I went to him a couple of times. Nice man, Doc Mapstone. He didn't hurt me. Made me hate dentists a little less."

This was once a very small state.

We walked a few more steps. His stride turned into a slight limp.

I asked him what he had seen tonight but he avoided the question.

"The West we knew is gone, David. Don't you know that? They even canceled the cowboy artists' show at the Phoenix Art Museum. That was the only reason I ever went down to that damned city."

Looking back, I could see Sharon's car under the streetlamp. I didn't want to get farther away. From where we stood, the broad starry sky demanded attention. I could pick out the Little Dipper. As a Boy Scout, I had won a merit badge in astronomy, but now I couldn't identify most of the other constellations.

Santa spoke again. "I sit at home and when I can't sleep…my wife died ten years ago and lot of nights I can't fall asleep…I walk around and watch. Watch the stars. Watch this dying little town."

"Like this evening."

"That's right. Haven't seen so many police in a long time and FBI, too. Knew it couldn't have been a burglary. Must be something mighty important. That Texaco belonged to Shorty

Hayes, you know. Shorty ran it forty-six years before he died. Hell of a poker player."

"Want to tell me what happened at Shorty's tonight?"

He stopped and looked back at the ruin of a gas station. We had gone about a block.

"Cops, cops, and cops. My boy wanted to be one, ya know? But he went off to Vietnam and didn't come back."

"I'm sorry."

"Yeah, me, too. Anyway, they were really interested in that Ford pickup that got towed off."

"Did you see how it got there?"

"Oh, yeah. Man parked it there. A big man, broad shoulders, black hair. Taller than you. He was smoking a cigar."

"Anglo?"

Grainer shook his head. "Could have been. Probably Mexican. I wasn't close enough to be sure and he stayed in the shadows."

Grainer was describing Mike Peralta.

I asked how far away he was when he saw the man?

"About a block away, standing behind a tree."

He contemplated as his jaw worked the chewing tobacco, then continued.

"It was too far away to make out his face. But the fella didn't act lost. He was careful to pull into the dark instead of sitting under the light. Got out of the truck. Lit his cigar. Walked around. I told all this to that big black G-man."

"Did the man at the truck seem nervous?"

He squinted, exposing dozens of little ravines on his face. "You sure you ain't the law?"

"Not anymore."

I had to wait for the conversation to work at its own speed. Grainer pulled a can of Copenhagen from his back pocket and stuffed another piece of chaw inside his rosy cheek. A sudden gale of cold, dry wind failed to make any impression on his wide hat.

"He didn't seem nervous. He walked my way a bit, so I was getting worried he'd find me watching him. Then he yawned and stretched and turned around. Went back and leaned against that truck, and enjoyed his smoke. He waited maybe twenty minutes and a car pulled up. White four-door, California plates. I couldn't read the numbers. Eyes are going. He climbed inside and they went back on the Interstate."

"Heading?" I hoped he knew their direction.

"Couldn't be sure."

"Do you know about what time he got here?"

"Little after ten."

That was several hours unaccounted for after the robbery. I asked if he had unloaded anything from the truck.

Grainer shook his head.

"Nothing?" I asked.

"Nothing."

Diamond couriers used a small suitcase on wheels. The FBI had played the tape for me, showing Peralta and the second guard going through a back corridor of the mall. They walked side-by-side—the hallway was made for deliveries, so it was plenty wide. The other guard had the wheelie bag.

Then Peralta suddenly spun the man off balance and snatched the case with his left hand. When the man reached for his gun, Peralta already had his Glock in his right hand and fired. One shot. The other guard fell back. Peralta took the bag and walked calmly out of the camera's view.

This was all the feds would show me. I asked about other cameras, other angles, and they went into the we-ask-the-questions attitude. But the reality was that they had lost him.

Then he got to Ash Fork.

But the weapons locker in his truck was empty. That was unusual. The man always drove around with multiple guns. I would have to do an inventory of the room-sized armory back at the office, which Lindsey's sister Robin had christened "The Danger Room." Now we had plenty of danger.

I thought about what Grainer had told me. The diamonds could theoretically be stuffed in his pockets, depending on the size of the settings. So he had decided to dump the suitcase.

"Did he do anything while he waited?"

He puffed out his cheeks and smiled at the miracle of a returned memory.

"Yep, yep. Now that you mention it, he did. Got on his haunches and fiddled with the back bumper of the truck."

I thought about that. Arizona only required one tag on a vehicle, not two. Peralta must have put on a different tag to get out of town. His real one would have been on all the police broadcasts. Otherwise, it was one of thousands of Ford pickups. Then he changed back to his real tag. He intended for the truck to be found and identified.

And he left the business card with the message for me on the dash.

"When the car pulled up, did anybody get out? Did it seem like he was being forced inside?"

"No, sir," he said. "The man got right on in and they was gone."

"What did the FBI tell you?"

He shook his head, the wind stirring the tendrils of his beard. "Not a damned thing. The Yavapai deputies think I'm a pest, calling about the burglaries, the crime around here. They have a trailer shack down the street here, but you hardly ever see a deputy. Budget cuts and all. I come to think, screw 'em. I can handle things if I need to."

He opened a button on the coat and patted the butt of a pistol. Of course.

I handed him my card and asked him to give me a call if anything else came to him, or if he saw that four-door car again.

He mumbled something unintelligible about private eyes, shook my hand, and limped back into his forlorn village.

Mapstone had nothing to do with this. Tell him not to try to find me.

Whatever Peralta really intended by the message, whether he meant it or somebody was leaning on him, he had worked with me long enough to know that sometimes I didn't follow orders. Even his orders.

Chapter Five

Back in the car, I slid on my holster. Sharon had brushed out her hair and, with the visor mirror down, was nervously freshening her lipstick. She had been agitated on the entire drive up. Who could blame her?

I asked her about Ash Fork and why Mike might have come up here.

She shook her head. "I have no idea."

"You still have the cabin in Heber?"

"Yes. The FBI was very interested in that. They're probably at the place now, hoping he'll show up. They spent hours at our house today—well, yesterday, now—with a search warrant."

I drove west on the one-way street, turned a block, then came back on the eastbound one-way that returned us to the Interstate. Grainer was gone and it was difficult to imagine the thriving town he had described.

"Did you expect to find him dead here?" I asked Sharon.

"No."

My body tensed even before she spoke the next sentence.

"He called me tonight."

Two obscenities came out of my mouth before I stopped myself.

"I'm sorry, David."

I asked her what time he called. Around eight-thirty.

"When were you going to tell me?"

She flipped up the mirror and the light went off. Her large brown eyes watched me.

"He said not to tell you anything."

"Sharon…" I stared at the highway, a stream of semis passing us as I stuck to the speed limit. "I can't believe it. You know the FBI has your phones tapped. You'll be implicated in this."

"They don't even know about this phone. Years ago, the county installed a second landline at the house as a backup in case of an emergency. Then they forgot about it. After he left the sheriff's office, I called twice to have them take it out. They never did."

"What did he say?"

She laughed, a surprising sound in this cockpit of tension.

"When I first met him, before I even knew you, I was this girl from the barrio. A nobody. He was a deputy sheriff, the son of a judge. He had grown up in a fancy house in Arcadia. My family had a four-room, tarpaper shack in Golden Gate, before they bulldozed it for the airport. He'd been to Harvard, for God's sake, and I barely got out of high school. But I was very vain. I knew men liked me. And he liked me. I didn't always look like an old lady."

"You're very attractive, Sharon. And you're the most accomplished person I know."

She waved it away. "I wasn't digging for a compliment, David. There is a point to the story."

I shut up and ten miles later she continued.

"He liked me, and we started dating. He was only one generation out of the barrio, but he would tease me. He enjoyed making me mad. One of his things was to impersonate a guy named Paco Sanchez. He made up this character that was a gardener who spoke terrible English but was going to take me away from that cop Peralta I was dating. It made me angry, that he was making fun of me. And it made me laugh."

"That's a playfulness I never saw in him."

"Well, you weren't a sweet young thing he wanted to get in the sack."

"Thank God for that. I'm still worried about the FBI listening in on your call tonight."

"All they would have heard is a call from my old beau Paco."

"What?"

She laughed again. "He used the same voice as back then. 'Hey, pretty one. You still with that cop?'"

Her voice switched into a high-pitched, heavily accented Spanglish.

"Don't think I wasn't worried about a tap, even though this phone number is lost somewhere in the Maricopa County bureaucracy. So I played along. I asked him how he was. He says, 'So-so, pretty one. I run with a bad crowd. You know that. Things are kind of *siniestro*. You be okay?'"

"Scary."

"Right. I told him I was home and safe and he'd better not let my husband catch him calling me. It was the same game we used to play back in the day when he was being Paco. He told me I might not hear from him for a while but it was going to be okay. In between, he did the old flirting in Spanglish."

"Smart man," I said. "But he didn't give you details?"

"None. I was afraid to be too specific in what I asked."

The big trucks left us behind and the road was black with specters of tall trees on either side.

"David," she said, "he said another thing. He asked me about my *gabacho profesor* friend. That would be you."

"I figured."

"He said the *profesor* needed to watch his *gabacho* ass." She slipped back into her impersonation of an impersonation. "'But don't tell him that Paco said it. Don't tell him about me at all.'"

I tried to shuffle the deck into order.

Peralta had shot the diamond courier at noon on Friday at Chandler Fashion Center, and then escaped before the police could arrive. By ten p.m., he was abandoning his truck in Ash Fork, where Orville Grainer saw him. Before that, at eight-thirty, he called Sharon on the forgotten landline. He used a play-act that only the two of them would know, yet he conveyed important information. Did he assume she was being tapped? Or was he under duress or otherwise compromised?

"Are you mad at me?"

"Yes."

"I didn't know what to do, David. Things were happening so fast. The FBI didn't let me go home until after six. I was going to tell you, and then I got the call that his truck had been found and we raced up here."

I let out a long breath and my anger fell away. I told her about Horace Mann and the business card, about Orville Grainer watching Peralta climb into a sedan. Then I shut up and watched the road for deer. Lack of sleep was starting to slow me down, make me jumpy.

"There's one more thing," she said. "When he called, I heard a train in the background. Very distinct."

We were breaking through the forest and entering Flagstaff, so I took the exit into downtown. It was three thirty Saturday morning and few cars were on the streets. Our FBI escort had disappeared.

At 6,900 feet above sea level and sitting beneath the San Francisco Peaks, Flagstaff in daylight was one of the most scenic places in the Southwest. At this time of night, we had to settle for the appealing little downtown with its pioneer-era brick and masonry buildings. Unlike so many places in Arizona now, it felt authentic.

It had been real to me when I came here as a child with my grandparents. It was cool and beautiful, like a small town out of a storybook. Flag was a real place with gritty jobs in timber and the railroad, along with a little college.

It had trains to delight the young me, all those Santa Fe Railway streamliners that stopped at the handsome depot with its Alpine chalet roof. Not only the young me. Anyone who really knew me understood that I still loved trains and especially the Flagstaff depot.

Now the town had spread out into the pines with subdivisions and shopping strips, a mall, and a Walmart Supercenter. The college had grown into Northern Arizona University. But the city had done a decent job saving downtown from the bulldozers, with the exception of erecting a hideous new city hall that looked like a second-rate suburban office building. Babbitt's was still here, gone from Babbitt Brothers Trading Company, to Babbitt's Backcountry Outfitters.

The old business district that ran along and north of Santa Fe Avenue—old Route 66—had been cleaned up. The cheap hotels that catered to railroaders had been spiffed up into offices or boutique lodgings. The smoky risky bars frequented by drunken Indians were gone. Even the seedy Hong Kong Café was now a more upscale cantina.

But the railroad remained. I pulled into the parking lot of the station. The Southwest Chief, the only passenger train left, had come and gone. Although the depot was lit, it was likely locked up until the next train came later this morning. Ours was the only car in the lot.

"David, you really believe he's on a special assignment..."

Sharon let the sentence hang, not quite a question.

"Don't you?" I said.

"Mike and I have had our bad times. You know that."

"You divorced him once."

She smiled and nodded.

I said, "I still haven't heard the story of why you two decided to get back together. The daughters are grown and gone."

"It's a long story. Maybe on another night drive. But you really believe he's a good guy, too, right? Still?" Although her voice was gentle, her eyes were black with emotion.

It seemed to be a moment requiring a speech to buck us both up, about Peralta's unwavering integrity, even when he could also be demanding and domineering and difficult as hell to work for. But the ground started shaking and suddenly intense light came out of the east, followed by six thundering locomotives and a freight train doing at least fifty.

When it was bit quieter, as container cars full of the scrap from de-industrializing America heading for Asia swept past us, I kept my response simple. "I do."

Then I ran through the scenarios, which were basically two. Either he was working a case for a law-enforcement agency that required him to go deep undercover. Or he was under coercion to steal those diamonds for reasons and persons unknown.

He must have had different license tags on the truck when he got to the mall—there wouldn't have been time to change them in the immediate aftermath of the shooting and robbery. So something didn't suddenly happen to cause his trip to the High Country. It was planned.

For whatever reason, the media still didn't know that the diamond thief was former Maricopa County Sheriff Peralta. He was one of the better-known people in the state. Merely walking into a mini-mart to use the restroom would be taking a chance. That this information hadn't been released made me think he was on assignment.

But one he couldn't, or wouldn't, tell me about.

Then there was the empty gun case. That made no sense under either scenario.

Finally, I told her about the woman who had stopped us earlier, what really happened behind the car as her finger was on the trigger of the semiautomatic pistol, and my doubts that she was really a DPS officer.

"Then," she said, " don't you think you should do as Mike wrote on the card, and as he said when he was playing Paco? Let it alone. Let it play out."

"Aren't you worried?"

She put her hand on my wrist. "I've never been more worried in my life."

"Me, too. What about his diabetes?"

"All his insulin is gone. So is his blood-sugar meter."

"So he planned this." The thought gave me no comfort.

Then I checked the rearview mirror and saw it—a pay telephone across the street.

The mile-long train was still loudly passing through as I whipped the convertible around, turned onto Santa Fe Avenue, made an illegal U-turn, and stopped in front of this artifact of twentieth-century communications technology. I was even old enough to remember phone booths. This was a simple hooded stand that held the phone.

I put on the flashers and stepped out. It had gotten colder. The hard plastic receiver was freezing, battered, would not pass a health-code inspection—but it carried a dial tone. I slipped it back in the cradle and looked around.

The slip of paper was slid into the top of the phone casing, sheltered from the wind by the minimalist stand. It was actually a business card. My business card. They got around. And to think I had wondered if I would even need them when I became Peralta's partner. I turned it over and read the familiar draftsman printing:

FIND MATT PENNINGTON

I pocketed it and stepped off the curb as a Flagstaff cop cruised slowly past. By the time I slid into the driver's seat, he had picked up a call and sped off silent code three, emergency lights but no siren.

I showed Sharon the card. "Ever hear him mention this name?"

"No. It doesn't sound familiar at all."

My phone vibrated. A message from Lindsey with three numbers.

It was time to get back to Phoenix.

Ninety minutes later and a mile lower, we passed through the enormous freeway interchange on the north end of the metropolitan area. Sharon was asleep. Some civic wrecker had climbed onto an overpass and written in black capital letters: OMENVILLE.

Chapter Six

The Westin was the one of the new swanky hotels in downtown Phoenix, occupying the lower floors of the bland Freeport-McMoRan building. The glass-sheeted box had been finished as the Great Recession blew up.

In the go-go years before the crash, one in three jobs had been connected to real estate. It was the only conversation at my gym in the basement of Central Park Square. Even the woman who cut my hair was flipping houses. For me, it was like Joe Kennedy's anecdote about shoeshine boys trading stock tips in 1929. Anybody could see it coming if they cared to look.

The result in Phoenix had been a straight-up Depression. Now it had mellowed into a prolonged recession, whatever the boosters said. Phoenix had seen nothing like it since the bad years of the 1890s. The perpetual-motion growth machine had broken down.

Thousands of people were still underwater on their mortgages, owing more than the houses were worth. Thousands more had simply walked away. Entire subdivisions within the "master planned communities" of suburbia had been empty. Then Wall Street had moved in and bought the houses as rentals. Even this didn't stop the economy's bleeding and many of the rental houses, already built on the cheap, turned shabby fast. Wall Street flipped the properties to new slumlords. Talented young people and empty-nest baby boomers with means were moving to cities with real downtowns, places like Seattle and Portland. Fewer retirees had the money to move to Phoenix and brag about not having to shovel sunshine.

Phoenix embodied Eric Hoffer's remark, "Every great cause begins as a movement, becomes a business, and eventually degenerates into a racket."

But the Westin's lobby looked modishly elegant, if empty, when I walked in at six a.m. The friendly young woman at the registration desk said hello and I responded as if I belonged there and went to the elevators.

When I stepped out on the eighth floor, the hallway was empty. The space was quiet. Not even a sound of a couple making early-morning love. I walked to the room number Lindsey had texted and knocked.

The door opened two inches, the security latch in place.

"House gigolo," I said.

"Please come in. I called hours ago."

Then she was in my arms and for that moment the world was right and safe. I felt the contours of her body through the plush white robe she wore.

I felt the hard plastic inside one part of the robe, "Is that a baby Glock in your pocket or are you glad to see me?"

"Both."

I kissed her and un-mussed her pin-straight dark hair. My eyes stayed on the simple diamond of her wedding ring.

Diamonds.

So much trouble.

"You look exhausted, History Shamus."

"Staying up all night doesn't have the appeal that it did when I was fourteen years old."

She led me into the room. It was a good deal nicer than a Holiday Inn, with expensive furniture and floor-to-ceiling windows looking north onto Central Avenue.

Phoenix is on the farther edge of the Mountain Time zone, so it was still dark outside. The view showed tired city lights but one of the first light-rail trains of the day was heading up the street. It was a view we didn't get from our house in the historic districts.

Neither of the queen-sized beds had been slept in. I slid off my jacket and collapsed onto one of the beds. Lindsey curled up next to me and I told her everything that had happened.

She was skeptical about my traffic-stop reaction, which irritated me.

"I'm not making it up."

"I know. But your tale…I'm sorry. Your description of the night has a dream quality to it. You were under tremendous strain. You were tired."

"That woman was going to shoot me."

"Strawberry Death." She gave me that ironic half-smile. My testiness evaporated. Lindsey had the ability to tease without hurting.

"She had strawberry blond hair, yes." I thought about it. Had I overreacted? "So you're pissed that I made you leave home?"

She propped herself on her elbow and swung a long, naked leg over me. Her skin was not quite porcelain, but very fair, a beautiful contrast with her nearly black hair.

"I'm never mad when you're concerned about me, Dave. This is a pretty nice safe-house, too."

"But you didn't sleep…"

"Could you have slept? You were a long way away and I didn't hear a word from you."

"I was afraid they were listening in."

"Dave, I altered your cell to make it a totally dark device. The data are encrypted and your conversations are scrambled. Nobody can listen in. Not even the feds."

She was right. She was put out with me. But she didn't move her leg. She was five feet eight and I was six two and we had the same inseam. I stroked the soft, perfect skin of her thigh.

She said, "Peralta obviously ditched his cell so they couldn't track him. He shot a guy in one of the most crowded malls in town and made a clean getaway. Mike Peralta, international jewel thief. Kinda sexy."

"Lindsey, this is serious."

"You have to smile or you'll cry, Dave. I don't think you have to worry about Strawberry Death. She was only a scared rookie on a traffic stop facing my dark dangerous lover. You're very intimidating, you know. You don't realize it."

She sat up on her haunches. "Take a shower and let's go home."

It sounded like a good idea.

I stripped down, stepped into the commodious shower, and let the hot water sluice off my aching body. In a few minutes, Lindsey joined me, and we got friendly.

Afterwards, we got in bed long enough to watch the sun come up. It was worth it. Light revealed Camelback Mountain, Piestawa Peak—formerly Squaw Peak—and the North Mountains. Sunrise draped a coppery glow over the Viad Tower, the only interesting skyscraper in the city. The air was clean enough that we could see the Bradshaws, the muscular blue mountain range where the High Country began. It made me think of my travels last night. Dreamlike, yes.

Once the sun was higher, it showed off the emerald carpet of trees running north to the bare mountains and Phoenix didn't seem so bad.

Lindsey had taken a cab to the hotel and Sharon had dropped me off. So we rode the light rail up to Park Central and ate breakfast at The Good Egg. While Lindsey waited at our table, content with the house coffee, I walked next door to Starbucks for a venti mocha. I smiled involuntarily at all the times Peralta had made fun of me for ordering the drink, wondering where he was now and whether he was safe.

Then I saw the stacks of *Arizona Republics* and the top headline on page one, "Peralta Linked to Gem Heist."

I was angry before I read the subhead, "Former sheriff shoots diamond courier at crowded Chandler mall." I bought a paper and got my mocha.

Lindsey read it on my face before she saw the newspaper. I tossed it into an empty chair. "I can't stand to read it."

She read the article. "Ah, they're calling it the 'crime of the century.' Don't we have a few more decades to go? Hey, doesn't your old girlfriend work at the *Republic*?"

"They pushed her out in a reorganization years ago," I said. "You know that."

"You know the drill, Dave. Keep asking the same question and try to trip up the suspect. Don't be so serious. An omelet will do you good."

"Showering with you did me good."

She smiled, then her brow furrowed. "Did you try to convince Sharon to leave town for awhile? She could be with her daughters in San Francisco."

"I did. She won't go. Said she wants to take care of you and me. Anyway, the FBI is staked out in front of their house."

"The media are going to be camped out for her, too."

"She'll be all right." I sampled the mocha. It had exactly the right amount of chocolate. I hoped Sharon would be all right. Even if the feds weren't there, the Peraltas' house, perched on a bluff overlooking Dreamy Draw in north Phoenix, was like a fortress and Sharon was a decent shot.

We were at a table on the front patio with the heaters going. It was in the fifties, nippy for Phoenix. I would have been comfortable taking my jacket off but I needed it to conceal the Python.

Birds sat expectantly on nearby bushes and light poles. The bird issue was large enough that the restaurant had resorted to putting sugar and other condiments in plastic containers to keep them from being carried off.

The other tables were occupied and the conversations loud. They were talking real estate at one table. At another, I heard a man say, "The bankers got away with the crime of the century and my family lost almost everything. I don't blame Peralta if he decided to cash in."

I didn't know any of the other diners, a good thing that day. My partner was front-page news. I was nobody. We were also the only diners reading a newspaper. It was unsettling...say, if you hoped to sustain a civilization or democracy.

Lindsey asked if I could stand talking about the "gem heist." I nodded.

"You're convinced Peralta is working deep cover."

"Yes."

She studied me. "Even though this new SAC you met said it's not true."

"He wouldn't tell me. He might not know himself."

The server brought our food with the place's customary efficiency. Lindsey had soft-scrambled eggs, bacon, and tomatoes in place of an English muffin. I had my usual Sun Devil omelet.

Lindsey ran her finger along another headline: "Texting While Driving, Woman Impaled Through Buttocks."

She said, "So, History Shamus, if Peralta really is on a case, wouldn't he have let you know beforehand? Somehow?"

I hadn't thought this through last night. Now I was glad she was encouraging it.

After a bite and some reflection, I said, "Not if it came up suddenly. He went into the office early yesterday, same as always. He texted me at nine to say he was going on a diamond run. By the time I got there, he was gone."

"Peralta texted?"

"Old dog, new tricks."

"Had he texted you before?"

I stopped with the fork in midair, then set it back on the plate. No, he had never texted before. I hadn't thought much of it because I was getting ready for the day and he had done half-a-dozen of these diamond jobs since we had become private detectives.

"So all you know is that the text came from his phone."

"True." I chewed eggs and second thoughts.

She ate and talked at the same time without it ever seeming unladylike. But I was partial.

"So if it was him, and this new undercover case came up suddenly, and all he could do was text you…" She paused. "That doesn't make sense for him. Not somebody who has never texted before. Somebody like that will stick with habit and call. The next you know, the FBI shows up at the office with a search warrant. That's the first you heard of the robbery."

"Yes."

"They interviewed you there, right?"

"Two hours worth, while they went through the files. Some nerd spent time with Peralta's computer before taking it."

"We nerds are useful, History Shamus. It's curious they didn't take your computer."

"That made me think this was all for show." I glanced at the newspaper. Maybe releasing his name to the press was for show, too. They didn't release Peralta's involvement yesterday when someone might have identified him driving to Ash Fork.

"So he leaves you a message on the first business card. Don't try to find him."

I nodded.

She put her hand lightly on mine. "I know you're tired, love, but if he really is undercover, shouldn't you leave this alone? If you muck around digging into the case, you might put it at risk and endanger him."

"You mean, be a hotdog."

I ate in silence. She was right. Perhaps. One of my many character flaws was getting into target-acquisition mode and immediately going to afterburners. Sometimes I needed to slow down.

I said, "But he left the second card. He knows I love trains. He knows I love the Flagstaff depot. He called Sharon from a pay phone there, made sure she heard the railroad in the background. Sure enough, he had left a message where I would find it. That would indicate he wants me to be involved."

"Why?"

"Maybe something went wrong. Or, he is not undercover but being coerced into this robbery."

She pointed to the newspaper. "Nothing subtle about it. If he wanted the diamonds, he could have overpowered the other guard before they got to the mall. Instead, he shot him there and did it on camera."

"That gives him more credibility going deep undercover."

"And ruins his good name."

"For now."

"But something went wrong and now he needs you?"

I shrugged. I didn't know. The more I ate, the more my body wanted to sleep.

She applied a dainty napkin to her mouth. Then she swigged the coffee like a truck driver. "What if he really did it?"

"Lindsey!" I lowered my voice. "How can you even think that?"

"The man gave his life to serving the people of Maricopa County." She looked around at the breakfast crowd. "And they kicked him to the curb because suddenly it's unAmerican to be Hispanic in Arizona. It'd make me want to get a little revenge."

"That's not him. He was philosophical about losing the election. We were the ones who were angry."

"We have to look at this dispassionately," she said. "That's the way you would approach any other case."

I nodded.

She leaned toward me. "Maybe he wanted to prove something."

"Prove?"

"The white supremacist took his gun, remember? You had to rescue him. That had never happened during his career."

Peralta and I had never discussed that incident, but what Lindsey said was true. Mike Peralta's credo was never give up your weapon. But in that situation, he had been blindsided, disarmed, and strapped to a chair in a room with explosives. By the time Peralta was unstrapped, two bad guys were dead. But all through it, he had been, for probably the first time in his life, helpless.

"He may be feeling old," she continued. "Feeling as if…"

After a few minutes, I finished her sentence, "Feeling as if he needed to prove he was still capable. So maybe that drove him to accept a dangerous assignment."

"Or," she sipped her coffee, "become a jewel thief."

We finished breakfast in silence. I knew what she was thinking: nobody really knows anybody else.

Afterward, we boarded the train and rode down Central to the Encanto station, we walked two-and-a-half blocks to the 1928 Spanish Revival house on Cypress Street. The street was blessedly free of satellite trucks, black SUVs, and strawberry blond DPS troopers.

The temperature had warmed into the high sixties and the air was dry and magical. It would be the kind of day when you could say, yes, this is paradise. When I was young, it had been a flawed Eden, a garden city surrounded by citrus groves, farms, and the Japanese flower gardens, and beyond that the empty majesty of the Sonoran Desert.

That was almost all gone now that the builders had turned the Valley into fifteen hundred square miles of lookalike housing developments, shopping strips, and tilt-up offices and warehouses built on spec. Even Baker Nursery, a reminder of the days when even the most humble place was lovingly landscaped, had closed. Newcomers threw down gravel and thought they were being responsible. "We live in a desert," they would say. They knew nothing about this wettest desert in the world and the oasis they were profaning. There was Scottsdale and Paradise Valley, if you had the money. But it wasn't my paradise anymore.

Time was, we had seven lovely months and five hellish ones. Now it had almost flipped. It didn't cool down until after Halloween and the heat kicked up in March. The temps had gone up ten degrees in my lifetime, and that was local warming, replacing the groves and farms with concrete and red tile roofs. Nobody wanted to talk about what climate change would do here. I kept friendships by not bringing it up

But on Cypress Street, in the historic districts, especially within this property line, here was the magnet that kept me in Phoenix.

Inside, I thought momentarily about driving into the office and going through recent cases we had worked, everything I could discover about the diamond runs. To find Matt Pennington.

But I made the mistake of going into the bedroom to change clothes and then I was on the bed. It took about two minutes for me to fall into a deep, dreamless sleep.

Chapter Seven

The sun was low by the time I woke up. It didn't seem as if it should still be Saturday, but it was. Lindsey was sitting beside me in bed with her laptop open.

"Any news?"

"Hashtag Peralta is the most trending item on Twitter in Phoenix," she said.

I asked if that was a good thing.

"Oh, Dave, not in this case. Most of it is ugly, racist stuff. So much hate in one hundred forty characters."

"Someday we'll have social media trials and summary public executions."

She cupped my face with her hands and kissed me. That always took away the darkness and made our little oasis a bright and hopeful place.

Afterward, we had cocktails, Beefeater martinis, stirred, with olives. It was one of our healing rituals against the crazy place that began outside the property line, where the voters were such fools that they had kicked my friend out of office. Cocktail time was sacred.

As we watched the last light outside the picture window, I told her what some sleep had enabled me to realize. I had kept saying that this was an ordinary diamond run. But it actually wasn't.

"There were two guards, not one. In the past, Peralta had gone alone."

I didn't know much about this part of our business, only that it was good money, plus the background that Peralta had given me.

Up until about 2000, the jewelers themselves had transported the diamonds. That stopped after a couple of robberies, including one where some Colombians had murdered a jeweler in the lobby of a Florida hotel and took his suitcase.

After that, many jewelers set up armed security teams in every state that picked up the diamonds, took them to the shows, and returned them to the jeweler at the airport.

But some firms hired two local guards to meet the jeweler at the airport outside the secure area—where they could still carry their weapons. They would take the diamonds, worth anywhere from three hundred thousand to a million dollars, to Kay, Zales, and other stores for special shows. Then they would return them to the jeweler, waiting safely at the airport.

"The companies didn't mind losing a guard but they didn't want to lose a jeweler."

Then, around 2005, they cut back to one guard, I told Lindsey. A few months after we became private detectives, Peralta won a contract from Markovitz & Sons to transport diamonds in the Phoenix area. The most recent job before yesterday had been to take special-show diamonds to an invitation-only event at the Royal Palms Resort. Peralta told me Charlie Keating had been there.

"Don't forget the 'savings-and-loan kingpin' part," she said.

"Peralta said Charlie was still complaining that the feds wouldn't pay for his knee replacement when he was incarcerated in Lompoc."

That transport had gone according to standard procedure. Peralta took the suitcase back to Sky Harbor and handed it to the jeweler, who went back into the secure area and discreetly examined the contents. I only knew the details because Peralta wanted to tell his Charlie Keating story.

"But this time it was two guards," she said.

"That's what the FBI told me. I assumed Peralta was going alone."

Lindsey asked who had provided the second guard. I didn't know. Mann had told me that he was a private investigator.

"Who Peralta shot."

"Winged," I said.

"I can find out who he is."

"Lindsey, your computer snooping worries me."

"Nobody can catch me, Dave. Trust me."

I knew she was the best. She had been the star of Peralta's cybercrimes unit and then she had spent a year in Washington working for Homeland Security. It still concerned me. The FBI would be all over us and in ways we couldn't tell.

She distracted me by suggesting fajitas for dinner. We sliced onions and peppers together in the kitchen. I made guacamole. Then I grilled the veggies, steak, and chicken inside the old *chimneria* in the backyard while she warmed the tortillas in the oven and assembled the salsa, shredded cheese, and sour cream.

I was way too full and loving it when Lindsey said, "I found Matt Pennington."

Before I could learn more, the front door registered a knock. Three loud thumps. Whoever it was didn't bother to use the wrought-iron knocker.

Maybe it was a neighbor. Maybe it was the tamale women selling door-to-door or a television crew wanting to know about the "gem heist." Whoever it was, I moved quickly to the front bedroom and peeked outside.

The porch light showed a black Ford Crown Victoria was sitting in the driveway.

Crown Vics with their wonderful Interceptor engines were on their way out as the standard police vehicle in North America. They were becoming rare. Ford had stopped making them. This one had an eight-inch scratch on the right edge of the push-bar that was attached to the front bumper. It was one of the vehicles of the sheriff's personal security detail.

The three thuds came again. That was the way cops knocked.

I opened the door to see one man. His partner had stepped into the flowerbed to peer in the picture window. One of Lindsey's impatiens was under his boot.

"May I help you?"

Peralta's old detail had been reassigned, of course. Still, I knew one of this pair, a sergeant named Gordon who had been in the patrol division under Peralta and was on the edge of being fired for what appeared to be a righteous brutality complaint. The other one, two decades younger than Gordon, came back to the step and showed his star.

As if I didn't know.

They could have been brothers. Both were about five eleven, wearing cheap Dockers and polo shirts to show off their biceps. Both had thinning-hair crew cuts. They looked like personal trainers at a second-rate health club. Gordon's partner was giving me the cop squint.

Gordon said, "The sheriff wants to see you."

Chapter Eight

I did not walk out to the Crown Vic without consideration.

They wouldn't say what "the sheriff" wanted of me—and it felt like a metal file being dragged across my teeth even to hear the title connected with anybody but Mike Peralta, certainly not this pretender.

Don't think I didn't consider that they might not really be deputies. Too much was in flux: Peralta on the run, his messages to me, and the mysterious traffic stop early this morning. But I recognized the car and I knew Gordon from my days with the department.

I decided to take the chance, but not before I excused myself. In the bedroom, I slipped my easily concealed BUG—backup gun—into a holster in the small of my back and covered it with a blue blazer. The Smith & Wesson 442 Airweight revolver held five potent .38 special hollowpoint bullets. If the worst came about, it would be my last resort.

Back in the living room, I looked at Lindsey. She smiled and winked at me, *See what they want.*

I paused in the long twilight to admire the cool breeze, and then I climbed inside. The personal trainers even let me ride in the front passenger seat, with Gordon driving.

"I didn't even know this neighborhood existed, Mapstone." Gordon took in the elegant period-revival houses as we went west on Cypress and then turned south on the one-way that was Fifth Avenue. On the other side of McDowell Road were bungalows more than a century old and beautifully restored.

"Thought everything downtown was a slum, but this is something. Reminds me of back home in Minnesota, the old houses and front porches."

"It's not downtown." My voice was friendly. "It's Midtown. Downtown only goes as far as Fillmore."

My pedantry shut Gordon up. We were passing Kenilworth School, where I had passed kindergarten through eighth grade, when I heard Gordon's partner behind me.

"So how is Miss Cheerleader Legs?"

In the history department, his query would have led to a disciplinary action for using sexist language and objectifying a woman, followed by sensitivity classes and perhaps therapy.

In the cop shop, the proper response would have been, "Your wife looked fine after I fucked her this morning, kid. Thanks for asking."

But I wasn't a cop any more.

I didn't answer.

Out of the corner of my eye, I saw Gordon give his partner a "back-off" glance and the voice behind me fell silent.

The kid was too stupid to stay on an elite detail. Soon enough he would find himself alone on a dark road with a guy less forgiving than me. One who would cause him much pain and require years of facial reconstruction and he would squint because it hurt to open his eyes.

Dark road—I thought again of Strawberry Death. I was still not persuaded by Lindsey's explanation.

At Van Buren Street, we jigged east to First Avenue. I dreaded seeing the new occupant in Peralta's former office suite, where I had spent many sessions hearing his demands for progress on a case. That seemed like another person's life now.

But the car turned left on Jefferson Street and pulled in to valet parking for the Hotel Palomar.

Nobody said anything. We merely got out and I followed them inside.

The Palomar was the crown jewel of CityScape, the latest attempt to revive a downtown that the city had nearly killed in the sixties.

The development had been presented in the newspaper with renderings of audacious skyscrapers. The reality was vapid and suburban, turned in on itself instead of recreating a walkable downtown commercial district. Still, it was better than the brutal empty plaza it had replaced, and Lindsey and I spent as much as we could at the limited selection of shops. We tried to be civic stewards, supporting downtown rather than driving to Scottsdale or the Biltmore.

Inside the hotel was another matter. The Blue Hound restaurant and bar had a flashy LA feel, with dark wood, swag lamps, large mirrors hung at menacing angles over the tables, leather sofas in front of a fireplace that was lit even in the summertime, textured walls, and a big crowd.

I followed the plainclothes deputies past the fun to the elevators. We rode up in silence.

The car opened onto a rooftop bar called Lustre. With the temperature still above seventy, it was a beautiful night to be here. But the place was empty. A sign said, "Reserved for Private Party."

That would be the casually dressed man at the bar with a messenger bag on the floor beside his feet. He stood up and smiled at me. Then he extended his hand.

And I shook it.

He saved me the impossibility of speaking his title by saying, "Call me Chris."

Then he dismissed the detail with a "thanks, guys" and led me to a table.

Christopher Andrew Melton was completing his first year as Maricopa County sheriff. Not being a big television watcher, especially what passed for local news, this was my first opportunity to really see him.

He was my size and my height. I had so hoped he was a short little guy. I had dreamed most of his hair had fallen out, leaving only dust bunny tufts. But, no, it was still there, golden and expensively cut. His voice was measured and harmonized with education, not the redneck twang I expected. He was further helped by the kind of limpid blue eyes that were ubiquitous in British costume dramas.

He had moved to Sun City West after finishing twenty-five years with the FBI. He invested in some houses and made top dollar before the real-estate crash. With his federal law-enforcement pedigree, he won consulting work for the homebuilders and the rock products association—the trade group that lobbied for the asphalt, concrete, and aggregate producers—doing what, I didn't know. I did know they were two of the most politically powerful entities in the state.

Then he ran for sheriff. An "impossible bid," the pundits had said. "Mike Peralta will be sheriff as long as he wants the job and then he can be governor." That was what they had said.

But Melton found his issue and his timing with illegal immigration, something Peralta was supposedly "soft" on, even though the Sheriff's Office had no authority over federal enforcement of immigration laws.

It was a dirty campaign, with Melton's surrogates playing to Anglo fears and emphasizing that the sheriff was "soft" because he was "a Mexican himself." "What part of illegal doesn't he understand?" one bumper sticker read, with Peralta's face on it.

Melton beat Peralta by ten thousand votes in the Republican primary where the turnout was twenty percent. The county's population was four million.

And now he sat across from me.

"I know this is awkward," he said.

The server arrived and saved me from saying many unhelpful things. In addition to the campaign, I could have mentioned the Justice Department investigation of the Sheriff's Office, brought on by Melton's highly publicized "sweeps" to round up illegals. This had destroyed years of effort by Peralta and the Phoenix Police to build cooperation in a community that was often victimized by crime. Now it was back in the shadows.

With deputies playing immigration police, response times had risen around the county, even for priority calls. Violent crime in the areas policed by MCSO was increasing. There were allegations of failure to investigate sex crimes. Jail conditions had deteriorated and prisoners had been abused. The county had already paid out three million dollars to settle lawsuits against the department. Local wags were already calling him "Sheriff Crisis Meltdown."

And this was only from what I had read in the struggling local paper. From a few conversations with old friends in the department, I sensed things were even worse. That the model law-enforcement organization built by Peralta had been trashed.

Melton had even changed the department's uniforms from light-tan shirt and brown slacks to intimidating LAPD black. He had moved into the new Sheriff's Office headquarters that was Peralta's handiwork, the product of years of fighting the county supervisors for funding.

In the newspaper, Melton had called the building, "A sign of the positive changes I'm bringing to this department."

The craziest part was that Melton was more popular than ever, at least among the old Anglos who voted. He probably reminded them of their favorite grandsons, in addition to being "tough on crime," as they imagined it.

A lazy thinker would fall for it. He didn't look like a bigoted Southern lawman from the fifties. No, he was svelte and boyish and well-spoken. It would be easy for a lazy thinker to like him.

I was pretty toasty from the martini with Lindsey but ordered a Four Peaks Hop Knot IPA.

"Make it two," Melton said.

I wondered what his constituency in the suburban mega-churches and LDS meetinghouses would think.

Looking around, downtown Phoenix seemed almost on the verge of being cool. From the rooftop bar, we had views of the Suns arena, multiple skyscrapers, and the South Mountains and Estrellas in the lingering twilight. Steps led up to an azure swimming pool. Gray columns were topped with ice-blue lighting that matched the color of the still water. Lindsey and I would have fun here.

His voice brought me back to the unpleasant business at hand.

"I'm sorry about Peralta." He folded his arms across his chest and sighed. "You probably think I'm a bad guy for the campaign. But it was politics. He understood that. Phoenix has changed and he didn't change with it. So voters wanted a change."

I stared at him.

He released his arms and shook his head. "But this jewel robbery. Bad stuff."

"A person is innocent until proved guilty."

The woman brought our beers and withdrew.

"I'm afraid it doesn't look good and the FBI will be digging very hard into Peralta's time as sheriff."

"They won't find anything but good police work." I took a big swig and let the liquid burn my insides.

"We can hope so," Melton said. "I wanted to talk about you."

I put the glass down and said nothing.

"I was sorry you left. I could have used you. Your ability to employ the historian's techniques to solve cold cases is very valuable."

"It was time for me to move on."

"Maybe not." He reached into the messenger bag and pulled out a book. I recognized it instantly because I had written it. *Desert Star: A History of the Maricopa County Sheriff's Office.*

"This is a fabulous book," Melton said. "Really great. I had no idea there was so much history here. Would you sign it?"

He slid it across and handed me a pen.

Play to the author's shameless vanity. I opened to the title page and wrote, "To Sheriff Chris Melton, making new history. David Mapstone."

He thanked me. Then, "Maybe you'd write a new preface. We could re-release it."

I didn't answer. As a historian, I had written only two books, thirty articles for historical journals. Not enough to gain tenure.

He put the book away and pulled out a file. It was about an inch thick.

"I'd like you to look into this for me."

My eyes lingered on the folder. It looked worn. I told him no, that I already had a job, and slid it back to his side of the table.

He smiled sadly. "I don't think there will be much private investigator work coming your way with your partner as a wanted fugitive in a violent crime. It wouldn't surprise me if the DPS revoked your license, as well as his."

"But you're here to help me…" I drained the glass halfway.

"Exactly."

So I gave it to him, exactly, "I don't like you, Sheriff. I don't like your politics. You and your people lied about Mike Peralta's record. You set people against each other."

Remembering the thugs that had shouted Peralta down at one debate, the vicious online comments about him from Melton supporters and all the "dark money" from anonymous out-of-state donors, I started to get wound up.

I forced my voice to stay even. "I don't approve of the way you won the election or how you run the department. And I don't take clients that I don't like and trust." I thought about it and added, "No disrespect."

"Call me Chris."

"If I did take your case, it would be a five thousand-dollar retainer up front, then five hundred dollars an hour after that. I would want total control of the case. No second-guessing."

He laughed from below his diaphragm and wiped his mouth with a paper napkin. His beer was still untouched.

"That's not what I had in mind."

His hand went back into the bag and pulled out what looked like a wallet. I realized what it really was only when he placed it on the table atop the file and opened it: a star and identification card. My old badge and credentials.

"You're coming back to the Sheriff's Office, David."

I sat back, feeling the little revolver against my shirt, and marveling at his chutzpah.

"And I would want to do this, why?"

"Open the file."

He slid the folder toward me again.

I swept the badge case aside and flipped to the first page. It was an incident report dated July 24th, 1984. It looked like a museum artifact. At the bottom was my signature and badge number.

He tapped the paper. "Do you remember this?"

I nodded. A body of a twenty-something male had been found in the desert not far from the Caterpillar tractor proving grounds in the White Tank Mountains west of the city. Today the area is overrun with subdivisions, but then it was empty. The dead man had parked his car and walked on foot without water before he had collapsed.

I had been the first deputy to respond to the call, the one who had secured the scene and written the incident report. There was no obvious evidence of a crime. People did strange things in the desert. And then the desert did unmerciful things to their remains. Then the case had been turned over to the detectives and I had lost track of it. This was when I was finishing my master's degree and preparing to leave the department and Phoenix.

Now, under the enchanted metropolitan sky with blessed ice water sitting next to the beers, I shrugged. "So?"

"There's been a new development in the case."

"Turn it over to your cold-case unit. I'm sure they're quite capable."

He shook his head. "I want you to investigate this. It requires your special skills." He leaned in and touched my arm. "David, this is your home, your hometown. You belong with us at the Sheriff's Office. I'll warn you, the county is going paperless. I should have given you the documents digitally. But I thought the paper files might be easier."

I drained the glass and stood. "Thanks for the beer, Sheriff."

I was halfway out when his voice stopped me.

"Lindsey."

I turned to face him. My feet felt heavy.

He beckoned me back with a flipping of his fingers, as if he were summoning a child. "Call me Chris. And you forgot your star, Deputy."

I walked back and stood over him. "Why did you mention my wife?"

"Sit down, David."

I did.

"Your wife is a hacker. She has been all her teenage and adult life."

"You're being cute with words," I said. "Lindsey was a sworn deputy in the Sheriff's Office cybercrimes unit and then she was recruited by Homeland Security. What made her so valuable is that she's a 'good hacker,' if you want to use the word. A knuckle-dragger going by some manual from Microsoft isn't going to have that expertise."

"That's what made her so effective. She's one of the best hackers we ever encountered."

A coldness spread in my limbs as I wondered who this "we" was.

"Your wife's time in Washington, D.C., was not what you believe, David. I hate to put it this way, but sometimes it's better get the truth out there. She wasn't faithful."

"My marriage is not your business."

"There were several instances where she strayed. I know it hurts, but my sources are golden. You need to know this."

"Good-bye," I said, but made no effort to leave the chair.

I knew Lindsey had played and strayed, knew it because I had found a confessional letter she intended to mail to me but never did—and then I had tucked it back in her things and never spoke of it. It had been a mad time for both of us. Her sister Robin had been alive then. If the sheriff was trying to mind-fuck me to do his bidding, this wouldn't work.

He lowered his head. "She was unfaithful to the country, too."

"What the hell are you saying?"

"You know about the F-35 fighter? It's our most advanced jet. We're fortunate that Luke Air Force Base was chosen as the primary training base."

I looked him in the eyes.

"You're giving me a chamber of commerce pitch," I said.

"Unfortunately not." He leaned in a few inches. "You may also know that China stole important information about it. An airplane we thought would give us a twenty-year advantage. Now the Chinese are incorporating its features into their advanced fighters, especially the Shenyang J-23. Try explaining that to the young men and women who will die in combat if push comes to shove in the South China Sea or over Taiwan…"

"This is a long damned way from being Maricopa County sheriff." I tried to throttle down the anger in my voice and failed. "Running the jails humanely. Serving warrants. Dull job, but necessary."

"Listen to what I'm telling you, David. The feds have reason to believe Lindsey actually helped the Chinese gain access to the F-35 designs. They know a man she was sleeping with did it and he is about to be indicted. They think she was involved, too."

"She was working for Homeland Security!"

His voice was calm, the eyes sympathetic. "There's so much you don't know."

"You're accusing my wife of treason." I couldn't stop the heat from burning my cheeks. I tried to center myself by staring at the empty swimming pool, the water as flat as glass.

Melton said, "You can help her…"

"By working for you? I've said too much already. You're probably wearing a wire. What I need to do is get the best lawyer in town and go to the papers."

His shoulders hunched in tension.

I said, "If Lindsey did these things, why isn't she in prison already?"

"Because federal investigations take time. There are open questions. But the White House is putting on pressure to go after leakers and spies, especially involving China. Listen to me, David. I can help you if you'll help me."

"Me, working an old DB case can somehow balance the scales of an active investigation of treason? Involving my wife?" I spat the words. It was not my best moment.

"This 'dead body' case, as you put it, is important to me. As for your wife, I can buy you some time. I know people, more than you realize, and they can work in her favor. That's a guarantee. And maybe with that time and influence, Lindsey can… well, do whatever she needs to do."

What the hell did he mean? Clear her name? Leave the country? Meet up with Peralta to split the diamonds?

"I want to know more about the accusations against Lindsey."

"I can't do that, David. I'm already out on a limb for you. Washington could come in with a National Security Letter. Do you know what that is?"

I nodded, not exactly sure but it wouldn't be good. It would prevent us from discussing the case, perhaps even deny Lindsey counsel.

"Don't think it can't happen. So you need to be very careful. The country changed after 9/11 and nothing got softer with the election and re-election of Obama. These are dangerous times and the government holds enormous power to protect us."

For a few moments it was silent enough to hear glasses clinking behind the bar.

Melton shrugged. "Me, I tell my wife everything that happens in my day. You'd better not say a word of this to Lindsey."

"So how can she help herself?"

"She can tell who she was working with inside the government…"

"Flip," I said. "Become a snitch."

"She might be able to work for the government again."

I wondered if he was wearing a wire. "She did nothing wrong. But if a person did what you claim, I don't think he'd get off so easy."

"Provide help and the charges could be reduced or dropped," he said. "I've seen it happen. She might have to work at the Genius Bar at the Apple Store for awhile but it beats thirty years in prison for espionage."

"And the sheriff of Maricopa County knows all this, how?"

He slapped the table. "I've said too much already. Are you in?"

"Goddamnit, slow down! I need to talk to Lindsey first…"

And then I was aware of the murmur twenty feet behind me. Turning, I saw dozens of people, young, beautiful, stylishly dressed, waiting to get into the bar.

"No time, David." His eyes bore into me. "Are you in?"

Thucydides, the father of historians, said that men are motivated by fear and then by honor and self-interest. And here I was.

But I was not beyond churlishness.

"I want my old office back."

He made an amused face. "The historic courthouse has been remodeled. I'm afraid your old space is now a courtroom." He smiled. "But there's another office on the fourth floor you'll find to your liking."

He fished a key out of his pocket and placed it on top of the file.

I signed papers from the Sheriff's Office and a certification document from the Arizona Peace Officers Standards and Training Board. Next came a Bible out of that damned messenger bag. We stood up and he swore me in at the rooftop bar. So help me, God.

He fished out a business card and scribbled numbers on the back. He held it up and I took it.

"You'll report directly to me. Read the case file and call me in the morning. We'll get started." He paused and then put his hand on my shoulder like we were good buddies. "It gets better, David. Trust me. You're from Maricopa County. This is your hometown. You owe, don't you think? To leave it a better place for our kids than we found it?"

I wanted to break his hand.

"Do you want a ride home?"

I shook my head. "I'll take light rail."

"Glad somebody uses it. I hear it runs empty all the time."

I picked up the file, slid the badge case in my blazer pocket, and walked away.

As I reached the elevators, the crowd was surging into the bar, and Call-Me-Chris Melton had disappeared.

Chapter Nine

I walked out of the hotel in a trance, oblivious to the perfection of the evening, crossing First Avenue mid-block. I was about to step over the light-rail tracks, across the low concrete barrier where it was stenciled DO NOT CROSS, when the horn shook me into the moment.

The train was no more than half a block to my right, the operator flashing his lights and laying on the horn. I stepped back and let the train come into the station, walking around it.

The majestic old county courthouse was as lovely, dignified, and enduring as when it opened in 1929, an art deco interpretation of Spanish architecture. It had been built as a combined city-county building. So, here, facing Washington Street, was the courthouse. On the west side, guarded by carved Phoenix birds, was the entrance to old city hall. With such attributes, it amazed me that Phoenix had not torn it down.

Enough damage had been done. When I was a boy, lush grass and shrubs, shaded by queen palms, surrounded the building. Now all that was gone, replaced by dirt and the skeletons of palo verde trees. Somebody thought they were saving water, even though it was being misused to fill artificial lakes in subdivisions thirty miles away.

I wondered about the workers that had ripped out those noble trees back in the 1980s and whether they had realized the damage they were doing.

Then I made the mistake of looking back at the graceless, sterile cube of CityScape and how it overpowered the flawless art deco Luhrs Tower in the next block, its fourteen stories with elegant setbacks built for a low-rise city that held 48,000 people. CityScape, heavily subsidized by the taxpayers, was doing fairly well for now. It had a comedy club and a bowling alley. The bottom of the Luhrs Tower was empty except for a Subway shop. This was Phoenix.

At the front of the courthouse, the old fountain was still there. A plaque read:

IN MEMORY OF
LIEUT. JACK W. SWILLING
1831-1878
WHO BUILT THE
FIRST MODERN IRRIGATION DITCH
AND
TRINIDAD, HIS WIFE
1850-1929
WHO ESTABLISHED IN 1868 THE FIRST
PIONEER HOME IN THE
SALT RIVER VALLEY.
ERECTED BY
MARICOPA CHAPTER
DAUGHTERS OF THE AMERICAN REVOLUTION
1931

I sat on the fountain's concrete lip and listened to the water.

"Swilling's Ditch" was one of the hundreds of miles of canals built by the Hohokam to divert water of the Salt River in this great alluvial valley. "Those who have gone"—the disappeared civilization, the canal builders. Then the Anglos came, found the ancient waterworks, the most advanced in the New World outside Peru. They cleared out the ancient canals, built new ones and the Phoenix was reborn.

Old Phoenix kept its secrets. Jack Swilling was one of the town's founders. He was also a scoundrel who helped betray the

Apache leader Mangus Coloradus, leaving him to be tortured and killed by the U.S. Army. It was an act of treachery that helped ensure twenty years of war. But this wasn't engraved on the fountain.

And people like Chris Melton didn't even know or care. They moved into their new subdivisions far from the heart of the city and thought the only history was back home in the Midwest. I would bet he had never read this plaque.

The water trickled in a melody that should have been comforting. Not tonight. Because I knew. Too much and not enough.

Maybe even Mike Peralta was a scoundrel who would throw everything away for a case of diamonds. And here I am carrying that damned badge. I never should have come back here. Not to this building. Not to this city.

Better to be teaching history in Southern California or Denver, Portland, or Seattle, even in a community college if need be. Anywhere but here.

Yet Peralta never stopped trying to get me back to the Sheriff's Office and he had finally succeeded. When I didn't get tenure in San Diego and returned to Phoenix, intending to sell the house and move on, he hired me to clean up some old cases. And I stayed.

I never should have stayed.

Phoenix is not my city now.

It belongs to the millions of newcomers drawn here by sun, a pool in the backyard, and big wide freeways to drive. To the ones that bulldoze its history and throw down gravel and concrete where there once were flowers and oleanders and canopies of cottonwoods, eucalyptus, and Arizona ash over open irrigation ditches.

I hear the ghosts of the Hohokam and love it when it rains. Newcomers want championship golf and endless sunshine.

They own this place now, not me.

They tell me every place changes, but why did my place have to get worse? It's not as if we traded the Valley of Heart's Delight to become Silicon Valley.

What right have I to hate them? They have no memory of my garden city when the air was so clear it seemed as if you could reach out and touch the mountains. They don't miss the passenger trains at Union Station or the busy stores and movie palaces downtown.

How could they miss what had been wiped away?

The problem is me, for loving Phoenix still.

The blame rests with me, for coming back, for staying.

I should have sold the house in Willo, where the historic districts carry strands of the old city's loveliness—sold it and left for good.

But it had been built by my grandfather, had always been in the family. How could I endure seeing a photo of it on the Web, knowing a stranger owned it, and had probably put rocks in place of Grandmother's gardens?

But it is a house, nothing more, and sentimentality disables me.

What fool would mourn Phoenix? It makes as much sense as pining for Muncie, Indiana, in the nineteenth century.

My fool's punishment is that I am from nowhere.

"David, this is your home, your hometown."

I have no hometown.

I am a fraud.

I'll never make it home again.

Had I not come back, I never would have met Lindsey, the young Sheriff's Office computer genius with the nose stud and wicked sense of humor. She would have been so much better off without me.

I should not be here.

It's not healthy.

It's not sane.

I am like a mad archeologist trying to conjure ruins back to their past glory.

Or like a dog that can't leave his master's grave, ending up a stray that howls all night in the cemetery, crying, *loss…loss…loss…*

So help me, God, I am so lost.

The water shut off, as if on a timer.

I made my legs stand and take the steps two at a time up to the grand arched main entrance where I buzzed the night bell.

"Mapstone! I haven't seen you in forever. How the hell's it hanging?"

The deputy didn't even realize I had left the department.

A metal detector and X-ray machine with a belt had been installed inside, but otherwise the lobby and airy atrium looked the same. No, better. The county had actually done a good job restoring the building to its period beauty. The brass elevator doors glimmered beyond.

Instead, I took the staircase that wound up the atrium, walking on the brown Mexican saltillo tiles, gripping the railing that so many thousands of justice-seeking hands had touched. The decorative tiles on the risers had been polished and replaced where needed. The wrought-iron chandeliers burned through yellow panes set off with colored medallions.

When Peralta had first put me over here, the building was an afterthought holding a few county agencies. Now, I guessed it was busy on weekdays. Tonight, it was silent enough for my footfall to echo. I reached the fourth floor and walked past the doors of dark wood, pebbled glass, and transoms. Overhead were white globes spaced every few feet.

My phone vibrated. A message from Lindsey: "You ok?"

I texted back, "Yes. Home soon."

I was anything but okay.

Then I found the correct door, slipped in the key, and went inside.

My new office was perhaps ten feet by twelve feet, a comedown from my old digs. But it had a large window looking north. I turned on the lights and there they stood, the antique wooden desk I had scrounged from the county warehouse, swivel chair, and two other straight-back chairs in front. Against one wall was the 1930s courtroom bench I also had appropriated. Another wall held the historic map of Phoenix that was yet another of my finds, one I didn't take with me when I left the job.

It was as if Melton had planned it all before we ever talked.

And I had fallen into the snare.

Treason, indeed.

I switched the lights back off, crossed to the desk chair, and slowly lowered myself to sit. The empty desktop received its first employment since I had resigned and cleaned out my old office—the case file Melton had given me. I thought about reading through the case now, thought better of it, and instead spun around to watch the cars moving along Washington Street.

I wondered where Peralta was, if he was safe, what the hell was going on. I needed to be working on finding him, deciphering the messages on the cards, not rehashing a thirty-year-old case.

The dread had hold of my throat and chest before I realized it. My heart galloped insistently inside my chest. I was conscious of every chamber of my heart opening and closing, opening and closing. In only seconds, it seemed, the trap door to oblivion would open beneath me. *Yes, Sharon, I still get panic attacks.*

The only remedy was to move, to get up and flee the building, get into the night air and see some other human souls. At Central and Washington, I boarded a train so full of them that I had to stand all the way home.

On the way, I tried to figure out what to tell Lindsey.

Chapter Ten

Our block was awash in white lights and hemmed in by the dark silhouettes of satellite trucks bearing the logos of television stations. As I drew closer, I saw that the lights were from television cameras and pointed at our house. The house looked good. Lindsey looked even better, standing on the front patio and talking into microphones that five reporters held to her very telegenic face.

Setting aside my initial alarm, I held back on the sidewalk.

"Sheriff Peralta is a man of the highest integrity," she said. "I worked for him for a long time and my respect for him grew with every year. I'm sure a logical explanation will come out about what happened."

Logical explanations. I was all for that.

"Why would he shoot a man and steal the diamonds?" A woman's voice.

"These are allegations," Lindsey said. "I only know what you people have reported. The police are investigating."

"Have you heard from him since the theft?" A man shouted the question.

"Of course not." Not a second's hesitation, her tone earnest. She turned her head to move the hair out of her eyes.

"Not a word? Your husband is his partner in their private detective business."

"Not a word."

She was a good little liar, my wife.

I walked on to the end of the block as they ran out of questions and packed up. Not one word I could say to them would make things better.

The neighborhood was as magical as the surprised deputy had found it. The period revival houses had all been restored and were some of the priciest real estate in the city now. It seemed as if only Lindsey and I had not put in a pool.

Willo had been built slowly, almost one house at a time, a huge contrast to the industrial-scale subdivisions laid down elsewhere, later in the life of the city. A couple of blocks over were bungalows that dated back to before statehood. Most of our block had been built in the twenties. The City Beautiful Movement even infused the sidewalks, which ran between small "parking lawns" on one side and the larger lawns that extended to the houses. Only philistines put in desert landscaping. This had always been the oasis.

Ten minutes later, the street safely in darkness, I unlocked the front door and stepped inside.

"You were impressive."

"Thank you."

She tilted her face up and I kissed her.

I said, "I wondered how long it would take for them to show up. Better you speaking to the media than me."

She looked at the brown file folder. "Is that from the High Sheriff of Maricopa County?"

I nodded.

"And?"

After hesitating, I showed her my star.

"No, Dave." She pushed it away and shook her head. "Why would you go back to the Sheriff's Office? For Sheriff Meltdown. My God, that's not right. What happened?"

I sighed. "Oh, Lindsey, talk to me, and I'll rub your feet."

The temper drained from her face. "Deal."

We went to the sofa and I pulled off her shoes, running my fingers along the perfect facets of her cheerleader ankles. I avoided her concerned look. I kissed the left foot, sucked her toes for a few moments, and began to massage.

"Ooooo, History Shamus…"

"Why is the FBI investigating this case?" The question suddenly entered my crowded mind.

"I don't know. It's not an interstate crime yet. The FBI has really changed since 9/11. It's very focused on counterterrorism. Now that you mention it…" She shook her head.

"This should be Chandler P.D.'s case. Not one Chandler detective was in Ash Fork early this morning."

"So I'll give you one, Dave. Why would Mike Peralta need a million dollars?"

I pressed my fingers into her calves and attempted to study her face. Only one lamp was on and her expression was shadowed. I turned away and meditated on the tall bookshelves on the far wall and the stairway that went up beside them.

Oh, for time to do nothing but read books and hang around with Lindsey, free from the outside world, free from the burden that had been hung around my neck beside that perfectly still rooftop pool.

"A million isn't what it once was," she went on. "Like when you were young, my older man. Not only that, but it's a million in stolen, traceable, hot-as-hell diamonds. You can't exactly take that to the pawnshop. So I did some digging around."

The bottom fell out of my stomach.

"Keep rubbing."

I did as I was told.

"The Peraltas have a net worth of 2.4 million," she said. "Part of that is in their home, which is paid off. Sharon still gets more than a hundred thousand a year from the sales of her self-help books, DVDs, and speeches. Mike's pension is ninety-two thousand a year. In the past six months, the private detective work has brought in a net sixty-seven thousand, twice what it did when you guys were starting out."

I moved to worshipping her right foot. I would never get used to the tattoo on the top. "Emma." She got it in D.C., after the miscarriage, after she nearly bled to death and saving her meant we could never have children, after she fled from me. But there was that ink, in one of the places where it was most painful to get a tattoo. And on her perfect fair skin. To me, tattoos were trashy or belonged on sailors, especially in *Moby Dick*. I was a dinosaur from the twentieth century. I also wouldn't have chosen Emma. But there it was. I had never mentioned it.

She said, "If you dig deeper—oh, right there, that feels so good—the Peraltas have 1.25 million dollars in what you would call 'investable assets,' money that can be put in stocks and bonds and mutual funds. And all this is as of the latest account statements. Nothing has been pilfered. No evidence of accounts being drained for, say, a gambling habit or to pay off a blackmailer. They have no debt. Imagine that in today's America."

I said, "So why would he need a million bucks in diamonds? It's more evidence he didn't turn rogue." Or, as Lindsey had suggested earlier, that he had committed the crime to prove something, to stick it to the voters that had betrayed him. But I didn't say that.

She smiled. "Are you proud of me? Wait until I tell you about Matt Pennington."

I nodded and rubbed her feet. Maybe that would be enough, we could wind down and go to bed, and none of this would be real in the morning.

Part of that might even have happened if I hadn't said another word.

Instead, I said, and I said it very carefully, lightly, trying to avoid a vowel of accusation in my voice, "Please tell me you weren't hacking the Peraltas' financial data, Lindsey."

After a pause, her voice was smaller but had an edge. "I talked on the phone with Sharon. Want to tell me what's wrong, Dave?"

And so I did.

All the way home, I had rehearsed a way to discuss our mess in a conversation that would be careful, nuanced, calm, and fluent. All that preparation deserted me the more I began to speak.

It took about fifteen minutes to get it out and by the end I was talking too fast and too loud.

Her perfect ankles and feet withdrew and she sat at the other end of the sofa, her arms wrapped around her legs.

"You don't buy any of this, do you?"

"Of course not."

"What else did he tell you I did in Washington?"

That was the leading question from the depths of hell.

I hadn't told her that he had mentioned her affairs. I didn't now, looking straight at her and lying convincingly, or so I thought. Her blue eyes darkened, never a good sign.

After a searing pause, Lindsey finally spoke, her voice as hard as, well, a diamond.

"He's using you, Dave. He's trying to scare you and he's trying to use me to get what he wants."

She walked off to the kitchen and began cleaning up, loudly banging pans.

Of course, he was using me. I was a fool on a hundred fronts but I knew this much. I walked to the kitchen and stood in the doorway.

"What should I have done?" I said. "I can look at the file. It can't do any harm."

She stared into the sink and scrubbed harder. "Don't talk to me like I'm a child, Dave."

That came out of nowhere and I started feeling the same anger that was motivating her manic kitchen cleaning.

She dried her hands with a striped dishcloth and turned. "You should have called me. We should have made this decision together."

"There wasn't time."

"Why not?" Her tone was sharp. "Did he have an arrest warrant?"

I struggled to find a response. She was right, of course.

I said, "I couldn't let him throw you to the wolves."

She smiled with cutting false sweetness. "Aren't you the white knight?"

Everybody has an interior jerk. Mine was about to lash back but I stopped it. For a long time the house enclosed us in a tense quiet.

She made a lithe move across the room and I stepped aside. When I followed, I found her sitting on the wide starting step. The staircase led to a door, then a walkway that spanned the interior courtyard to the garage apartment. She put her head in her hands. I touched her shoulder.

"And you're a deputy sheriff again. Working for this racist pig."

"It won't last," I said. "I wanted to buy time."

She turned her shoulder to avoid my hand. I sat in the leather chair and pressed ahead.

"We need to talk to a lawyer. This is serious stuff, Lindsey. I'm worried."

When she spoke again, the sarcasm was gone. "I was loaned out to an interagency unit, CIA, NSC, DIA, that's the Defense Intelligence Agency."

She looked up. "Did you think I was in D.C. dealing with Nigerian email scams? My God, you're naïve."

"I guess so. You told me it was a temporary job at Homeland Security."

"Look, Chinese hackers got a bunch of information on the Joint Strike Fighter, the F-35, by penetrating a British contractor. That's not news. You can find stories about this on the Web, at least the defense press."

"So you don't have to kill me if you tell me?"

She didn't laugh and I regretted interrupting.

After a moment, she continued. "The efforts to steal information didn't stop there. Our job was to find out who were the bad guys, how big the breach was—what had they learned? Then the task was trying to feed them false information, flawed design elements. I also created a back door into their network and a malware bug that would have rocked their world, but they wouldn't let me use it. Said it was shot down by the White House."

I wasn't surprised her work would attract attention in high places. She was so damned smart and good at what she did.

She sighed. "The damage was much worse than the brass feared. They stole design elements and critical systems information involving not only the F-35 but the F-22."

"Did you find out who they were?"

"Unit 61398. No surprise, probably."

When she saw the My-God-you're-naïve expression on my face, she explained.

"It's one of the most important hacking groups of The People's Liberation Army. The Internet is a battlefield."

I let out a long breath.

"So why would Melton have his story backward? Why did he say I needed to buy you some time because you had given the Chinese information?"

"Because he's evil. Because he's using you!" Her shoulders stiffened and she used both hands to whip back her hair. She stood and walked past me to the picture window, staring out on Cypress Street.

She whispered, "My God, you believe him!"

"I do not." I said it forcefully. And I meant it.

I stood up and embraced her from behind. She pulled away.

"Part of you believed him when he was telling you about… whatever he told you went on with me in Washington. I could see it in your face, Dave. I know you."

This is where I should have stopped it. Diffuse the situation. Go to bed, safe in our cocoon, you and me against the world, babe. But the alcohol truth serum was still in my bloodstream.

I said quietly, "Maybe he was misinformed. When you came home, you told me that your security clearance had been revoked and they confiscated your laptop. Can't you understand why I was concerned after what Melton said? Somebody could be out to get you. Blame you for something that went wrong. I'm not so naïve that I don't know how shit rolls downhill in government agencies."

"You don't know anything," she said, her voice rising uncharacteristically. "Jesus, David..."

It was the first time I could recall her ever using my full given name.

"Lindsey, please sit down. Let's work this out together. I only mention the security clearance because..."

"Oh, now you want to work it out together. Why didn't you tell Meltdown to stick it and come home so we could work it out together then? But, no, you believed what he told you about me and you rolled over like a coward. Where else do you think I'm a liar?"

"Hang on."

"Fuck you, David! You were screwing my sister right in our home." She shook her head. "You must have felt like quite the stud."

I slowly shook my head. "It wasn't like that."

She dropped to her haunches and stared at me.

"Really? Tell me what it was like? Tell me everything. All the details. What it felt like. Then tell me what it felt like when Robin died."

I turned away from her glare, felt my cheeks burning.

"It felt like hell."

There was no avoiding it.

Robin. Lindsey's half-sister was a curator for the art collection of a rich man in Paradise Valley. The job went away with the real-estate collapse, when his empire proved to be built on nothing but debt and promises, and he used a revolver to blow his brains all over a Frida Kahlo original hanging in his living room.

The collection went to his creditors and Lindsey insisted Robin move into the garage apartment.

Then a family tragedy estranged us and Lindsey fled to D.C. For months, I was sure I had lost her.

Robin. She was a fairly close match for the actress Robin Wright with long hair, when she was younger and not anorexic. But this Robin had no glamour. She was a storm child. She always called her older sister by her first and middle names, Lindsey Faith.

There was no excusing my part in what happened next, not Robin's aggressiveness, not the fact that Lindsey insisted she stay here, rebuffing my suggestion that Robin move.

Robin and I happened.

Whatever Lindsey did in her personal life during those months, I had no right to whine or pry. I had never judged her.

My offenses became unpardonable the night that Robin and I were in the backyard and she took a bullet intended for me. She died in my arms. The vengeance I took, on that last case as a deputy sheriff, didn't bring her back. For a time, I wondered if Lindsey would leave me, not for having an affair with Robin but for losing her.

Now I said, "Every day, I wish that bullet had hit me." My voice was too loud.

She sprang up and turned away. "Oh, please, quit feeling sorry for yourself. You did what you did, feeling like the big stud. Now you have the balls to question my integrity? To believe that badged ego telling you I'm a traitor!"

"I don't believe it!"

"She loved you."

"What?"

"Are you a stupid person, David? Did you not hear what I said? Robin fell in love with you. She told me. I thought I'd lost you."

"You would barely take my phone calls then," I said. "This is not about Robin. This is about whatever it is that Melton thinks he knows and how it could hurt us."

"It hurt us that you believed him."

"I don't!"

She muttered another profanity and strode across the hardwood floor to the desk, opened a drawer, and produced her blue pack of Gauloises Blondes cigarettes and lighter. Some people smoke after a meal or sex. Lindsey mostly smoked when she was under great stress.

She said, "I don't have to explain myself..."

"I didn't ask you to. I'm not the enemy."

"Then why are you willing to lie down with the devil!"

We were both shouting now. Shouting fights were very rare in our marriage.

"Now you know national security secrets I swore not to divulge. I had to tell you because you don't trust me!"

Re-crossing the room, she stood before me, one hand on her hip, her eyes now wide and full-on angry violet.

"I'm going for a walk. I need to take a break from this."

Lindsey was almost always preternaturally calm. Not now. The tone in her voice was boiling.

She quickly slipped on her shoes and headed to the door.

"I never doubted you. Not for a second."

"Right." A sardonic half-shout.

"Lindsey, please. Please don't…"

The door closed and I spoke the last word of the sentence to myself.

"…leave."

Chapter Eleven

Later, I reflected on how a lover's quarrel never takes a logical course and for each of us, a perilous combination of fissile materials—shame, jealousy, and regret—was waiting to create a destructive chain reaction. Later, I would wonder why, why I agreed to accept the star from Chris Melton, and boil it down to one prime motivation: fear. Unreasoning fear for Lindsey. I was ambushed and made the bad call. I was usually good under pressure. Not this time.

But that was later.

Now, I stewed for maybe thirty seconds and stood up.

Outside, it was full dark, moonless, and most of the neighbors had their lights off. But I could see Lindsey, thanks to her white blouse. She was on the sidewalk almost a block away.

She had already crossed Third Avenue and was past the judge's house. He and his wife sang in a band.

The night held no band noises, barely any sounds at all. A bell from a light-rail train clanged two blocks east on Central, the direction Lindsey was heading. If you listened very carefully you could hear the continual grotesque moan of the Papago Freeway to the south.

The street held no FBI watchers, no reporters. Not one car was parked at the curb in our block.

I wanted to run after her but stopped myself. It would only reignite the argument. I started walking east slowly. Maybe I would catch up, maybe I would walk off my own brew of anger, confusion, and neediness. I needed her to understand why I took that file, took that oath.

This would be a good time for one of those business cards from Peralta to turn up and tell me what the hell to do.

I watched as Lindsey reached the gate and wall that closed off Cypress from cars at the end of the block. Pedestrians could walk through openings that lined up with the sidewalk. The wall ran nearly the length of the mile-long historic district. It was one of the horrid changes forced by the neighborhood association—I called it the Willo Soviet—to gain its support for light rail.

The result made the neighborhood, where streets had always run straight through to Central, and when this part of town was much more crowded and busy, into a "gated community." At least on one end.

The gate across the street supposedly allowed emergency vehicles to come through if need be. But one day a fire truck had stopped and the firefighters had asked Lindsey if she knew the "code" to open the barrier. There was no code. It was a damned locked gate.

The goddamned walls and gates made me angry every time I saw them. If I wanted gates and walls, I'd move to the suburbs.

Lindsey didn't like walking through the Wall of Willo, either. "I always wonder if somebody is waiting to mug me on the other side." She had said this more than once.

At least an ornamental light had been placed beside the sidewalk entrance on Cypress. It illuminated Lindsey clearly as she stepped through and disappeared on the other side, where First Avenue ran north and south. A block beyond that stood the open arms of the mid-century Phoenix Towers on Central Avenue.

Steps on the grass made me turn.

And there she was.

"Fight with the wifey?" she drawled. "But you want to make it all better."

The woman Lindsey had nicknamed Strawberry Death was two feet away, that semi-automatic pistol of a make I had never seen before pointed at my chest. This time, no DPS uniform—she wore a black turtleneck, black jeans, and black running shoes. I wondered how long she had been watching.

I opened my mouth and closed it. I was not thinking of clever comebacks.

She drawled, "She's pretty. A little of the Goth girl left in her. If I had time, I'd suicide you both. Suicided is better, cleaner. But I don't have time. Where are my stones?"

"What?"

"Are you hard of hearing? Where are my diamonds?"

So that's what this was about.

"I don't have them."

"Then I'm going to have to keep the promise I made."

"To who?"

"Whom," she corrected. "You should know better, Doctor Mapstone, being an educated man. Whom."

My feet felt very heavy as I spoke. "To whom?"

"Peralta."

Gun in your face. Buy time.

"You told him this?"

"I didn't have time," she said. "But a girl's got to keep her promises. Now, where are my stones?"

She smiled, showing a perfect set of white teeth, and made the mistake of taking two steps toward me as she answered.

I quickly stepped in close, as if we were about to dance. By the time she realized what was happening, it was too late. I planted my right foot and calf behind her left leg and used this as a lever to push her backwards.

At the same moment, I grabbed her gun hand with my left hand while notching my right hand under her elbow. It incapacitated the arm, pushed the gun aside, and helped propel her off balance and down hard.

Thanks to this straight-arm-bar, the gun came loose before she could pull the trigger and I fell on top of her.

This should have knocked the air out of her, but it didn't. She wrestled, punched, and made grunting and growling sounds.

She also wore Chanel Number Five.

My face was instantly on fire. It took a couple of seconds to realize this was a result of her raking fingernails across me. She tried a kick in the groin, but I blocked that by turning to the side. Then she bit me on the wrist.

That let her struggle toward the pistol on the grass while I grasped the waist of her black jeans to hold her back. Her hair had come loose and I pulled on it hard. She screamed and cursed me. My reach was longer and with my other hand I tossed the gun into a hedge. Something black and sudden came into my vision, followed by pain and starbursts. She kicked me in the face with her running shoe.

Her move toward the bushes and her weapon caused me to pull my .38. Before I could even raise the revolver, she sprinted away, leaving her pistol on the ground.

It took me a few seconds to get my balance. She had nailed me good with that kick.

By the time the dizziness faded, she held a good head start and she was fast.

She ran east on Cypress.

I pumped my arms and hammered the asphalt across Third Avenue, over the curb, and across the uneven, eighty-year-old sidewalk. But she was younger and I couldn't catch her.

Her lead extended. She wove in and out of palm trees on the parking lawns, making me momentarily lose sight of her.

Suddenly Lindsey stepped back inside the wall, headed back in the direction of home, and saw us.

Strawberry Death paused beside a palm long enough to reach toward her ankle.

A backup gun.

But she didn't turn on me. Instead, she started running east again. She was thirty feet from the wall.

I shouted, "Lindsey, run! Go back! Run!"

Lindsey froze and stared at me, unsure of what she was seeing.

I tried to get a clean shot but the two women were aligned and now not more than a few steps apart.

"Deputy Sheriff, halt! Drop your weapon! I will fire!"

Hearing this, Lindsey instantly withdrew to the other side.

"What's going on out there? Are you all right?" A man's voice from a porch.

"Get inside and call the police," I yelled.

Then I stopped, dropped to one knee, made my breathing slow down, and lined up the barrel on the back of the woman, the gold and red of her hair shining under the streetlight.

I slowly let out a breath and started the trigger pull.

But then she passed through the cut in the wall.

And three seconds later, I heard the shot.

Chapter Twelve

Lindsey lay face down on the pavement.

The back of her white blouse was red and wet with blood.

I swept the surroundings with my .38 but the woman was gone. Then I knelt beside my wife and gently turned her over.

"Dave…"

"I'm here."

"Your face is bleeding."

"I'm fine."

"Bad time for a walk, huh?" Her lips tried to smile.

I looked around again, but the parking lots across the street were empty and the edges of the wall looked clear of any lurking killer. The half-smoked Gauloise was burning five feet away.

"Don't leave me." Her voice sounded groggy.

"No. Never."

"It hurts. Hurts."

The entry wound was in the middle of her chest.

I needed a trauma kit.

I needed a trauma team with surgeons.

Her breathing was rapid and shallow. I took her pulse. Weak, thready. Classic shock symptoms. She was bleeding out.

"Stay with me, Lindsey. I love you. Stay awake."

She stared at me, tried and failed to speak while I shakily dialed 911 on my iPhone, gave our location, my badge number from memory, and called for help.

"My wife has been shot. She's badly wounded."

Fire Station Four, with a paramedic unit, was only five blocks away. I heard the sirens from McDowell. It took somewhere between forever and eternity for the first emergency lights to appear on First Avenue.

The memory of Robin dying in my arms was banging in my vision. I couldn't let it happen again.

Couldn't.

"Keep breathing, baby. In and out."

She nodded.

"Hold my hands tight." She did, but her strength was fading. Then her eyes closed.

Stripping off the blazer, I carefully rolled her to one side and used it as a makeshift dressing against her back. I wouldn't let the word enter my mind: useless.

Firefighters and cops were arriving. Red and blue lights bounced off the wall, doors opened and closed, and uniforms approached. I moved aside and let them work, giving a description of the shooter to an officer who broadcast it on her portable radio. A helicopter appeared overhead and blasted us with white light.

More sirens were approaching from the distance.

Chapter Thirteen

St. Joseph's Hospital, a Level One Trauma Center, was half a mile away.

An hour later, Lindsey was still in surgery. "Critical condition." That's all a doctor had told me as I was sent into in a long, largely empty waiting room with a television at one end bolted near the ceiling. A Hispanic family, mother and three small children, sat near it, staring silently.

God didn't owe me anything. That didn't stop me from praying for Lindsey.

A man came in to have me sign paperwork as Lindsey's next of kin. I had her Social Security number memorized. He seemed amazed that we had insurance. I remembered when St. Joe's was a hospital for the elite. Now most of the patients must have been on Medicaid or nothing.

It wasn't even connected to the Catholic Church anymore. After an abortion was performed to save the life of the mother, the bishop retaliated by cutting off church ties that went back to 1895. Now the local wags called it Mister Joe's and the moneyed Anglos had long abandoned it for Mayo. But it still was one of the best hospitals in the Southwest.

After the doctor left, it was quiet except for the television and a page for "Trauma Team Two." I assumed that "Trauma Team One" was busy with Lindsey.

My face was still burning from the scratches. My left cheek

and eye felt swollen from where the woman's running shoe had connected. I didn't want to look in a mirror.

I was bargaining with God like a panicky twelve-year-old, staring at nothing, when Phoenix Police Sergeant Kate Vare strode in, wearing a stylish short leather jacket and carrying an expensive leather portfolio.

She sat next to me. The butt of her Glock protruded from the jacket.

How I wished Lindsey had taken her Glock instead of a pack of cigarettes for that walk.

"I'm sorry, Mapstone."

It was the most human thing she had ever said to me.

Vare and I were once rivals, or at least she saw it that way when I worked for Peralta and she was a cold-case expert for Phoenix P.D. But the new chief had reorganized the department and now she was a night homicide detective. Otherwise, she looked the same: petite, ash-blond hair in a short bob, tightly wound.

Homicide. I pushed that word away. That was only the name of the unit she was assigned to, the kind of detective sent on this type of call, GSW, gunshot wound, victim in critical condition. Assault with a deadly weapon.

GSW to the chest, exit wound, massive blood loss. I knew the score.

My wife was in there dying.

I put my face in my hands but the pain from the scratches and kick roared up like a wildfire. The wound on my wrist where Strawberry Death had bitten me was red and painful but the skin hadn't been broken. I rose up again.

Vare cleared her throat. "You know we have to do the drill."

She opened the portfolio and prepared to make notes as I retold my encounter on the lawn with Strawberry Death, disarming her, and chasing her toward Central where Lindsey had the bad luck to turn around and come back our way.

I had already given this information, along with as complete a description of the attacker as I could muster, to a uniformed officer. But this was the drill, as she said.

Then I went through the events of the early morning traffic
stop headed into the High Country, the same woman in a DPS
uniform drawing down on me and only stopping when the FBI
tail vehicle came behind us.

My mind was bouncing in so many directions that for a few
seconds I wondered if she really was a DPS officer and a part-
time hit woman. Weirder things had happened and Arizona
grew weirder by the day. It probably paid well and she had the
perfect cover.

"We'll check to see every DPS patrol officer who was on duty
last night and this morning around Camp Verde," Vare said.
"But I don't think she was a cop."

"Why?"

"I'll get to that. Why would this woman be trying to kill you?"

I shook my head. "I have no idea." I tried to focus. "I've never
seen her before. Didn't receive any threatening calls or emails.
Nothing I've been working on seemed dangerous."

I added, "She's done this before."

Vare cocked an eyebrow.

"She said it would be cleaner if she 'suicided' me, as she put it."

Vare wrote it down.

"We recovered a semi-auto from the shrubs near your house."
She tapped her pen on the legal pad. "It's a Heckler and Koch
Mark 23, chambered for a .45. That's a Special Forces weapon.
It can work with a laser-aiming system and a suppressor. Who
the hell did you piss off, Mapstone?"

"Can't civilians get them?"

"In this state?" She sniffed. "You can get anything. Maybe it
can give us some fingerprints. What about Peralta?"

That didn't take long. I was surprised it hadn't been her first
question.

It was a good question, *the* question. But I had already decided
not to mention that the woman had told me she was there for
"her stones," that she had made Peralta a promise. There were
good reasons to be honest, chiefly that it might give me police
protection. But the reasons to hedge were more compelling. The

first reaction of Vare and the FBI would be that I was involved in the diamond robbery.

I chose Door Number Two.

"I'm more shocked than anybody," I said. "I also don't know why the FBI would be working a diamond robbery."

"And shooting."

I nodded.

She set down her pen and thought, then started ticking items off on her bony fingers.

"Maybe the robbery was planned in another country? Or it involved a federal agent or a postal worker? The diamonds might have been from another country and they asked the FBI to investigate. Or Chandler P.D. wanted the bureau's forensic expertise on a major jewel heist. The feds have diamond experts. They have art theft experts."

"But I didn't even talk to a Chandler detective when I was called up to Ash Fork this morning."

"What's your point, Mapstone?"

I rubbed my hands, feeling the dried blood on them seeming to cake up into little flakes.

"My point is this whole thing stinks."

God, why didn't I keep us in the nice hotel downtown with the friendly shower?

I watched the entry to the waiting room, hoping to see a doctor who might tell me something, something good. Every scrub-clad medico walking past drew my eye, but each merely continued going.

Vare stood and pulled out the chair, then placed it directly in front of me and sat again. She pulled closer until our knees almost touched.

"Did it ever occur to you that Peralta might have sent this woman after you?"

You mean the woman who keeps her promises?

I said, "That doesn't make sense. He's my friend..."

She immediately talked over me, like old times. "I thought he was a good cop, too. Obviously we didn't know him. Maybe he's tying up loose ends. Maybe he thinks you know something. It's strange he left a note specifically about you on your business card in his truck."

Word traveled fast.

She leaned in. "Have you heard from Peralta since the crime?"

I looked at her without blinking, forcing discipline into every cell of my body.

"Kate, my wife is in critical condition and I've had my ass kicked by a girl. So anything I do right now might be grief, or because my face hurts like the devil. But you'll consider it a 'tell.'"

Next I looked down and to the left, blinked rapidly, and cleared my throat. "See what I mean?"

Her cheeks turned red with frustration.

I said, "The answer is no, I haven't heard from him."

I was a good little liar, too.

"Do you know something about the diamond robbery, Mapstone?"

I knew the woman wanted the diamonds. Before that, I had found another business card Peralta had left for me across from the Flagstaff train station. "Find Matt Pennington." Lindsey had been about to tell me about Pennington when I provoked our ruction and she walked out.

I knew Orville Grainer had seen Peralta exit the truck, change the license plate, and get in a sedan. And Peralta, playing lawn boy on what I hoped was a forgotten landline, had told Sharon that I needed to watch my ass. I hadn't watched it very well.

I said, "No. I want Lindsey protected."

"It's already done."

I let out a long breath.

Vare made me go through it all over again and I did. Lindsey leaving to go for a walk, me following.

"Why did you follow her?"

"At first I didn't want to go walking, then I changed my mind."

No way was I going to tell her we had a fight. For any cop that provided a sweet, low-hanging fruit—alleged marriage trouble. *Maybe Mapstone was screwing this woman and she got tired of hearing him promise to leave his wife. Or Mapstone actually encouraged or even paid her to kill Lindsey and set it up to look like a random crime.*

She let it pass. "You should know we found a burglar bag near where you encountered her. It had lock tools, an alarm bypass, handcuffs. You pissed somebody off."

This information passed into my nervous system and chilled me.

Five beats. "Any marital troubles, Mapstone?"

"No."

I didn't hate her. Faced with the same facts, I would have asked the same question.

Next Vare wanted to know about recent cases I had investigated as a private detective and what Lindsey had been doing. I kept my answers calm, short, and factual. They filled three handwritten pages of notes.

"That's all for now. There have been a bunch of felony paroles and early releases to save the state money. So we'll check for bad guys you arrested or testified against who might have gotten out recently."

"Thanks."

Four women walked past in purple scrubs. None looked in the waiting room.

Vare closed the portfolio, pushed the chair back into place, said they would send over a sketch artist, and handed me her card.

I didn't immediately take it.

Chris Melton was on the television across the room. "Live," the banner said at the bottom on the screen. "Downtown Phoenix Shooting."

The TV morons didn't even know it was Midtown, not downtown, if they were talking about what happened to Lindsey.

Melton was standing out in front of the St. Joe's E.R entrance.

"Turn that up, please. Please!"

The Hispanic woman at the other end of the room complied and I heard him talking.

"The Phoenix Police are the primary department investigating this case. What I can tell you is that the wife of a Maricopa County deputy was shot while she was taking a walk. Obviously I can't identify her. She's fighting for her life and I ask everyone to send their prayers."

My face started throbbing violently. As reporters shouted questions, I could see Vare stiffen.

"No questions," Melton said. "Here's what I can say, any attack on a family member of a Maricopa County deputy sheriff is an attack on all of us, on the entire law-enforcement community, on the community as a whole. We will not stop until this animal is run down and brought to justice..."

Maybe there had been another shooting of a deputy's relative. But no. The shooter was identified as an Anglo woman in her thirties with reddish blond hair, who remained at-large.

"Goddamn him," I hissed.

Vare stood over me and her sharp features darkened. "Are you with the Sheriff's Office again, Mapstone?"

"It's temporary."

"Fuck you," she said, then lowered her voice. "Why didn't you tell me you were working for Meltdown right off?"

I reacted with equal fury, standing, and towering over her. "He swore me in tonight, damn it! I've been a little distracted, if you didn't notice. My wife is in there..." I threw an arm in the direction of the trauma suites and my voice broke.

But I forced some composure, sat, and spoke slowly. Kate Vare could help me or really hurt me. I needed her help. "He wants me to look into an old dead-body case."

"What case?"

"I haven't even begun checking out the file. It was a body I found back when I was a patrol officer. I was in my twenties, Kate. In the last century. I don't remember much about it. Some guy who went hiking in the desert, got lost, got dead. It didn't seem suspicious. I turned it over to the detectives and thought it was closed."

"So what's his angle?"

"I wish I knew. He said there's been a new development. He wouldn't tell me what until I had studied the file he gave me. This happened literally three hours ago."

I had so lost track of time that probably wasn't "literally" true. Close enough. I wasn't grading freshman essays.

She put her hands on her hips.

"I want to know what it is."

"I'll tell you when I find out. You should be more concerned about Melton trying to grab publicity by horning in on your case."

She nodded, went over and muted the television, then sat back down and reopened her portfolio. All the damaged tissue in my face silently groaned.

"I want to go back through this," she said. "So this woman pulled a gun from an ankle holster."

"That's what it looked like."

"Why didn't she shoot you?"

"I had my .38 on her. She saw it and ran. Or maybe she heard the neighbor call from the porch and didn't want to risk a witness."

"So she ran through the opening in the wall and shot Lindsey. Why?"

I thought about that and told her she knew Lindsey was my wife. And Lindsey was in the wrong place at the wrong time.

"Hmm." She closed the pad again. Her voice shifted cadence and what came next almost sounded like an afterthought.

"Lindsey lost her sister in a shooting."

"Robin." I stared at the wall texture.

"And the woman who murdered Robin is doing life now because you happened to be driving down Maryland Avenue a few days later and identified her..."

I knew and she strongly suspected that was only part of the truth.

Vare didn't know that I had been about to execute the woman who killed Robin when my cell phone rang, the screen had said "Lindsey," and the few better angels I had left by that time stopped me.

Some days I still regretted letting her live. On those days, days like today, I was on the knife's edge, justice had not been done and I sure as hell was not noble.

Robin. And now Lindsey…

Vare leaned in and whispered, "The women in your life have bad luck, huh?"

It took every bit of self-control to not leap over and strangle her.

I said, "I want my wife to have protection, twenty-four hours…"

"I already told you." She rose and started to leave. But after two steps she turned and came back, stabbing her index finger in my chest, right about where the bullet entered Lindsey. "Stay the hell out of my investigation, Mapstone. If I find you using that badge to play vengeful husband, I swear to God, I'll ram my fist so far up your ass, I'll make you pay for breathing."

She stomped away. She weighed a hundred pounds wet but she was a good stomper.

My anger breached the levees and I yelled after her, "Then find who did this, Kate…." But she was already in the hall and gone.

I touched the point of pain she had left on my sternum and thought of Lindsey.

I looked up and Vare was standing over me.

She cleared her throat and spoke slowly. "I'm sorry, Mapstone."

I started to say, "Don't worry about it," but she talked over the first syllable.

"It was uncalled for. Look, I've got a new boss. He talks a good corporate game but I don't think he's ever gotten his handcuffs dirty. City Council wants to cut our pay and take away our pensions. It's shitty all over. All I'm asking is, don't make my job harder."

When she had wound down, I nodded. "Fair enough."

She patted my shoulder, an astounding gesture of rapport for her, and cocked her head.

"What kind of leather did your DPS officer wear?"

I closed my eyes and tried to remember. It had been dark. The gun had held most of my attention.

"Webbed," I said finally. "She wore a webbed equipment belt."

"Then she was fake," Vare said. "DPS wears plain Safariland leather."

Five minutes later, Melton appeared at the doorway. Four gold stars gleamed from the collars of his crisp black uniform. I was up and headed toward him. He must have seen the blood in my eyes so he stepped forward and hugged me.

The son of a bitch hugged me.

I didn't hug back.

"We're going to get this shooter, David. Don't you worry about that."

He studied me. "You're covered with blood. Can I have someone bring you a change of clothes?"

I stepped back, wishing the blood hadn't dried, wishing it could have stained his immaculate uniform. I thought of Jackie Kennedy after the assassination, when she had worn that blood-stained suit all the way from Dallas to Washington. "Let them see what they've done," she said.

I said, "Why do you care about a woman you called a traitor?"

"David, you're overwrought. Do you have kids?"

"We don't have children."

He looked at me like an alien being, then tried to smile sympathetically.

"Take a few days. Then look into the case. You're going to need the distraction."

My hand made a fist and I forced myself to relax, open up each finger.

"She's in good hands." He clapped me on the shoulders. His eyes swept the room and settled on the Hispanic family at the other end.

"My God, they cost so much. Our health care, our schools. I bet they're illegals and we could arrest them right now."

Yes, and some resort would lose its housekeeper who worked a second job as a fry cook at another business. I kept my response simple. "Leave them alone." And almost gagging, I added, "Sheriff."

He smiled. "Call me Chris."

Halfway out the door, he added, "And call me by Tuesday. Let's talk about this case."

Chapter Fourteen

The next day didn't pass in a blur. It went by in agonizing minutes, every sixty seconds scalding me. My body felt as if every nerve was jangling on the surface of my skin.

The Saturday night mayhem began to fill up the waiting room after eleven. Finally, a doctor came for me, took me into the fluorescent-lit hallway, and told me the only thing that really stuck. Lindsey was alive.

The rest I remembered in pieces. I should have been taking notes.

She had suffered massive blood loss and they had put her into an induced coma to protect her brain. I remembered the words "hypothermic treatment."

How long would she be this way? As much as two weeks.

She had been lucky, the bullet passing through her without fragmenting, missing her aorta by half an inch. She was also a healthy woman, which would help. But it was too soon to know about "impairment" of her brain and heart. The next twenty-four hours would tell us much.

At four a.m., I was allowed into the ICU to see Lindsey. A pair of uniformed Phoenix Police officers stood outside and one checked my identification. Then I was led into a nursing station that was the center of activity with desks and monitors. All visitors had to pass through this area. That was good.

From there, it took a keypad code to enter Lindsey's room, one of several pods separated by large windows from the nursing station. The unit was also monitored by video cameras. The setup looked between a cross of a spaceship and a high-end prison.

My wife was on her back, a ventilator tube in her mouth, three IV lines attached to her arms and one running inside her gown, and no pillow under her head. The pillows were supporting her arms and legs. Gauze pads were taped over her eyes.

Heart and respiratory monitors were attached and beeped softly. A blood-pressure cuff was around her right arm and periodically it automatically inflated and deflated. A second nurse came in to check the plastic IV bags hanging on stainless steel rods above her bed.

I talked to her, certain she could hear me, told her I loved her, but they didn't want me to get too close. Her hand was cold. It didn't return my grip.

The room held no hospital smell. No smell at all. That was good, right?

When I saw the dried blood in her hair, I became "agitated," as the nurse put it. Could they wash her hair? No. At least they could use a wet cloth to wipe away the blood. Lindsey was the opposite of vain in almost every way, but she was proud of her hair.

After ten minutes, another medico with a cart came in and I was guided back out. The nurse gave me Lindsey's wedding rings, the simple narrow platinum band and the engagement ring with a princess-cut diamond. "A timeless modern style," Lindsey called it.

When I stepped out of the ICU, Sharon was waiting with her daughters, two beautiful, high-functioning Latina lawyers from the Bay Area. Melton and his crew wouldn't dare ask them for their papers. The anti-immigrant sentiment was as much about class as anything else.

They all hugged me and for a few seconds I thought I would shatter and cry in their arms. But it didn't come. My emotions pinballed inside. Outside, I felt numb, underwater…

Still, I let them tell me everything would be all right. Mike had been shot and put into a coma, remember? And all turned out well. I was vulnerable to comforting lies at that moment. I welcomed them.

After awhile, Sharon and I took the elevator to the first floor and walked through the corridors of the older part of the hospital. I used my left hand to hold a cold pack to my battered face, kept my right hand free. Historical photos were displayed on the walls. The hallways were wide, dimly lit, and deserted. It made me focus, check sightlines and sounds, feel the companionship of the .38 inside my waistband.

And suddenly, I was facing a wall, touching it lightly, feeling the texture, lost in losing Lindsey. Fortunately, the fugue didn't last.

But Sharon began sobbing. I took her in my arms.

"I'm so sorry, David...So sorry..."

I whispered, "You didn't do anything wrong."

It felt good to comfort someone else, to be outside myself if even for a few minutes. Still, I was back to hyper-awareness, too, a good thing.

I expected her to talk about the uncertainty of Lindsey's recovery, say how I didn't have to think about getting through the next two weeks or the next day, but only the moment I was in right then...that sort of thing. I expected her to say shrink things.

Instead, she couldn't form a word. I took her hand and we walked.

We were past the closed cafeteria before she spoke.

She asked what I was thinking.

"That Lindsey is dying. That it's my fault."

"How can you blame yourself?"

So I told her. It took awhile. I could hear noises coming from the kitchen, preparing breakfast for hundreds of patients.

She sighed and shook her head in a narrow, slow axis. Her large Mexican Madonna eyes working not to judge me.

"You did the best you could with the information you had. I wish you hadn't let that rat bastard Melton box you in a corner."

"I know."

"Maybe it's for the best, give you a distraction during the wait for Lindsey. And she is not dying, David."

She squeezed my hand.

"I remember when you left Phoenix to become a professor," she said. "We were all young then. You would visit us at Thanksgiving and Mike would always try to convince you to come back to the Sheriff's Office. And he finally got you and everything seemed right."

"I failed in academia and my first marriage. He took pity on me."

"You didn't fail," she said. "You put your skills to their best use. You solved the first case, where the woman got off the train and disappeared?"

I nodded. "Rebecca Stokes. She was a victim of a serial killer that had never been identified before." If anything, the victims deserved for us to remember their names.

"And you sure didn't fail personally," she said. "Patty was never right for you. Here, you met Lindsey and you were a big success clearing old cases."

Then her tone changed. "I'm not sure this PI business is good for either of you. This violence…" She shook back her hair and stared down the dim hallway. "It's worse than when you both were at the Sheriff's Office. When Mike lost the election, he could have become a consultant, pulled down six figures, and never worn a gun again."

"I know."

"Why did he want to become a private eye? Why did you go with him?"

I didn't answer.

"It started with your first case, that girl that was murdered in San Diego. When the bad guys took Mike prisoner, you killed both of them."

"They drew on me."

"And there was no other way? No other way to de-escalate the situation."

"No. Have you ever had a gun in your face?" I forced my voice back to normal. "Civilians think you can shoot the gun out of their hands or divert the poor misunderstood person into social services."

"I'm hardly a civilian, David. I lived with a cop for forty years…"

"With a break here and there."

She smiled weakly.

"Anyway, they were domestic terrorists. I'm all out of compassion considering what they did, and what they would have done if we hadn't stopped them."

I couldn't tell her the rest of the story, how I had called in Mike's old friend Ed Cartwright, an undercover FBI agent who lived out in the desert and sold weapons to the survivalist crowd and gangs. He was a full-blood Apache and in their twisted way they trusted him as the Noble Savage. Cartwright took the gun I had used and made me leave, saving me trouble from the police. I wasn't a deputy anymore.

"David, promise me your first reaction won't be violence."

I promised. There were too damned many promises out there.

After another dozen steps in silence, she said, "Why don't you go back to teaching? When this is all over. Lindsey could do anything with computers. It would be a good life for you both. And Mike could become a consultant."

I said, "That sounds like bargaining."

"I'm not on the clock. Psychologists are human, too."

"So you're telling me you had no idea he was going on this diamond run?" Even I was surprised at how quickly I had shifted gears.

"I already told you, no." Her voice had an edge and she dropped my hand.

"But he calls you on the phone. He says I need to watch my ass. Something went wrong."

"David, if I had realized that he meant you and Lindsey would have this woman show up at your door, of course I would have…I'm not a goddamned mind reader here. He's not exactly the most forthcoming man in the world. He doesn't talk about his work. What did he tell you about the diamonds?"

"Nothing."

"And now he's gone and he's in trouble."

We reached the expansive new lobby, where a janitor was running a floor-polishing machine. Such a pleasant job, nobody shooting at you.

I asked if the FBI was still outside their house.

"Two SUVs," she said, "and a Crown Vic that tailed me all the way here. I'm very safe, David. I have a Glock 26 subcompact in my purse. Why wasn't the FBI watching your house?"

I shook my head.

I told her that Strawberry Death was somehow connected with her husband and the diamond theft. She had first appeared after the crime, when we were on our way to Ash Fork.

"That was the DPS officer?"

"Yes. Same woman. This was not a coincidence. When she confronted me on the front lawn, she said, 'Where are my stones?' She said she'd made Mike a promise. What the hell does that mean?" I described her and asked Sharon if she remembered Peralta mentioning anyone like that.

"Does she sound like anyone you know? Anyone you remember seeing?"

"No, David. Why are you badgering me?" She started crying again, but when I reached out she pushed my hand away. "I'm trying to help you. I think I understand the stress you're under but you need to let the FBI and the police do their job."

"Well, the FBI is officially labeling Mike an armed fugitive."

"That's absurd!"

"I believe that. I think he's working undercover. But if he is, this new Special Agent in Charge doesn't know about it or he's a damned good liar."

I didn't know who to trust. I said, "You need to go back to the Bay Area. It's not safe here. This woman who shot Lindsey deliberately came after me. She's still out there. You are probably next on her list."

She stood straighter. "We're not leaving. I can take care of myself. Jamie and Jennifer can, too. We'll take shifts with you watching Lindsey."

I said, "At least don't be exposed at night. This woman likes the night."

"So do you," she said. And she was right.

Back upstairs, we waited. I was allowed in to see Lindsey four more times. IV bags were changed. A blood-pressure cuff was attached to her arm and periodically inflated and deflated, sending the data to the monitors. A nurse with an elaborate cart containing additional monitoring equipment came in once—another time I was instructed to leave the unit. I napped for short periods in chairs, leaving kinks in every muscle.

A police technician used a laptop computer to generate a likeness of Lindsey's assailant. The problem wasn't the quality—it was a pretty good rendering. The problem was that she looked like scores of other average-attractive thirtysomething women walking around the malls of Phoenix. This was no doubt an advantage in her trade.

At seven p.m. Sunday, the three Peralta women sent me home to rest, promising to call if anything changed.

Sharon walked me to the door. It was black night outside and I realized I hadn't seen the sun for more than a day. Then the question that had been sitting under my feet like a land mine finally detonated.

"Why are you here?"

She looked at me strangely. "For you and Lindsey. Why?"

"No, I mean what brought you to the hospital? How did you know we'd be here?"

"The call."

I was suddenly twitchy. The feeling of imaginary ants marching up the back of my neck was so pronounced that I reached back to brush them off.

"What call?"

She said, "I got a call from the hospital. They said you asked them to call me and say Lindsey had been shot and please come. What's wrong?"

"I didn't tell anyone to make a call. Man or woman's voice?"

"A man."

I stared through the glass door at the night street. "Accent?"
She shook her head.

I looked back at her. "Could it have been Mike?"

"No."

"People can change their voices, Sharon."

"I know my husband's voice."

I asked to see her cell phone, but the supposed call from the hospital only showed "602," the area code. When I attempted a return call, it provoked the familiar three tones followed by "Your call cannot be completed as dialed." Whoever had called Sharon had concealed his tracks well. Lindsey knew how to pull off such a trick. I didn't.

I said, "It wasn't the hospital."

"Well, thank God someone let me know," she said.

"How many people have your number?"

She thought for a few seconds, stroking her hair. "Maybe two hundred in five states and D.C."

I cursed, handed her phone back, and studied her.

"What are you not telling me?"

Her eyes widened in exasperation. "I'm telling you everything."

I tried to make myself stop, but I couldn't. "Sharon, are you in on this with him? Did he call you about Lindsey being shot?"

"No! David, you're traumatized."

I couldn't tell if she was being truthful. Sharon was usually as straightforward as her husband and thankfully lacked his manipulative streak. But who knew better how to lie than a shrink?

I repeated, "What are you not telling me? Whatever it is, another miscalculation by him and we'll all be dead."

She turned away and placed her hand against the wall, lightly at first and then with such force that it was if she were trying to push the building off its foundations. When she faced me again, her eyes were still wet with tears.

I had never seen Sharon cry in all the years I had known her, all the years she heard other people tell their psychological nightmares, all the years she had endured her husband's moods and tirades.

"I didn't know what Mike meant," she managed in a husky voice. "When he called on the old county landline as Paco and told you to watch your ass. I should have done more. Should have realized. Now Lindsey is hurt."

"It's not your fault. I'm to blame."

"I'm afraid…" she began. Then she lowered her head for a long moment before finishing. "For the first time in my life, I'm afraid he's in over his head. We can't lose both of them, David. And you lost Robin, too."

"We won't lose them," I whispered without conviction.

"He's in trouble, David, and he needs you."

I suddenly felt angry again. "If he needs me, he has to do more than drop a cryptic note on a business card."

"I know, I know." She put both hands on my shoulders, calm again. "I don't know how to ask for your help because you're totally focused on Lindsey. As you should be. But…"

"We can help each other." I said it not knowing what it meant, what I was promising. "I'll try to find him."

"Thank you." She pulled my face close. "You're exhausted. Go home and get some sleep. I promise we'll call if anything changes here."

She turned me and pushed my numb body forward.

The automatic sliding glass doors gave their kissing sound and I walked through. When I looked back, she was watching me with those wide brown eyes. I shook my head and forced myself to move along.

Chapter Fifteen

A cop had given me a ride to the hospital, so I crossed the expanse of Thomas Road and walked the nine blocks home, past the narrow streets I had memorized on my bicycle as a child. Edgemont, Windsor, Cambridge, Virginia, Wilshire, Lewis, Vernon, Encanto Boulevard, Cypress.

Hardly anyone lived in the neighborhood from those days. One friend from grade school went into the Diplomatic Service and was posted to Budapest, another was a lobbyist in California. Yet another was living in London. So many had left town.

Willo was one of the safest neighborhoods in the metropolitan area. If I didn't live here, if I hadn't brought trouble, there would barely have been a violent crime in years.

There was no time for those thoughts. No time to appreciate the distinctive character of each house or mourn about the idiots who had put in desert landscaping where this had always been the oasis. No time, for now, to worry about Lindsey. All my senses had to be on high alert.

It was Sunday night in the heart of the city and few cars passed me on Fifth Avenue. A couple walked their dog. No assassins were hiding behind oleander hedges in the service alleys. Overhead, high thin clouds lingered, turned pink by the reflected city lights. A slight breeze tousled my hair.

At home, I armed the alarm and took a long shower, locking the bathroom door and setting two guns and my iPhone on the vanity. I let the needles of hot water pummel my battered face, let the room fill with steam.

I dried off and approached the dreaded mirror. Even after using several cold packs at the hospital, the tissue around my right eye was colorful and swollen, plenty of purple, red, and orange like an Arizona sunset. It hurt in colors, too, all in the red zone. My left cheek bore the slashes of the killer's fingernails. I popped four Advils.

The little meteor strike of skin was four inches above my right nipple, the remains of the only time I had been shot. It had come on the first case Peralta gave me to clean up. I lost enough blood to pass out and they airlifted me from Sedona to St. Joe's. I was lucky my lung didn't collapse. When I woke up, Lindsey was there. We weren't even married. Sometimes when we were in bed, she would lightly worry the scar with her fingertip, trying to erase it. Fragments of the bullet were still inside me.

"Lord, have mercy."

I spoke the words to myself and said them conversationally, not exactly as a petition to the almighty but a stress valve letting off. The moment stunned me. My grandmother, a daughter of the frontier who knew much loss in her long life, had used that phrase often and in exactly that tone of voice. Now I said it.

A few years ago, I realized that if I were in a relaxed situation, especially sitting down, my hands would join in my conversation. This was not wild gesticulation. It was hands and wrists. Grandmother had done the same thing. When I was a little boy, I had thought it was strange. Now I did the same thing all the time.

The grandparents who raised me were long dead and yet they lived on through me. I considered how I had underestimated Melton. Yes, I had taken the badge out of unreasoning fear, to buy time for Lindsey, even though I didn't believe a word he said about her. But he had also gotten to me about how "I owed" my hometown.

Grandfather talked that way. He told me stories of the early pioneers, the heroic acts of dam and canal building that had turned a wilderness into a garden. That's how he told it. "Never forget that you owe," he said. "Never forget that you are from Maricopa County, Arizona."

Grandfatherisms, I called them. Melton had made a snare for me with those sentiments.

Even though it was Sunday night, I dressed in a pinstripe blue suit, starched white shirt, and muted red tie. For the first time, I noticed the pattern—tiny diamonds. My new watch, the one Lindsey had given me for Christmas, went across my wrist. I stashed a pair of latex evidence gloves and badge case in my pocket, slipped on the Colt Python and the backup gun. I was a deputy sheriff again.

The case file from Melton was sitting in the living room. I decided to let it be for a few hours. I would do three more tasks associated with Peralta and then pause, if not stop.

It was not clear to me that he was safe. The man was very capable on his own—I was not indispensible. For years, he had given the orders and saved the day. But on a case a year ago, I had saved him. Now he had left the cryptic second business card. Whatever trouble he was in required my assistance.

That's what I told myself.

His undercover adventure, predicament, descent into lawlessness, whatever it was, also twined up with the assassin who met me on the front lawn last night. I wasn't going to get in Kate Vare's way, as long as she did her job. But the shooter remained at-large and anything I could learn about her connection to Peralta would help.

It couldn't be a coincidence that she had come after me after he made off with the diamonds.

The first task was quickly foiled.

Find Matt Pennington.

Lindsey said she had news about this, but before she could tell me more we had begun fighting about the new job with Melton. I sat at the desk and carefully folded Lindsey's glasses, studying the acetate tortoiseshell frames with round lenses and small earpieces that perfectly fit her thin face.

"My nerd girl look," she would say.

Unfortunately for me, Lindsey's computer was password-protected.

I tried every word and number combination I could think of and got through with "Dave" and the date and year of the first time we had sex. That delightful memory, and the fact that she recalled it, was followed by anxiety that I should call Sharon to check on her. I resisted the temptation. I had only been gone for forty-five minutes.

The computer screen was neither sentimental nor anxious. It brought me to a gray backdrop with a red box demanding "Keystroke Authentication Pattern."

She was too clever for me. I gave up. I could at least Google Pennington later. Hell, I might even Bing him. But I needed answers no search engine was going to supply.

I went outside, the Colt Python in my hand. The air was magically dry and pleasant.

The darkened carport was clear of assassins, so I climbed in Lindsey's old Honda Prelude, and drove west.

Our office on Grand Avenue, a squat adobe that was about all that remained of a once-charming 1920s auto court, looked quiet. The neon sign of a cowboy throwing a lasso, the other survivor of the motel, blinked benignly. Otherwise, the place was surrounded by a twelve-foot steel fence and watched by surveillance cameras.

I pressed the remote in the car to open the gate, let it close behind me, then got out of the car and went in, unlocking two heavy deadbolts and disarming the alarm.

Inside, the front office held its usual smell of dust and old linoleum. I turned on the banker's lamp atop my desk and for a long time merely listened. Everything sounded and looked much the same as when the FBI had arrived with a search warrant Friday afternoon.

Why was the FBI investigating this case? For that matter, why did they arrive so soon after Peralta's robbery?

The walls stubbornly refused to give me answers.

Next I went into the Danger Room, unlocking the steel door. I compared the assault rifles, sniper rifle, machine guns, shotguns, and pistols in their neat racks and drawers with the firearms inventory from the files. Over time, the bookish David Mapstone had learned all the details and capabilities of each weapon. Nothing was missing.

Peralta had gone on the diamond run carrying only his .40-caliber Glock sidearm. Not only that, but he had emptied out the weapons locker in his truck.

I retrieved a shortened M-4 carbine—the technical term was close quarter battle receiver—and extra magazines. Don't forget a Remington pump shotgun with a belt of shells. No party is complete without one. Rounding out my kit were two pairs of binoculars, one with night-vision capability. I zipped them up in a black duffle bag and set it aside.

Next, I sat at the small desk in the far end of the small room. It held a laptop connected to the video cameras.

I quickly spun through forty-eight hours worth of digital information, learning nothing new. At 8:15 a.m. Friday, Peralta came in the gate, parked his pickup, and walked inside. Unfortunately in this case, we lacked cameras watching the interior of the building. Thirty minutes later, he left. At 3:12 p.m., the cameras showed the FBI arriving and, two hours later, leaving. Images of me appeared, walking out and driving away. Otherwise, not a single car pulled to the gate even to turn around.

Back in the main room, I pulled out Peralta's plush chair and sank into it, studying his desk. The top was as usual immaculately empty. The FBI had gone through the credenza behind his desk, taking his laptop and the files in the credenza cabinet as evidence.

"Good luck with that computer," I said out loud, thinking of how little he used it.

Then my eyes settled on the dictaphone, still sitting atop the credenza. It was at least twenty years old, the same one he had used when he was sheriff. I suppose the county had so little need for it they let him take it when he left office.

The feds probably thought it was an objet d'art and left it alone. They were wrong. He used it almost daily, despite Lindsey's efforts to match him with a voice-recognition app.

She had considered it a breakthrough when she success-fully walked him through setting up a Gmail account. On the other hand, she had also taught him about GPS tracking of cell phones, and how to remove the battery and SIM card to avoid it. That, he had immediately absorbed and put to use on Friday after leaving the mall.

I pressed the "play" button but immediately stopped the machine. Who knew, the agents who searched the office might have been givers as well as takers, and now were listening on the bug they had left behind. Putting on the spindly headphones, I started the dictaphone again and his deep voice immediately echoed out only for me.

"Mapstone, it's Friday morning and I need this letter to go out today."

I thought again, *Jeez, we need to hire an administrative assistant.* If we live through this.

Over the headphones, I heard, "Date today. To, Mister Dan Patterson, Three-fifty East Encanto Boulevard, Phoenix. Look up the ZIP Code. Dear Mister Patterson. Thank you for your inquiry about our services. However, we do not handle marital disputes or surveillance. I would recommend these firms that might be of assistance…"

I listened as he droned on, sounding routine and even bored, not like someone about to steal a million dollars in diamonds. But there was nothing routine about this dictation. My stomach tightened the moment I heard the address. Encanto Boulevard only runs west of Central. On the east side, it becomes Oak Street.

He finished the letter with "and that's all for today. Aren't you happy?" and the machine was silent except for a subtle scratching every fifteen seconds or so.

I let it run.

"Mapstone." Now his voice was different, dead serious. "By the time you find this, things will be pretty crazy. You're going to hear a lot of things about me. Don't believe them. The FBI has probably questioned you. I kept you out of this so you wouldn't have anything to tell them. Also, you and Lindsey would be safer."

The machine scratched and seemed to hesitate. I hit it, the universal fix for all things mechanical, and Peralta continued.

"Don't trust anyone. If things go according to plan, I'll be back in the office Monday morning. If they don't..." After a pause, the voice said, "If they don't, find a man named Matt Pennington and he'll know how to contact me." He gave Pennington's number and address. "There's no time to tell you more and it's better that you don't know. Run frosty, Mapstone."

After more silence, I whispered. "Easy for you to say."

Things had obviously gone wrong as early as Friday evening, hence he had left the note to me on the business card in Flagstaff.

I would find Matt Pennington. First, I decided to play a hunch.

Ready to leave, I thought about turning off the neon sign, but didn't. Robin had insisted that Peralta restore this little remnant of old Phoenix, when the blue highways ran past miles of neon-lighted motels. We could keep paying the electric bill for this little bit of whimsy on what was now an otherwise dismal stretch of roadway.

With the extra firepower now inside the Prelude, I drove out Grand. It was the only major street that cut at a southeast-northwest angle through the monotonous grid of Phoenix.

Once, Grand had been the highway from Phoenix to Los Angeles. Railroad tracks still ran beside it. Now Grand would take me to Indian School Road where I turned west again.

Indian School was another bleak six-lane Phoenix raceway across flat land bordered by pawn shops, payday loan offices, tattoo parlors, strip joints, empty buildings with for-lease signs out front, and even an outfit in a defunct Wendy's that promised money in exchange for your auto title. Little shrines decorated the joyless landscape, commemorating the loss of loved ones in a traffic mishap. Off on the curvilinear side streets were the cinderblock houses of Maryvale.

This was Phoenix's first mass-produced single-family-home development, John F. Long's American Dream in ranch houses built atop former fields of cotton, alfalfa, lettuce, and beets. It was the opposite of Willo, but in the 1960s it was new, with all-electric kitchens and backyard pools.

Builders such as John Hall, Ralph Staggs, and Elliott White-house copied Maryvale on various scales all over the Valley. Del Webb built Sun City. They drew an Anglo middle class and retirees from Back East and growth paid for itself. That's what the city leaders said.

The last of that generation, Whitehouse, had died only a year ago.

Some areas fared better than others. In Maryvale, the Anglos moved out and the poor Hispanics moved in. Many of them were followed by successive waves of illegal immigrants that staffed the hotels, restaurants, and lawn services. It was suburbia aging badly, a linear slum.

People called it Scaryvale.

I found what I was looking for south of Indian School on Fifty-First Avenue, a shopping strip hard against the bank of the Grand Canal. The canal itself looked nothing like its namesake in Venice or the massive channel in China.

Carrying water from the Salt River Project dams and reservoirs in the mountains east of the city, this canal was bounded on both sides by a maintenance road, forty-five feet or so across total. It was the oldest in the system, one of the first Hohokam canals cleaned out by Jack Swilling in the 1870s. Like the Arizona Canal to the north, it extended all the way to the Agua Fria River.

Shady cottonwoods once bordered this Grand Canal, but the mighty SRP had cut most of them down by the time I was born. In some nicer areas, people hiked along the maintenance roads, but most who drove across the canals daily never noticed, never thought about the miracle of being able to turn on the tap without worry.

The shopping strip, thrown up in the eighties, was two-thirds empty. Its anchor tenant, if you wanted to call it that, was called El TobacCorner, a nice little Spanglish mash-up name. A red sign bordered by blue flashed "open."

But I didn't turn in yet. I drove across the canal and continued on for almost a mile, checking the rearview mirror. Without signaling, I accelerated and spun left into a residential street, wound around past falling-apart homes, and rolled slowly back out to the main thoroughfare. Nobody seemed to be following me.

The parking lot of El TobacCorner was nearly empty. One dirty pickup truck and a tricked-out Honda lowrider sat directly in front, beneath the digital sign that urged passersby to "Have a Smoky Day." Otherwise, half an acre of asphalt was badly in need of business.

I parked in the first row away from the shopping strip, facing toward the road.

Shadows approached and I tensed, reaching for the Python.

Dogs. A pack of five mutts trotted past the Prelude and kept going east. With the combination of people losing their homes in the recession and the immigrants moving out, or deeper into the shadows, Phoenix had a serious stray dog problem.

Another night in paradise.

A bell by the double glass doors and an electronic beep somewhere in the back announced my arrival. I was the only customer.

Del Shannon was singing "My Little Runaway" on the sound system. The shop was brightly lit and the first thing you noticed were walls covered with large colorful posters advertising Zig-Zag, Marlboros, Kool menthols, and brands I didn't know. I doubted they carried Lindsey's brand. Only on a second look did I notice a drop ceiling dating from the Carter administration with yellow stains from water leaks.

The shop was laid out like an "L," with rows of waist-high, glass-fronted display cases running on either side of the long end and tall cases and a cash register closer to me. A four-sided, vertical plastic case held Zippo lighters with all manner of artwork. One showed a figure with a skull head drinking a glass of wine.

Behind the cases, the walls had been drilled to hold clear racks showing more product—individual packs of cigarettes, e-cigs, rolling papers, gum, and chewing tobacco.

That last made me think momentarily of Orville Grainer up in Ash Fork.

But only momentarily.

A big man sat on a stool ten feet away at the long end of the "L." Beside him was a comic book. He was ethnically ambiguous, at least thirty, at least three hundred pounds, and dressed like a baby. In other words, the giant, sagging T-shirt and long-short pants gave the effect of a four-year-old with short legs and long torso. The look was completed with a cholo cap turned sideways and a riot of aggressive tattoos on each arm and one climbing up one side of his neck.

These ubiquitous outfits accompanied a society where most of the men, at least, seemed to postpone adulthood indefinitely. I thought about photos of working men and even criminals fifty years ago, how they would be in suits and ties. When Americans read books besides *Harry Potter*. But there was no time to linger on that thought.

The big head cocked and he spoke over Del Shannon. "Lookin' at something?"

I thought about responding to his growly question. He looked like a clown. I was looking at a clown. His intention in all the "body art" couldn't have been to make people look away. Then I remembered Lon Cheney's observation that "there's nothing funny about a clown in the moonlight."

I looked away and approached a woman sitting in a low chair behind the register.

She was Anglo and might have been fifty, with gray hair that looked like a bathroom rug, a dead-fish complexion, mean porcine eyes, and a sleeveless size twenty-five housedress decorated with sunflowers. Only her head and shoulders were visible. Her hands were beneath the waist-level nook that held the register.

"Yeah?" An Okie twang.

That was customer service.

"Is Jerry here?"

"No." She pulled out a burrito and took a large, messy bite. "His pickup truck is parked out front."

The pig eyes met mine, the Platters came on with "Only You," and we stared at each other while she chewed. Phoenix used to have a big cohort of Okies, Texans, and Arkansans, but they had been lost in subsequent waves of immigration. I kept my peripheral vision open to movement from the man on the stool.

"What's up, Belma?"

Jerry McGuizzo emerged from the back, stopping when he saw me. His face was as flat as a dinner plate and it didn't look happy to see me.

He looked me over and whistled. "You look like shit, Mapstone. The old lady give you that shiner? How come you're dressed so funny?"

"We need to talk."

He suddenly laughed like I was the funniest guy on the west side, pulled out the kind of plastic comb I owned when I was ten, and ran it through what little hair he had. He used his left hand, the one with two stumps where complete fingers had once been. Then his hands went into his pants pockets.

"I don't have to talk to you." He sneered and leaned forward from the waist when he spoke. "You're not a deputy anymore. I can call you Asshole, asshole."

I said, "Sure, Jerry."

"So without that badge, you're only some asshole trespassing on private property, asshole."

He stepped around Belma and let loose a large gob of spit. I turned in time to keep it out of my eyes but it went low and landed on my tie.

Lindsey gave me that tie.

Jerry laughed harder.

I laughed, too. We both had a grand old time.

Then he leaned over the counter to speak or spit again and I broke my promise to Sharon.

I suddenly grabbed him by both shoulders and pulled his face hard into the top of display counter.

He let out a pained squeak as an elaborate spider web of broken glass grew around his head.

He was a little guy, so it was easy.

So was shoving him backwards into the wall, where he collapsed on the floor followed by a cascade of dozens of packs of Camels, Pall Malls, and Newports dislodged from their homes.

It was as if he were at the bottom of a slot machine and had won the jackpot, only doing so might require reconstructive surgery to his cheekbones and jaw.

He fell back moaning, and I produced the Colt Python, traversing the barrel to my left.

"Stay on that stool, fat man."

He stayed on the stool.

My eyes caught a slight movement right. I brought the barrel to Belma.

"I don't like it that I can't see your hands," I said.

The burrito was sitting beside the tip bowl.

Jerry moaned, "Leave it alone, Ahu. Don't do nothin', Belma…"

She slowly placed chubby little hands on the cash register while Jerry pulled himself up. He looked better than I expected, a puffy nose constituting most of the damage.

"Stand up and back away."

She did.

I stepped behind the counter and retrieved a sawed-off, double-barreled shotgun from a space below the register. From the tip of the barrel to the end of the stock, it was about fourteen inches long.

Jerry tried to explain. "We've had robberies…"

This was sweet deterrence. Shoot straight through the cheap facing of the counter while some dirtball was demanding money.

"It's okay, it's okay!" Jerry had his hands out, palms facing me. Now he was the peacemaker.

I holstered the Python. Breaking open the sawed-off, I saw two twelve-gauge shells in the chambers. Those would have torn me in half. Why was my breathing so even?

With my other hand, I produced my badge case and held it out low.

Lindsey's blood was on the star, the identification card, and the leather. The badge case had been in the pocket of my blazer, which I had used as a trauma dressing.

Let them see what they've done.

"Your information was wrong, Jerry, and you assaulted a deputy sheriff."

"I didn't know. How would I know?" He was talking fast, using his hands to make a calm-down gesture. The clown on the stool had not moved a millimeter and stared at me with flat eyes. I snapped the twelve-gauge back in place, cocked the hammers, and let it rest in the direction of his bulk.

"Honest mistake, Mapstone. Let's talk. Come in back, to my office. I'll get you a towel to clean up."

"Maybe I'll take you downtown. Couple of years in prison, in general population, would do your asshole good, Asshole."

"Oh, c'mon, Mapstone. I was only jokin'."

"You know your rights, correct?"

"Sure, but…"

"Read your damn rights!"

"I have the right to remain silent…please!"

"Keep going."

He rubbed his bashed face. "Anything I say can and will be used against me."

I stared at him. The Miranda Warning was one of Phoenix's gifts to the world. After the Supreme Court let him off because his constitutional rights had been violated, Ernesto Miranda would sell signed Miranda Warning cards for five bucks. Until he wound up on the wrong end of a knife fight in the Deuce.

"I have the right to an attorney and if I can't afford an attorney, one will be provided for me. I understand each of these rights as I have explained them to me."

I nodded approval and he looked sad. Belma, likely standing for the longest stretch in years, added a long fart to the proceedings.

For a few minutes, I let him think about being arrested as not a single customer came in. For all the silence, the place had a jumpy oppressiveness, like even the packs of smokes wanted to bolt for the parking lot, and I was not the cause.

Then I let him take me to the back office.

Three-Finger Jerry was a former Phoenix cop and a Jack Mormon; in other words he had backslid out of the church. He earned his nickname when he blew two digits off in a firearms accident. With his own police shotgun.

After he was bounced from the force, he set up El Tobac-Corner and seemed to fade away unless you had business with him.

The one exception came a couple of years ago, when his estranged wife called 911 to say he was having sex with a rubber pool raft in the common area of his apartment complex. She filmed the act on her cell phone and it went viral on the Internet, battlefield of angry spouses and spies.

Jerry got probation for indecent exposure and for a while was another dubious celebrity in the Arizona freak show.

He was also the only person I could easily find on a Sunday night who was a bona fide member of the supply chain involving stolen goods.

In other words, Three Finger Jerry was a fence.

Chapter Sixteen

I followed him into the hall, twenty feet past cigarette cartons stacked against the walls. Jerry was a short guy with a blond crew cut, wearing a gray T-shirt that was too big for his spindly arms. He did a "Walk Like An Egyptian" dance and laughed. I didn't.

The hall opened into a larger storage area with pallets of more cigarette cartons and Tide detergent. At the back were two metal doors. One, which he opened, had a black plastic OFFICE sign. The other was unmarked and secured by a heavy padlock.

The music switched over to "Rockin' Robin," the Bobby Day version. I hadn't heard it or thought about it in years. I was thankful that it was shut out when he closed us inside the little room, bid me have a seat, and settled behind a cheap, small desk.

The walls were unpainted Masonite and covered with old *Hustler* centerfolds in all their gynecological meticulousness.

"Thanks for smashing in my face," he said

"You brought it on."

He looked at me earnestly. "I mean it. Had to spit on you, see? Nothing personal but I had to put on a show. You didn't disappoint."

A drawer opened and his hand reached in. I started bringing up the sawed-off but he came out with only a dry face cloth. I used it to wipe off the ruined necktie.

I asked him why we needed to put on a show. His eyes avoided me and he pulled on the T-shirt, his loopy arm muscles standing out. Sweat stains were darkening the garment.

"How's your buddy, Sheriff Peralta? I hear he became a private eye."

The question surprised me considering Peralta's newfound notoriety, but I made my face express boredom.

"He's doing well. How's the fence business?"

He studied me with sad gray eyes. I was one of the few people who knew he had been one of Peralta's CIs or confidential informants.

He lightly rubbed his mashed face. When he took his hands away, his drawn appearance was evident. Since the last time I had seen him, he had probably lost twenty pounds he couldn't afford.

"Business is shitty. That's how it is."

"Is that what made you pick up the muscle out front?"

He stared into his lap. "He picked me up. He's MS 13, so you'd better watch your ass. Goddamned Salvadorans. I'm into 'em deep. Look, I've got to close pretty soon, so what's on your mind?"

He pulled out a Marlboro and lit it with trembling hands, offering me the pack, but I waved it away and said nothing.

He smoked with his bad hand. The shooting accident had shorn off most of the index and middle fingers. So he smoked by holding the cigarette between his thumb and fourth finger. The effect was half Sinatra and half circus geek.

After a few moments, he shrugged. "This business used to be simple. Junkies and burglars bring in electronics, I pay 'em shit, send the stuff to Mexico where it's repackaged and resold."

He smoked and stood. His small body seemed incapable of idleness, but what had that gotten him? When I kept staring, he sat back down and continued.

"Here's what made it work. Stuff goes to a pawnshop and it's liable to attract the cops. A legit pawnbroker has to log it in the computer system. Here, I got a smoke shop in Maryvale. Who's gonna think? Simple business model. I connect buyers and sellers. How am I different from an investment banker or a hedge-fund guy? We're a coarse, shitty land run by criminals. I go with the flow."

While he philosophized, I gently uncocked the little shotgun's hammers, broke it open, tossed the shells on the floor, and set the empty firearm beside his desk.

"So what changed?" I asked.

"The fucking Internet, for one thing. E-sellers, they call them—craigslist, eBay. Scoop up a lot of the really good stuff, so I'm dependent on the dude who's too stupid or too poor or too jonesing and impatient to go online."

He had given this much thought.

"Plus, there's too much crap today," he said. "Thieves don't know the PC era is over, see? Don't even try to bring in a PC nowdays, much less with Windows XP. Macs, iPads, iPhones, and Androids—those I can use."

He pouted.

"And?" I said.

"The fuckin' Salvadorans."

"You have to go through them now?"

"Shit, they don't care about stolen iPads. Stolen guns, they like those if they're the right kind. No, they use my humble, locally owned retail establishment the way they want."

He wiggled his arm to see a silver watch.

I put my hands behind my head, exactly the way Peralta used to do when he was either relaxing or trying to irritate me. It had the latter effect on Jerry.

"What do you want from me, Mapstone? Use your fucking imagination. Money and drug drops. Stuff I don't want to know about, okay? If there's heroin coming through here to be broken up and distributed, it's not my problem. The less I know, the less chance they'll feed me to their pit bulls." He paused. "Cigarette smuggling is the biggie. That I have to know about."

"What about the tax inspectors?"

"Haven't seen one in years," he said. "State cutbacks. Anyway, some of the inventory is legit. Go look, you'll see tax stamps. The rest goes into the black market. I don't get diddly as a cut even though I'm the one taking the chances here."

"How'd they take over?"

"I needed a loan fast, okay? Goddamned Indian casinos, all around the city now. It's their revenge on the white man. Anyway, I was fifty thousand short and a guy told me about a guy. You know how it goes. Next thing I know, Ahu is my babysitter." He used his good hand to wipe away sweat. "Are we done?"

I thought about that. Ahu's tattoos didn't look like MS 13, one of the most dangerous criminal organizations in the hemisphere. He didn't fit the profile ethnically, either. Jerry, as a former cop, should know that. But somebody was leaning on him and Phoenix had no lack of gangs.

Even if Ahu didn't belong to Mara Salvatrucha, this was cause for concern. CIs always went to the highest bidder. Peralta had taught me that. Now somebody was able to put in a higher price for Jerry than keeping him out of jail on condition that he provide information and not murder anyone, Peralta's old deal.

I thought about the Tide. It was tough on stains, a cash cow for Procter & Gamble, and in recent years had become a street currency used to buy drugs. Addicts shoplift the 150-ounce bottles and at the most risk a shoplifting charge, way better than a felony count for burglarizing, say, a television. Organized groups called retail boosters have gotten into the racket, and not only with detergent. Fences buy the items at a discount and resell them, even to major retailers.

Jerry's simple business model was keeping up with the times.

I said, "We're not done. You have some place you need to be?"

"I need to close, Mapstone. Really."

"Your sign says you're open until eleven."

His new partners probably had a shipment on the way. I affected nonchalance.

He blew a plume of blue smoke over my head, stood up, turned around, and studied one of the pinups. He sighed and faced me. "God, this town was way simpler when the Italians ran things, you know?"

I nodded sympathetically.

"Tell me about diamonds."

He looked at me like I was insane. "Diamonds? What?"

"You heard me, Jerry. Tell me about diamonds and I'll let you close or whatever you need to do."

He plopped into the chair. "Diamonds. They're hard. They're forever. They're a girl's best friend. Color, cut, clarity, and carat. Who cares? Some lowlife brings in a stolen engagement ring and I'll give him a hundred bucks. And that's if it's a good ring. The resale market stinks."

My swollen eye and cheek throbbed in realization.

I smiled on the inside.

He doesn't know about Peralta and the robbery.

This was a good thing, or so I calculated. If he knew, he might have somehow used it against me. For the first time, I was thankful for a society of ignoramuses that didn't read newspapers or even watch television news.

He stubbed out the Marlboro. "I don't deal in 'em."

"How would a person fence valuable diamonds, in unique settings? Hypothetically speaking."

"Way over my pay grade," he said. "Diamonds make people crazy. The 2003 Antwerp heist? A hundred million. They got caught. Absolutely insane plan. But it didn't keep them from trying. You get into that kind of shit, you better pick out your dirt furniture."

I raised my eyebrows.

"Dirt furniture," he repeated. "Goes well six feet under."

When I spread out comfortably in the chair, he talked again.

"Here's what I've read, okay? Uncut diamonds are the easiest to resell. They're tough to trace. The buyer could cut them, change their characteristics, and make it hard to track them. Nothing worth more is as small and easy to move. No mineral is worth more per gram. Now, cut diamonds are a different breed of cat. If they're expensive enough, they might be laser-inscribed, with a number or name. De Beers does that. I'm no expert, but that's what I've heard, see."

For somebody who claimed little knowledge of diamonds, he knew quite a bit.

I said, "So they're not fence-able?"

"I'm not saying that." His pride kicked in. "The smart thief would wait. Let the cops move onto other stuff. Then find the right wholesaler. You know, with the right set of ethics. They'll still get a fraction of what the diamonds are worth. The wholesaler will resell 'em to retail jewelers who don't want to ask too many questions."

He picked out another smoke with the remarkable dexterity of that shot-off hand and lit up.

He continued, "Wholesalers make the money. But understand, they're after diamonds worth millions, not the engagement ring your girlfriend gave back, see? That's what I've read, at least. Honest to God, I don't deal in diamonds. If I did, I wouldn't be in this fuckin' mess."

"So who would know about these wholesalers?"

He watched me closely. "You'll leave if I give you a lead?"

I nodded.

He reached for a notepad with his good hand and scrawled an address. He tore off the page and slid it across to me.

"I handled a delicate matter once," he said. "Let's leave it at that. I delivered a package to this office."

"Who works here?"

"I don't know. I didn't want to know and my client wasn't going to tell me. My instructions were to walk into the outer office at a certain time and put the package on the secretary's desk and leave. I didn't see a secretary or anybody. Don't think that wasn't intentional. After I got back in the hall, I heard the door being locked behind me. Look, I'm taking a chance even giving you this much."

As he checked his watch for the tenth time, I unfolded the computer-generated color sketch of Strawberry Death.

"Ever seen this woman?"

"I thought you said you were going?"

I tapped on the sketch.

He actually took a moment to study it. "Nope, but I'd like to. She's cute. Not exactly the kind of clientele we get in here, you know? She lose a diamond?"

"Something like that."

I thanked him. And although I already knew his answer, I told him we could help, get him into witness protection in exchange for his cooperation.

He waved me away with his three-fingered hand, the Marlboro held firmly.

"Go. Go."

Halfway down the corridor, I turned back to him.

"Where would a person go in this town to hire a hit on somebody?"

He rolled his eyes. "Anywhere. Depends on whether you want it done right, and don't want to get caught in a sting by law enforcement."

"Can you be specific?"

"No." He lowered his voice beneath the sounds of Chuck Berry. "If I had that answer, I might take out my baby sitter. Hey…"

As "Johnny B. Goode" ran on, he gripped my shoulder. "Be careful with that name I gave you. Word is he's close to the cartels."

As I walked back through the store, the fat man was where I had left him. Only his tombstone eyes moved, tracking me.

Jerry, for show, followed me to the door, shouting. "Beat the shit out of me. Go ahead and watch the claim I file against the county! This is an honest business. I don't know anything about any goddamned computers…"

"Okay, Jerry…"

"Tell me I'm clean, you bastard! I want to hear it."

"You're clean. It was a misunderstanding. Thank you for your cooperation."

He was still yelling from the door when I got in the Prelude.

It was better not to linger. I drove to the corner, pulled into another asphalt lagoon. Say what you will about Phoenix but you can always find another parking lot.

There, in the lonely dark, my heart started hammering and I could hear the blood pulsing through vulnerable arteries and veins in my neck and temples. I could hear my breathing, hot and dry. Taking my hands off the steering wheel, I watched them tremble.

All this foolishness over what for me was a garden-variety panic attack.

I hesitated to even use the expression, for they were truly debilitating for most people. I was very high functioning. Panic skirmish? Anxiety Cold War? They never kept me home under the covers.

Still, it put a name on the periods of high melancholy and anxiety that had struck me periodically since I was nineteen, the day after my grandfather died. I didn't know what they were for years. They were one of my eccentricities I kept to myself.

Then, one day I read an article about panic attacks and the symptoms seemed to fit. I felt better when I learned that Lord Nelson and Sigmund Freud probably suffered from them, too. The knowledge didn't make them go away. Lindsey did.

Now, alone in the car, I scanned the lot for trouble. Finding none, "Rockin' Robin" replayed in my mind. It would be there for days.

Robin loved me, or so Lindsey had said. Robin was not the falling-in-love type.

I tried to unspool the snarl that had drawn Robin and me together. Danger, need, passion, electricity. It was all that and more. Beware the cunning and treachery of memory, especially concerning lovers.

Would I have left Lindsey for Robin? Never. But how could I know all the contingencies, all the counterfactual history? Lindsey might have left me for one of her lovers in D.C.

All that was in the past. In the present, I might lose Lindsey after all. The thought paralyzed me.

My head was hammered by pain. It was from the very real damage the hitwoman had done to my face, but also from the fear that I would lose both of them, Lindsey and Robin. Especially that Lindsey would never wake up again. Cliché but true, she was the great love of my life. And, yes, fear that I would lose Mike Peralta, too.

"Quit feeling sorry for yourself."

There, I was talking to myself.

This would be an opportune time for Strawberry Bitch to take me out.

I distracted myself by imagining the criticism I would face for such a statement in the faculty lounge.

When a hitman does his job, he's praised for being independent, assertive, and effective, but when a woman does the exact same thing you call her a "bitch."

"I suppose you're right," I said out loud.

We hope you will be more gender-sensitive in the future, Professor Mapstone. You enjoy a position of white male gender-privilege that's not even apparent to you, you bastard.

"Thank you for pointing out my failing. I'm sorry, although I suppose tenure-track is kaput for me. I will not use the term Strawberry Bitch."

Until her gender-power is being used on me from the business end of another H&K Mark 23.

Then I thought about the situation more seriously. A .45-caliber Special Forces pistol was not an assassination weapon. Hitmen favored .22 caliber pistols firing sub-sonic rounds. These were easy to silence.

So why was she carrying the big gun? For intimidation purposes, perhaps.

Kate Vare had described the bag she had dropped outside our house containing burglar tools, handcuffs, and tranquilizers. Maybe she had intended to stage a murder-suicide—as if I had shot Lindsey and then myself. With the handcuffs, perhaps she intended to torture one or both of us.

For her stones.

As the cars sped past like comets in search of a star, I thought again about her other words, to the effect that she would kill me to fulfill a promise to Peralta.

In her anger, Lindsey had chided me for being naïve, but would Peralta have unleashed this reaper on me? Was I kidding myself about the man I thought I knew? But then I remembered his words on the Dictaphone, "You're going to hear a lot of things about me. Don't believe them."

I rolled down the window and took in the breeze, thought about how close I had come to being blown apart by Belma's sawed-off shotgun, and my hands became steady. I pulled out my iPhone, and dialed to ask about Lindsey.

Chapter Seventeen

I stopped at the house and changed into casual clothes for the overnight shift. The file from Melton was still there, demanding my attention. Not for the first time, I wished I had told him no, whatever his threats to Lindsey. Everything might be different now.

Or not. We had been on Strawberry Death's to-do list that night.

Lindsey's rings went into a sock, which I rolled up with its mate and dropped back in the sock drawer. I slid a couple of books off the shelves and put them into my briefcase with the MacBook Air. Then I put a light jacket on to conceal my big Colt revolver and headed up to the hospital.

There it was so quiet and deserted that I was able to find a space in the two-block-long parking garage close to the skywalk entrance. I checked out the concrete expanse carefully but no killer was hiding in wait. I walked through the automatic doors and headed toward the massive complex of buildings. The skywalk was empty and Tom Petty's voice was coming over the speakers, singing about learning to fly without wings.

Sharon had nothing new to tell me. This time it was my turn to shoo her off to get rest. She said I looked exhausted.

Two new Phoenix Police officers were outside the ICU. I checked them out long enough that they started giving me the cop eye. This caused them to take extra time looking at my driver's license—no need to bring my badge into it—before I was buzzed into the unit.

It was almost ten and I was given a lecture about visiting hours, but they took pity on me and allowed me inside Lindsey's room.

I sat by her high-tech bed and held her limp hand, reading Billy Collins poems aloud. He was her favorite poet. IV bags were changed. A nurse looked at me indulgently, as if to say, *She can't hear you.* I knew that she could and kept reading.

After my ten minutes were up, I sat down in the waiting room with the file in the chair beside me.

It was still there when I woke up.

The wall clock showed five after three and I was momentarily disoriented and frightened. The room was empty. No one passed in the halls.

I picked up the file folder, snapped off the rubber band that held it together, and began to read. Pretty soon I was making notes.

Seeing my old handwriting in the cramped boxes of the original incident report made me think of that David Mapstone. Doing the calculations, I seemed impossibly young. I was juggling being a deputy with working on my master's degree.

I had taken my own apartment at the edge of the lush Arcadia district and had left Grandmother alone in the house on Cypress. She understood a young man's desire to be on his own. At that time, when the state was determined to ram the freeway through the old neighborhoods, they were in decline. More than once, I found a homeless person sleeping on Grandmother's lawn.

I drove a ten-year-old Firebird that I was inordinately proud of. I should have kept it—I would have owned a classic. My girlfriend was named Deb. She's a history professor at Cornell now. I thought Heineken was a sophisticated beer and I knew too little of jazz. The bad recession of 1981 was still lingering.

The service weapon I carried as a deputy was the same one as today, the Colt Python .357 magnum with a four-inch barrel. It wasn't regulation but the supervisors let it fly. They knew I wanted the stopping-power of the big gun, something the .38

didn't have. If a hopped-up criminal came at you, the .38 would eventually kill him. But he might keep coming and kill you, too. The .357 magnum would knock him down. I was a believer in stopping-power.

A month before, Peralta had become the youngest captain in the history of the Sheriff's Office, an obvious comer. He kept pressuring me to stay in the Sheriff's Office, not become an academic. Sharon had completed her Ph.D. in psychology. They had two young daughters. We had become social friends and would eat Mexican food he cooked every Wednesday night.

The nasty recession of the early 1980s was still hanging on. The metropolitan area was two-and-a-half million people lighter than today.

I was different from the other graduate students. For someone my age, I had a real job that mattered, one with adult responsibilities, one with duties that carried consequence. On the other hand, most of the other deputies held me in some suspicion. A college degree was rarer then in law enforcement, much less somebody who wanted to be a history professor. It made for an ongoing tension, this living two lives.

That July day, the midnight-to-eight shift was slow. The schedules worked for me so I could go to class and handle my slave-labor grad-student teaching load during the day. Who needed sleep at that age?

I was on patrol far from the city, west past mile after mile of farms and into the desert that framed the White Tank Mountains. I was there because Caterpillar, which ran a desert proving ground up the side of one steep rise, had been hit by a series of burglaries.

The area was popular with high-school keggers and the occasional body drop, whether done by the mob or freelance killers working for money or trying to conceal the consequences of their murderous passion. They assumed we wouldn't find a body out here. We nearly always did.

Otherwise, it was the desert: silent, incomprehensible, teeming with wildlife at night while on the surface, to the untrained eye, a creation of brute simplicity where saguaros that could live for centuries looked at you as nothing more than a passing trifle.

At 6:07 a.m., with the angry summer sun already thirty degrees above the horizon, I found a car sitting off a dirt road a mile from Caterpillar. It was a faded green 1967 Dodge Monaco with Arizona plates and no one visible inside. I pulled behind and radioed in my location—ten-twenty—and the tag number. When the dispatcher told me it wasn't stolen, I stepped out and checked the vehicle.

It was empty and unlocked. Inside, I found no weapons or drugs. The keys were in the ignition and when I turned them to bring up the alternator, the dashboard showed me a full tank of gasoline. The tires were worn retreads.

The trunk held a spare tire, jack, and a large first-aid kit, nothing more. It was neat and had been recently vacuumed.

I thought about backing away and waiting, in case these were burglars. But the break-ins at the proving ground always involved cars pulling right up to the fence. Recreational hikers this far from town were rare in those days. I pocketed the keys and decided to check the area on foot.

The monsoon season hadn't started yet, so the chalky soil was hard-packed and didn't show tracks well. But I spotted some light foot treads leading out into the desert. From the cruiser, I slung a canteen over my shoulder and put on my Stetson to shield me from the sun. I followed the footprints.

They disappeared as the land became rocky. I took a chance and went straight, finding them again thirty feet away on sandier soil. I was hardly an expert tracker. In this case, I was lucky.

Maybe twenty minutes later, as the land dipped in a graceful slope, I saw him face down and maybe five feet away from a large stand of cholla. He had dark-brown hair and wore yellow running shoes. When the direction of the breeze changed, I knew he was very dead.

What a great way to end the shift—with a stinker.

I pulled out the heavy portable radio on my belt, a new innovation, and called for the medical examiner and detectives.

As a uniformed deputy, my job was pretty simple. Secure the scene. That was easy, given that we were in the middle of nowhere. Today the area is overrun with houses, including the fancy subdivision of Verrado. Back then, it was silent emptiness.

My other memories were few. Because of the incident, I had to get a friend to cover for me in teaching my undergraduates that day and I made good overtime from the county.

As I read on, I learned more about my stinker.

His name was Tom Frazier and he was twenty years old, an emergency medical technician for Associated Ambulance and completely alone in the world. His mother had died of a heart attack three months earlier. He had no brothers or sisters and his parents had apparently divorced years before.

Aside from his work colleagues, who spoke well of him, he seemed to have no friends. He had no girlfriend. In those days, no detective would ask about a boyfriend unless it was a vice investigation.

If the file ever contained a photo of Tom Frazier, it was gone. All that remained were shots of the scene and the autopsy.

The detective wrote that Frazier was saving money for college and his bank account held five thousand dollars. But that, aside from the old Dodge, made up his assets. He rented an apartment, not far from where I lived at the time, was up-to-date on his rent.

The last person to see him alive, at least according to the reports, was his ambulance partner at the end of their shift. When he didn't report for duty twenty-four hours later, the Associated supervisor called his home but the phone went unanswered. No answering machine, much less today's cell phones.

The medical examiner estimated he had been out there for a little more than thirty hours. In high summer, that was plenty of time for the sun and heat to do its damage to the corpse.

This meant he drove out into the desert and then walked away from his car in darkness. The car was in running order.

He didn't walk back toward the city, which was curious. The land sloped up toward the mountains there giving a nice view of Phoenix to the east. He could have seen the city lights in the distance.

Instead, he walked south for more than a mile. Nowadays that would be heading toward Interstate 10. Then, only farm roads and a two-lane highway lay in that direction and miles away.

Two weeks later the toxicology findings came in and the detective stopped his efforts to find out about Tom Frazier and why he had left his car and walked into the wilderness with no water.

I read the three-page tox report, marveling at how primitive it was compared with today. But it was modern enough make the cause of death definitive: a heroin overdose.

The case was closed as a probable suicide.

The theory was that Frazier was despondent over his mother's death and decided to push himself over the edge with too much H.

This was the conclusion of the eighty-seven pages of documents before me. The case was listed as cleared but much about it didn't make sense to me. I wanted to think that even the young me would have known it, had I circled back around to follow up.

For one thing, why didn't Frazier simply stay in the car and die? Also, given the amount of the drug in his system, it was amazing he walked as far as he did.

The reports contained no evidence that Frazier was a drug abuser. His body was decomposing and had been snacked on by coyotes, but the medical examiner found no evidence of multiple needle holes. He wasn't an addict. His colleagues said he didn't even smoke pot.

So maybe he chose to use heroin once as his ticket out.

Maybe. But where was his paraphernalia? When I had searched the car, I had found nothing. Addicts, especially with decent-paying jobs, had shooting kits nearby, all the time.

The detective surmised that Frazier must have sat down and shot up once he was out in the desert. But no needle, cooking spoon, lighter, or tourniquet was found.

By the time all the official cars have arrived and deputies had tramped through the area surrounding where the body and car had been found, it was impossible to even know for certain if Frazier had really been alone.

I was as much to blame as anyone. I didn't suspect a homicide. I only saw another example of a fool walking into the desert in the summertime.

The desert makes people do strange things. But this was a suspicious death not a suicide. Tom Frazier had no one fighting on his behalf to find out what really happened out there, not even the Maricopa County Sheriff's Office.

Did he have enemies? Why would he spend money for a tank of gas if he intended suicide? Who else saw him on his day off? What was his demeanor in the days before his death? How did he spend his days off?

The biggest problem was that his wallet was missing. For the second time, I went through the inventory of items found. The wallet was neither on him, in the car, nor in the desert between the vehicle and the body.

This was long before the immense migration of illegal immigrants headed *el norte* through the desert, many dying there. The land was astoundingly empty by today's standards. Someone wouldn't have happened upon the corpse and stolen the wallet.

In addition, a skirmish line of academy students had swept the terrain searching for anything, finding nothing.

His car tag and dental records had identified the corpse.

He was buried in the Green Acres cemetery in Scottsdale, the arrangements paid for by an unidentified family friend.

I opened my MacBook Air and wrote up my assessment. To: Sheriff Melton. From: Deputy David Mapstone. It was like the old days, only the wrong man was sheriff. I blind copied Kate Vare. It also wasn't my "history thing," as Peralta called it.

The history thing. It had set me apart from an ordinary cold-case detective, using a historian's techniques to dig deep into the case and its times.

Now I wasn't so sure. I had been in law enforcement longer now than I had been teaching. It felt so strange, so wrong. When I was twenty, I meant my time at the Sheriff's Office to be a youthful adventure, a stint of public service, something I could tell my grandchildren about. Now, here I was, still, and there would be no grandchildren to tell.

In any event, Melton didn't deserve the history thing.

I would email the report to him, fulfilling the county's paperless ambitions. Then I would FedEx a resignation letter with my star and identification card.

Doctors swept into the waiting room. One was a tall man about my age, the trauma surgeon. He looked and acted like a fighter pilot. The second was an Asian woman, introduced as the "hospitalist." I had no idea what that meant. It was only a little past six a.m.

Again, I should have taken notes, but I was too distracted by the presence of the docs and my hopes and fears.

The surgeon was pleased Lindsey had made it through the first twenty-four hours.

"That's crucial for controlling shock and stabilizing cardiovascular and neural functions…"

She showed good brain activity. She wasn't paralyzed.

But we weren't past the crisis, he said—that would last through the first seventy-two hours "at least."

They talked about reversing the shock and dealing with any extra fluid swelling that occurs with trauma.

The doctors wouldn't make any predictions. I didn't ask.

"We continue to hold out hope," the woman said.

I realized that was meant to be honest yet comforting but it almost pushed me off the edge of a very tall cliff. I nodded.

Did I wish to speak with a social worker? No.

They swept off to do doctor things. Had I even gone to use the restroom, I might have missed them.

I waited for visiting hours and sat with Lindsey. I left reluctantly. I wanted to stay, sleep in a cot next to her, never let go of her limp hand. But I didn't have that choice.

So I decided to take a walk.

It was Monday.

Chapter Eighteen

The address McGuizzo had given me went to one of the skyscrapers in Midtown Phoenix. Once it had been the headquarters of a bank.

The bank was long gone, one of the many casualties of the 1990 crash. Since then, much of corporate Arizona had either been bought up or migrated out to Twenty-Fourth Street and Camelback Road or to north Scottsdale. That left Midtown with half a dozen zombie towers. This office was in one of them.

It was close enough to walk on a morning like this, when the temperature was barely sixty and the dry, clear sky ridiculed the plight of Lindsey and me and hundreds of other patients and family members at Mister Joe's. The sun was its intense self. I slid on dark glasses. They also helped conceal my black eye.

I trooped across the parking lot of Park Central, past the Good Egg where Lindsey and I had eaten breakfast what seemed like years ago, when we were fresh from our fun in the hotel shower and the biggest problem was a missing Mike Peralta and the diamonds. It seemed like a big deal then.

The tower was a bland sheet of blue glass, turned at an angle to the avenue, utterly dead at street level. The architect, if you could call him that, had intended the building to have a relationship only with the automobile. Like all its siblings, it was attached to a long, multi-level garage that sat on its backside.

That's the way I made sure to come in with others. My timing let me catch up with a half dozen of the few people that still worked there. It was eight-thirty. I was the tallest in the group, dark hair, broad shoulders, too memorable. I was the only one who pressed the elevator button to the eighteenth floor.

When the doors opened, a sign directed me to a law office in one direction. He was not a lawyer. I went the other way until I found the suite number that Jerry had written on the notepad. It went to a door, five long steps on the carpet and ten more on tile, making the turn that the building's cube shape demanded. The door was only adorned with a number, no nameplate. Across from it was a fire extinguisher set into the wall, nothing else. Not even restrooms or a drinking fountain. It looked like a dreary place to work.

I listened for a few minutes, pretending to study the note. Only the electrical hum of the tower's core spoke back. Was the occupant a guy who rolled into the office early to talk to clients on the East Coast, or did he keep 'Zonie *mañana*-time hours? There was only one way to find out.

I put my hand on the door and turned it.

The door opened.

The view was dazzling through large windows. The outer office was empty and the lights were off. A receptionist's desk was unstaffed. Two chairs and a sofa held no customers. On a low table, several celebrity magazines were neatly laid out.

The art on the blond wood walls consisted of colorful, vintage travel posters: "visit the Pacific Northwest wonderland—travel by train," "Grand Hotel Roma," and "the Dune Beaches by the South Shore Line."

It was difficult to tell what business resided here.

I decided to wait by the glass, taking in the South Mountains and Sierra Estrella. The air wasn't too dirty this morning. I prevented my gaze from going lower, where it would find the white hulk of the hospital.

And like the hallway, the room contained only the silence of human-made spaces, especially the whoosh of the air conditioning.

"Anyone here?" I finally called out. The reception area had two doors. One, I had used to enter. The other was between the sofa and a sickly looking potted tree. I knocked and no one answered.

I said "hello" as I opened the door inward. No one responded.

This office was large but spare. The walls held more of those travel posters with fantastical images of trains, ships, and bathing beauties from the twenties and thirties. Two dark wood chairs sat in front of a desk that might have been new when the building went up. An executive chair with the stuffing coming out of a tear beside the head completed the ensemble.

It was dim with shades down keeping out much of the light. I stepped in.

"Hello?" Out of old habit, I added, "Sheriff's Office."

It looked as if I had beaten everyone to work this morning.

Then I saw the shoes attached to legs hanging at a low angle in a doorway to my left.

The legs were attached to a man who was attached to the doorknob by a necktie. Make that two neckties, one solid blue and the other a red rep pattern. I was all for wearing ties in this barbaric age, but this was a little overboard. His face was one foot from the floor and his arms were stiff at his sides.

On one hand was a 1995 class ring from the United States Naval Academy.

I snapped on the lights to the bathroom but there was no need to check a pulse. He was as straight as a well-planed two-by-four. Rigor mortis sets in within three hours of death and fades away after twenty-four. Given his stance of attention at the absurd angle, I would say he had killed himself twelve hours ago.

A more thorough sweep of the office revealed nothing special, certainly not safes containing stolen diamonds for wholesale.

I slipped on the latex gloves and locked the door from the office to the hallway. Then I went back into the private office.

The corpse's wallet contained credit cards, a health-insurance card—little late for that now—two twenties, and a few business cards that only gave his name and phone numbers. Stuck to a credit card was a driver's license. I disentangled them and held it up to the ambient light. The license was issued to Matt Pennington. He was forty-five and showed a Scottsdale address.

"Find Matt Pennington," Peralta had written to me. Here he was.

Using the memo app on my iPhone, I wrote down the information. Then I slid the wallet back and went through his front slacks' pockets with more difficulty. His bladder had emptied and, surprisingly in the dry climate, the pants had not dried. Keys in one pocket. A pack of cigarettes in another.

No cell phone. I ran my hand around his belt, and there was no phone case on it, either.

I went back to the pack of smokes, reached in, and pulled the box out.

It was the distinctive blue hardpack of Gauloises Blondes, the same brand Lindsey sometimes smoked. She bought them online because they weren't imported into the country anymore.

The health warning was inscribed in French at the bottom of the azure front panel.

"No kidding." I muttered quietly. Talking to dead people was something I had learned as a young deputy, the black humor that saved us. Tom Frazier and his fellow EMTs probably did the same thing. Always out of earshot of civilians, of course.

The pack had been unwrapped and I opened it. Half the cigarettes had been smoked and a matchbook was inside. I dug it out, hoping it advertised a bar or restaurant where Pennington might have been a regular. It was blank.

But not on the inside.

In blue ink, someone had written a phone number. I copied it on the iPhone and replaced the cigarettes in his damp pocket.

Down on one knee, I could see his face. "What the hell did you have this for?"

I asked. The face, purple from lividity, blood collecting after the heart stopped, did not answer.

Chapter Nineteen

The air conditioning switched off and the rooms grew very quiet as I studied the scene. There's no easy way to die but this was particularly...I searched for the right word. Something between "gutsy," the ability to hang yourself from a doorknob and not stop when all you had to do was lower your arms and hands and take the pressure off your neck, because this would not be a fast way to kill oneself.

That, and "preposterous." If you wanted to kill yourself and you are on the eighteenth floor of an office tower, why not leap through the window, or toss a chair through first and follow it down to the pavement? This building was a creation of the 1980s and I doubted the windows were that strong, particularly since it was thrown up on the cheap during the years of the savings-and-loan racket.

Unless you didn't kill yourself but had help.

You were "suicided."

I was very conscious of the sound of my breathing as I checked his wrists.

Pennington looked a little under six feet and in good shape, easily strong enough to fight back against a five-five woman. Unless she had a gun on him.

What if he had been handcuffed from behind and left to slowly strangle? Or tortured for information, a little bit of pressure applied from the back, as he slowly suffocated from the neckties. He would have held out hope until the darkness closed around him and slammed shut for the last time.

His pale, stiff wrists showed no cuts from being handcuffed. But there were ways around this, such as putting something like a washcloth between the skin and the hard metal of the cuffs. That way, any evidence the person had been shackled from behind as he slowly suffocated and struggled would be more difficult to detect.

Plastic Flexcuffs were another option. Use a gun to intimidate, make him get on his knees, restrain him, put the ties around his neck, start asking questions.

Strawberry Death probably had better tricks than that.

My tricks were limited by time, by who might be expecting Pennington's office to be open. I quickly went through his desk drawers, the most interesting item being a nine-millimeter pistol in the top right-hand drawer, for all the good it did him. Or, if he really wished to kill himself, why not use that?

I did a quick study of his desk. The top was cleared of everything but a blotter and a telephone. Not even a laptop. In fact, there was no computer in the office, although there was a charging cord and a T1 cable. Strawberry Death took his laptop.

If it was her. Historians are warned against something called confirmation bias, where every piece of information backs up your existing hypothesis. It's a big no-no. Pennington might have made many enemies. But she was the killer at-large whom I knew.

There was something else: besides the faint but growing odor of death from Pennington's corpse, I detected traces of Chanel Number Five.

Coco Chanel had been a Nazi collaborator during World War II. She had hired a former perfumer to the Tsar to create the scent that would bear her name. Five was her lucky number. "Your mind is an amazing thing," as Peralta told me.

That meant Pennington was connected to diamonds. Perhaps a fence.

The closet showed me a tantalizing file cabinet with combination locks on each of the four drawers. No time. I needed to be out of this office.

Still, I lingered.

"Well, I found him, what next?" I whispered.

Hearing nothing in the ether from Peralta, I played the best hunches I had in a dim room with a dead man. I studied the edges of the filing cabinets. It appeared as if they had been built into the closet itself. Only an inch of the heavy metal was sticking out of a black wooden frame.

I tapped on the drawers. They sounded empty. But diamonds weren't likely to take up much space inside.

I spun the dials, pulled on the drawers, and nothing happened. Four drawers.

I tried setting each dial to coincide with the last digits of Pennington's birthday. Not one drawer opened. On each one, I ran his birthday as a four-segment combination. They stayed locked.

Being there was growing from foolhardy to insane to linger this long. But only the quiet kept me company.

Then I remembered the class ring and started setting the four combinations from the top town: one, nine, nine, five. I don't know why I tried it, but when I slid the last dial over to five, the wall clicked and the file cabinets popped ever so slightly toward me.

Reaching around again, I pulled on the left side. It gave way and I was staring at the door to a safe. The safe had a digital keypad and an inset handle that looked as if you turned it, the result would be a missile launch. "Valberg," a modern black-and-orange label said. The file cabinets were a false door.

Another ten minutes went by as I tried putting in different combinations. Each time, a small light went red and who knew what might have happened if I kept at it.

I closed the false door and it sealed with a soft but definitive sound. I spun the combination knobs around to random numbers.

When the phone rang it was a low, muted tone. But you might as well have attached jumper cables to my spinal cord, connected to a fully charged battery. I stared at the desk phone. The digital read-out glowed lagoon green. It said, UNKNOWN.

I approached it warily. Two rings. Three.

My hand touched the receiver.

Then I picked up.

"Pennington," I said.

A long pause followed and I was instantly sorry I had answered.

Then a man's voice said, "What's wrong, Mister Pennington? You're late. "

"I was tied up."

"Is everything in order?"

The voice was a medium timbre, speaking standard American English, no movie villain German, no cartel Spanish.

He didn't know Pennington's voice.

So far, so good.

Now the real gambling began.

"A woman tried to kill me."

A long pause. Maybe I had made a bad move. I expected the line to go dead.

But he came back on. "Her name is Amy Morris. That's what she goes by, anyway. She's after the diamonds, too."

"You should have warned me."

A pause. Then, "We thought you were safe, out of the loop."

"I don't like being out of the loop," I said. "What about Peralta?"

"Peralta is a different problem, and it's better for you not to know. He's our problem. Did you kill the girl?"

"No," I said. "She got away. She's a fighter."

"She's well trained. They say she was a Mountie, you know."

"Hell! She's a cop?"

"Not anymore," he said. "It may not even be true. There are many stories about her. If they sent her for you, we need to meet quickly. At the place you designated."

"No. That's not safe now. I don't like this." The agitation in my voice was easy to manufacture. "Not if this Morris woman knows about me. Makes me wonder who else knows. We need a new meet point. And what about the FBI?"

Another pause, longer this time, and I worried that I had finally stepped out of bounds.

But the voice came back yet again, a taut tone. "Mann's window is closing."

Mann. I thought about Peralta's recorded warning.

I said, "How much time? This has all gone to hell. I don't feel right about this."

"Calm down, Mister Pennington. Let's meet. It would be good to finally see you."

I tamped down the flood of adrenaline in my system.

When I didn't answer, the voice turned angry. "You're acting pretty foolish if you're going to let your fear of that girl keep you from the million dollars you stand to make on this deal. You came highly recommended, but we can go somewhere else if we have to."

A million dollars? Off a million-dollar diamond robbery? How did that work out?

I said, "This is business. I want it done right."

"That's better." His tone returned to normal. "So when do we meet, and where?"

"Soon. I'll call you." I paused. With the blocked number, I didn't know how to reach him. I said, "Give me a new number. I don't trust the old one."

"You're being paranoid. But if it will help…" and he read out ten digits.

"Thanks. I'll call."

Before he could protest, I hung up.

A few seconds later, the phone rang again. UNKNOWN. I didn't pick up.

I wiped down any surface that I might have touched before putting on the gloves. Then I checked the peephole into the hallway. The corridor was empty. I unlocked the door again, stepped out, and softly closed it. I put on my sunglasses.

One benefit from the building being on hard times was that the security desk downstairs was empty.

Later, I would find one of the few remaining pay phones in the city and call the fire department: I noticed a strange odor on the eighteenth floor. Coming from the office at 1806. You might want to check it out. Maybe it's a gas leak.

I was glad to be out in the January air.

Chapter Twenty

When I returned to the hospital, a woman in a gray pantsuit with short red hair intercepted me at the elevators. Her face was full of freckles and smiles. So this was not the social worker who would tell me that Lindsey had died while I was gone.

I let loose the breath I had been holding.

Then I noticed the gold shield and gun on her belt.

We shook hands and she introduced herself as Megan Long, a Chandler Police detective. She had an engagement ring with a large clear diamond in the main setting and smaller ones on the band. I had come to notice such things.

"Buy me a cup of coffee," she said, and we walked to the Starbucks near the main lobby and sat at a table.

"I thought you'd want to know that we found the diamonds."

"Yes," I managed, my mind scrambled by what I feared would come next: *and Peralta is dead.*

But the phrase didn't come. Out of a dry mouth, I added, "Where?"

"Apparently in the parking lot of the mall."

She watched my expression. Her eyes were jade. I tilted out my hands in bafflement.

"Yesterday, a woman brought a small wheeled suitcase to the station. She put it beside the front doors and left. We thought it might be a bomb so everything went on lockdown and the bomb squad was called. 'Shelter in place.' What a stupid-ass expression."

"But it wasn't a bomb…"

"It was the diamonds meant for the jewelry store, packed exactly as they were shipped. We showed them to the jewelry store people at the mall. Then they called the man from Markovitz and Sons who had brought them to Sky Harbor and handed them off to Peralta. He stayed in town after the robbery. Anyway, he came to the station and verified that they were real. He put them under a microscope. Very fancy-looking thing."

"Nothing was missing?"

She shook her head. "Nope. We captured the woman's image on the cameras and the license of her car. A SWAT team arrested her last night."

I asked who she was.

"A housekeeper at the San Marcos."

It was the oldest hotel in town, established in 1912 by Doctor Alexander Chandler and built in the Mission Revival style. For decades, it had been the centerpiece of a little town on the Southern Pacific Railroad surrounded by farms. That was before the trains went away and Chandler turned into an affluent "boomburb" with almost a quarter million people and Intel semiconductor plants. The Crowne Plaza was now running the San Marcos as a golf resort.

I said, "You're kidding me."

She shook her head. "Catalina Ramos. She has a second job at the Johnny Rockets by the Harkins Theatre in the mall. She had parked at the far edge of the lot, as employees are required to do. She claims that after she got off work, she drove home, and discovered the suitcase in the trunk of her Toyota."

"Why didn't she call the police?"

"She's undocumented. Been in the country since 2001. But after SB 1070, she was afraid that if she went to the police, we would deport her. This kind of thing has happened all over, especially since the new sheriff began his 'immigrant sweeps.' We had a good relationship with the undocumented community before that."

SB 1070 was the law that cracked down on illegals, or, as some critics said, merely drove them deeper into the shadows.

Nationally, it made Arizona into a place of bigotry and hate. It was good politics. Ask Chris Melton. Peralta opposed it and lost the election.

I said, "And you believe her? She had nothing to do with the robbery?"

"We do. She has a totally clean record and children in school. No brothers in prison. No boyfriend. Her employment checks out and she was at work when the robbery went down. She decided to leave the jewels at the front door of police headquarters."

I asked if the Toyota had been locked. It had. But it was a twenty-year-old car without an alarm and could have easily been opened with a Slim Jim device.

That would have taken some brass: shoot the second guard, take the diamonds, get in your truck, take the time to stop at an anonymous Toyota, break in and pop the trunk, drop in the suitcase, lock up, and drive away. All this while police were converging from every direction.

It was the kind of brass that Peralta had.

Detective Long said, "What are you thinking?"

"Where this leaves Peralta."

It wasn't exactly a lie.

"He's still wanted on warrants for robbery and assault with a deadly weapon." She paused. "I know you worked for him and he's a friend. Everybody in our department is stunned that he did this. But I'm still going to find him and put him in prison. He was caught on the camera. The evidence is definitive."

Definitive. Hardly anything else in this case was.

She sipped her coffee and continued. "He probably expected to come back and get the diamonds once the initial response died down. Or, he had her tag number, so he could have come to her house. She might never have known the diamonds were there if she hadn't checked her trunk.

"I was wondering where you were," I said. "The FBI called me up to Ash Fork in the middle of the night when they found Peralta's truck. I kept looking for a Chandler detective."

Her face scrunched up.

"What bullshit. I've dealt with fed interference before—they never play well with others—but nothing like this. They swooped in and took the case. I protested and got stuck deeper on the bad-girl list. Command folded like a cheap suit, is that the expression?"

I nodded.

"I didn't get it," she continued. "What was their jurisdiction? But we were forced to back off. Since 9/11, their powers have expanded to the moon. When they found the truck, they didn't even tell us until twelve hours later and by that time they had towed it back to Phoenix."

The green eyes lasered me. "Why do you think they took my case?"

"You're giving me more credit than I deserve. Peralta was close to the old SAC, Eric Pham. It was an unusual collaboration with a fed. After he became a private detective, Pham threw him a few jobs."

"You, too," she corrected. "You're his partner."

"Fair enough." Then I felt obligated to say I had been brought back to the Sheriff's Office. It's temporary. To consult on an old case. I'm not a racist. I don't hate Hispanics.

She laughed, a fine melody that reminded me of Lindsey. "Is that going to be how you identify yourself every time? It might take awhile to get all that out when you're breaking down a door."

Before I could do more than smile, she added, "Horace Mann is an asshole."

"Yes," I said. "How did he react to you finding the diamonds?"

"Like an asshole." She looked at the ceiling and blew out a sigh of exasperation. "He came out with his entourage, waited long enough for the diamonds to be verified as the stolen property."

"How did he seem?"

"What do you mean?"

"Happy? Relieved?"

"Not at all. He was pissed. The hicks in Chandler solved the case."

There might have been other reasons he was vexed but I kept them to myself. A dead man was attached to a doorknob in an office half a mile north of us. Somebody on the phone who was expecting those diamonds had told me that "Mann's window was closing." I didn't know enough yet to advance a theory and didn't want to dig myself in deeper.

She chuckled.

"Do you know what this was?"

I shook my head, unsure of which "this" she was talking about.

"When the call first came in, I expected the shipment was a bunch of engagement rings, something like that. But the jewelry store manager told us it was a closed show for their most exclusive customers."

"Chandler has changed," I said.

"Lot of money," she said. "Not quite Scottsdale, but getting there."

"Enough rich women to be exclusive customers."

She frowned. "That's a sexist thing to say."

I started to apologize, but she tapped my knee. "I'm kidding. Relax. You know what you call a woman flying an airplane?"

"No."

"A pilot, you sexist pig." The fine laugh rang out again, and then her face grew serious. "Here's the thing. This wasn't any ordinary diamond show. It was ice. Bling. Hip hop stuff. Amazing, gaudy, huge. The big deal was a pair of rings that Tupac Shakur had worn, 3.6 carats, top clarity and color. You know who he was?"

"Even I know."

I told her it didn't fit with the white-bread image of the suburbs.

"That's probably where most hip-hop music is bought," she said. "It's all my son listens to. Ugh. How many talks have I had with him about the misogyny and hate for the police in the lyrics. He thinks I'm so out of it. He talks about how it's poetry of struggle and oppression. Do you have kids?"

"No."

When I said the word, something closed in her face and she thought differently about me. In Chandler, what married man wouldn't have children? She didn't know anything about Lindsey or me. Now I was simply strange, beyond comprehension.

I pushed the thought away and said, "Hip hop has gang connections. Tupac was somehow tied in to the Bloods. Or maybe it was the Crips. Could they have initiated the robbery?"

"Maybe," she said. "I did some research. A couple of years ago a music producer was robbed of a fifty thousand-dollar diamond necklace, plus a Rolex worth another fifty K. But I didn't find anything this large or audacious. Anyway, the people invited to this show are all respectable, rich, white. For all I know, real rappers aren't so much into bling any more, so it's become a collectable for the housewives who watch reality television."

"And all this was worth a million dollars?"

"That's what the expert from New York said."

"Only a million..."

"Yes. I don't know about you, but in my life that's a lot of money."

I took it in and we settled into silence.

"Well, thanks for telling me," I said, extending my hand.

She took it. Her skin was smooth and cool. "Have you heard from Peralta?"

"No." I said it without hesitation. But this is what I had been waiting for. Megan Long wasn't here for a courtesy call. Rapport had been established. She was now down to business. So I ran through my Friday, how I knew Peralta had agreed to do a diamond run, but told me nothing more. The dictaphone message, that part I left out.

She nodded as I talked, not writing anything down. This didn't deviate from the statement I had given the FBI on Friday.

"They tell me your wife is in critical condition," she said. "Do you think this shooting is related to the robbery? Sergeant Vare thinks it is."

And she would be right. But once again I said nothing about Strawberry Death and the demand for "her stones." After a moment, "I don't know what to think. I'm focused on Lindsey getting better."

"Here's to that." She toasted me with the cup, stood, and gave me her card.

I said, "May I ask a stupid question?"

She cocked her head.

"Didn't the rolling bag have a GPS tracker?"

Her eyes narrowed, trying to conceal her emotions.

She held up her index finger. "Would you give me a minute?" Then she stood and walked twenty paces into the high-ceiling lobby, pulled out her cell phone, and engaged in an animated conversation. She closed the phone and paced, not looking in my direction. In five minutes, the phone rang and she hastily answered.

Sitting down with me again, she looked flushed and was shaking both her legs.

"It's not a stupid question. The case did have a tracker and it was working. I don't know why the FBI didn't turn it on. Or, for that matter, why Peralta didn't cut it out and get rid of it. He had guarded diamonds before. He knew it was there."

"So maybe he didn't intend to come back for it."

"Which means what?" Her response was heated. "And why the hell didn't Horace Mann activate the tracker?"

"Maybe he did," I said.

She stared at me a long time before running a pale hand through her hair.

I ran the scenarios through my mind. Maybe Mann saw the tracker indicating the parking lot and assumed Peralta had ditched the device there while keeping the diamonds. Maybe he put the Toyota under surveillance hoping this Pamela Grayson would show up to claim the bag.

She mumbled, "This is fucked up" and looked at the people around us. I understood. Who the hell knew what had gone down? Who was involved and who could be trusted?

"There's something else." She bit her lip, wondering whether to tell me more. "The rolling bag had a hidden compartment.

Mann found it. Nothing in it. But when I talked to the guy from Markowitz, he said their bags didn't have hidden compartments. It's strange."

"What about the other guard?" I asked.

She turned and faced me. "He's out of the hospital, wearing a sling. The bullet went through his shoulder but didn't hit any bones."

I nodded. Peralta was that good a shot.

I said, "Which shoulder?"

"His left."

"Which is his gun hand?"

The freckles on her forehead scrunched together. "His right."

"And he couldn't get off a shot?"

"No," she said. "He said Peralta's shot knocked him down, stunned him. He's an older gentleman. But my partner checked him out and he came back mostly clean."

"What do you mean mostly?"

"He lives out in the desert by Wickenburg and there's some intel on him being suspected of selling guns to felons, but nothing proved. He has a valid PI license. He's a Native American gentleman."

My freckle-less face must have shown something.

She asked, "Are you all right?"

I nodded, trying to remember what I had seen in the video of the robbery. The second man was wearing a red ballcap, his back to the camera. My attention had been on the image of Peralta, grabbing the bag, turning, and firing. The feds wouldn't allow me to replay the scene.

In a low voice I asked for the man's name, even though somewhere inside I knew the answer.

She assessed me. "I shouldn't, but what the hell. You're a deputy again. His name is Edward Cartwright."

Chapter Twenty-one

Ed Cartwright.

FBI Special Agent Ed Cartwright, deep undercover.

Valid PI license. Native American gentleman. Fade into the background.

It had been a setup from the start. But for what?

There were too many FBI agents, I knew that much.

I took the elevator up to the ICU swimming in anger.

But when I stepped out, I saw Sharon. The expression on her face turned me to ice. I started to speak, but no words came out.

"Where have you been?" she said.

"Looking for your husband. What's going on? How is Lindsey?"

She simply hugged me and I felt my body go numb. I felt her warm breath on my ear as she whispered, "David, I am so sorry."

Lindsey was dead.

The obscene ease with which the thought came surprised me, as if I had earlier decided to take the stairway in the office tower as high as it would go, break open the locked door, walk across the roof, and step into the air. Lindsey and I had been twinned for so many years, the only surprise was that I hadn't felt something, an extrasensory squeeze of the heart, something, as I was prattling on with the red-haired detective downstairs.

I didn't hug Sharon back. My body was slack. *Widower,* my God. Yes, I would find the strawberry blond assassin and kill her. For that matter, I would find and kill Mike Peralta, too, for thoughtlessly precipitating this catastrophe like the diplomats and generals and plumed emperors had done with the Great War a century before.

Sharon led me into a consultation room where an older woman in blue scrubs was waiting. She had a face that was both kind and had seen it all. Her identification tag read "RN." I heard the door close.

Then I was sitting there with no memory of my body having moved from the elevator to this chair.

The woman said, "Your wife has a serious fever."

I let out a heavy breath of relief. Lindsey was alive. How bad could a fever be?

I said, "I want to see her."

"Talk to me for a minute, Mister Mapstone."

I regained my fear and stammered, "She's felt cold to me."

"I know," the nurse said. "That's normal because of the shock and the blood loss."

When she paused, I forced myself to take out a notebook and a pen. I wrote what she had told me, my shaky hand leaving the first few sentences looking as if they had been written in some strange, ancient alphabet.

"In general, fever is not altogether a bad thing," she said.

"Is Lindsey okay?" What a foolish, immature question. I asked it anyway.

"No."

"Sorry," I said. "So, 'not altogether a bad thing'…"

"Right. So far as fighting infection goes, it's better for the body to run a little hot because the 'bugs' can't survive above a certain internal temperature. So maintaining ninety-nine to a hundred-and-one degrees Fahrenheit is considered not out of the question."

Her voice was calm and businesslike and I was screaming inside with impatience. If it wasn't out of the question, what was the problem? But there was a problem, of course.

"She had a dirty wound," the nurse said. "For the past hour, her temperature has been one-hundred-four. That's dangerously high for an adult."

I made my hand write. My letters became more intelligible.

"We're using antibiotics and taking other steps to knock it down."

I stopped writing and rested my hands on the table. "What if you can't?"

"I'd rather think that we can. She's a fighter and we're helping her. She was healthy and is fairly young. It's a much better scenario than if she had been elderly or in poor health."

I wrote again like a dutiful student, which was ironic because as a professor I was suspicious of the ones that wrote down every word I spoke. I was pretty sure they weren't getting the broader themes and most important points of the lecture, wrestling with them, thinking critically.

I put the pen down. Sharon took my other hand.

The nurse looked at me straight on. "You deserve to know that a very high temperature could be extremely serious, even critical, depending on whether the organism she has is, or is not, susceptible to the antibiotics."

The hits kept on coming.

"Organism?" I asked.

"Some are resistant big-time." She shot out some acronyms, some of which I had heard of, some not, none sounding good: MRSA, MERS, VRSA. "We have to rule those out."

"I want to see her."

"Not yet. Give us some time. We need to get the cultures back from the lab so we know what's causing the infection. I'll come and get you."

Back in the ICU waiting room, Sharon asked me what she could do. I shook my head.

"Go home and get some rest," I said.

"Let me stay."

I didn't answer.

After a few minutes, she stood, told me she would return in a few hours, and made me promise to call her if Lindsey's condition changed. She didn't ask about Mike and I was in no condition to debrief about what I had learned.

After Sharon left, I sat among four other bereft souls in the room, all as incapacitated with worry as me. The room was turbulent with a blaring television and the nearness of death. I thought of Kafka's words, "The meaning of life is that it stops," and I hated him for writing them.

After two aimless walks down the hall, I settled back in and slid low in the chair.

It was so wrong not to be totally concentrated on Lindsey. But I couldn't even get in her room.

I felt like I was drowning.

To save myself, I called a criminal defense lawyer at Gallagher & Kennedy where we'd done work as private investigators. Before I got too far into my problem, Lindsey and national security, she stopped me.

"This is not something to discuss on the phone," she said, and then sent me to her assistant to make an appointment.

I should have told Melton to go to hell and made this call instead of taking the badge. But maybe Strawberry Death would have broken into the house after we were asleep and killed us both. I was drowning in contingency.

It would be next Monday before I could see the lawyer.

Then I tried to sort other things out, the ones that didn't involve secrets to the Chinese, dirty wounds, and deadly acronyms. Were she awake, Lindsey would save me from such situations.

What would she say now?

She might say, "What's it all about, Dave?"

It was about…

Peralta and Cartwright, pulling off the diamond robbery and making it look oh-so-convincing by Ed being winged. They were both in on…what?

Horace Mann of the FBI taking the investigation from Chandler PD with no explanation.

Whoever was in the car in Ash Fork, picking up Peralta and returning to the Interstate.

It was about Amy Morris, the hitwoman who shot you, my love, with her "promise" to Peralta.

Matt Pennington in his anonymous office, a safe hidden behind fake filing cabinets, "suicided" in his bathroom.

The man who had phoned Pennington's office, who was now expecting me to call him back.

Who was working together and at lethal cross-purposes?

And all this for a million dollars in gaudy diamond jewelry that was now in the Chandler Police evidence room, safe in the rolling bag they arrived in. Except this bag was special, rigged with a hidden compartment.

My understanding of this case is coming in slivers, a sliver at a time, and every time they seem to make a whole, another sliver is taken away.

Except…

Except the value of the jewelry stolen and recovered didn't jibe with the information from the caller to Pennington's office, who promised that Matt was getting a million-dollar cut for participating in their heist.

Of a bag with a hidden compartment.

Even this liberal arts major realized that was one hundred percent of the stated value of the stolen property.

In other words, Peralta was involved in a job valued at much more than a million. And that meant that Strawberry Death's stones weren't the ones stuck in the trunk of Catalina Ramos' Toyota. Those diamonds had been left in the rolling suitcase with the GPS tracker, easily found.

The real stones worth killing for were still out there.

"Lord have mercy."

Out loud, I involuntarily channeled my grandmother again. No one else in the room looked at me.

Chapter Twenty-two

After an hour, they let me in to see Lindsey. Her police guard had been cut to one officer. Inside the intensive care unit, I had to wear a gown, gloves, booties, and a mask. "Nothing from the outside goes in except to stay," I was told. "Nothing from the inside leaves." I packed my jacket and guns in a locker.

Tubes were still running in and out of her, connected to IV and plasma bags, and she was still on the respirator. A couple of additional machines kept watch. Her catheter bag was half-full of urine and I thought how horrified my immaculate Virgo wife would be to know this.

The medicos explained the plastic blanket that shrouded her body: it had water running through it to help her cool down. I could feel the heat of her hand even through the gloves.

Her beautiful hand was different, palm clenched inward, digits at odd angles. I tried to keep my voice from shaking when I asked about this and they told me it was normal. What about this was normal?

I rubbed her thumb, squeezed her misshapen hand. She didn't squeeze back. No miracles today.

Through the mask, I whispered, "Please come back to me."

To the nurses, I said, "Does she dream?"

"Probably."

I stared at the floor and prayed for her to enjoy sweet dreams. God doesn't owe me anything.

But maybe for her...

I stayed as long as I could. Unfortunately, they were very punctual monitoring the time. After I retrieved my stuff from the locker and left the ICU, I stepped into the hall and had walked twenty steps when I heard the ruckus coming from around the corner.

Several people kept saying, "Sir!"

As I got closer...

"Sir, you're going to have to leave. You can't be up here."

My pulse jacked up and I reached inside my jacket for the Python but kept it in the holster as I heard slurred profanities.

Someone whispered, "Hell, drunk Indian."

Another voice: "Call security now, please."

I walked to the L in the corridor, turned, and saw Ed Cartwright.

"Not goin' anywhere. Trying to keep the red man down. Stole our land. Sons of bitches. But the Apache were never defeated! You needed Apache scouts to beat the other Indians!"

He was weaving among three nurses and aides, putting on a great show. He wore a red ballcap and a blue sling, neatly pressed Western shirt and new blue jeans, tooled cowboy boots. His right hand held a pint of cheap whiskey.

"I'm a deputy sheriff." I flashed the blood-caked badge. "I'll take care of this man."

"Hey, watch the shoulder, po-po!"

"Come with me, sir," I said, steering him by the uninjured right arm toward the elevators.

"Racist!" he shouted toward the audience, his face a mask of tragedy. "You heard what he called me! I'm gonna get rich off this! Sue the Sheriff. Sue the County. Sue this pale face! You're all witnesses. Racist po-po! Oh, feel like I'm gonna throw up."

He weaved and bent over.

I whispered, "If you puke on me, I'm going to break your good arm."

The car arrived empty and I pushed him inside. Instantly, he stood in a posture suggesting authority.

"You make a subtle entrance," I said.

He smiled.

"It's a good thing the Phoenix cop guarding Lindsey didn't get involved."

"Where'd you get that deputy's badge?" he said.

"Long story." I pointed to his cap. "Redskins" was emblazoned across the front. "Political statement?"

"Huh? I'm a Washington fan. Have been since I was assigned to FBI headquarters in D.C. I can't find any love for the Cardinals. Who beat the crap out of you?"

"The same woman who shot Lindsey."

He assessed me in silence. Cartwright must have been very handsome when he was younger, with his high cheekbones, black oval eyes, dark sandstone complexion, and rugged look. Now, in his sixties, his face was cut into hundreds of rivulets and the eyes were bordered by puffy skin that left him with a permanent and intimidating squint. His hair was the color of lead, tied back in a ponytail.

"How is she?" he said.

"Bad."

He patted my jacket.

"Still carrying that wheel-gun artillery?"

I nodded.

"You have a backup?"

"On my ankle. The woman who shot Lindsey had one, too. That's what she used."

My mind was back on Cypress Street, Saturday night—why didn't I take the shot?

When we reached the first floor, he dropped the whiskey bottle into a recycling container and I followed him outside into the perfect day. We moved at the fast stride that I remembered from the first time I had met him, when he had showed me his survivalist bunker built into the side of a hill. Back at his house, he had a formidable library. I liked him instantly.

"Wait," I said. "I can't leave Lindsey."

"This is why I had to put on the act to get you out of there. You love her. Family is everything. I get that. But I need you to walk with me. Give me ten minutes and then you can go back. There's nothing you can do for her now."

"What if she dies and I'm not there?"

"She's not going to die." Any passerby would think he was looking at me, but I saw his eyes subtly scanning the street, something I should have been doing. Then he spoke again. "Have you heard from Peralta since Friday?"

"Not exactly." I told him about the business card in Ash Fork, the disguised voice on Sharon's landline, and the message on the dictaphone.

I asked if Peralta had made contact with him.

"No." He spat on the sidewalk and watched it evaporate in the ten-percent humidity. "Three days now and no contact. This has turned into a real goat fuck."

I stopped. "*This?* There's a this?"

"Walk with me."

I reluctantly complied. When Third Avenue was clear of cars, we crossed without speaking. Stepping off the curb seemed like a betrayal of Lindsey. Her skin was so hot. I stared at my feet moving through the crosswalk across the asphalt. *So damned hot.*

Now my eyes were scanning the street and buildings, too. I felt jumpy. I was seething, too. That Cartwright had been a part of this scheme with Peralta and I was left in the closet like a discarded garment. That Strawberry Death had disappeared and Kate Vare had, too. Where was my update on Lindsey's assailant? Let her come for me. Give me another chance…

On the other side of the street, Cartwright broke through my brooding.

"Three weeks ago, the Russian mafia contacts me. Fifteen million in gem-quality rough coming through town. Could I steal it?"

"Rough?"

"Uncut diamonds," he said. "What you see on an engagement ring or in a woman's earlobes has been cut and polished.

Rough is the way they come out of the mines. You probably wouldn't recognize it."

I was hardly shocked to hear about the Russian mafia. Phoenix was a mob town going all the way back to Al Capone's organization during Prohibition. It was a convenient back office to tally Las Vegas casino skimmings after World War II. With so many people coming and going, Phoenix was an easy place to reinvent yourself and remain hidden.

Today, in addition to the cartels, it was hard to imagine a gang that didn't have an outpost in the metropolitan area. Crips, Bloods, outlaw bikers, Mexican mafia, tongs, and other Asian criminal organizations. We were so diverse. All this and Phoenix had a lower violent-crime rate than most other large cities, despite the occasional hysteria from some politicians. Maybe it was because of this. Too much killing was bad for business.

Cartwright seemed to read my thoughts.

"Things are getting worse," he said. "Budget cuts. Cops laid off. The aviation unit cut back. Phoenix PD disbanded the old Organized Crime unit for the flavor of the month. Violent Crimes. Homeland Security. Organized crime investigations pretty much died."

I sighed. "So much for the people who voted in Melton because they were afraid of their Mexican gardener."

"Don't even get me started on Crisis Meltdown. He disbanded Peralta's OC unit."

"He's one of yours. Retired FBI."

"Not mine," Cartwright said firmly. "Younger generation and different Bureau. When he was running for sheriff, he made such a big deal about being a decorated FBI agent. I had never heard of him. Turned out he never did shit as a field agent but he was quick to claim the spotlight for small busts. They called him D.Q. Melton."

"D.Q.?"

"Drama queen. He couldn't find a real collar in a shirt factory."

I laughed but he spat again and continued: "Russians. You drive to the right places in this town and it's like out of that movie, *Eastern Promises,* I shit you not. They own barbershops, nail salons, and other fronts, taking in all kinds of stolen goods, but mostly precious gems, diamonds, gold. They steal credit card and debit card numbers. The younger ones stake out public Wi-Fi locations and grab user information. We have a ton of other ethnic mafia crime, including the traditional Italian gangsters, and nobody is doing anything about it. Makes me fucking disgusted."

"What about the FBI? Why don't you do something?"

"Terrorism sucks most of the manpower. And most of that turns out to be a BFWAT." He pronounced it as BEE-fwat.

I cocked my head.

"Big Fucking Waste of an Agent's Time."

"They have you."

"Doing what? Domestic terror cases, mostly." The three wrinkle-ravines deepened. "Nobody here knows I'm FBI— except Pham, Peralta, and you. Sharon doesn't know, right?"

"She doesn't."

The ravines disappeared. "Make sure it stays that way."

"What about Paradise Valley?" I said. "There were two dead bad guys. You made me leave and you stayed."

"Two bad guys *you* killed," he corrected. "I untied Peralta and gave him the gun you handed me when I told you to get the hell out of there. I told the cops I was homeless, camping out on the property, and that was that."

I shook my head.

"Play to people's prejudices and it gives you an advantage, David. I'm the crazy old drunk Indian living out in the desert, selling guns, and working as a private eye who can get things done."

"And you don't care if your clients are aboveboard?"

"That's how you catch the bad guys."

The breeze made the palo verde leaves quiver. He stopped and looked at the hulking buildings and abundance of asphalt. Half a block ahead, a young Hispanic woman in scrubs jaywalked where Third Avenue made a wide curve around Park Central.

"Look how ugly this town has become. This was a better place when the Apache ruled."

"No doubt," I said. "Tell me about the Russians."

"We met at a café in Wickenburg, me and two Russians. They knew I acted as a courier for Markovitz and Sons when they brought in diamonds for shows. They'd give me a hundred fifty thousand dollars if I'd handle the shipment for Chandler Fashion Mall on Friday. All I had to do was retrieve the rough, which would be concealed in the suitcase."

"How did it get there?"

He shook his head. "They wouldn't tell me. Markovitz is one of the top outfits in the country. Vertically integrated manufacturing, design, and distribution. But every organization has its bad apples. However it happened, the Russkies knew that rough was going to be there. They wouldn't tell me how they knew, or who it was intended for. Once a shipment is delivered to the jewelry store the salespeople lock it in a safe until it's time to set up the displays. The empty suitcase sits in the back. It's supposed to be empty, right? Grab the rough and nobody would be the wiser."

"And give it to the Russians."

"Right," he said. "So I took the job. Easy money for the U.S. Treasury and the Russians would never know what hit them when they were eventually arrested."

I asked him how Peralta got involved. Cartright steered us north, across another street and into the big parking lot that had once served Park Central when it was a shopping mall.

"After I met the Russians, I ran the deal up the chain of command and got a call from the director. Not every day I get a call from the director. He tells me fifteen million in rough had gone missing three months ago from the evidence control unit."

"Inside job?"

"Had to be," Cartwright said. "I don't even need to tell you the kind of bad press this would cause for the Bureau. Remember the forensics lab scandal? *The Washington Post, New York Times…*"

I said, "There were also wrongful convictions based on tainted evidence."

"I'm trying to explain how they think at the top. They're thinking about the press, being called before congressional committees, seeing their careers implode. So, back to the evidence theft. A very quiet investigation was launched and produced a list of ten agents and technicians that had the clearance, opportunity, and skills to have done it. They were about to go after each one hard-core when my little Russian deal popped up. "

"So they wanted to set up a sting." I said.

He nodded. "The trouble was, the thief might have been high enough in the Bureau to know that I was deep undercover. Unlikely, but we couldn't take the chance. So we needed a distraction that took the spotlight off me."

"Peralta."

"Yes," he said. "The concealed rough would only come if I was at Sky Harbor to receive it. Otherwise, the Russians would get suspicious. But if I stayed in the loop too long, the suspect within the Bureau might see red flags. So the plan was for Peralta to steal the entire shipment and get the rough. Make a big deal of it in the media. See how each suspect was reacting to the news by monitoring their phone calls, emails, and movements. Watch the Russians. Peralta would contact them, demand a cut, and set up a meet. We'd roll up the Russians, recover the evidence, and have enough to arrest the insider who stole it."

He ran through the robbery scenario. Once they were inside the service hallway at Chandler Fashion Mall—and on camera— Peralta was supposed to shoot Cartwright to make the theft look real and establish his bona fides as going rogue. Peralta had hand-loaded the bullet he would fire into Cartwright's shoulder so it would pass through cleanly without fragmenting. Without making a dirty wound.

"Still hurt like a son of a bitch," he said. "I think he actually enjoyed doing it."

Cartwright bought Peralta time to escape by acting more injured than he was. It was more than two hours before the courier-turned-robber was identified. To further camouflage the sting, the FBI instantly removed Eric Pham because he was Peralta's friend. They brought in a senior agent from the outside to take charge.

"Horace Mann," I said.

"He's a supervisory special agent. Flew in from Minneapolis on a Bureau jet and took charge."

"Does he know who you are?"

"He might find out I was quietly forced to retire ten years ago or face charges for bribery."

That was the cover story that allowed Cartwright to go undercover. I said, "No chance he could know you're still on the job."

"There's always a chance." He momentarily looked back at the hospital. "But it's a reasonable risk. Remember, the idea was to get be out of this early so I'd be nothing but a bit player, a victim at that."

"Is Mann a suspect?"

"That's an interesting thought, but no," Cartwright said. "The prime suspect is named Pamela Grayson. She's a senior agent in evidence control. Two years ago, she was investigated when eight pounds of very high quality heroin went missing, but she was cleared. So she was already on the radar for the diamonds."

"Already?"

Cartwright nodded. "It gets better. She served as a field agent in the Central African Republic. That's one of the centers of diamonds used to fund wars, drugs, you name it. Here's a sweet part: she was already in town when the robbery happened, staying at the Phoenician. Vacation, she said."

"What color is her hair?"

He looked at me curiously. "Brown. I've only seen the pictures."

People can color their hair.

I thought more about all he was telling me. "But this meant she had to know what the Russians knew. So either she had lost the diamonds to the Russians and was trying to get them back. Or she was working with the Russians, and why did they need you? Plus, all this drama would make me stay as far away as possible."

"Maybe you'd make a bad thief, David. When this much money is the itch somebody needs to scratch, he—or she—will take chances. Get reckless."

It sounded too complicated. Too many unanswered questions. Too much that could go wrong.

I said, "But what if the real thief was Mann?"

Cartwright squinted at me. "Why do you have a hard-on for him?"

"We had a nice little chat," I said. "I don't like him. He also strikes me as a control freak. Did he volunteer for this, or was he assigned?"

"Cartwright said, "He volunteered to a priority request but..."

"So if he stole the diamonds from evidence and was working with the Russians, he'd be in the perfect position to steer the investigation wrong. As it is, Grayson has been tipped off by the robbery and if anything happens to her, she can claim entrapment."

"Don't play high-school lawyer, David. This was moving fast. I wasn't totally comfortable with the plan."

Then I told him about the voice on Pennington's phone. "Mann's window is closing."

"Are you sure you heard right?" he said. "Horace Mann has a clean record. He's been decorated for valor. Maybe your caller said 'the man.' Something like that."

"I know what I heard. If Horace Mann is dirty, what next?"

"If that's true, Pham has it covered."

"Pham's not in Alaska?"

"Hell, no. That's disinformation, same as using the media to make sure the Russians and the bad fed knew Peralta was the robber. The director wanted redundancy and secrecy because this evidence theft involved a compromise of Bureau security. So he had Pham handpick a very small team that could go dark and be Peralta's guardian angels. Mann doesn't know."

"What could possibly go wrong?"

"Smart ass. Peralta has a GPS homing device concealed in his shoe but it never activated. The trackers on his vehicle didn't function, or he removed them. We haven't heard anything. The messages he left for you at least show he was still alive as of Friday night. I have no idea why he went to the High Country."

"And he willingly got into a sedan that headed back to the Interstate. That's what the witness told me. He could be in Southern California by now."

"Hell."

I recounted my conversation with the Chandler detective, how the official shipment had been found but the hidden compartment was empty. He said he already knew.

Then I asked him who was shadowing Sharon. Phoenix field agents working for Mann. That gave me little comfort.

"But nobody was watching our house. Why not?"

"I'm not sure. Might be a manpower issue. Peralta was trying very hard to keep you out of this, keep you safe."

A stream of bile started creeping up from my stomach. "That worked really well. If they had been there, Lindsey wouldn't have been shot."

"I'm sorry, David. There's a lot of moving pieces."

"Yeah. This was a pretty damned big moving piece. What about this woman," I pulled out the Phoenix PD sketch. "Pamela Grayson?"

"No."

I pointed at Strawberry Death. "How does she fit?"

He shook his head. "I saw that on TV. I have no idea."

"That's not good enough." My tone was full-on angry now. "She's connected to this. When she confronted me in the front yard, she said, 'Where are my stones?' When I told her I didn't have them, she talked about having to keep a promise to Peralta."

"Did she sound Russian?"

"Southern accent."

"There was nothing in the intel about her."

"Well, your intel sucks. Somehow she's connected with Peralta. She knew his name. She knew he had the diamonds. What is this promise?"

I told him about first meeting her when she impersonated a DPS officer. And about Kate Vare finding a kit on the lawn that the woman had left behind, with handcuffs and tranquilizers. About her preference to "suicide" her targets.

"She's a professional," I said. "She's done this before."

Cartwright took it in without speaking.

I said, "Who is Matt Pennington?"

Although his eyes didn't change, I saw the tension knotting up the small muscles in his neck. "Where'd you get that name, David?"

I told him about the message Peralta had left for me in Flagstaff, my walk to the zombie skyscraper, and what I had found.

We paused in the shade and he put his hands on his hips.

"You're full of surprises, David. For years, we had heard that the biggest diamond fence in the Southwest was operating here. Mostly selling gem-quality diamonds to retailers. There was a list of potential suspects Pham's people was working on. Pennington was not one of them."

"But you suspected him?"

"I heard his name from some of the circles I run in. I did a little checking and never found a thing. He worked at a call center. Led a boring life. His back story interested me."

Cartwright told me how Pennington had served as a liaison officer with a Mexican Navy drug interdiction unit. The Sinaloa Cartel penetrated it, a major intelligence breach, and Mexican marines ended up getting killed on a raid where the cartel had advanced notice. Although nothing was ever proved, Pennington was sidelined and left the U.S. Navy. That's when he moved to Phoenix.

I said, "Now the man who called me in his office thinks I'm Pennington and he's expecting me to call him back."

"And you will."

"No." I stopped and forced down the volcanic anger inside. My voice was dishonestly steady. "I won't. Lindsey was nearly killed and I'm only now learning this is all because of an internal FBI fuckup? And you don't even know who shot her? This is where I get off."

I started to turn back when he grabbed me hard by the shoulder with his good hand. His grip was strong enough to push me down if he'd been inclined.

"Look, boy," he shouted like a drill sergeant, "Mike Peralta loves you like a son!"

His words stunned me. That word again, *love*, coming from the most improbable source.

His grip tightened until my shoulder, arm, and hand were immobilized with pain. I would have hated to be on the receiving end of his strength if he hadn't been shot three days before.

The onyx glare fixed on me. "We're not going to leave him out there. *You* are not going to leave him out there."

He let go and walked ahead. "He'd do the same for us."

By this time, we were fifty yards into the parking lot and approaching an ancient RV. A bumper sticker said, "Ask Me About My Grandkids."

I followed and caught up with him.

He put his hand on my back and in a gentler voice said, "Come sit with me for a few. Then you can get back to the hospital."

Unlocking the side door, he beckoned me in with a tilt of his head.

I reluctantly stepped up and inside. A poster directly ahead showed a nineteenth-century photograph of four warriors with rifles. It was bordered by the words, "Homeland Security. Fighting Terrorism Since 1492." It wasn't easy to read because the shades were drawn, including flaps to keep anyone from seeing in through the windshield. The air was stale.

A sound—was it a sniff?—caused me to turn my head left and through the gloom see the figure sitting on a bench. A black hood was over his head.

Something in the primal brain reacts to a hooded man whether he is the reaper or the reaped.

I started to turn back and speak, or flee, but Cartwright gave me a decisive shove and slammed the door behind us.

Chapter Twenty-three

As my eyes adjusted to the dim light, Cartwright's prisoner jerked at his restraints knowing we were in the RV. It sounded like a show from a horror house but he wasn't going anywhere. The shackles allowed his legs to move an inch at the most. His hands cuffed behind him were useless. A seat belt completed his imprisonment.

Ed motioned for me to sit on the opposite bench, then he approached the man and slipped off the hood, revealing a black blindfold tight around his head. Next, he ripped open the man's shirt, sending a little hailstorm of buttons onto the yellowing linoleum floor.

He was muscled up and his sunburned skin was about seventy percent tattoos. Prominent among them was a scroll with Cyrillic letters, two skulls with crowns and, running down his abdomen, an enormous onion-domed cathedral.

This was not the kind of thing you found on the average ASU student.

Or perhaps it was—I was out of it on the contemporary culture front.

In any event, the abundance of tats had overpowered a wider assessment of the man. He was in his thirties with short blond hair, a rawboned face, and thin lips. An X of duct tape covered his mouth.

"Ain't he pretty?"

I said nothing. He looked hideous. If he wasn't Russian mafia, he had paid thousands to a local ink-slinger to get the same effect.

Cartwright reached toward the man's right ear and pulled off the duct tape in a slow sawing sound. The results showed the downside of wearing designed stubble. Scores of little hair follicles violated by the tape started bleeding.

The man flinched but made no sound.

Cartwright leaned close. "We had a deal. I get your diamonds and you pay me a hundred fifty grand. Now the diamonds are gone and the Mexican tried to kill me. You fucked me, Bogdan, and you're gonna make it right."

The head tilted up. "How do you know my name?"

This brought an open-handed slap across the man's jaw.

Cartwright demanded, "Where are my stones?"

I suppressed a shiver.

"You're a dead man, red savage." His voice was a baritone with only hints of a Slavic accent. "When my people…"

Another slap, harder. The Russian fell sideways and Cartwright sat him back up. My black eye began throbbing in sympathy pain.

"Your people are dead." Cartwright said the words matter of factly. "You won the lottery, Bogdan. You're alive because you get to give me answers."

The Russian coughed up some phlegm and was about ready to spit when Cartwright snapped his fist against the bottom of the man's jaw. The move was so quick it caught the tip of his tongue between his teeth.

This time silence was not possible. Bogdan screamed.

"Don't you bleed on my stuff, you commie bastard." Cartwright used both hands to tip the man's head up. "Swallow it all, blood and spit. How'd that work out for you, genius?"

Three minutes.

Five minutes.

I watched the time pass on a wall clock that needed to be straightened. Housekeeping was not the strong point of Ed's RV. The heat increased and the air was stagnant.

The man swallowed, his Adam's apple moving like a rickety elevator.

Cartwright reached back into a cabinet and brought out a flimsy dirty brown something. He pushed it against the Russian's face until he gagged.

"You know what that is, smart guy? That's the scalp I took of a Russian adviser behind the lines in North Vietnam. Sliced it off with my Ka-Bar while he was still alive. Then I gave him an Indian lobotomy. Might have been your daddy or uncle."

I caught a whiff of rotting meat and suppressed a dry heave of my own.

Cartwright tossed the scalp aside and leaned in, "Why did you send the Mexican to rip me off?"

"Don't know what you're talking about." The Russian's answer was slurred by the damage to his tongue.

"Yes, you do. We had a deal that I would pick up the shipment from the jeweler at Sky Harbor on Friday morning. When I got there, the Mexican had been hired as a second courier. Nobody told me. Why'd you do that?"

Bogdan shook his head.

"Here's my theory," Cartwright said. "You brought him in to take the rough for less money, cut me out of my commission. Too bad he was a crappy shot."

"Fuck you."

Crack. Ed's open hand knocked the Russian nearly off the bench. He pushed him back into place and cinched up the seatbelt.

Another long silence, before Cartwright spoke again. "The only way out is for you to tell me the truth, Bogdan. You knew the diamonds were coming in. You knew they were hidden in the suitcase."

The tattoos on Bogdan's chest rippled and his face reddened but he said nothing.

"Enough of this." Cartwright reached into a cabinet behind him and held up a black cylinder with holes in the sides and heavy multi-sided top and bottom. It was about the size of a travel container of shaving cream. But the shaving cream didn't have two safety rings on the top.

My un-muscled-up abdomen tightened and I looked longingly at the door.

Cartwright ran the device across the Russian's face.

"You know what this is, Mister Badass Russkie Criminal? An M-84 stun grenade. A flash bang. It's a non-lethal weapon. Unless…"

He slipped on evidence gloves, deftly passing the grenade from one hand to another. My eyes were fixed on the pins, making sure they were still there.

"What are you doing, you goddamned faggot!?" It was Bogdan's voice and he was not happy.

Cartwright had unbuckled the Russian's pants and dug a hand down in his crotch.

"I wanted to see what you had down there, little guy. Here's the deal, this is a non-lethal weapon unless I set it off between your legs." His voice was barely above a whisper. "Now open your mouth."

"Fuck mmmfff…"

Cartwright pulled the secondary safety pin and slipped it in Bogdan's mouth as he started to curse.

Next Cartwright rattled off a long sentence in Russian—the only word I could make out was "Apache"—and Bogdan's shoulders stiffened. He frantically struggled against the shackles, getting nowhere.

"Yeah," Cartwright said in English, "You cocksuckers didn't know the red savage could speak Russian." He looked at me. "I told him he's about to get some high-tech Apache justice. When I let go of the safety, we'll have enough time to leave and then Bogdan's manhood is going to be turned into pudding."

This was not the Reid interrogation technique. A very long half-minute passed in silence. Bogdan's face shone with a layer of sweat.

"Go to hell."

He spat out the little metal triangle.

I looked at Cartwright and mouthed, *What are you doing?* He ignored me and pulled the primary pin.

It hit the floor, making a sound reminiscent of a tuning fork. Cartwright used one hand to hold the Russian back against the seat, while the other, slipping out of the blue sling, inserted the grenade between his legs.

"That's it, Bogdan. It's live. Look on the bright side. You'll never have to worry about prostate cancer."

To me: "Take down that poster. I wouldn't want to lose it when this thing burns down and the gas tank blows up. Do it!"

I pulled the poster down and rolled it up. Loudly.

Cartwright said, "Time's up," and started to flex back his arm, letting go of the grenade.

"Stop, stop!" This from Bogdan.

"Why?" Cartwright said.

"I'll tell you. Get that thing away from me. I want to have children! Get it away."

He slowly pulled out the grenade.

I picked up the primary pin and handed it to Cartwright, who inserted it. He smiled and tossed the thing at me.

I caught it.

The grenade was wet with Bogdan's urine.

Chapter Twenty-four

"They'll kill me if they know I talked."

It was ten minutes later, after Cartwright had redone the Russian's handcuffs so his hands were in front, in his lap. A little reward for cooperation. He was stretching his arms and rolled his shoulders. But he remained shacked to the floor, blindfolded, and buckled in.

"You'd better worry about your nuts staying attached to your body," Cartwright said. "Nobody's going to know about our conversation. I killed your associates."

"You say. There are more. And they always know."

"They don't have your ass right now. I do, you commie."

"Why do you keep calling me 'commie'? We're capitalists. If we were a bank on Wall Street…"

"Stop," Cartwright commanded. "Right now your job is to prove to me you're more than a *shestyorka*."

"Hey, fuck you, red man!" His arms became animated and I worried he might undo the seatbelt and make a move. Instead, he thumped his chest with both manacled fists. "You think an errand boy has these? These are earned."

"How did you know about the rough?" Cartwright opened a notebook balanced on the top of his right thigh and sucked on a pen like it was one of Peralta's cigars.

The Russian shrugged. "There's a man who signs off on the shipments for the Jews in New York City. He has a gambling problem. He's working off his debt to our organization."

"He works for Markovitz?"

The Russian nodded.

"So he received the rough and placed it in the suitcase."

A slight nod.

"Where did he get it? Those diamonds came from somewhere."

"I don't know and I swear to God. I'm Orthodox, so that means something."

Cartwright gave me a tight smile. "Bogdan, here, is a religious man, you hear that?"

"You're gonna need religion, Indian," he said. "My people believe you used the Mexican to steal the diamonds. They're coming for you."

"Ooooo, I'm scared." Cartwright wrote some more, about what, I couldn't tell. Then, "Why do it that way, sending the shipment all the way here? Why not steal the diamonds in New York?"

"Too much heat," Bogdan said. "If we stole them there, it would be too obvious. The security is too much around the Jews, the Diamond District. I know. I used to live in Brighton Beach. And you want us to rob the jeweler while he's at JFK?" He laughed. "It would never work. The cops, the FBI…too much heat. Better to get it down here."

Even in the shabby confines of the RV, with this dangerous character no more than six feet away, I couldn't escape Lindsey. I remembered a trip we had taken to New York, going to Brighton Beach and eating at a Russian restaurant. I noticed the many made men like Bogdan. Lindsey, who had learned the language in the Air Force, had ordered for us in Russian.

Cartwright's voice snapped me back.

"What next?"

The Russian grunted.

"What the hell next?" Cartwright pushed a finger into the man's sternum. "What if I had gotten the rough and given it to you? What were you going to do with it?"

He shook his head. "I don't know."

He reached his cuffed hands up, rubbing the dozens of little wounds on his face where Ed had ripped off the duct tape. "They never told me."

"Oh, bullshit." Cartwright's natural squint narrowed further.

"Real shit, man. I don't know." His voice rose, and then dropped to a near whisper. "They don't tell me everything. That's the way it works. They compartmentalize information." He leaned forward, wrinkling up all the stories told on his chest.

Cartwright pushed him back, made a few more notes, and let the silence accumulate like heavy weights.

"You Americans know nothing about the world," Bogdan finally said. "Five million people have been killed in Congo since 1996 and all you care about is going to the mall. Five million!"

He worked his jaw. The tongue was still in pain. But he continued. "You go to war over three thousand dead from Arab jihadis that you armed in the first place, back in Afghanistan in the eighties, but you know nothing about the genocides that bring your diamonds. The diamonds on your wives' fingers probably came out of those wars and you'd never know it. Your wives have blood on their hands. Diamonds aren't even that rare, you know? We invented a machine that makes synthetic diamonds, as good as what comes out of a kimberlite pipe. But people give them such value. I don't get it."

"The man's a philosopher," Cartwright interrupted. "So let's say these stones came out of Congo."

Bogdan paused and let out a long breath. "Sure." He smiled. Movie-star teeth as white and even as keys on a new piano. "Let's say."

"That's still not a who," Cartwright said. "Who gave the rough to the guy who packed it in New York? Where did he get it?"

The smile went away. "I. Don't. Know."

"You know the Mexican who shot me." Cartwright said, his voice rising. "You hired him. Where did you find him? Why did you set me up?"

"If he's not your partner, then he stole from us!" Bogdan said. "Nobody betrayed you."

Cartwright sniffed. "Do you believe him?"

"Nope," I said, speaking for the first time.

"I don't either. I'm gonna take him out into the desert and blow his nuts off and leave him for the coyotes."

"Sounds like a plan," I said.

"Goddamn you!" Bogdan said. "I'm telling you the truth. Why would we hire you and then have somebody shoot you…?"

"Because you're Russian mafia scum, " Cartwright interrupted, although he continued writing in the notebook. "Your Mexican probably agreed to do the deal for a quarter of what you were going to pay me. Probably an illegal alien. For all I know, this helped conceal the robbery so that whoever was expecting that rough thinks I took it. You threw suspicion off yourselves."

"No…no…" Bogdan gesticulated wildly. "Don't you read the papers? This man was the sheriff here. I am telling you, my people think you set this up and you have the rough."

"All the more reason to leave you for the varmints."

Bogdan dropped his hands heavily into his lap. "Then do it. Be a fool."

This was when the fury that had been building in me for days broke down the door of my discipline. I sprang on the Russian and gripped him by the throat. He tried to bring his arms up but I was too close, leaning on him with my knee in his crotch. He flailed and made guttural sounds. I stared at the blindfolded face, blind myself.

"The woman." My voice was a snarl. "Red-blond hair, Southern accent, professional killer. Give me her name and where I can find her…"

This was not the lateral vascular neck restraint, as the police euphemism goes for a chokehold that can disable an adversary and sometimes accidentally kill him. My hands were out for pure murder, crush the windpipe, devil take the hindmost.

I let up the pressure enough that he could breathe and talk. He inhaled with the desperation of a man who had been chained to the sea floor and suddenly reached the surface. But then he tried to ram his arms upward to break my grip, a good martial arts move. It was what he should have done in the first place. Except that I was ready for it and moved back. His fists and arms connected with air.

Cartwright tried to pull me back but I pushed him away. I slammed the fleshy part of my hand into Bogdan's nose. He screamed in pain and his muscles went slack. I used the interlude to handcuff him tighter, jamming the metal into the flesh of his wrists. Then I leaned back in.

I could smell the cigarettes and stale food on his breath but I wasn't really seeing him. All the literature showed that torture was ineffective in interrogations, in addition to being immoral. I wasn't seeing that, either. My mind's eye was where Cypress Street met First Avenue, Saturday night, Lindsey bleeding out, my blazer as a hopeless trauma dressing. Hearing her voice, *Don't leave me…it hurts…hurts…*

I put the vise of my hands snug around his neck and again began to apply pressure with my fingers. My fingers are very strong.

"Tell me about the woman."

"What woman?" He croaked a whisper.

"Give me a name or I'll crush your windpipe. I don't care…"

But by this time my rage had subsided and I let Cartwright pull me back. He brought my face close. "Stop this," he whispered.

I slumped into the opposite bench, watching the bright red blood stream out of Bogdan's nose.

"My associate is excitable," Cartwright said. "I'm sorry about that."

"You're all savages!" Bogdan sounded as if he had suddenly contracted a head cold. "When Russia conquered Siberia, the Cossacks exterminated the natives!"

I didn't have the energy for a history lesson.

Cartwright pulled a cold pack out of a first-aid kit, struck it with his hand to mix the chemicals, and held it against Bogdan's face.

"We're looking for a woman," he said. "Thirty years old. Good looking. She's a professional killer. Does she work for you?"

"No."

"Did any of your people recently commit suicide?"

"What are you talking about?"

"You'd better take good care," Cartwright said good-naturedly. "She seems to think those diamonds belong to her. She likes to kill people by making it look like a suicide."

"Suicide is a sin," he said.

"So Matt Pennington is in hell?" I said.

"Pennington?" Bogdan almost pulled off the blindfold but didn't. Maybe it was a survival mechanism. He knew who Cartwright was, but not me. The fewer faces he saw, the better his chances he might get to live.

"You know him?"

"I've heard the name," Bogdan said.

"Do you use him?" Cartwright asked.

The Russian shook his head. "He works with the Zetas. Our partners are Sinaloa. I'm telling you what I heard. He's a good fence. Patient. Discreet."

I said, "Now he's got a lot of time to be patient because somebody hung him from a doorknob with a necktie. My bet is the woman did it."

Bogdan spoke some words in Russian. The expletives weren't difficult to translate.

Cartwright loosened the handcuffs and put the cold pack in Bogdan's hands so he could hold it in place across his nose. His wrists were bruised from where I had notched up the cuffs.

Ed eased himself onto the bench beside me. For the first time, I saw his notebook. He had been sketching the tats on the Russian's chest.

"Bogdan doesn't know. He doesn't know the woman. He doesn't know what his bosses were going to do with the rough. I believe him. Probably give it to one of the cartels for drugs or to settle debts. You can move diamonds easily. They hold their value in cross-border transactions. They can't be traced back to the source."

Suddenly Abba was singing "Dancing Queen."

It took a few seconds for me to realize it was a ringtone. By that time, Cartwright had taken away the cold pack and pulled the cellphone from Bogdan's pants. He placed it in his bound hands. Then he produced a Beretta Storm subcompact pistol and ran it across to the man's face before nudging it into his crotch.

"You're going to answer, Bogdan, and you're going to be a good little commie. Remember…" The phrase that followed sounded like *Ya gavaryu pa roosky*.

The meaning was clear enough: *I speak Russian*.

Abba stopped singing and Bogdan said, "Da?"

He listened and answered with more words, many more, but Cartwright didn't seem perturbed.

"I found the Indian." Bogdan switched to English. "He fought pretty well for an old man but I got him…"

Cartwright winked at me as we listened to unintelligible chirping from the other end of the conversation.

"No, I didn't kill him. He didn't have the diamonds. He thinks we have them, that Peralta is working for us…"

More from his interlocutor.

"I believe him. Peralta is working for himself and he has them…" His face reddened. "You don't tell me what to do! We know where to find the Indian. He's not our problem…I know it's fifteen-fucking-million!"

Then he switched back to Russian and the conversation went back and forth for another two or three minutes. Cartwright listened carefully but never removed the pistol from the Russian's jewels.

After the phone went dead, Cartwright holstered his weapon and returned the cold pack to Bogdan, who once again held it against his nose with two cuffed hands.

"Very good," Cartwright said.

His slid the cellphone into his pocket with difficulty.

The Russian's voice came beneath the cold pack. "What kind of deal are you prepared to make with me?"

"That depends," Cartwright said. "You're handcuffed and blindfolded. That's a pretty weak hand."

"I play blackjack," Bogdan said. "Out at Talking Stick and Fort McDowell. I count cards. They never catch me. Stupid Indians. No disrespect. The trick is knowing when to leave."

Cartwright shrugged. "You've still got a weak hand and you can't leave."

"You let me live," he said. "You never tell what happened here. And I'll give you information."

I felt Cartwright's hand touch my leg. *Don't answer.* So we sat in silence. Whatever resort temperature was outside, here it was getting stifling.

Finally, Cartwright said, "If your information checks out, we have a deal."

He was about to say more but Bogdan started laughing. It began as a muffled giggle completely out of proportion to his powerful build. It turned into a mix of hilarity and hysteria that filled the dim interior.

"You are fools." He pulled away the cold pack. "That rough was taken from the FBI. That's right, genius. FBI diamonds. So when they catch you, they'll send you off to be tortured in the American gulag. Unless this woman you are afraid of catches you first."

Chapter Twenty-five

Cartwright followed me outside, closed the door.

Whatever the particulate matter counted by the weather service today, the air around us smelled as sweet as Eden compared to the prison cell-like odor of the RV.

We walked a few paces, close enough to the door for security's sake and far enough away to speak in low voices and not be heard by Bogdan.

The sun was high now, the intense glare spooling down on us, the asphalt magnifying the heat. It was a reminder of what was to come starting in May.

I slipped off my jacket, exposing my holster. Sure, Arizona had a national reputation as a land of gun nuts, but you rarely saw someone open-carrying in the central city. So I slid my badge onto my belt. If it didn't keep a cop from drawing down on me, at least it might make civilians less nervous—or less reckless.

"Thanks for not killing my Russian," Cartwright said.

"You were going to blow his testicles off."

"That was a planned interrogation technique. You were running on emotion when you need to run frosty."

"That's what Peralta says."

He looked down. "It's good advice. Emotion won't help you. You know that."

I did. I still wanted to strangle the Russian or anybody else who could lead me to Strawberry Death.

He kicked the asphalt with his expensive boot. "You know, even with all the bullshit I went through in the war, when I joined the FBI I was so starry-eyed that I thought I'd become the first American Indian director. I was that naïve."

"You would have made a good one."

He ignored the praise. "I was more interested in putting away criminals than kissing ass. They were never going to let me in their country club. But I was so committed to the Bureau that my wife left me. My children are grown but for years they wouldn't talk to me. Who can blame them? I was on the job. I wasn't there for them."

"I'm sorry."

"Don't be. I made my choices. The last five years, my daughter and I have rebuilt something. She had a baby last year. I'm a grandpa, can you believe that?"

I smiled and nodded.

"All my career, I saw the worst of people every day. It was hard to see the good, to trust anyone. So here I am. Taking the undercover job...Well, when I decided to go that way, I didn't feel like I had anything to lose."

"Do you still feel that way?"

"No, actually. You hear a lot about how deep undercover people lose their way. Some do. They become what they set out to fight. Doing this has actually grounded me in a way that wearing the suit and tie every day never did. I have to keep myself tethered to reality, to the mission. So that's my advice for you."

"Point taken."

He said, "You reading about the Great War?"

"It's all that's on my bedside table."

"Be sure to read *The Sleepwalkers*. It's the best book on the causes of the war that I've ever seen. It will completely change your perspective."

"It's waiting for me at home."

Then he asked me why I was still wearing the deputy's badge and I told him about my meeting with Melton on Saturday night. I felt such a deep shame that my face burned.

"He manipulated you."

"I know. That's what Lindsey said."

"Smart woman. Keep her. Look, I can make some discreet inquiries about what Melton told you. See if it's real."

I thanked him. Then, "Is that really a Soviet scalp in there?"

"Naw." He smiled. "It's an old chamois I used to polish my car. I stuck it in my compost barrel for a few days and then put it in a plastic bag to preserve the gamey smell. Figured it might come in handy someday. Remember what I said about playing to stereotypes giving you an advantage?"

I wondered what mine was now, my wife shot, my partner missing, me carrying a star issued by Chris Melton. Stereotypical fool, sounded accurate.

"What are you going to do with him?"

He pulled the cap down, shading his eyes. "Drive him out to some Walmart lot, take off the handcuffs, and tell him to slowly walk a hundred paces before he removes the blindfold. By that time, I'll be gone."

"They can find you."

He didn't answer.

"Do you believe what Bogdan told us?"

"No reason not to." His shaded eyes scanned the lot. "This confirms the diamonds are the ones we were looking for, stolen FBI evidence. It doesn't tell us where they came from in the first place, how the Russians knew the diamonds were coming here, or who was the intended recipient."

"It also doesn't explain why Peralta left me the note to find Matt Pennington. According to Bogdan, Pennington wasn't part of the heist…"

Cartwright saw the expression on my face. "What?"

I suddenly remembered the matchbook in Pennington's pack of cigarettes and the telephone number written inside it. I called up the note on my iPhone and read the number to him.

"Doesn't sound familiar," he said. "Call it."

I hesitated. Then I pressed the number and held the phone to my ear.

On the second ring, a man's voice answered.

Peralta.

Several dozen exclamations fought for attention in my brain, relief, joy, anger, anticipation. I pushed them away and said, "It's Matt Pennington."

"You have the wrong number," he said and hung up. It sounded like the same old blunt Peralta. I didn't detect fear or coercion in his tone.

I had finished telling Cartwright about the brief exchange when my phone rang. Not Abba. An old-fashioned phone ring. It was the number I had just dialed.

"Wait," Cartwright held out a hand. "Give it to me."

"Apache Mortgage," he said in a happy sales voice. It was a radical change from his normal tone. "May I have your account number, please?"

He handed it to me.

"Whoever called back hung up."

"He's alive!"

He nodded slowly. "But he's with somebody. Not the Russians. Not Pamela Grayson. And whoever it was, he couldn't talk around them. The woman who shot Lindsey?"

I shook my head. "She confronted me demanding the diamonds. She said she had made Peralta a promise, whatever that means. But it didn't seem like a pleasant one. I don't think he'd be alive if he was with her."

He kicked the asphalt again.

"Then there's another player. The man who called Pennington's office. Maybe the original owner of the diamonds who somehow tracked them here."

I was eager to get moving, out of the sun, back to the hospital, and, as soon as I could, send the badge back to Chris Melton with my resignation letter.

Cartwright stopped me after I had taken two steps.

"Don't be too hard on yourself, David. If your wife hadn't gone for that walk, you might both be dead. This woman might have come in while you were sleeping. End of story." He slid his left arm back in the sling, wincing. "Oh, I'm getting too old for this."

The pain-creases in his face relaxed and he spoke again. "Don't cut your ties with Sheriff Meltdown yet. They might be useful to us."

"I was afraid you were going to say that."

He stared at me for a long minute.

"You know, David, it ain't what you don't know that gets you in trouble. It's what you know for sure but just ain't so." He winked. "Mark Twain."

I reluctantly nodded and walked away. By the time I was across Third Avenue, the RV was gone. All that remained was a blue cloud of carbon monoxide.

Chapter Twenty-six

When I reached the ICU, Sharon was back with her daughters. Lindsey's condition hadn't changed; none of her physicians were there; and the closest I could get was watching her through the window. So I took Sharon down to the Starbucks in the lobby and told her what I could.

"At least he's still alive," she said

She seemed distracted. I studied her face but could only see her struggling to keep up the strong front. I had expected her to be happier, but she looked gaunt with worry.

I said, "No calls on that landline?"

She looked at me curiously, then shook her head.

I asked if the FBI was still tailing her.

"Like white on rice," she said. "We've started taking coffee and sandwiches out to the unit watching the house. I'm not worried about us. I am worried about Mike. And you, David. When was the last time you slept?"

I shrugged. "I've been taking catnaps."

"You look awful. Go home and let us keep watch. I promise to call when something changes."

"Sharon, you only left a little while ago." I was about to protest more but the exhaustion hit me deep in the bone. I was struggling to keep my head up.

So I left and the farther away I drove, I became strangely happy to be momentarily freed from the hospital.

Back on Cypress, I had to fend off concerned neighbors. *How is Lindsey? How are you holding up? We saved your mail and newspapers. What can we do to help?* Willo was that kind of place.

Then I scoped out the property, finding nothing amiss. The landscaping service had come and gone and the winter lawn looked glorious.

Inside the bedroom, I locked the door and slid a chair against it, set an alarm for two hours, and collapsed into the bed. For a few seconds, I looked at the stack of unread books on the bedside table. Then I was gone.

By three thirty, I was out the door in a light gray suit and navy blue rep tie. I drove over to our office on Grand Avenue and went into the Danger Room. There, I ran through the surveillance tapes on fast-forward. At two a.m. today, a dark four-door Chevy pulled sideways beside the gate and a woman emerged.

Strawberry Death.

Looking for her stones.

She was dressed entirely in black and put a dark watch cap over her distinctive fair hair. Then she stepped onto the hood, mounted the roof of the car, and draped what looked like a comforter over the spikey top of the security fence. One smooth move and she was over, pulling off the comforter and moving toward the office door. The entire maneuver took less than a minute. She had been trained.

Any passing patrol car would merely see a parked vehicle. The angle kept me from getting a tag number.

I switched to an outside camera that showed her disappear around the northwest corner of the building. The back door was secured with a heavy gate meant to defeat the most skillful burglar. Nor would that burglar find the concealed alarm box. Sure enough, she emerged on the other side in a few minutes and went to the front door.

She suddenly looked toward Grand Avenue and fell to the ground. That passing police car might have appeared. She stayed there for seven minutes, not moving.

Finally, she stood and again approached the door. I tried another camera, one mounted to the edge of the roof. She was working with small lock-picking tools. Her head swung around, then went back to her attempted break-in.

"Good luck with that," I said out loud.

I grew more concerned when I saw a small crowbar in her hand. But she backed away and moved lithely to the edge of the building. The parking lot was already illuminated cadmium orange by two sodium lamps. A bright white spotlight joined in, sweeping the front of the building. I switched to the camera that showed Grand. Sure enough, a PPD unit had pulled in behind the Chevy.

Calling up the rear-facing camera, I watched her sprint to the back fence. It was ten feet high, but she shimmied up the steel, stood with her feet between the spikes, and launched herself into the darkness. She was in amazing shape.

I fast-forwarded the front camera. Within a half-hour, the single police cruiser had been joined by two more, then a tow truck departed with the Chevy. She lost her wheels. Was it too much to hope they had caught her nearby? Probably. But I could check with Vare on the provenance of Strawberry Death's car.

I should have been frightened. I was elated.

I was edgy enough, though, to jerk when my phone rang. It had a Sheriff's Office prefix.

"David, it's Chris. How is Lindsey?"

We were so damned casual and friendly. I told him.

"I read your report. It's exactly the kind of excellent work I expected. And I appreciate you doing this at a time of tragedy."

I mumbled a single-syllable response, wondering if he always spoke as if he were on television.

"Let's talk about it. I know this is a tough time, but maybe you could come down to headquarters. Better yet, I can meet you at your office in the courthouse."

I wanted to protest but didn't, mindful of Cartwright's admonition. I sure didn't want to go to the new headquarters building at Fifth Avenue and Jackson Street, in what was once the downtown warehouse district. The ninety-three million-dollar building looked like an alien battlecruiser was mating with a 1970s shopping strip. But ugly as it was, it was Peralta's baby: he conceived it and fought for the funding and now it was Chris Melton's temple. The idea of going inside made me sick.

"How about the courthouse?" I said.

"Does twenty minutes give you enough time?"

I told him that it did.

On the way downtown, I called Kate Vare and told her what I had found.

Her voice was icy. "Are you working my case, Mapstone?"

"No, this is why I'm calling you. I stopped by our office and checked the surveillance tapes."

"Why?"

"Because I was the victim of a crime. Because I wanted to make sure our office was secure. Because I wanted to. Why does that have anything to do with what I'm telling you?"

"I've seen your act, Mapstone."

What the hell did that mean? I started to speak but she cut me off.

"I want to see these tapes."

"Sure, fine."

"And why were you there?"

I went through it again. To me, the point was easy: The woman was not only in town, she was still stalking me, trying to burglarize our office. Not only that, she had almost been caught and the police would have the car, the license. Hell, they might have even picked her up a few blocks away, or at least done a field interview until Strawberry Death sweetly talked her way out of it.

I said, "She was here early this morning, trying to break in. If you check the logs and find the suspected four-five-nine call, where a vehicle was towed from our address on Grand, you might find the identity of this woman."

"Quit telling me how to do my job," Vare said. "You have bigger issues. You have something she wants."

"I don't know what," I said, trying to keep any "tells" out of the timbre or rhythm of my speech. "Any thoughts?"

She chuckled joylessly. "I know you're into history, so I'll tell you a story. When I was starting out, they told stories about the old police headquarters. It had an elevator up to the city jail. It was a really, really slow elevator. And when they had a suspect who was holding back, the detective might ride up with him and carry a rolled-up phone book in his hand. By the time that really slow elevator reached the jail floor, the suspect would be talking like his life depended on it. I always liked that story."

She would love for me to be the guy handcuffed in the slow elevator and her with the phone book. Properly used, it could inflict terrible pain and never leave a bruise. Or so the old-timers had told me. I didn't take the bait.

I said, "The Chandler detective told me they recovered the diamonds."

"I know. Too bad for your buddy. He did the crime and he didn't even get to keep the diamonds." Another chuckle. "I read the report you sent to Meltdown on your old case. You fucked up."

"The detective fucked up."

"You were the first officer on the scene, Mapstone. The Sheriff's Office was pretty shoddy back then. They let you be a deputy, right? Now they've brought you back, so that tells you a lot about Sheriff Meltdown."

"Kate, what are you doing to find the woman who shot my wife?"

"I'll let you know when we have something concrete. I've picked up three homicides since Saturday night, okay? So you're not the only family member asking for help from the police."

I struggled to keep my voice even and professional.

"Any luck with fingerprints from the gun she lost? Or the burglar bag?"

"No prints," Vare said. "She probably wore tactical gloves and you didn't notice. Not even one hair from the bag."

I suppressed a sigh.

"Look at it this way, Mapstone. You disarmed her of the big gun. What shot Lindsey was smaller caliber. We recovered a .32 shell casing. So things could have been way worse if the woman had fired her primary weapon."

"Yes."

"If she's a pro, the Beretta Bobcat or Tomcat is fashionable now. Small, concealable and it can carry a silencer. So we are working this case."

I thanked her and asked again if she would check into the impounded Chevy from Grand Avenue.

But I was only speaking to myself. She was gone.

I wondered how long it would take her to make a connection to the late Matt Pennington. "Suicided."

But by that time, the FBI would already be involved and Kate Vare's life would be a jurisdictional goat fuck, as Peralta would say. Peralta, who had answered the phone that went with the number on the inside of Pennington's matches. The number his killer had been seeking.

Downtown, I parked the Prelude in the CityScape garage and crossed to the courthouse, showing my identification and being let past the metal detector as if I really worked there.

Beside the door to my office, the county had placed a new placard:

DAVID MAPSTONE
Sheriff's Office Historian

It was much like the one that sat on the wall outside my old office, including the MCSO star emblem. Below was added: Christopher J. Melton, Sheriff. Even Peralta hadn't thought of that granular bit of self-promotion. Seeing the thing made me queasy.

For ten minutes, I admired the restoration—high ceiling, art deco light fixtures, dark wood moldings, frosted glass panel of the door. Someone had hung a large photo from the 1950s showing citrus groves spreading out below Camelback Mountain, not a house in sight. Behind my desk was a photo of Chris Melton in his black uniform, furled American flag in the background, Hollywood smile.

Then when there was a tap, like a doctor about to come in the exam room, and Melton stepped in.

"You didn't have to dress up," he said.

"I like to."

Melton was dressed up in black BDUs—battle dress uniform—with baggy cargo pants, combat boots, and ballistic vest. Cops playing soldiers. I thought about Peralta's rising concern about the militarization of law enforcement, and that was even before the Department of Defense started showering even the smallest police forces with gear.

"I was tagging along with SWAT." He pulled up a chair.

"Everybody safe?"

"Sure. We were serving a warrant."

I remembered serving warrants alone, but said nothing.

"Turned out there were no weapons," he said. "But we got fifty dollars' worth of marijuana."

I wondered how much it had cost the taxpayers to mobilize the SWAT team for a petty drug raid. He went through the motions, asking about Lindsey, and I went through the motions, telling him the basics. He wanted to know if I liked the "historic photo" and I told him that I did.

"You did an outstanding job digging into that case." He slid a UBS flash drive across the desk. It was black, like his uniform.

"What's this?"

"Paperless office, remember? The new county policy. So this," he tapped it, "is the murder book for your case."

"Wait a minute, Sheriff…"

He smiled and switched his index finger at me.

I tried again. "Wait a minute, Chris. You have a homicide unit this should go to if you think Frazier's death was suspicious. I'm not a homicide investigator."

"You sell yourself short, David. How many murders did you solve for Mike Peralta? Fifty?"

"Sixty-two."

"There you go."

I felt as if I had rubbed against poison ivy but the itch was deeper than my skin. I wanted him out of this office. I wanted out of this office.

He pulled a clear plastic bag out of one of his commodious pants pockets and placed it beside the data stick. It said EVIDENCE in red. Inside there appeared to be a wallet.

"Check it out," he said.

I held up my hands. "No gloves."

He fished a pair out of his pants. Of course he had some. He probably had a complete crime-scene kit in those cargo-pants pockets. I reluctantly slid them on and opened the evidence envelope.

The wallet was blue nylon with a Velcro seam. It was dated only by its design and materials. Otherwise, it was in surprisingly good shape for being so old. I already knew what it held before I pulled it open and saw Tom Frazier's driver's license. He had dark hair and the card said he was six feet, two inches, two hundred pounds, brown eyes.

"He's not so different from your build," Melton said. "About the same age. He had lost his mother, his last family member. You only had your grandmother at that age."

He had done his homework on me. I didn't like that.

I made a quick inventory of the other contents: an emergency medical technician card issued by the state, an Associated Ambulance employee identification, thirty-two dollars in currency signed by Donald Regan. No credit cards, but hardly anyone that age back then would have qualified for one. No photos.

Other things seemed missing, too: dirt or sand from the desert, and faded material from being out in the sun.

I said, "Where did you get this?"

"Are you interested in the case?"

"Mildly."

He leaned forward. "Enough to have a conversation with the person who found the wallet?"

"I'm a historian," I said. "That's the way I approach cases. It seems like you need a real homicide detective who works cold cases." I mentioned a couple of names.

"So what's the difference between a historian and a detective?"

I had been asked this so many times, thought about it when Peralta first brought me aboard, that I should have had a neat elevator speech. But I didn't.

Good detectives and historians had much in common. They wanted to find the "how" as well as the "why." Both gave heavy weight to primary sources—whether witness interviews documents, diaries, and other reminiscences of the people actually involved in the event—as opposed to secondary sources such as newspaper accounts. Both were mindful of bias.

There were important differences, too. A good historian wanted to understand causality and complex underlying social and economic forces and pivotal personalities, not merely assemble evidence. He or she was open to new interpretations as fresh scholarship emerged, formerly secret archives were opened and key players who had kept silent decided to talk.

Understanding history meant acknowledging when the facts didn't go your way, when they challenged or undermined your thesis. Some detectives would cherry-pick facts to assemble a case. Only shoddy historians did that. History was an argument without end. A criminal investigation resulted in a conviction that was rarely overturned, even if the suspect was innocent.

History was especially about distance and objectivity. Unfortunately, I had lived part of this history, being the first deputy on the scene.

"Sounds good to me," Melton said. "Sounds like what I need here. But don't worry about footnotes."

The man had such a wry wit.

I said, "What about the chain of command?"

"You'll report directly to me," he said, "like you did with Peralta."

That was good. Melton had brought in or promoted thugs to the highest ranks of the department. Hard asses with a history of brutality complaints who relished his campaign against illegal immigrants and poor people in general. And as a former academic, I had never really been welcomed by many of Peralta's commanders, either. The only thing they hated worse than a meddling professor was a reporter.

"You can't help him, you know. That's an FBI case, and you can only get in the way. Or worse. You could be charged with obstructing if you start digging around. These feds, believe me I know, they see the suspect's friend meddling and they don't like it. It might even cause them to think you're an accessory."

I nodded. "How do you know I'm not?"

"Because I've checked you out. I know your work. I trust my gut."

"And you blackmailed me over Lindsey."

He shook his head and blew out a breath. "No, David. I was trying to help you. I'm going to help you and Lindsey."

My ass, I thought, wondering about his real motivations besides self-aggrandizement. Sliding the wallet back in the evidence bag, I asked him about forensics.

"I'm going to send it to the lab to test for latest prints and DNA," he said. "It's hard to know what we'll find. But there are photos of the wallet and its contents in your murder book."

I folded my hands and leaned back. "What's next for me?"

He pulled out a notepad and scribbled, tore off a sheet of paper in the paperless county office, and placed it on the desk.

"She found the wallet. Go talk to her. That's all I'll say. You can approach it with fresh eyes." He pulled a box out of his cargo pants and handed it over. Business cards. "Do you have a check?"

"A check?"

"So I can get you in the system for direct deposit."

I pulled one out of my wallet and gave it to him. Keep your friends close and your enemies closer—and get paid for the trouble.

He stood and started to leave. "I'll hook you up with an IT person so we can get you access to the MCSO computers. A few things have changed since you left. Got a Homeland Security grant to upgrade the system." He smiled. "Good hunting, David."

As the door closed, I slipped some business cards in my pocket and remembered the person who had first taught me the Sheriff's Office computer system, a young deputy named Lindsey Faith Adams.

This was the first time in a couple of hours that I had really thought of her. It made me wonder if this was a natural recharge mechanism or if something was missing inside me. Or, worse that a cold, detached spectator was living in my soul.

"Lie down with the devil," Lindsey had said.

And wake up in hell.

Chapter Twenty-seven

A century earlier, the Great War was raging. It swept away four empires, sixteen million lives, the first great era of globalization, and it changed everything. The belief of constant progress in the West was forever destroyed. A foolish, harsh peace set up an even deadlier world war twenty years later.

We live in the shadow of the Great War still, even if most people don't realize it. Right down to the vernacular: no man's land. Trench coats. Blotto. Brass Hats. Shell shock. Push up the daisies.

It was the last war fought by poets.

In Flanders fields the poppies grow…

Dulcet est. Decorum Est.

Kipling, who lost a son in the war, echoed the book of Ecclesiastes, providing the words engraved in the ubiquitous British monuments: *Their name liveth forevermore.*

He also captured the cynicism of the later war-poets and the Lost Generation:

If any question why we died

Tell them, because our fathers lied.

My grandfather was too old to be drafted and already married. Grandmother told me much about the war when I was a child, especially how she blamed it on "Kaiser Bill." Newer scholarship would dispute it but I doubt that would change her mind. She was ahead of her time in blaming Woodrow Wilson for the flawed peace. Some revisionists argue that the United States should not have entered the Great War at all.

Arizona was only two years past statehood when war broke out in Europe. Phoenix's population was about fifteen thousand. The cotton farmers made big money from the war. Frank Luke, born in Phoenix, became the state's first ace and the first airman from anywhere in America to win the Medal of Honor. He died in action in 1918. He was twenty-one years old.

Their name liveth forevermore, but Kipling has been out of fashion for decades and is mainly remembered as an apologist for British imperialism.

I meditated on these events as I crouched behind a neighbor's bougainvillea with a clear view of our house. In my hands was the close-quarters battle receiver M-4 carbine with a night scope. To that I had added a titanium suppressor so I could work with as little noise as possible. I locked and loaded a thirty-round magazine and clicked the fire selector to semi-auto.

It was two a.m. Tuesday.

Earlier, walking back to the car beneath CityScape, the parking garage had been empty of people. Too empty. No one was following me, right? I couldn't be sure. I was glad to drive out of that vast concrete crypt.

It was too late to visit the address Melton had given me. So I went to Durant's and sat at the dark, comfy bar, let them fix me a martini and steak. It was the first real meal I had eaten since Saturday night.

Sharon called to tell me nothing had changed in Lindsey's condition except that they had ruled out the worst viruses. The fever persisted.

As the Beefeater burned my throat, there was no risk of being that cold, detached spectator. The world is full of imponderables but that never stopped me from stewing, especially as some of the doctors' warnings and comments came back. How the surgery had removed torn flesh and bone. How another round on the operating table might be required to drain the wound, to "revise" it for clean edges to promote healing...

"You okay, David?"

It was the bartender. I nodded and realized my shoulders and head had dangerously slumped.

"Yes."

Better to channel Lindsey's uncommon blend of wit, intelligence, and street sense. What would she tell me now?

Stay safe.

Come home to me. (Back at you, baby).

Don't wait for Strawberry Death to find you.

Find her first.

The only way to do that, lacking Kate Vare's cooperation, was to lay a trap. So after relieving Sharon at Mister Joe's, I stayed only thirty minutes and left for home. I parked the Prelude prominently in front of the house, went inside, and took another nap.

Strawberry Death liked to work under cover of darkness. The night before, she had visited our office on Grand Avenue. Maybe tonight she would come here. As Vare said, I had something she wanted.

At a quarter to two, I dressed all in black and set up my sniper's position. It was down in the forties, cold for Phoenix. A wind was coming from the north, fresh and enchanting. I had always loved these winds from the High Country, but there was no time to dream.

The bougainvillea was more than three feet tall and lush. I smelled the dirt beneath me. This had been farmland a century ago, with the closest houses being the bungalows that still stood, beautifully restored, two blocks away. My spot was only a few feet from our carport. If all went according to plan, I could claim I was in the carport. No Maricopa County jury would convict me. Kate Vare could suck it.

The neighbors were long asleep and had no dogs. The street was empty except for the Prelude and the comforting yellow glow of two streetlights. No FBI watchers. Maybe Horace Mann had a tracking device on the car and didn't think he had to worry about me. That was fine.

It was 2:42 by my watch when headlights swung off Third Avenue and a car crept down the street. It was another dark Chevy four-door, the kind of car you got at a rental outfit. Passing our house, it sped up, crossed Fifth Avenue with a rolling stop, and continued another block to Seventh where it signaled a right turn.

The night-vision binoculars allowed me to get a tag number.

I was about to relax for a long night when headlights came from the west, from Seventh Avenue. The driver approached very slowly, stopping for a full minute at Fifth Avenue even though there was no cross traffic. Then the car crossed Fifth and coasted through our block. A person could walk faster.

Arizona was a cheapskate state with no front tag. But the car looked the same. My heart was thudding against my breastbone even though I was sure my position was hidden. The car came to the stop sign at Third Avenue, signaled, and turned north.

Five minutes, no more, and headlights again painted Cypress Street from the east. Same Chevy, same tag. It pulled to the curb two houses beyond our place and the lights switched off.

I watched through the binoculars, which were little help against the darkened glass of the vehicle. Nobody got out. This was not a neighbor getting home from a party in Scottsdale or late-arriving guests.

The muted sound of a car door opening. A head emerged and looked directly at me. Beneath the watch cap, was the wholesome pretty face of the assassin. There was no uncertainty. It was her.

The sensible response was to call the police. Surely I wasn't going to start a firefight on Cypress Street. Instead, I set down the binoculars, picked up the carbine, and steadied it for a good aim and to prevent it from kicking up once I opened fire. My back was against the neighbor's wall and my knees were raised to support my hands gripping the weapon.

Strawberry Death was forty feet away, all in black, moving in my direction. She walked down the sidewalk toward our house as if she were taking a very early morning stroll. I could have taken her down right then but waited. I was in the bushes of the house to the east; she was coming from the west. Then I realized my mistake.

Our Spanish-Colonial Revival style house faced Cypress Street in a backward L shape, with the short leg of the L being the master bedroom sticking out beyond the living room. It was closest to me and would block my view of her at the front door.

I could have set up at the house to the west, but the shrubbery was not as full. I could have set up across the street, but they had a dog. I was stuck.

Sure enough, when she made a ninety-degree turn and walked up our front walk, I lost contact.

I made myself stay. The front door was solid wood from 1928. Even if she were successful in prying it open, the alarm would go off. So what would she do? What would I do? Knock to see if anyone was home. If they were there and answered, shoot them, and call it a night. But that wasn't her style. Too much potential noise. Not enough fun.

She had promises to keep.

So she would look through the picture window, see the darkened house, and make her way to the backyard to disable the alarm and come through the back door. To intercept her, I would have to leave my shooting position and go through the carport on my side of the house. But that was only if she went on the far side of the house, which would require climbing a higher wall that was close to the neighboring windows.

Suddenly, she reappeared, coming across our lawn toward me. She crouched and moved under our bedroom window, careful not to step in the flowerbed and leave tread marks from her shoes. She briefly rose up and peered inside. I had left the lights off and the blinds drawn, so she would see nothing but darkness.

Another ten feet and she would reach the dark sanctuary of the empty carport and beyond it a rickety fence with a gate to the backyard.

I could have painted her with the laser, ordered her to freeze. No.

My mouth silently formed the word, "police." And then, noiselessly, "halt." I aimed for her chest, took in a breath, let it out slowly, and smoothly squeezed the trigger.

Three rounds came out fast as a lightning strike.

Sure, I wanted to empty the magazine into her, but that would have risked stray rounds going through the houses of neighbors. This rifle was good to five hundred meters. So I did one pull, fired a short burst.

With the suppressor, the carbine made a sound like pebbles falling.

The impact threw her backward like a discarded doll. She landed on her back in the grass and didn't move.

I picked up the spent cartridge cases and slipped them in my pocket. I would place them in the carport to support my story for the police: I fired protecting my home from an armed burglar.

Then I heard a sound that was half gasp and half muffled scream. I wondered if the neighbors were enjoying middle-of-the-night sex.

In that instant of absent-mindedness, flashes came from the woman on the ground. Was she using a flashlight?

No.

The arms and leaves of the bougainvillea shattered. Something heavy and fast sped past my cheek. Something pulled quickly on my sleeve.

It all happened in silence, except for a slight spitting sound, the snap of shrubbery, and the smashing of bullets on the wall behind me.

The heap on the lawn had rolled over and was firing at me, using a silencer.

I fell to the ground, tried to make myself part of it, remembered everything I had read about the infantryman and the dirt below him.

She was wearing ballistic armor. The sound I had heard was her recovering from my bullets hitting her vest but only knocking the air out of her.

They made fun of my Colt Python, my "wheel gun," but if I had shot her with the .357 she wouldn't have gotten up, ballistic vest or not. Now it was too late.

My heart was about to gallop out of my chest but I steadied the M-4 and squeezed off another short burst. It stitched up the lawn. But she was already up and moving. I aimed but she dodged. The risk of a stray shot was too great. That wasn't even my biggest fear. That would be that she was coming to kill me. She was better than me. Way better.

By the time I could get a good aim, she was in the Chevy. The brake lights glowed red. I dropped to one knee and fired at the back window. It crumpled and the sound of more pebbles broke the silence of the street. My wits returned and I put another round in the left taillight. Then I was running for the Prelude as she sped off. The sidewalk was painted with a blood trail. I had hit her with effect at least once.

The first time George Washington saw combat, he commented, "I have heard the bullets whistle, and, believe me, there is something charming in the sound." I hated to disagree with the Father of Our Country, but there was nothing charming in the whistling I had heard. It was somehow made more sinister by our firefight with suppressors. I checked my sleeve. It had been sliced as with a knife. Fortunately, I wasn't bleeding.

She turned south on Fifth Avenue, screeching rubber, by the time I had the Prelude cranked up. I followed with my lights off. She was nearly to McDowell, her lights on, but the telltale rear light shot out. The car swung east onto the thoroughfare.

I could call 911, but that would eventually bring Kate Vare and questions I didn't want to answer now that I was in pursuit. So I left the phone in my pocket and jammed the engine up to seventy to make the green light. I flipped on the headlights and slid in a CD of Ornette Coleman. Charlie Haden was on bass. "Change of the Century." "Lonely Woman." The improvisation, eccentric chord structures, and dissonances calmed me.

From the time we began dating, I taught Lindsey jazz and history, how to make and enjoy a dry martini. She taught me about computers and contemporary music, good stuff not pop crap. She taught me about Russian literature. It was a profitable exchange. We laughed a lot. God, I wanted her back.

The light at Central almost caught me but I made it through on yellow, the Phoenix Art Museum flashing past. Light rail wasn't operating this late and few cars were on the wide roads. The north-south grid changed from numbered avenues and drives to numbered streets and places.

I closed the distance with the Chevy to three blocks. Strawberry Death drove straight east, keeping to the speed limit. I did, too. The secret to driving in the city of Phoenix was if you stayed at the speed limit, you would hit all the green lights. There were exceptions—the Piestawa freeway, Forty-fourth Street, a few others—but in general it worked.

I fingered the tear on the left sleeve of my jacket where a bullet had passed through. A few inches in the other direction and I would be dead in the neighbor's shrubbery. Why didn't I think to put on a bulletproof vest?

In only a few minutes, we had traveled nearly three miles and she turned left on Twenty-fourth Street, another insanely wide highway masquerading as a city street. If she was wounded, it wasn't serious enough to affect her driving. My fusillade into the rear window apparently hadn't harmed her further.

A Phoenix Police SUV slipped past me as we crossed Thomas Road and for a moment I thought he would pull her over for the darkened taillight, the suspiciously missing rear glass. Then I could back him up and this nightmare would be over. But he turned onto a side street. Going to a call.

When I was a little boy, much of this area had still been citrus groves with creeping subdivisions and good new schools attracting the middle class. You could still buy oranges and grapefruits at roadside stands. Now much of it had turned shabby, lawns gone weedy or left to become dirt, another linear slum in the making.

The toffs who made it a point of pride never to go south of Camelback, or even Bell Road many miles to the north, called this area "the Sonoran Biltmore," a slur for the changing demographics.

The real Biltmore was getting closer. We hit green at Indian School, Campbell and Highland, then the fancy midrise condos, offices, and Ritz-Carlton at Twenty-fourth and Camelback Road loomed up.

Camelback turned red and I slipped onto a residential side street behind the glassy Esplanade office tower. The low-slung houses here once had views of the mountains. Then a future governor, developer Fife Symington, built towers terribly out of scale with their surroundings and this street began a slow decline. Symington later got in trouble with the law but he'd made his money and wrecked a neighborhood. So very Phoenix.

For me, the street provided a sanctuary as I turned off the lights and did a one-eighty, then slid slowly back toward Twenty-fourth.

The light was green now and the Chevy was a block ahead, passing Biltmore Fashion Park. Where the hell was she going?

Less than half a mile on, I got the answer: She turned right into the entrance to the Arizona Biltmore. I saw that the guard-house was unmanned and flipped off the headlights again. The Chevy drove on. We were enveloped in shadowy trees, perfectly manicured lawns, and very expensive real estate.

The hotel was some distance from the street. Many people thought it was the work of Frank Lloyd Wright, but the architect was actually his former student Albert Chase McArthur. Either way, the resort was a jewel. Fancy houses surrounded it, too. The Chevy took a right on Biltmore Estates Drive, a parkway that wound a lazy half-circle around the golf course and was lined by expansive older mansions. Plenty of diamonds here. Historic diamonds. Conflict diamonds. Legitimate diamonds.

What the hell was Strawberry Death doing here?

A few years ago, some of the local leaders had convened a series of salons to discuss big ideas for Phoenix's future. They had been held at a developer's house on this street and I had been invited as the token historian. Not much had been accomplished other than good booze and company. This particular house had hosted Ronald and Nancy Reagan as guests in the 1950s.

We drove past that place and the Chevy slid into a circular drive of another property. I coasted to a halt, car lights still off. I was unable to see through the landscaping but soon lights started coming on in the house. Making note of the address, I turned around and left, amazed that this fifteen-year-old Honda Prelude hadn't attracted attention.

A mile south, back in the Sonoran Biltmore, I pulled into the parking lot of a tumbledown shopping strip and tried to figure out my next move. The answer came with a tap on the driver's window. It was a skinny young man in a hoodie, an Anglo. I almost shot him.

"Do you have any cash to spare?"

"No."

"Is there anything I could do to earn it?"

I looked him over. He couldn't have been more than twenty years old but he was getting by hustling on the streets.

"Get in the car," I said. As he walked around, I stowed the carbine in the back seat.

He sat in the passenger side and used his hands to slick back his onion head of dark hair.

"Are you a cop?" He zeroed in on the Python in its holster on my belt.

I shook my head. "Do I look like a cop?"

He studied me. "I don't know."

"Maybe *you're* a cop."

He pulled up his hoodie and shirt. "I ain't wearing no wire. I'm not the police. I used to be a student."

"Why did you quit?"

"The money ran out," he said. "I got to like the meth way too much. Let's drive somewhere private."

"We can do this here. How much?"

"Twenty-five bucks to suck your cock, forty if you want me to swallow. It's better than you'll get from your wife."

I doubted that. As I wrote on a notepad, he shivered in the seat. I peeled off four twenties and held them out.

I said, "You have a phone?"

"Yeah."

"You can have the money if you call this number and read these words, only these words, and then hang up." I flipped on the dome light.

The number went to Silent Witness, which was less likely to have advanced tracing equipment than calling 911 directly. His time on the phone would be short, but long enough to say that he had spotted the woman who shot the deputy's wife Saturday night, the one on television, and she's at this address right now.

He read the note, moving his lips. "Seriously?"

I ran my fingers over the twenties. "Easy money. Then you get lost and forget you ever saw me."

He reached for the bills but I pulled them away. "After you make the call."

The boy pulled out a cell phone and started to dial.

Chapter Twenty-eight

I returned to the hospital and settled into an empty ICU waiting room, dozing intermittently. Lindsey's doctors woke me a little before seven to say that the fever had broken.

My face felt strange. I was smiling.

After being allowed ten minutes beside my sleeping beauty, I found Sharon waiting outside and told her the news. She gave me a hug and sent me home for rest. That was one thing I was not allowed at the moment.

Outside, clouds had come in and it smelled like rain. People were smiling. Rain had that effect in Phoenix.

Home. The first thing I did was to make sure any evidence from early this morning was gone. I picked up Strawberry Death's shell casings. They went with a .32 caliber pistol. The neighbor's shrubbery appeared in decent shape.

Inside, I scanned the *Arizona Republic*. It had a story about how the Sheriff's Office was missing a number of weapons issued by the federal government through a surplus military gear program. As a result, the feds were cutting off MSCO from future deliveries. There was also a follow-up story on a federal probe of the Sheriff's Office for racial profiling. My new boss.

By now, a Phoenix Police SWAT team would be interrupting the morning walks of the people along Biltmore Estates Drive. Maybe they would already have the woman in custody or dead. I showered and waited for a call from Vare.

In another suit, starched white shirt, and Salvatore Ferragamo tie from Lindsey, I returned to the Prelude and drove to the address Melton had given me. Exhaustion weighed on my limbs but I couldn't stop.

It was deep in Arcadia, a district in Phoenix that ran against Scottsdale and contained some of the most beautiful properties in the city. It still benefited from the flood irrigation that remained after the groves were bulldozed. The older houses were long rambling ranches surrounded by mature trees. Camelback Mountain presided over the oasis of orange, lemon, and grapefruit trees, cottonwoods, willows, and sycamores, towering oleander hedges.

You can still drive north on Arcadia Drive at night, turn onto Valle Vista Road clinging to the edge of the mountain and see the vast carpet of city lights below you. Lindsey and I would go up there and make out like high-school kids. Not far away is the Camelback Falls mansion, where I once worked a case after Peralta had been shot and was in a coma.

But Arcadia was changing. New owners were tearing down the older houses and putting up tall McMansions, tearing out trees and foliage that had thrived for decades and throwing down haphazard desert landscaping and concrete for more cars. It added to the heat island. It wasn't authentic. If you asked me, it was a crappy investment of water to throw down gravel here so developers could add artificial lakes and golf courses out on the fringes. But nobody asked me. Why was everything lovely and historic in my city at risk, all the time?

The only comfort from this vandalism was that the ongoing real-estate bust was keeping the destruction at a slow-mo pace.

I turned north, with the head of Camelback directly before me. It was formed a few million years before the rest of the mountain but wasn't showing its age. Another turn put me on a street with a long row of ficus trees, two stories tall and meticulously trimmed to make a privacy hedge. Amid them was a gate. I pressed the button on the call box, gave my name, and watched it slowly swing open. The car passed through the copse of trees and oleanders before opening up on a three-story French chalet surrounded by at least two acres of grounds. From the street, you would never know it was here. Which was, of course, the idea.

The house was white—of course, it would be white—with gabled windows on the top floor and three tall chimneys. It was built to look old. A turret completed the facade on one end. With the overcast, I could see lights on in every room, warm, welcoming, giving money to Arizona Public Service.

It was sprinkling when I walked up three low steps to a double front door. I would have preferred to remain outside and feel the rain, smell it, and smell the reaction of the land. But I pressed the doorbell. A Latina housekeeper led me inside and said she would fetch "Miss Diane."

The foyer was overpoweringly white—walls, tile floor with black diamonds embedded, baby grand piano, marble table topped by a vase of white lilies, multiple arched entrances and a staircase circling overhead. Color was added by tasteful antique chairs, a dark cabinet, black wrought-iron candelabra, oxidizing copper sculpture, and a light-brown fireplace with a mirror on the mantle.

It was a long way from Cypress Street. But the room felt both overcrowded and sterile.

I heard footsteps on the grand staircase, caught a flash of legs, and forced myself not to look up.

Soon a young woman appeared. She was twenty or so, athletically put together. The first thing you noticed was the long tawny hair, then the long tanned legs set off in a casual short dress. Her eyes were a rich brown. She came close enough that I could study her long lashes.

"Well, well." Her smile was powerful enough to light the house, her teeth the color of polished porcelain. "Aren't you dressed up? You don't look familiar. Diane's had so many lawyers through here since Daddy died that I know them all."

"I'm not a lawyer."

"I didn't think so. You don't have that transactional look. You're very tall."

She placed her hands on my shoulders. "You're a little old to be Diane's new distraction but I suppose you'll do. Yes, you will do. She usually likes them young, after she snagged Daddy, of course. Maybe she's turning over a new leaf. I find young men boring."

She was inside my comfort zone. I took a step back and she stepped with me, as if we were dancing. Later, I thought how she was close enough to try to disarm me or run a blade into my stomach, but I put down my defenses because she was pretty and the surroundings moneyed.

She kept her hands on my shoulders long past appropriate and looked at me smoothly.

"Who did that to your eye? You don't look like a brawler."

"I'm not, usually. Who are you?"

"Zephyr." She tossed her hair, which glistened in the bright room.

"The west wind."

Her lips curled up. "You know your mythology. I like you."

I knew more about trains. The Denver Zephyr had been a premier passenger train before America decided it wanted to throw away its great rail patrimony. They stayed on life support with Amtrak, which operated the California Zephyr. Lindsey and I had ridden it through the Rockies.

This Zephyr started to say more when a new voice came behind us.

"Zephyr, dear, leave the gentleman alone. He and I have to talk."

She finally removed her hands. "Of course, Mother. Have fun. He's good looking and I bet he knows it."

Now I was being played. Women her age had rarely found me attractive, not even when I was twenty.

Zephyr sauntered through an archway and disappeared.

"She's very mischievous. Do you have kids?"

"No." I introduced myself and showed her my badge and identification.

She gave me a firm handshake. "I'm Diane Whitehouse."

Diane Whitehouse was petite with thick dark hair cut to her jawline and parted on the left. She wore black Prada jeans, a simple white sweater, and diamond studs in her ears. She appeared to be about my age, with big eyes behind the black plastic-framed glasses that were fashionable again.

Her forehead was defined by natural wrinkles. I respected that. Being rich in this town almost mandated a trip to one of the pricey plastic surgeons in Scottsdale, "Silicone Valley." A large solitary diamond sat on a ring, the only other piece of jewelry she wore.

She was also the widow of Elliott Whitehouse, the last of the old generation of local residential builders, who had died last year.

I had never met the man but he made his fortune laying down suburban tract houses all over the Valley. When I was young, his corny flag-draped billboards promised, "You don't have to be president to live in a Whitehouse."

I was surprised he had chosen to remain here after selling Whitehouse Homes and retiring. The usual playbook was to leave the city for coastal California or the San Juan Islands. Of course, this was probably only one of his homes.

Like so many of its custom-designed cousins that ran from here across to Paradise Valley and up into the slopes of the McDowell Mountains, this one managed to appear expensive and trashy at the same time.

Diane led me through one of the arches into a study lined with light-brown built-in bookshelves, interspersed with a marble fireplace, a large mirror, and French doors leading to a terrace. All of this except the mirror was colored butterscotch. A heavy black wrought-iron chandelier hung from a snowy ceiling. The room had too much furniture. She invited me to sit on a sofa and settled across from me in a chair, crossing very slender legs.

"This rain is so depressing."

"I love it," I said.

She nodded like a scientist whose experiment had produced something unexpected. "You must be a native."

"Fourth generation."

"Not many of you," she said. "That must be lonely."

I thought about that and decided she was right.

"I've lived here long enough that I should appreciate the rain," she said. "But I don't. What do you think about that?"

That had nothing to do with the weather. It was signaled by a pedigreed toss of her head. Like mother, like daughter. She indicated a glass display case holding a very old piece of pottery, geometric design, with a shard broken out near the middle.

Or it was a very good fake. Yet considering Elliott White-house's wealth and the abundance of various styles of large, ornate native pottery, Hopi Katsinas, and Mexican Day of the Dead figurines on the shelves, I knew it must be authentic.

"Beautiful," I said. "Mimbres, with a kill hole."

The Mimbres were part of the Mogollon culture, one of the prehistoric peoples of the Southwest. The "kill hole" was part of the burial tradition, placed with the deceased so his spirit could escape through it to the next world.

"Very good," she said. "I asked Chris to send me his best detective. He told me he had a professional historian on his staff. I'm impressed but not surprised."

I was not an archaeologist and the three thousand years of human habitation of Arizona was not my specialty. I had dated an archaeologist once, or at least that's what she claimed to be. Instead, I was pretty sure she was a murderer and I very nearly fell in love with her. Talk about a footnote. No, I knew only enough in this field to be dangerous and yet impress Diane Whitehouse. But her comment made me wonder if she ever read the local newspaper when it reported on my successes working for Peralta?

"Chris is going places, you know," she said. "You stick with him. Governor is next and beyond that, who knows?"

So she was a campaign donor. That was why Melton had roped me in.

"He's such an improvement over Mike Peralta." Diane recrossed her legs, idly stroking an ankle with her fingers. "I can't believe Elliott contributed to his campaigns all those years."

Every muscle in my face remained relaxed. Her expression grew intense. "I had intended to go to that jewelry show, you know? And Mike Peralta, our former sheriff, shoots a man, steals the jewels. This is such a dangerous place. One doesn't want to be called a racist, but…"

She sighed and smiled.

Of course *one* didn't even need to finish the sentence.

"Elliott took me to Antwerp once. I visited the old diamond district. Amazing place. The deals were done with a handshake. And generations of craftsmen did the cutting and polishing. Much of that has moved offshore now, where it can be done much cheaper."

Like Jerry McGuizzo and Bogdan, she knew a good deal about diamonds.

"You don't strike me as someone who would be interested in bling," I said.

She laughed. "No. I thought Zephyr might like something. Maybe Tupac's rings on a chain to take back to Stanford. Her birthday is coming up and it's only been a year since Elliott died. She's terribly spoiled but what can you do?"

Stop spoiling her, I wanted to say. Instead, "Is she your only child?"

Diane hesitated and pushed back her hair. "She was my child with Elliott. We were twenty-five years apart in age but it never felt that way. He had two sons by his first wife."

"Do they live here?"

She shook her head. "It took some getting used to, for all of us. When Elliott and I started dating, I was seen as the home-wrecker. The boys resented me. How could they not? They couldn't see into the reality of that marriage, how dead and passionless it was. Anyway…now they have their own families. There's respect between us.…"

In another setting, I might have said something to show I understood or sympathized. But I was here on police business. Not only that, in the eyes of Diane and Chris, I was here as the hired help in his political aspirations, tending to a wealthy patron. It made me feel dirty.

I said, "The sheriff told me you found the wallet."

Her forehead furrowed. "The wallet. Yes."

She sat straight and stared into the white ceiling and her face relaxed. "You know, when the real-estate bubble collapsed in 1990, Elliott was one of the few local homebuilders who wasn't wiped out. He was a survivor."

"He was the last of his kind," I said. "Now it's all national builders."

She nodded enthusiastically. "He had amazing business acumen. When I met him, I was only twenty-five and I thought he walked on water. The sophisticated older man and the malleable young woman." She paused and watched over the big glasses to see my reaction. I was a model of empathy.

"That's what it looked like on the surface," she said. "He was weaker than the world knew and I was stronger. But we had a good marriage. A complicated marriage, but isn't that redundant? I know this must sound terribly boring. An aging woman who's lost her looks and can't stop talking."

"Not at all," I said. The reality was that I didn't want to be here and didn't care about this case compared with Lindsey's survival, finding her killer, and getting Peralta out of this jam. Less than a mile from here, I hoped, a SWAT team was taking down Strawberry Death at this moment.

But I had to play along for now, couldn't let my agitation show. I gallantly added, "You are very attractive." And she knew it.

"You're so kind," she said. "Do you have a Ph.D.?"

I nodded.

"So I suppose I should call you doctor…"

"No. I'm not a physician or a dentist. And you're not one of my students."

She smiled. "I imagine you were a fine professor. Where did you graduate?"

"Miami of Ohio."

"Ah, one of the 'public Ivies.' I took Zephyr there. Such a lovely campus. She had the grades for it, but she wanted to be on the West Coast. She doesn't read books, you know, other than *Harry Potter*, even though she's smart as hell. Don't let her beauty fool you. I was very different. I loved books and history. Did you have a specialty?"

"The Progressive era in America through the New Deal." All my academic insecurities were bubbling up, so I felt the need to justify myself. "My doctoral adviser had studied under Arthur S. Link, so the apostolic succession was continued."

It was unclear if my name-dropping mattered. Her smile turned impish. "Was there a laying on of hands?"

"A Ph.D. dissertation defense isn't so spiritual. Anyway, he died a few years ago."

"Somebody said that every time a professor dies, an entire library burns. So why aren't you teaching? Why become a cop?"

I told her it was a long story. The short version was that academia didn't like me as well as I liked it, and now there was such a surplus of history instructors that I'd be lucky to get a job at a community college in Lawton, Oklahoma. Then I tried to steer us back to the business at hand. I had more important things than chatting with a rich woman.

"It took me a long time after his death to start to go through his things. But I finally did, and I found the wallet."

"Can you show me?"

Chapter Twenty-nine

We climbed the circular stairway that Zephyr had descended and Diane Whitehouse led me down a hallway and into an expansive bedroom. It held more pottery. More kill holes. French doors led to a balcony and a view of Camelback. The rain had stopped.

"This was Elliott's bedroom."

I raised an eyebrow.

"As we got older, we slept in separate rooms. He snored. I wanted my privacy." Her eyes assayed me. "Don't judge, Deputy."

"Just taking in facts."

She turned quickly and led me into a walk-in closet that looked as big as our guest bedroom, all dark wood and smelling of cedar. Golf shirts and slacks on stainless-steel hangers lined one side. Opposite these were floor-to-ceiling drawers and cabinets. Our reflections showed in a huge mirror at the back.

"I found it here." She pulled out a drawer. "Under socks."

The drawer was empty now. Or it appeared that way. She reached across me and pressed on the bottom, which popped up a panel. She pulled it out revealing a hidden space beneath. A file folder was the only object there now, secured by a black band. I asked what it was.

She shrugged. "Have a look."

I put on a pair of latex gloves and pulled it out, slipping off the band. The folder held what must have been a hundred photos in color and black-and-white. Most were eight-and-a-half by eleven. Each showed a man posed naked, all of them young, all very fit with well-endowed erections. Their hairstyles ranged from perms of the 1970s to contemporary looks.

It wasn't mass-market gay porn and none showed a sex act. One or two men covered their faces. Most smiled. Each photo looked as if a lover had taken it as a keepsake. None had dates on them, but the photographic paper on the permed guys was brittle.

"I am not a homophobe," she said. "But this isn't what I expected to find in my husband's closet. I was hoping for girlie magazines or something like that. Even *billets-doux* from women would have been better."

"Where did they come from?"

"They were his. That's what I assume. It was his drawer. Only he came in this closet. He was an amateur photographer." She shook her head. "Trophies."

"This is where you found the wallet?"

She nodded. "Underneath them, wrapped in paper."

One photo fell to the floor. It was the size of a snapshot. I picked it up and studied it. Tom Frazier smiled at the photographer in an outdoor setting, palm trees in the distance. Unlike the others, he was fully clothed.

I held it up. "Did you see this?"

She shook her head. "After I saw the first photo, I couldn't bear to go further. I'm not a bigot, Deputy. It's tragic if Elliott had to stay in the closet all these years." She looked at our surroundings and giggled. "Sorry. 'Highly inappropriate laughter,' as Zephyr would say."

"This is the man whose wallet you found."

The little crow's feet around her eyes deepened. "My God."

"Do you have something I can put this in? I need to take the file with me."

"I understand." She opened another drawer and handed me a battered tan leather portfolio with Elliott Whitehouse's name embossed on the cover. "Please don't bring it back."

I slid the file inside and pulled off the gloves. Then I asked if she knew the name Tom Frazier, if her husband had ever mentioned him? Both answers were no and we were dancing around an important question. She bit her lip and fell silent.

"Tell me about you?" I tried to move things along.

"Me? My family moved here from Chicago when I was ten. We lived in Maryvale. It was very different then, of course."

"What kind of work did you do?"

"I was pretty aimless when I was young. Nobody paid for me to go to Stanford." She laughed without humor. "I went to ASU, working my way through college. Had plenty of friends. I guess I was about as wild as anyone my age. Didn't you go through that kind of period?"

"Sure." In my twenties, I had been driven and focused, missing out on the young lives of my friends, but what was that to her?

"I was working at Diamond's when I met Elliott. You know, Diamond's Department Store at Park Central? I haven't been down there in years."

"It's closed," I said.

Her shoulders rose and fell. "Anyway, Elliott was a self-made man and pushed me. So I went to graduate school. Started my own interior design company. Then when Zephyr was born, I enjoyed being a stay-at-home mom. Elliott let me collect pottery. I suppose he thought I needed an outlet of some kind."

"Ever married before?"

"I came close." She touched my left ring finger. "I see you're married. Happily?"

"Yes."

"Have you ever been unfaithful?" She let her small hand rest atop mine and the atmosphere in the big closet closed in on us.

I gently pulled my hand away.

"So you have." She smiled. She had a very nice smile. "Men have secret lives."

"Women, too," I said.

She sighed. "True enough."

I turned with my back to the drawers and faced her. "Did you suspect your husband was gay or bisexual?"

She smiled again, sad this time. "Elliott was a man's man. He was of that generation. So much of him was hidden. Again, I think it's a generational thing. Men his age didn't talk about what was going on inside. Men your age can be different, thank God."

I started out of the closet but she blocked me.

"Do you want to know what he was like in bed, David?"

That smile again. Not the sad one. The one with chemistry and danger. The kind that had taken me many years of experience to decipher its meaning. I still felt the electricity of her hand atop mine. She took off her glasses and tilted up her chin. I felt a finger in the pleat of my slacks. Then it ran down my leg.

I could have picked her up and fucked her against the wall right then. She was small and I was tall and as our romp continued we would knock down the dead man's golf shirts, rolling around on them.

I crossed my arms.

"I was a horny young woman, David. I still like sex. I need it. Don't you?" Her voice was husky. "Elliott liked that at first. After we'd been married for a year, we might have sex every eight months. If I was lucky. Believe me, I counted. But I liked the life he paid for. Do you think that makes me a prostitute?"

"No."

"Then Zephyr came along. I didn't want her to be raised in a broken home. I suppose that was foolish. There was no prenup. This is a community property state and I could have taken half of everything. But I stayed."

I nodded.

She ran her other hand through her hair. It fell back in place perfectly. "You know what's strange? He always had male assistants. Good-looking guys. I mean real hunks. I never gave it a second thought at the time. I was happy that he didn't have little babes that would bring out the green-eyed monster. Women who might replace me if he grew bored. But when I saw those photos, it all made sense. I wanted to throw up."

"Why did you bring the wallet to Sheriff Melton?"

She dropped her hand from my slacks. The electricity shut off.

"I looked at the driver's license and did a Google search. I found a little article about this young man being found dead in the desert in 1984. It was his wallet. I thought his family might want it."

She walked out, brushing past me, now more with impatience than flirtation.

I followed her into the bedroom.

"Do you suspect your husband was involved with Tom Frazier?"

"Who the hell knows?" She sat in an armchair and crossed those slim legs. "I don't even know Elliott, I realize now."

"He never mentioned the name?"

She shook her head.

"This is a suspicious death," I said. "Probably a homicide."

Her face lost color. She stared at me, opened her mouth but no words came.

"Was your husband violent?"

She nearly jumped out of the chair. "What the hell are you implying, Deputy?" The "David" stuff was gone. "How dare you? Who do you think you are to say that Elliott could have murdered this young man?"

"You said that. I asked if he was violent."

She whirled around and strode to one of the French doors. For a long time she stared out at the mountain. The top of the camel's hump had disappeared in the clouds.

Finally, a small voice: "Elliott was a man of extremes and he could be very generous. When I told him that I hated north Scottsdale, he bought this property and built this house for us. The more I learned about Native American and Mexican art, the more he bought me pieces. Very expensive ones."

She turned back and her face was composed.

"I'm terribly rude. May I get you something to drink?"

"No. Thank you, though."

She fixed me with her enormous beautiful eyes. "The answer to your question is that Elliott had a bad temper. It was worse when he was drunk, which was a lot. He hit me more than once. My dad had been an alcoholic, too. He beat me with a belt when

I was fifteen years old! Shit, I thought it was normal. With Elliott, he would slap me and the next morning turn sweet and give me an expensive present. He'd want to take me out to dinner even if I had a black eye. I had worse than yours, believe me."

"If he was involved with Tom Frazier and something went wrong, do you think he was capable of hurting him?"

Her shoulders rose and fell. "We always want to think the best of the people close to us, don't we? But those pictures showed me how little I really knew the man. So the honest answer is, I don't know."

I handed her my card and started to leave.

"David, about what happened back there in the closet…"

"Don't give it a second thought, Mrs. Whitehouse."

That smile again. "It's Diane. I wasn't going to apologize. I see something in you, David. You're special. I feared that Chris would send some knuckle-dragger and he sent you, instead. I always fell for brains. It's not as if I throw myself at men."

I tried to smile back. "I'm very honored. I also love my wife."

"To whom you've been unfaithful before. Only children confuse passion with love."

She handed me her card and stroked my fingers. I let her do it.

"Call me if there's something you want, David."

What I really wanted was someone who could find millions in missing rough diamonds and lead me to Peralta. Most of all, I wanted Lindsey to get better.

She watched me closely, this compact still-lovely woman, in her expensive black jeans and huge house and ancient pottery with kill holes, who had deposited this secret on Chris Melton's doorstep.

Until Ed Cartwright told me otherwise, until we knew Peralta was safe, it was my doorstep, too.

I left her in the bedroom and let myself out.

Chapter Thirty

I got half a mile when the phone rang. Kate Vare. Would I meet her?

She was sitting in an unmarked Chevy Impala in a parking lot off Twenty-fourth Street and Osborn. The homely one-story building nearby had once been a home-cooking restaurant named Linda's. Now it was a Mexican eatery. I pulled next to her in the timeless cop fashion, driver's door to driver's door.

Her elbow was resting on the doorframe, window down, and she looked me over. "Why are you so dressed up?"

"I went to see Diane Whitehouse."

She cocked her head and I gave the elevator speech about Tom Frazier's wallet.

"Jeez." She laughed, a strange sound coming from her. "Old Man Whitehouse in the closet? He hit on me once, you know. Years ago when I was a uni. Went to a burglary call at one of his subdivisions under construction. He talked to me about how hard it must be for me, being tough all the time, and I wouldn't have to be that way with him. It was a smoother come-on than it sounds."

I took it in and said nothing. Even though it was getting toward noon, the streets were slick and moody, the rain clouds low and misshapen like boiling lead.

"I'd love to be there when you log in those photos as evidence," Vare said. "Do you like him for this?"

She meant did I think the late Elliott Whitehouse, the legendary Phoenix homebuilder, had murdered his lover. Oh, and the lover was a young man.

I shook my head. "Frazier was found dead of a heroin overdose, but there's no evidence he was a user. If he was Whitehouse's lover, this seems like a lot of bother. Why not simply bludgeon him with a piece of rebar and dump the body in a mineshaft or bury it under a concrete slab? Hire a hitman. It doesn't make sense."

"And why keep the wallet?" she said. "Maybe he thought it would make identification more difficult."

"Except Frazier's car was within walking distance."

"We almost caught your girl." She changed the subject suddenly.

"Almost?" My stomach felt as if it had dropped five inches.

"She was at a house by the Biltmore. Up on Biltmore Estates Drive, with those lovely older places? This one was foreclosed on during the worst of the bust, only the neighbors wouldn't allow a sign out front. It was bank-owned and sat empty. Somehow she found it and was using it as her base."

I looked straight at her and asked how they almost found her.

"Crime Stoppers call early this morning. We set up a perimeter and called in SWAT. Made entry at eight a.m. She was gone. But she'd been injured. Maybe a gunshot. She had performed surgery on herself, stitched it up. Left a bunch of bloody gauze and a suture kit. She was moving fast. Looks like she made it out through the golf course before we secured the perimeter."

I leaned toward the steering wheel and let out a long sigh. It was not theater. My best hope for catching Strawberry Death had failed and she was on the loose again.

"Did you shoot her, Mapstone?"

I pulled out the Colt Python and held it up. "If I had shot her, she'd be dead, blown six feet back from the point of impact. Anyway, you told me that if I worked this case, you'd…"

"Yeah, yeah." She shook her head dismissively. "I've changed my mind. This woman is dangerous as hell. I know Lindsey's in the hospital and for some reason you've got this special from Meltdown. But I need your help."

"You? Need my help?"

Her sharp features tightened. "Don't fucking congratulate yourself, Professor. Help me."

I could give her real help, but that would compromise the operation that Peralta and Cartwright were running. Too many secrets, too many compartments.

She said, "Why are you working for Meltdown?"

I told her the truth.

"You're an idiot, Mapstone."

"I know." It started to sprinkle. I watched the drops heal my dry hand.

"Lindsey wouldn't betray the country."

"I know." My voice was louder this time. "It was Saturday night and he was leaning on me. I needed to buy time."

Vare shook her head. "And you went home, told Lindsey, had a fight, and she left to take a walk and cool down."

"That's pretty much it."

"You asshole," she said. "Why didn't you tell me this to begin with?"

"It didn't seem relevant."

"Let me tell you about relevant. Twenty minutes after we made entry to the house on Biltmore Estates Drive and secured it, Horace Mann showed up with a dozen agents. He ordered me to turn over control of the scene. My fucking scene! When I refused, he called the chief and…" She punched the steering wheel. "That was that. Why?"

"The woman must be connected to the diamonds."

"Exactly. And she thinks you're connected, too. I checked the logs and we did impound the car you described. It was a rental, made with a credit card to a woman named Amy Morris. Have you heard that name before?"

"No."

"You're not helping."

"I'm trying." Actually, I was lying again. Amy Morris was the name I first heard from the man who called Matt Pennington's office. That man was still waiting for me, as Pennington, to call him back.

Vare said, "I ran her and nothing. Nothing! The credit card had only been used once to rent that car. She used a North Dakota driver's license that was fake."

"She's a professional assassin. She's got the tradecraft."

"But who the hell is she and why is she here?"

"I think she's here to kill Mike Peralta and everybody close to him."

"Sharon's okay…"

"She has FBI agents all over her. But when did the woman first show up? On the road to Ash Fork Friday night. I was driving Sharon's car and she was with me. This Morris woman was dressed like DPS, pulled out her gun and was ready to shoot me. She would have killed us both if the FBI unit following us hadn't pulled off the freeway at that moment. Morris gets in her car and leaves. The next time I see her is Saturday night outside our house. By that time, Sharon had a protective cordon outside her house. We didn't."

Vare actually let me complete several sentences. She drummed her right fingers on the steering wheel, stared ahead. I could see the gears turning and that made me uncomfortable. Kate Vare had good gears.

"None of this makes sense, Mapstone. Peralta shot a guy, some old man who has a PI license, he stole the diamonds, stashed them in some woman's old Toyota, and disappeared. He doesn't even have the stones."

Maybe Strawberry Death doesn't know that. Maybe she's simply out for revenge, whether the diamonds were recovered or not. I speculated out loud without giving away too much. I was relieved that she discounted Ed Cartwright as "some old man."

She said, "Where is that suitcase? Does Chandler have it? I want to go through it. Maybe the shipment wasn't even the real diamonds…"

The gears were catching correctly. I told her Horace Mann had taken it into evidence.

"Fuck! Is Peralta guilty or is he running some kind of operation?" Her eyes bore into me.

I didn't dare even blink. "He's not guilty of a robbery. Lindsey checked his finances on Saturday. He's got plenty of money. There's no motive. If he's running an operation, he never told me."

"FBI?" she said. "Peralta and Eric Pham were tight."

"Pham's been sent to the Arctic Circle."

"Then DEA or ATF. The ATF chief lives right down the street from you."

"She took a post in France."

"So what?" Vare said. "This thing has cartel written all over it. They use diamonds as a substitute for currency to pay for cross-border shipments of drugs, or to settle drug debts."

"Peralta hates the cartels," I said. "But he never told me he was doing anything more than working as a guard on the diamond shipment."

"Maybe he wanted to protect you?"

I shrugged. "It didn't succeed." I waited a few beats. Then, "Who is the go-to diamond fence in Phoenix?"

I already knew the answer. The only surprise was that she wasn't already thinking that way. She shook her head and promised to find out.

"If you find that person, the pieces might come together," I said. "But you're poaching in a federal case."

"Fuck them." Her tone was adamant. "This is my town."

She started the car but didn't leave.

"Did you know that Mann and Sheriff Meltdown are friends?"

My cheek and eye started burning insistently. "No."

"Oh, yeah. They were in the Bureau together, both stationed in Minneapolis and Chicago at the same time. They were partners for seven years. Meltdown was best man at Horace Mann's wedding. I asked around. Something is really wrong here. No offense, but Meltdown didn't bring you back to the Sheriff's Office because you're such a brilliant cop. He…"

This time I interrupted to finish her sentence: "He did it because Horace Mann wants me out of the way."

I stared out at the shabby streetscape, felt like the idiot she had described.

Vare pushed my elbow. "You are good at finding trouble, Mapstone. So go do it. Get in the way. But keep me in the loop. One more thing. If this Amy Morris is out there, she's not going away and she's coming for you. So as much as you love that wheel gun, you'd better carry more firepower. Now go find trouble. Call me, Mapstone."

She stomped on the gas and fishtailed out onto Twenty-fourth heading south as the sprinkles turned into a hard rain.

Chapter Thirty-one

Lindsey's color had returned and the medicos were happy with her vital signs. For the first time, the hard realist inside me began to have hope.

I read her some favorite Emily Dickinson. But not about death kindly stopping for me.

When the nurses left, I said, "I almost got her. But she escaped. I let you down. They say her name is Amy Morris. But the name doesn't lead anywhere. Her driver's license is bogus. If you were up and around, you'd identify her in a heartbeat."

The ventilator's rhythm was the only reply.

I was about to continue when a nurse returned to show me out.

As I sat down in the waiting room, my phone rang.

"Are you alone?"

It was Cartwright.

"Yes."

"There's good news and bad news. Which do you want first?"

"Good, please." I felt my body bracing against the institutional furniture.

"Lindsey isn't under investigation for anything. Melton lied to you. It turns out he was partners with Horace Mann…"

"I know. Kate Vare told me they worked together."

"Vare? The Phoenix detective?"

"She's pissed. She doesn't like being shut out by the feds."

"Melton wanted you distracted. He's obviously working with Mann. Maybe your instincts weren't wrong."

"Meaning?" I asked.

"Meaning Pamela Grayson went back to her hotel. She visited her father in north Scottsdale. He retired and sold his business back in Ohio. We didn't know she had a family connection here. Her visit might not be connected to the diamond theft. Now I wonder about Horace Mann, too. He might be a suspect, after all. The man was very prompt to volunteer to take over this investigation. Back in the Army, the first thing I learned was never to volunteer."

I asked for the bad news.

After a long pause, "Lindsey had an affair with her boss."

And several lovers while I was letting Robin seduce me. It was our time of madness. I didn't tell him that or that all I wanted was to have her back with me. So I said I knew. No stranger can really see the inside of a marriage.

"I'm sorry, man. Anyway, time for you to make the phone call to the guy who contacted you in Matt Pennington's office."

I was suddenly exhausted again.

"Go have a hotdog at Johnnie's across the street," he said.

"Johnnie's is closed."

"Go to Johnnie's," he said. "Knock on the back door six times and be prepared to show your identification."

"Should I come highly armed?"

"That would be a bad idea. Remember, back door."

I thought he was going to end the call, but I heard a sigh. "One more thing, David. Don't contact me again. I need to lay low for this operation to work and for me to keep my cover."

I said, "I'm going to find Peralta. And I'm going to find the woman who shot Lindsey."

"I know." And he was gone.

Chapter Thirty-two

Johnnie had made the best dogs in central Phoenix but now his shop was another empty storefront facing Thomas Road. The windows were covered with brown paper. Still, I did as Cartwright told me and walked around back. Puddles had gathered in the rutted asphalt.

I stood against the wall behind the liquor store and waited. Situational awareness: No one seemed to be following me. The alley was empty.

The back door to Johnnie's was white and battered, with a slit of a window guarded by bars. A sign was pasted to the center, black with orange letters, the kind you could buy at a hardware store: "Construction workers only."

I rapped six times slowly.

A piece of paper peeled back from the slit, as if I were trying to get into a speakeasy. I held open my badge case until I heard a lock turn and the door opened long enough for me to step inside.

A big man with an assault rifle and ballistic vest told me to turn around and put my hands in the air to be searched. The lanyard around his neck showed an FBI identification.

"That won't be necessary."

It was Eric Pham.

"Anchorage is hell this time of year," I said. "But with climate change, it will get better up there."

He didn't laugh. He had no sense of humor in the best of times. But in the best of times, he also dressed like a fed with a fussy streak. If it was a hundred ten degrees, he wore a suit, dimple perfectly centered in his tie, gold-and-blue FBI pin properly centered on his lapel. Today, he inhabited jeans and a baggy gray sweatshirt. It made him look much younger and not in a good way.

He and his team were also perfectly concealed. The FBI had recently built a huge new Phoenix field office, but it was way up north by Deer Valley Airport. The Bureau had been located in Midtown all my life, but even it had become another hustle in the sprawl engine tearing the city apart. Now this was the last place anyone would look for the feds.

"You weren't supposed to be part of this." He glared at me.

"Peralta made me a part." I could glare, too. "He left the business card that said, 'find Matt Pennington.' Then this hitwoman…"

"We don't know she's a hitwoman or even a part of this operation."

My temples started throbbing. I couldn't believe what I was hearing.

"Walk across the street to the ICU and tell that to my wife. Oh, you can't because she's in a coma after the hitwoman shot her and nearly killed her…"

"Calm down, Doctor Mapstone."

So I was a doctor again.

I was about to go from zero to asshole in 3.6 seconds so I forced my temper down.

The room was dim, lit by a few overhead fluorescent lights long past their prime. The dingy tables from the restaurant had been set up with computers, two and three screens each, with four agents at work. All wore hoodies or T-shirts. They looked me over and went back to their screens.

Other than the computers, it looked nothing like an FBI control center from the movies of television. No expensively designed techno-wonder. A white board stood at one end of the room. Someone had sketched boxes with lettering inside:

PERALTA
RUSSIANS
SUSPECT AGENT
PENNINGTON
OTHER?

Lines connected some of the boxes. It didn't seem very helpful.

Pham said, "Our asset tells me you found Pennington dead, a suicide."

The asset being Ed Cartwright. Pham wouldn't say his name even among this trusted group.

I said, "That's what it was made to look like. The woman…"

"I understand why you're obsessed with her, but there's no evidence she has anything to do with this case."

"Outside our house on Saturday night, she stuck a gun in my face and said, 'Where are my stones?' I don't think she meant her rock collection. She said she would have preferred to 'suicide me.' Exactly what happened with Pennington. I disarmed her but she fought and ran. She had a backup gun and shot Lindsey."

Pham's finely chiseled features exuded skepticism.

"Are you sure that's what she said? You had a gun pointed at you."

"Yes!" The agents looked at me again and I lowered my voice. "She said something else, too. That she made Peralta a promise and killing us was part of it."

"Let's talk privately." He led me into a cubbyhole made by two six-foot tilt-up panels. Inside was another table where Lindsey and I had probably eaten Chicago dogs many times. Now it was covered with files surrounding a desktop computer. On the wall was an FBI seal and framed photo of the president. Were it not for these totems, I would have thought we were in a mortgage boiler room from the days of the subprime boom.

Pham sat forward on his chair, perfect posture, and waited until I took the seat across from him.

He slid a paper toward me. It was from the Department of Corrections and showed a woman with stringy long hair and cellblock eyes.

"Fourteen years ago, her boyfriend beat her little girl to death. She helped him bury the body in the desert. Shallow grave. She called the police and told them her daughter had been taken by a Mexican man. This was while you were away, but it was a big deal in the media. Peralta interrogated her personally, played it perfectly, got her to confess and testify against the boyfriend. He went away for life and she was sentenced to fifteen years as an accessory."

I held up my palms: so what?

"Look at the sheet again."

I scanned it. The woman's name was Amy Sue Morris. But she didn't look anything like the woman who had shot Lindsey.

"Women can redo their hair," he said. "Here are the two salient facts. First, in the sentencing, she went nuts. Peralta was in the courtroom and she threatened to kill him and his family. Second, she was released a week before Christmas from the Perryville prison."

"Eric, it's not the same woman. The one who nearly killed Lindsey is after the diamonds. She wore Chanel Number Five. How many released prisoners do that? I smelled Chanel Number Five in Pennington's office. She had been there."

"You're a perfume expert?"

He was almost making me start to doubt myself. But the woman I had tangled with had moves they don't train you for in prison.

Pham cut me off. "I don't want to get distracted here. The asset told me that the phone rang while you were in Pennington's office, you answered it claiming to be Pennington. The man expects you to call him."

I nodded.

"What did he sound like?"

"No accent. Baritone. No background noise. When I asked about Peralta, he said that he was 'a different problem,' that it was better for me not to know. Also, he told me that Mann's window is closing."

Pham stiffened. "He named Horace Mann?"

I nodded and he wrote it down on a legal pad.

"What about Pamela Grayson? Did that name come up?"

I shook my head. "But he also knew about the hitwoman. He named her. Amy Morris. That's the same name that Phoenix PD identified when they raided a place up by the Biltmore this morning. She's been wounded but she was gone."

"Wounded?" Pham raised an eyebrow.

"I shot her last night but she was wearing body armor. I followed her to the house. If she doesn't have anything to do with the diamonds, why did Horace Mann show up there this morning?"

"Because you called it in."

"But…"

"You're creating a feedback loop to bring everything back to the person who shot your wife. It's understandable. You're emotionally involved. You're also blinded by it." He tapped the corrections report. "That's your female. Give that to Phoenix PD."

"I know what I know." Still, I forced my breathing to slow down and took a careful, objective look. It wasn't her. The eyes, mouth, and cheekbones were all wrong, even if she could have changed her hair so radically.

I said, "Why are you so goddamned uncurious about this woman?"

He was unruffled, his voice the schoolmaster dealing with an unruly and not-so-bright pupil. "Do you have any idea how serious it is for evidence to be stolen from a secure Federal Bureau of Investigation facility?"

"I know it's embarrassing."

Now he did a little stretch with his head and neck, a man struggling with his temper. I was half a second from being thrown out of his sanctum and pushed away from the case.

He said, "This is very real, Doctor Mapstone. Someone with the clearance to smuggle out that evidence might be greedy. Or she could have the means to penetrate other highly secure Bureau operations. This is a national security matter."

I tried nodding with great seriousness. Then, "Where did these diamonds originate? Before they were in your evidence room?"

He squared his shoulders. "It's not a 'room,' and I can't disclose the origin of the evidence. Retrieving the diamonds and arresting the rogue agent is Washington's top priority, right from the director."

"And Peralta's safety?"

"He volunteered," Pham said. "I have confidence he can take care of himself."

"Even though you don't know where he is?"

"You talked to him." The schoolmaster's tone again. "He sounded like a man in control of the situation."

God, I hated the feds, most of them anyway. Peralta could conceal his troubles better than anyone I ever knew. The only thing I learned from calling him was that he was still alive.

Pham said, "I know you have many questions."

That was an understatement.

"I'll tell you what I can. The Bureau owes you as the one who wrapped up the only unsolved murder of an FBI agent in history." His eyes bore in. "But goodwill only goes so far, and I need you to make that call. Are you on the team?"

I pressed my jaw together and nodded. "I do have a few things to clear up." Best to start with a relative softball. "Why were you fired as the SAC, at least that was the cover story? Seems to me it might telegraph to your suspect that the Bureau was waiting for him."

"We thought about that but decided the suspect wanted her diamonds so much she wouldn't be thinking that way. She would likely know we were tracking the gems and knew they were coming here. She'd find a way to create a distraction and get them."

"Pamela Grayson."

Pham tapped on a six-inch set of files. No paperless office at Johnnie's "We're talking about a senior person with plenty of access to evidence and intel. She fits perfectly. Look, if we had played it straight, we might have gotten the Russians. But there's a very good chance we wouldn't have caught the rogue agent or anyone else she was working with. This could be a conspiracy within the FBI."

"'Anyone else.' The question mark on the white board."

"Exactly. Removing me as SAC sent a powerful message through the Bureau. I was to blame for the failed operation. The suspect would let down her guard. We've got her phones and computers under surveillance."

"But Horace Mann fits this profile, too," I said. "He fits it better."

Pham shrugged. "The asset told me you believe this."

"So did the guy who called Pennington's office." I studied Pham's face and decided not to push it. "So let's say I'm wrong. Mann is totally legit. Why is he leaving me alone? I haven't seen him since Friday night in the High Country."

"He doesn't take you seriously," Pham said. "Don't be offended. You're a former history professor who worked for the local Sheriff's Office. He's done enough checking to believe you didn't know about the robbery in advance and Peralta won't be contacting you. Your phones might be tapped but that's it. He's only got so many agents to stake out locations and follow people."

Once again I was grateful Lindsey had turned my iPhone into an impenetrable dark device. No reason for Eric Pham to know this.

I tried something tougher. "So how was the operation supposed to go down?"

He hesitated and drew a deep breath. "All right, Doctor Mapstone. But this is confidential FBI information. Do you understand?"

"Sure."

He swung his computer screen so we could both see it and tapped on the keyboard. A color video appeared.

"This is Terminal Four at Sky Harbor on Friday morning. As you can see, Peralta and the other guard approach this man."

He pointed to a nondescript middle-aged Anglo in a cheap suit. "That's the jeweler. He's passed through security to the main terminal. Peralta signs for the shipment and takes the rolling suitcase. It has the diamonds inside."

More tapping and black-and-white images came up. "This is from the service hallway at the mall."

Here was something I had already seen. A mall security guard lets in Peralta and Cartwright. There's a conversation and the mall guard walks ahead several paces and disappears around the corner. Then Peralta pushes Ed back and draws his weapon. He fires and Ed goes down. Peralta walks quickly toward the camera, pulling the suitcase, and going back the way he came.

I said, "So far, so good?"

"All according to plan."

Another view appeared on the screen, this time in color. Peralta was walking fast, carrying the suitcase now. He opened the door to his pickup, tossed the bag inside, backed up, and drove toward the street. It is a huge parking lot. Almost every space was taken. Two, no, three shoppers walked by as he cruised past.

"Here."

Pham froze the screen. Peralta had stopped at the outermost bank of parking. The truck was beside an old Toyota. The one belonging to Catalina Ramos.

The action moved forward slowly. As I had suspected, Peralta used a Slim Jim to open the driver's side, from which he could pop the trunk. He dumped the suitcase inside, closed the trunk, and drove away.

"This is where things went sideways?" I asked.

"No," Pham said. "We planned for him to do this so the GPS tracker in the suitcase would be useless."

"That doesn't make sense," I said. "If you think Grayson is the bad guy, why not let her follow the tracker? She'd have access to that technology."

"It would be too easy." Pham's hand was tightly gripping the computer mouse. "Grayson might suspect something."

As he talked, I thought about Horace Mann. He would be even more bulletproof. If he recovered the diamonds aboveboard, he'd be a hero. Even if the rough were in the hidden compartment, there would be no probable cause to arrest him. Quite the opposite. If he found the suitcase alone, he would have time to take the rough unobserved. But Peralta beat him to it.

He continued to talk about Grayson. "She needed to see that Peralta had found the hidden rough and taken it. That would rattle her. So we planned for Peralta to dump the suitcase."

"It's a hell of a gamble when Chandler Police was converging on the mall."

"Peralta is a cool cat."

He was that.

Pham continued the footage as the truck rolled out on Chandler Boulevard, pulled to the curb as two police cruisers raced past with lights going—there was no sound on the video. A quick left turn and he was on the 101 freeway traveling north in moderate traffic.

I asked, "Where did you get this?"

"A drone."

The video continued to follow him as he drove north, taking the interchange to the Superstition Freeway and popping out of the concrete spaghetti going west. Another four miles and he hit wide Interstate 10. The immediate direction was north into Tempe, then it would veer west into Phoenix.

Pham said, "The city cops don't even have a description or tag of the truck by this point." He seemed very proud of himself and his plan.

Next, something odd happened. Before the interstate curved west, Peralta got off on Broadway and drove north into mundane, low-rise office buildings and warehouses. No, he was going to Rio Salado College, one of the branches of the huge community college system. It was also where KJZZ, the NPR station, had its studios. The drone hovered and zoomed in on the truck entering the parking garage.

"By this time, we calculated that the scene would start to be sorted out. The asset was not going to talk. He was wounded, after all. He played even more disoriented. But the cops would eventually know Peralta was the other guard. So this seemed like a good place for him to change his license tag."

He fast-forwarded to the truck leaving and returning to the freeway.

"Wait," I said. "How much time elapsed?"

He pointed to a small digital readout on the corner of the screen. "Twenty-one minutes."

I said, "That's a damned long time for a gear-head like Peralta to change one tag."

He let the question pass.

"So you want to know what went wrong," Pham said. "Peralta had a tracker in his boot. It never activated. The next sign we have of him is in Ash Fork. He was never supposed to go to the High Country. He was supposed to dump the truck and hole up in a motel room with us watching him."

"And?"

"The Russians. Peralta would wait three days and contact the people who engaged our asset as diamond guard. Offer to sell the diamonds back to them. We have all their phones and computers monitored. So either they would call the person from the Bureau who was their partner or she would call them. By that time, she'd have seen the news coverage. She'd know the diamonds she worked so hard to steal and get this far were gone. When Peralta set up the meet, we'd get them all."

"Did Peralta know the names of the suspected agents?"

Pham shook his head.

"So if he heard Horace Mann briefing the press on his truck radio, that name wouldn't mean anything? It wouldn't cause him to change course?"

"No. Why would it? Horace Mann is not a suspect, Doctor Mapstone."

"Then why are you here? Does Mann know you're running this?"

He hesitated, then shook his head. "This is about redundancy," he said. "About compartmentalization. Washington insisted on this. It says nothing about Horace Mann's competence."

The Russian had spoken of compartmentalization, too. What could go wrong? I could imagine two sets of FBI agents getting into a gunfight.

I wasn't reassured about Mann, either. One reason why Peralta had left the first business card, the one saying I had nothing to do with the diamond robbery, might have been an attempt to protect me from suspicion. On the other hand, why would the FBI believe the writings of a wanted man? Maybe that first card was meant for me, to telegraph that all was not well with this very complicated operation.

I said, "What about Matt Pennington?"

"That came from Peralta via you," he said.

"He wasn't in the mix? He's on the white board."

"Only because of Peralta's note to you, which you informed our asset about. As you know, when Pennington was in the Navy he worked with Mexican authorities on drug interdiction. I'm trying to find out what happened with Pennington in Mexico. It's a DEA matter and they're not being forthcoming."

I suspected that I would never find out. Pham had been as forthcoming as he would be and only because he wanted something only I could do.

I leaned in again. "So show me more of the drone footage."

He looked down and spoke quietly. "I can't. The drone couldn't pass over Sky Harbor airspace. We lost him. Now it's time for you to make that phone call."

Chapter Thirty-three

Afterwards, I stood on the sidewalk by Thomas Road watching the traffic roll by, counting the number of giant pickup trucks that looked exactly like what Peralta drove.

My mind was fried and then sent back to the kitchen to be scrambled.

Lindsey was only a couple of hundred strides from where I stood, but every time I left the hospital I felt as if I was committing a small act of betrayal. Yes, there was nothing I could do to help her. Yes, I had promised Sharon I would find her husband, promised Ed Cartwright I would find his friend. It still felt lousy.

If Strawberry Death wanted to get me at that moment, all she needed to do was be behind the wheel of one of the trucks or SUVs traveling at fifty on Thomas and conquer the curb on the way to splattering me like a bug on the grille.

Pham would dismiss it as another 962 involving a pedestrian, radio code for accident with injuries. Or 963, accident with fatality. Such tragedies happened daily here, where the civic layout had become wide highways called city streets connecting real-estate enterprises. Nothing to see here. Move along.

I had spent my day at the extremes of the city, the mansion in Arcadia and the shabby former hot-dog place. Sure, it got worse. There were shanties in south Phoenix with dirt floors and homeless camps by the river bottom. There were thirty thousand-square-foot mansions on the sides of mountains. Neither extreme talked to the other.

Walking back into the hospital, I felt the anger in my steps. Why was Pham not buying my theory of the hitwoman? In fact, he had gone to the trouble of having his minions find a parolee that debunked my version. But the woman on the corrections sheet wasn't Strawberry Death. One only learned her moves thanks to professional training and constant practice, and never being caught. She operated in the shadows.

He also didn't believe me about Horace Mann. I knew what I heard. I knew Mann was dirty.

Pham's inattention stank: the hubris of a boss who had his mind made up, a massive amount of FBI ass-covering.

Another possibility chilled me. What if Pham was perfectly acquainted with her because Amy Morris was a government agent? She didn't even have to be FBI. We had so many agencies guarding the so-called homeland now.

Like Cartwright, Pham had dismissed me but in his case with an odd mix of formality and fake-casual management jargon. "So don't come back to this location, Doctor Mapstone. Don't try to contact me. You don't have the bandwidth to help in this space. So stay away."

Stay away, my ass.

I retrieved my briefcase from the ICU nurses and went to the waiting room. I should have written up my interview with Diane Whitehouse to add to the murder book. As far as Eric Pham was concerned, I was done.

The phone call back had seemed to go well but the technicians weren't able to get a fix on the man's location. We agreed to meet at six tonight by the fountain in Scottsdale Fashion Square. Except I wouldn't be there. I described one of Pham's FBI agents as me, as Matt Pennington.

But I wasn't done.

I thought about the white board at Johnnie's, the boxes drawn in blue marker and labeled PERALTA, RUSSIANS, SUSPECT AGENT, PENNINGTON, OTHER?

It looked as if it had been drawn up and abandoned like some corporate initiative that went nowhere. And what was "other"?

I pulled out a pad and made some drawings of my own.

One was a starburst with Peralta at the center. I sketched lines out to boxes for me, Ed Cartwright, Eric Pham, Matt Pennington, and the unknown people Peralta had joined in Ash Fork after abandoning his truck at the derelict gas station on Route 66. These represented direct relationships to Mike Peralta.

I added a perpendicular line from the Russians to Cartwright. They had contacted him.

Next I added a box for Strawberry Death with lines to Pennington and me. I made dashes between her and Peralta. I had no physical proof they had made contact or knew each other, but she had told me she had made him a promise.

To be complete, I drew a connection between Horace Mann and me. He had interrogated me on Friday afternoon, summoned me to Ash Fork that night to unlock the gun compartment of the truck, and then didn't order FBI surveillance of our house. That last had proved very useful to Strawberry Death.

What if she were working with him? If so, why was he so interested in having me dead? It had to be something more than what Kate Vare considered my ability to get in the way.

But the diagram wasn't quite right.

The only immediate connection to Pennington was Peralta. I pulled out the business card and studied his printing: FIND MATT PENNINGTON.

The dead man wasn't on the FBI's radar. But he sure as hell was on somebody's or Strawberry Death wouldn't have "suicided" him only a few hours or even minutes before I found him. Who gained from his death? Nobody I could see. But he had information and either gave it up before he died, or…

Or he was that tough and committed. Why not? He was a Naval Academy grad who apparently worked on dangerous assignments.

Or he didn't know and she killed him anyway.

I looked at the drawing, came up empty, and set it aside.

On the next sheet, I tried different thinking. If the crooks think of themselves as businessmen and some businessmen are crooks, why not look at the supply chain?

This produced boxes along a line. Inside the first was a question mark. After all, Pham wouldn't tell me where those diamonds in evidence came from. From there, the line went to the FBI evidence control facility to Markovitz in New York to Chandler.

Going only that far raised questions. Why wouldn't the rogue agent keep the diamonds himself? One obvious answer was to avoid being caught up if a search warrant was served on him. Maybe he didn't have the contacts and distribution network—I was still thinking supply chain—to turn the rough into cash. That's where the Russians came in.

And why did I know this much about the journey of these diamonds? One of their advantages was how they could disappear. They were small, easy to conceal, and carry across borders. Were we such great detectives in having this much information? Or was something else going on?

Perhaps I was being paranoid. Being shot at will do that.

After Chandler, I sketched the supply chain diagram in greater detail. Cartwright is shot and Peralta steals the suitcase. He pulls the switch in the parking lot, leaving the suitcase with the tracker in the trunk of Catalina Ramos' Toyota and taking the hidden rough. He travels the freeway system to Rio Salado College where he goes in the parking garage for more than twenty minutes.

I drew a box for Ash Fork but only added a line of slashes. Too many unknowns.

My hand was about to draw more lines and boxes but it lingered on the Rio Salado box. Twenty minutes. A very long time to change a license plate, especially for a guy as mechanically skilled as Peralta.

I pulled out my iPhone and called Rio Salado College security.

Chapter Thirty-four

The badge did have benefits.

Within an hour, I was still sitting in the ICU waiting room but video camera footage from Friday was streaming on my MacBook Air as I talked to the security chief at Rio Salado.

We started with the camera trained on the entrance to the multi-story parking garage. It faced outward, so we saw the entrance to the parking and beyond it the street and front doors of the college.

At precisely 11:37 a.m., Peralta's truck turned into the garage.

"Freeze that, please."

He did and I studied the image. It was definitely Peralta. He had put on a Phoenix Suns ballcap.

I said, "Do you have cameras inside the garage?"

"On every floor."

He flipped through several cameras and let them run. Peralta appeared on the third floor, drove halfway up, and backed into a parking space. I asked that he slow down the speed and watched as Peralta stepped out and went to the back of the pickup.

"Can you zoom in?"

He could. The light was bad and the image grainy, but Peralta stooped down behind the truck. Here he was changing the tag.

The footage continued to run. A shadow slipped under the camera and became a Chevy Impala. My stomach tightened.

"Slow it more," I said.

The Chevy stopped directly in front of Peralta's truck, blocking it. Strawberry Death stepped out. She was wearing a white top and blue jeans, her hair was down, falling below her shoulders.

She walked around the car and ran her hand on top of the truck's hood. Checking to see if it was still warm from the engine.

She didn't know he was there.

And then he popped up with his Glock drawn.

It was 11:42.

She had followed him, keeping enough distance not to be suspicious. I wished I could go back and study the tape from the FBI drone. It might have shown her tailing him from the mall.

Through the grainy footage I could see mouths moving. Her hands were empty. He had the drop on her.

"Rookie mistake…"

"Come again?" the security officer said.

"I'm talking to myself."

She reluctantly turned around and walked to the front of the Chevy, Peralta behind her. Then she spread her feet and bent far forward on the hood, empty hands straight out. This was on his commands, no doubt, even though there was no sound. It put her at a disadvantage, being so off balance. If she tried to fight, he could kick one leg out and send her to the ground.

Something flashed. He produced handcuffs. And like thousands of times in his career, he cuffed her. Next he did a quick search and pulled something out of her back waistband. Some kind of pistol. He slid it into his own waistband and roughly pushed her to the passenger door, opened it, and tossed her in.

Then he crossed to the driver's side and got in. The Chevy slid forward into a parking space.

They sat there as the clock ran. Maybe she was making him a promise.

Finally, Peralta's head appeared. He walked over to his truck and retrieved the old license tag from the garage floor by the back bumper. Then he was inside the cab and pulling out.

The digital readout on the camera feed said 11:58.

Afterward, I put on my earbuds, leaned back, and listened to Susie Arioli, Billie Holliday, and Frank Sinatra…

Chapter Thirty-five

I awoke suddenly in a panic attack. The playlist had run through and shut off.

The waiting room was empty, silent, the perfect petri dish for my corrupted brain chemistry. My heart banged against my breastbone, every breath seemed fraught, and I felt as if I were being buried alive.

Pull off the earbuds.

Stand up.

Breathe and walk.

Engage in the movement of the living.

I went to the elevator and rode to the lobby where the crowd snapped me out of it. Then I found the meditation garden. I wasn't alone. A couple of nurses were talking on one bench. I sat away from them, the dream still vivid in my memory.

I was in Matt Pennington's office again. Outside, it was night and through the windows the city was glowing like thousands of Christmas lights. I could smell the body decomposing. I could hear his Naval Academy ring scraping the floor from the movement of a dead hand. The phone rang and it was the same man as before, talking to me…

Fully awake now and calmer, I studied the landscaping and the slant of the sun. It was a beautiful place. My neck ached from where my head had fallen forward as I had conked out. My watch said three p.m.

But what the man in the dream said...
And he said it in a voice I nearly recognized...

Then I realized, part of this was not a dream. He had actually said it yesterday on the phone in Pennington's office. I only remembered it now.

"They say she was a Mountie, you know."

He had said that about the hitwoman, that and her name.

It didn't jibe with the Southern accent, but people can imitate dialects.

Ottawa, headquarters of the Royal Canadian Mounted Police, was on Eastern Standard Time, two hours earlier. I didn't know who to call or what to ask and anyone in authority was probably going home right now.

Instead, I pulled out the MacBook Air and started searching for keywords.

"Amy Morris" and "Mountie" wasted several minutes. "Amy Morris" and "RCMP" only showed me some news stories about a dog bite in Surrey, British Columbia. This Amy Morris was "policy and outreach officer" for the local Society for the Prevention of Cruelty to Animals.

So I dropped the "Morris" and spread a wider net. After twenty minutes of different keywords, I found the first promising lead. The Google summary was about the murder of an RCMP officer's husband and daughter in Calgary.

I pulled up the story and there she was.

The news was three years old, but the photo was unmistakable. A woman with straight, reddish-blond hair parted slightly to the right and falling to spread out a couple of inches onto her shoulders. Heart-shaped face, blue eyes, so-so nose, and full lips in a slight smile. She was wearing civilian clothes.

The girl next door, teacher of the year, young mom at the park.

She would catch your eye and you would think she's attractive, but the memory wouldn't last. Men caught a glimpse of Lindsey and didn't forget her.

The caption said, Sergeant Amy Lisa Russell.

The woman in the photo was Strawberry Death. There was no doubt.

I read the story, read it twice. The sergeant had been on duty when her husband and child had been found "slain" at their home in the Bridgeland neighborhood. I had visited the city only once, years ago, to lecture on the Great Depression at the University of Calgary. It had reminded me of Denver.

I searched for more stories about the homicides but there was nothing but rewrites of the original news.

Then I matched "Amy Russell" and "RCMP." Her name came up in some official documents regarding something called the Immediate Action Rapid Deployment unit. It sounded like a national SWAT team, very elite. If she had served in this branch of the Mounties, she would have learned the moves she showed when we fought on the front lawn and I lost.

By this time the garden was empty, so I called the RCMP headquarters and got the runaround, nothing could be done until Wednesday at the earliest, I would need to speak to superintendent so-and-so, did I want to leave my name and agency? I did.

Then I went to the RCMP home page and tried to find some other options. The Mounties were organized into four separate districts for the province of Alberta. Calgary had its own city "police service." It had investigated the killing of the husband and child.

The next call went straight through to the Calgary homicide unit. I gave my name, department, and badge number. Two minutes later, a man picked up and identified himself as Inspector Joe Mapstone.

We spent a few minutes trying to find adjoining branches in our respective family trees. When we discovered no common ancestors, I asked him about the Bridgeland murders.

"They were never officially solved," he said.

That was a telling word. "Officially?"

"Amy Russell was in the RCMP organized crime task force. Her work sent three members of the Malicious Crew to federal prison, box cars for every one of them."

I asked about the slang. "Box cars" meant two consecutive life terms.

"The Malicious Crew is one of our worst outlaw motorcycle clubs," Inspector Mapstone told me. "Our theory was that the homicides were revenge. Amy might have been killed, too. She should have been home but was called to her headquarters that day. Her husband picked up their daughter at school and went home. That's where the killers were waiting. We never released the details but it was nasty stuff."

"Which was?"

His tone stiffened. "What exactly is your interest in this case, Deputy?"

There was no reason to soften it. "She's a suspect in a murder here."

"Amy?" He almost shouted her name. "That's preposterous. I worked with her. Everybody loved Amy."

"That may have been true but there's no question. The identification is positive. It's the same woman pictured in the *Calgary Herald* story about the murders."

"How can you be sure?"

"Because she pointed a gun at me. She said she would have preferred to 'suicide' my wife and me. Then she shot my wife."

"My God…"

It was a good two minutes before he spoke again. I waited him out in silence. By then he had mastered his emotions.

"Her husband was bound with duct tape," he said. "He was forced to watch their six-year-old daughter raped, burned with cigarettes, and then slit up the middle from her vagina to her sternum. Six years old. Who would do such a thing? They covered him with her intestines. Then they started on him. It took awhile. A message was being sent."

"Who found the bodies?"

"Amy did, when she came home that night. We haven't been able to make the case yet. This is still active and open. Because it involves a police officer, it continues to merit special attention."

Civilians didn't realize how often cases were called "open," but the cops were pretty certain about the suspect. Certainty didn't always make a case.

There were probably hundreds like that here. Bob Crane of *Hogan's Heroes* fame had been killed in Scottsdale in 1978. Add in videotaped sex and it had caused a national frenzy of news coverage. Almost from the start, the detectives had identified a suspect and had begun gathering evidence.

But convincing a prosecutor and a grand jury is another, more difficult matter. They finally had enough evidence to take the suspect to trial in 1994, but the jury acquitted him. The case remains officially open.

I asked, "What kept you from making arrests?"

"The prime suspect killed himself."

My breath caught in my throat.

He said, "Legal name Aaron Henry Edmonds, street name Chaos. He was the top enforcer of the motorcycle club. We had him in our sights as the prime suspect. But two weeks later, he slit the throats of his two children and his old lady, the common law wife. Then he shot himself in the temple."

Or he was "suicided," Amy's first.

"Is Amy still a Mountie?"

"No," he said. "She resigned afterwards. You can understand why."

"You said you knew her."

"Yes. A fine officer and she served in top units. We had occasion to work together. Everybody respected her. After this… Well, she had to get away. She took a private-sector job. Making more than the Mounties could ever pay. At Yellowknife in the Northwest Territories"

I felt cold merely hearing the words.

The microwaves carried the sound of him turning pages of a file and then he gave me her telephone number.

"What's in Yellowknife?" I said.

"The Ekati diamond mine," he said. "She became chief of security."

Chapter Thirty-six

After I set down the phone, I made a note of our entire conversation.

Then I heard my name and turned to see Lindsey's top surgeon. I had never seen him at this time of day and a spike ran into my solar plexus, my hand gripped the wooden arm of the bench.

Maybe if I didn't acknowledge him, didn't turn around and stand up…

He said, "I have good news."

I almost leapt off the bench but he sat me back down.

"I don't use the word miracle lightly but your wife's recovery comes pretty close. A medically induced coma and hypothermic treatment…In other words, lowering her body temperature. It can take up to two weeks. But we're ready to start bringing her out now."

"Let's go!"

"Hang on." He put a firm hand on my arm.

"This will be very gradual and intermittent. In stages. Think of it like a deep-sea diver being brought up."

I curbed my enthusiasm, at least on the outside.

He said, "The goal is to bring her to general sedation until she has recovered enough to sustain herself. She'll come off the ventilator as soon as she's strong enough to breathe on her own. We're thinking twelve to twenty-four hours, but if anything looks bad, we'll need to resume the hypothermic treatment."

I nodded too many times. I must have looked like an idiot.

I said, "What will she be like?"

"Her brain didn't sustain any oxygen loss. That's very good. Toward the end, she should be able to respond normally. Her memories may be affected."

He sat with me for a surprisingly long time, saying nothing.

Finally he stood. "We can't declare victory quite yet, Mister Mapstone. But your wife is a very strong woman."

I knew that.

Chapter Thirty-seven

After a few minutes, I had to get out of the hospital. The claustrophobia was overwhelming. In the waiting room, the television made it impossible to think, sleep, or write a report.

I needed to walk. So I went two long blocks to the light-rail station and rode the train down to the courthouse. Stepping off, I passed through a joyous flock of young girls in colorful *quinceanera* dresses, laughing and talking. I steered my briefcase through the extravagant flowing skirts. When I was fifteen, I couldn't have imagined the adult me in this mess.

In the atrium, I saw a young woman in a miniskirt arguing with the guard. Seeing me, he said, "Here he is."

She turned around. It was Zephyr Whitehouse.

I suppressed a sigh and said, "Come up to my office."

She followed me to the elevator and we walked down the long hallway in silence.

That changed once I closed the door.

"I owe you an apology for this morning," she said. "I didn't realize you were a deputy sheriff. I had to rifle through Diane's purse to find your business card. Then I called Chris and he told me you are a historian, too. I'm impressed."

Good old Chris.

"No apology necessary." I sat behind the desk. "No need to be impressed."

"My therapist has told me about sexual competition between mothers and daughters," she said. "It's always been there between me and Diane."

She called her mother by her first name, like Lindsey and Robin had done. Did anyone say "mom" anymore?

I invited her to sit but she walked around inspecting, pausing to look out the restored 1929 windows. She had that combination of beauty, grace, money, and—if she didn't read serious books—at least a feral intelligence that allowed her to effortlessly be the sun of any solar system she entered.

She alighted on the 1950s photo of Camelback Mountain with nothing but citrus groves flowing out to the south.

She pointed. "Our house is right here now. Amazing. You must despise my father. Even though I loved him, I hated growing up with his last name. I thought about taking Diane's maiden name, Jacobi. You know last names only became common in Europe in the sixteenth century, as people left their home villages? Of course you do."

I would have nodded but her very nice back was still facing me.

She turned. "We both have the same middle name, mother and daughter. Colleen. Do you like that?"

"Colleen is a lovely name."

She smiled. "But I'm a Zephyr."

"Yes, you are," I said. "What do you want, I'm-a-Zephyr?"

She straightened her shoulders. "You're very direct, Professor. No time for postmodern irony and cynicism? Or maybe that's what you did and I missed it."

I put my hands flat on the desk. "This is not Stanford and these are not office hours. Please sit down and tell me…" I smoothed out my insides and finished with "…how I may help you."

She sat, the skirt rode up, and long tanned legs crossed. I kept my eyes on her face.

"Your investigation of Chip. I'm assuming that's why you came to see Diane this morning."

"Chip?"

"Elliott Whitehouse, Jr., my half brother. Chip. He and James are sons of Daddy and the sainted first wife, Kathryn. The woman done wrong when Daddy left her for Diane, who was nothing more than a secretary in his office. It was a scandal. Very sexy. Kathryn and my half brothers hate me. James goes by the nickname Tanker, don't ask me why."

Diane Whitehouse had told me that she met Elliott while she had been working at Diamond's.

I asked Zephyr to tell me about Chip.

"Nothing you probably don't suspect." She played with a thick strand of tawny hair. "He did bribe county officials to get land rezoned for his warehouses. He's mean and lazy, but he's also careless. I have copies of the checks."

She reached in her purse and slid across sheets of folded paper.

I scanned them. They showed checks written on E2 LLC and signed by Chip Whitehouse. Each was made out to a different individual. I recognized one name from the Planning and Zoning Board and another who was a county commissioner. Each check was in the amount of ninety-eight hundred dollars. The payment was below the threshold where the bank would be required to report it to the feds.

I said, "Why are you doing this, Zephyr? He is your brother. What's your angle?"

Her face flushed. "Chip destroyed an eight-hundred-year-old Hohokam site to build those warehouses. Never disclosed it."

"You're that passionate about historic preservation?"

Her face assumed an adult seriousness. "As a matter of fact, yes. And about the environment. Chip did all this and flipped those ugly tilt-up warehouses for twelve million dollars before the bust. He didn't even have tenants. I don't need an angle, David. It's the right thing to do. It's what I was taught by my father." The legs uncrossed and her perfect knees met demurely.

"May I keep these copies?"

"Please," she said.

County corruption didn't figure into the wallet Diane had found in Elliott Whitehouse's closet. I did come down here to write up the report for Melton, so I decided to turn the conversation to my needs.

I said, "Why would I despise your father?"

She nodded to the photo. "He's one of the developers who took all this away. I'm a serious environmentalist and it's hard for me to reconcile."

I thought about that issue, not for the first time.

"Historians might call that 'presentism' and it gets in the way of understanding," I said. "Men like your father were part of a moment in history."

"Meaning?"

"The mass-produced subdivisions that started with Levittown back East were in vogue. Gasoline was cheap and driving was pleasant. Phoenix had a serious housing shortage after World War II and plenty of land."

I paused to see if she was bored. Her eyes were engaged and bright. Or she was a good actress. Either way, I continued, "It was growing, and men like Elliott Whitehouse and John F. Long provided good housing for the former GIs who were starting families. Not only that, but Arizona was rife with land swindles. These men operated honestly."

"So they didn't know what it would become, or the external economic and social costs of sprawl."

"That's the objective way to approach it." I said. "What's happened in recent years is more unforgivable. Now we know the consequences. It became a Ponzi scheme."

"The American Dream." Sarcasm tinted her voice. "And look at all that's lost. I wish I could have seen it the way you must have when you were young. The Japanese flower gardens. Superstition Mountain without all the houses."

"It was a beautiful place."

She gave an exaggerated shiver. "I would never live in the Valley again. Once I graduate, I'm staying in the Bay Area. None of my friends are coming back, either. Why do you stay?"

I didn't answer.

Her lips made a sad smile. "You're a sucker for lost causes, David Mapstone."

I asked Zephyr what her father was like.

"He doted on me." The smile widened, showing perfect teeth. "I was a daddy's girl. Diane was jealous of me. But what was he like?" She stared at the high ceiling. "He was sixty when I was born, so I get the sense he had mellowed. He was very kind. I got a very different father than Chip and Tanker grew up with. He would get down on the floor and play with me. This big man playing like he was six again. He built me a very elaborate dollhouse. I still have it."

"Was he faithful to your mother?"

She nodded to my ring finger. "Have you always been faithful to your wife, David? Don't worry. I won't put you on the spot. I know he and Diane fought about one woman she was sure he was having an affair with."

I wrote down the woman's name.

"What about men?" I asked.

"Men?" She laughed and stroked her knees. "Are you kidding me? Daddy was a terrible homophobe. Racist. Anti-Semitic. He was a privileged white man of his generation. My half brothers aren't much different and they don't have any excuses. They support the 'Papers Please' law, think all our problems are because of illegal aliens, even though they employ them and pay them dirt. Hypocrites. You probably think I'm a hypocrite, too, growing up in the big house, copping to environmentalism from privilege." She paused. Then, "What's Daddy got to do with this?"

A shadow appeared behind the pebbled glass and I tensed. Then Kate Vare burst in without knocking. I made introductions.

"Is she leaving?" Vare said.

"Yes," Zephyr said, standing. She was a head taller than Vare. "It was very nice to meet you, Sergeant Vare. Thanks for all that you do, David. I'll text you my number."

When the door closed, Vare put her hands on her hips and smiled with malice.

"Your next girlfriend? She's too young for you."

"You wouldn't believe me if I told you. But she's Elliott Whitehouse's daughter."

"Well, enjoy it before she kicks you to the curb."

"She's not...!"

Vare held out a hand. "It's your business, *David.*" She imitated Zephyr, with an extra dollop of sweet sexuality, no mean accomplishment for Kate Vare. Her voice sounded like a completely different person. Back in her normal tone, she continued, "Walk right into the propeller. I won't stop you."

Before I could say more, she changed the subject. "So the boys pick up a suicide in Midtown, an office in the old United Bank tower on Central. Subject named Matt Pennington. He hanged himself from a doorknob with two neckties."

My middle wound in a knot but I kept my face neutral. "Did he?"

"They were willing to buy it. I called it bullshit. No note. His computer is missing. No cellphone. Who doesn't have a cellphone attached to them at all times now? I thought about your girl, Miss 'Suicided.' Then I found the fake file cabinets. I pulled them open with a pry bar. It wasn't easy. But there's a very elaborate safe behind them. We've got techs working to open it right now. What do you want to bet we find some diamonds?"

I said, "Who's Matt Pennington?"

"You tell me." She sat and leaned forward on her elbows.

"The name hasn't come up."

"Liar."

I kept my eyes straight on her and repeated the sentence.

"Well, you're not making enough trouble, Mapstone. Pennington was a Navy SEAL assigned to the Mexican marines on drug interdiction. Five years ago they tried to nab Chapo Guzman, the head of the Sinaloa Cartel..."

"I know who he is."

"Intel said that he was staying at a mansion on the Gulf of California. They went in from the ocean and immediately came under fire. Two Mexican marines were killed. Chapo got away. The bad guys had advanced information about the raid. The marines are the best agency in Mexico. I don't know what went wrong, but Pennington was assigned to a desk job and then left the service."

"So he was blamed."

She nodded. "I called in a favor from an old boyfriend in the DEA. Don't look at me that way, you jerk. Lots of men find me attractive. I wouldn't sleep with you if we were the only two humans left on a dying planet. If I hadn't had sex for a hundred years and you showed up at my doorstep naked with a rose in your teeth. If you had Old Glory draped over your face…"

"I get it," I said. "Your DEA buddy."

"He said Pennington was in the cartel's pocket. Specifically Sinaloa. But they could never prove it."

"So why did he end up here?"

"His mother was sick. Get this, he worked in a call center. The turnover rate at most of those places is one hundred percent. But he drove a new BMW every year and he had this secret office in Midtown. No name on the door."

"Now a dead man inside."

She leaned back.

"I showed you mine. You show me yours."

So I did, with only a few omissions.

When I was finished, she liked me a little better.

"That explains a lot," she said.

"Such as?"

"Such as the call I got this afternoon from Horace Mann. He wanted to know the whereabouts of a man named Matt Pennington."

"What did you tell him?"

"I said we'd check."

I asked her why she didn't tell him that Pennington was dead.

"Because I don't trust feds. Everything you told me shows why I'm right."

After she left, I made some phone calls, used the badge, and took a drive.

Chapter Thirty-eight

When I went in Lindsey's room after seven the next morning, she was breathing on her own. The ventilator was still there, but the tube was out of her mouth. The gauze patches were off her eyes.

If anything had come from last night's scheduled meeting in Scottsdale between "Matt Pennington" and the man on the phone, nobody had told me.

This was infinitely better than clearing a case. I sat and said, "Thank you, God."

Thumbing through Emily Dickinson, I found what seemed appropriate: *Angels In the Early Morning*.

It was only eight lines. I read them with a slow, exhausted reverence.

"…the flowers they bear along."

Those last words were in Lindsey's voice.

I raised my head and saw those blue eyes I loved, looking at me.

"Dave, my chest hurts…a lot. What happened?"

"I'm going to get the nurses."

She reached feebly and I took her hand.

"Wait. Stay with me, Dave. What happened to your eye? Where am I?"

"Mister Joe's"

"What happened?"

"You were shot. Do you remember?"

Her eyes closed and my first reaction was fear, but the heart monitor was steady and her chest and rising and falling.

Her eyes fluttered open.

"It hurts, Dave. I remember…fajitas. And you went with the deputies…" Her voice was raspy and she licked her lips.

I was relieved. I had been so afraid her last memories would be of our terrible fight.

She said, "Wait. Where's Peralta?"

"I haven't found him yet."

She struggled to keep her eyes open.

"You've got to find him. He's in great danger. Pennington…"

I prompted. "Matt Pennington?"

She nodded. "While you were gone to see Meltdown, I did some searching. Don't be mad."

"I'm not mad."

"He's DEA. Pennington is." She laughed and winced. "I sound like Yoda. Pennington is deep cover. Nobody but the top echelon of the agency knows."

I thought about Ed Cartwright.

She struggled to get the words out. "Pennington is close to the cartels and handles diamond shipments. But it's a cover. He's active DEA. You're crying, Dave."

I had been too transfixed by Lindsey awake and talking to feel the tears running down my cheeks.

"My mouth is so dry."

"Let me get a nurse," I said. "I love you more than anything. I promise once we get through this we'll live a different life. We'll read books." I was babbling.

She tried to smile. "Love you, too, Dave. I'm sorry I ruined your dark blue blazer. I know you liked it."

"Lindsey, don't worry about…"

Suddenly her words caught up with me. She had already fallen unconscious Saturday night by the time I thought of using the blazer to staunch the bleeding. She was out. I could barely feel a pulse.

I must not have heard her right.

She tightened her grip on my hand.

"I saw you pull it off and roll me to the side...put it under me. I was floating. Sounds crazy, right? And I saw your parents... and Robin and my mother. Dave, I saw our daughter. It was so sweet and I knew things were going to be all right." She talked faster and faster, then dropped to a whisper. "You think I'm..." She searched for the word. "...hallucinating. I'm not. It was real. But I had to come back to you."

"Thank you."

In the next seconds, nurses were hovering.

"We need to control her pain," one said.

"Dave," Lindsey stroked my hand. "Find Peralta."

"I don't want to leave you."

For the first time, she was able to look around and take in all the tubes, cables, and machines. That sweet, sardonic smile returned. "Doesn't look like I'm going anywhere. I'll be here...."

Then the pain med was flowing into the IV and she went back to sleep.

Chapter Thirty-nine

Sharon was waiting when I stepped outside. I told her about Lindsey and she hugged me so tightly I could barely breathe.

"David, this is the best gift. It's worth more than all the rough in the world."

Her arms fell away and her face suddenly went slack. My black eye, which had been feeling much better, was the target of thousands of little arrows.

"What did you say?"

But I had heard her fine. A tight circle knew the diamond shipment was valuable, gem-quality rough. There were her husband, Horace Mann, and Strawberry Death. The Russians and Cartwright. Me. Sharon was not among them.

Sharon began crying. "Oh, David. I messed up so bad."

"What the hell?"

"This wasn't supposed to happen."

I grabbed her arm hard enough to leave a bruise and steered her twenty feet down the hall, out of hearing of the uniformed officer by the ICU entrance.

"What wasn't supposed to happen? And how the hell do you know about *rough*? You said rough."

"Lindsey was never supposed to get hurt…"

"You were in on it with him."

She shook her head. "No. Not at first." She stammered. "Well, not much. Friday morning, he told me he was going on a special case. He gave me a prepaid cell phone and told me to only use it if he called or texted me on it. He told me not to be home between ten a.m. and two p.m., to be near the Piestawa Parkway, and not to trust anyone but you. Then he was out the door."

"But you didn't think to tell me this until now?"

"He didn't want you to know about this case. He thought you'd be safer if you didn't."

"And dumb." I shook my head.

She said, "He called me on his new cell around noon Friday. Now I know it was a little after the robbery. Something had gone wrong. A woman had tried to take them while he was changing the tag on his truck. I met him in north Phoenix and he gave the diamonds to me."

"Where are the diamonds right now?" I demanded.

"They're beneath the spare tire in my car. In socks."

My whole face throbbed. "What about when the FBI-executed the search warrant?"

"They were all over the house, but didn't spend much time on my car."

I tried to shake off the shock of the lie. I asked her what Peralta's plan was.

"I don't know. He said wait for his text. If everything was clear, he would call."

I hemmed her in with my arms and called her a liar.

"I'm not! He said the less I knew, the better. And there wasn't a lot of time. He wanted to get on the road."

I asked if it were possible he meant for her to give the rough to Matt Pennington? She said she didn't know, only that she was to follow his instructions. He was afraid the FBI might be able to pick up her prepaid cell if she used it more than once or twice.

When he thought things were safe, he would send her a text with the words, "ready for dry cleaning pickup?"

If someone else saw her phone, it would seem innocuous. If she were in trouble, she would respond "no." If she were safe, she would text "yes," and he would then call with fresh instructions for her. It was a more elaborate version of the asterisk signal between Lindsey and me. But his text had not yet come.

For me, pieces came together.

Not only had the original plan been blown when Peralta encountered Strawberry Death, he also began to doubt even Eric Pham or one of his agents. Peralta was careful that way, seeing possibilities five moves ahead. So he had gone to ground. His worry must have only increased when he didn't hear from the real Pennington.

I pulled out my iPhone and read out the number I had called and Peralta had briefly answered.

I said, "Is that the number you have?"

She nodded. "He made me memorize it. It's not even in the new phone."

"I called that number and he acted as if he didn't know me."

"He hadn't texted me and I hadn't responded," she said. "He probably thought you were under duress to make the call." She thought about it and asked how I found his secret cell number.

I told her.

She dropped her head. "Oh, no. No!"

"Why didn't you tell me?"

"I couldn't," she said. "Then you would have known I had the diamonds."

"So all the way up to Ash Fork and back, we had them in the trunk."

"Yes."

"In Ash Fork, the old cowboy told me he got into a car with some men. What about that?"

She sighed. "He told me there was a man up there who would let him borrow a car and lie convincingly to the FBI about him getting in a car. He used to run a hunting lodge near Hell Canyon where Mike would go, back before I made him stop killing innocent animals. They remained friends."

Orville Grainer. A patient of my grandfather, Doc Mapstone, my ass.

I slapped the wall in frustration, but my voice was resigned. "Oh, Sharon…"

"The landline was a lie, too. There is no landline. I made up the Paco stuff because he was adamant about you knowing there was real danger, after he was nearly ambushed in the garage."

Who could lie better than a shrink?

"What about Saturday night, when somebody called you to the hospital?' Was that Mike?"

"No," she said. "I swear, David. That was a voice I didn't recognize."

She kept apologizing, tried to put her hand on my shoulder, but I brushed it away. I made no attempt to comfort her.

"So why the hell did you beg me to find him? What was that about?"

She shrugged. "I lost my nerve. He didn't say anything about going to the High Country. I panicked."

"But not enough to tell me the whole truth."

She shook her head.

I said, "What happens if you text him the key word first, before you hear from him?"

She hesitated. "I don't know. He was afraid the whole plan is compromised. He made me promise to wait for his signal before I did anything, including involving you."

I thought about that. This would be a good time for a sensible person to walk back over to Johnnie's and knock on the back door. Peralta must be overreacting. Or contact Kate Vare, bring in the entire cavalry. There was Ed Cartwright, too.

But for various reasons none of those options felt right. Cartwright had said he needed to lay low. The local law would muscle me out of the way and wreck the mission, which was to bring down the person who stole the diamonds. Pham…He was trustworthy, right? After the past six days, I trusted fewer and fewer people. I recalled the agents inside the former hotdog place watching me. Pham might be penetrated and not even know it. Then there was Strawberry Death. She belonged to me.

So I told Sharon to text "DM is bringing the dry cleaning per the dictaphone." That should make it clear enough.

I watched as she typed the words and pressed send.

In only a few seconds the text appeared. "Yes."

"What are you going to do?" she asked.

"Bring the rough."

"But I don't even know where he is."

"I have a good idea," I said. "Give me your car keys." After I pocketed them, I added, "Watch over Lindsey."

"But what if someone follows you?"

"That's the idea."

As I walked away, she was leaning against the wall sobbing.

Chapter Forty

I took the long skywalk to the parking garage, pulled the black duffel bag of weapons out of the Honda Prelude, and found Sharon's car. I resisted the temptation to open the trunk. Out of the corner of my eye was a black SUV. So I tossed the duffel into the passenger's side and settled into the driver's seat. The fine German engineering cradled my hindquarters and made me realize how old everything in the Prelude was, right down to the seats.

When I pulled onto Third Avenue going south, the SUV was right behind me. But I made it a point to put down the ragtop so it was obvious Sharon was not behind the wheel. Here was a test about whether Mann's FBI watchers took me seriously. Sure enough, by the time I had gone five blocks, the SUV turned left. Somebody had given an order.

Somebody might have a tracking device on the car anyway.

At the house, I changed into black jeans, black turtleneck, and Timberland boots. I moved quickly. That was a very expensive car sitting in my driveway.

Back in the convertible, I adjusted my cell so its GPS was working. My dark device was now trackable. Then I put the top up and drove, crossing over to Third Street and taking the ramp down to the Papago Freeway, which ran though Midtown under a park. Crossing all the lanes of traffic, I made it to the Loop 202 exit and went straight east on the Red Mountain Freeway, past the north end of Tempe, Town Lake, Sun Devil Stadium, lots of shopping schlock, and getting off at Country Club Drive in Mesa. I turned left, crossed the Salt River, and the road became the Beeline Highway.

The rain had scrubbed away the smog and the day was spectacular. Ahead of me towered Four Peaks and the Mazatzal Mountains. Ahead of me were the High Country and the town of Payson.

At the top of the hour, I listened to the radio news. Fresh developments on the Saturday night shooting of a deputy's wife. The suspect was Amy Lisa Russell, a former Mountie. You could go on the station's Web site to see her photo. Police were "tight-lipped" about a motive.

The motive that would satisfy a prosecutor was the stones.

Vare had invested hours in badgering the truth out of RCMP headquarters in Ottawa. Canada is a major producer of dia-monds. While Amy Russell was chief of security at the Ekati mine, she compiled an impressive record of installing ever-better anti-theft technology and detaining employees who tried to sneak out little bits of rough.

It was only months after Russell resigned that mine officials realized that over a year between fifteen million and twenty mil-lion dollars in gem-quality rough had gone missing. The thefts happened a little at a time, but they added up impressively. Further investigation showed that the new security measures had proved essential to cloaking the drip-drip-drip heist. Only then was Russell seen as the obvious suspect and the RCMP was called in.

But she was missing, last known address in Vancouver.

I didn't know how her stones ended up as FBI evidence. Or how Horace Mann figured in. Was he working with her and the Russians? Or Pamela Grayson really was Suspect Number One. Maybe Mann was innocent.

As to Amy Russell's motive that would satisfy curious fellow humans…perhaps even she didn't know. If I were a hot-shit Mountie, I wouldn't throw away my career for diamonds. But then I hadn't suffered through finding my family massacred. I didn't feel this supernatural pull of the stones that locked onto so many, made them willing to steal, kill, take every risk. Changed them. And who the hell knows why anybody does anything?

The next few hours might tell.

My phone rang. Kate Vare.

"Where are you?" she asked.

"Lindsey woke up," I said.

"That's good," she said. "I want to interview her."

"Tomorrow. She's in a lot of pain. They only let me talk to her for a few minutes before she fell asleep. She didn't remember the shooting. Where are you?"

"Pennington's office. We got in the safe. He had fifteen million in cash, twenty million in euro bearer bonds, some diamonds."

After a long pause, she added, "He had a list of numbers. I'm guessing they're offshore bank accounts."

"I bet you find one for an FBI agent named Pamela Grayson. Or Horace Mann."

"That will require bringing in the FBI, but yes." She sounded very happy.

Then I told her what I had learned about Pennington's actual job.

She didn't answer.

I said, "So contact your DEA friend. They're not going to like losing their own."

She gave a heavy sigh. "This is a hell of a mess."

The desert lowlands fell away as I passed the abortion of Fountain Hills—I remembered when it was a lovely saguaro forest—then the rugged enchantment of Red Mountain and the Indian casino and the cottonwood-lined Verde River at Fort McDowell.

The car climbed effortlessly through millions of years of geology. Fantastic shapes appeared beside the highway. Cones and ribs, spires and mesas, crags that looked like human faces and nearly vertical walls. Steep climbs reached thresholds, followed by wide expanses and then more steep hills, ravines, and tight passages.

It was all here to see, the way time had pitted one element against the other to create our fleeting moment. Broken ground was cut by dry washes and arroyos. As I drove, precipitous cliffs and sharp drops and fold upon fold of rough mountains constantly remade the vista. Cactuses gave way to scrubby trees and grasslands fighting for their share of water. Overhead, the sky was enormous and deep blue.

I was lousy company on an Arizona road trip. Lindsey loved for us to drive around the state, armed with a detailed atlas and books on roadside history, geology, and Audubon guides. Yes, when it came to pleasure, she often liked physical books. But she was younger. I knew what was lost, what this country was like before six-and-a-half million people moved here. Fountain Hills was only one example. I became especially surly in Sedona, which I remembered as an empty place without a single traffic light. Alone, I was little better. The Beeline had been re-engineered into a divided-highway marvel. But that only allowed more people to profane the desert.

Around me was the Tonto Basin, land of many stories and much history. Zane Grey had written a novel of the same name. This had long been ranching country, once the whites had wrested it from the Apache. There were a few old mines, but they didn't have the riches of the territory to the west, around Prescott and Jerome, so they quickly played out. It had also been a hiding place for outlaws and rough territory that a lawman entered at his peril.

The Tonto National Forest began a few miles back and, for now, kept out the developers. The Bush Highway connected. To the south was Punkin Center. As a boy, I had loved stopping at the little store there. It was like something out of a cowboy movie. Ahead, the former cavalry watering hole of Sunflower was gone in a few seconds

Up here, if you looked past the divided highway, it was still possible to catch glimpses of the majesty of the land, the lonely, sublime American West and Arizona High Country. Here were fleeting vistas—once they were so abundant—without a single thing made by humans.

When Theodore Roosevelt had come to the Grand Canyon more than a century before, he had said, "Leave it as it is. You cannot improve on it. The ages have been at work on it and man can only mar it."

Now some grifters wanted to develop land right outside the Grand Canyon National Park boundary. How long before they privatized the park itself?

I had no time to dwell on the land or the past. The present demanded my entire attention.

Traffic was very light. A few hotdogs in big pickups blew past at ninety. If anyone was deliberately following me, he was very good.

Peralta had intended for me, and by extension, Lindsey, to have nothing to do with this operation. But, as Trotsky said, "You may not be interested in war, but war is interested in you."

Now I was at war.

If my hunches proved wrong, this war would be lost.

I thought about a book I had recently read on the Donner Party, trapped in the Sierra Nevada in 1846, reduced to cannibalism. The author had argued that many of the people made decisions that seemed rational at the time, until it was too late and winter caught them early. Then they had to forge on, no matter.

One of the sentences stayed with me: "The trap clicks behind."

When did the trap click behind me? Somewhere on this highway? Or much, much earlier?

I touched the car window. It was cold. Now all I could do was forge on.

Chapter Forty-one

The highway made one last upward leap and I entered the forest and then Payson. When I was a boy, this had been a trifling place with maybe a thousand residents. I remembered log trucks rumbling by. The town, with its storied cowboys and saloons, had only recently been opened to the outside world, the highway being paved in 1959.

Now logging was long gone, the population was fifteen times larger, and Phoenicians used it to flee the bludgeon of the summer heat. This had not made it better.

The forest looked sickly. Climate change and the bark beetle were slowly killing it. To the north was the largest virgin stand of Ponderosa pines in the world. How many times I had gone camping there with the Boy Scouts and later as an adult. Now I wondered if it would still exist in a couple of generations.

Mammoth wildfires were common now, another difference from when I was young. Land swaps in the National Forest had allowed subdivisions to be built in the pines. Almost every year, millions of dollars were spent to keep these tract houses from burning down.

A few years ago, the state's worst fire up to that time erupted to the east. It began after a woman had a fight with her boss, or was he her boyfriend? She stalked off into the woods in shorts and flip-flops with only a towel, cigarettes, and a lighter. When she became lost, she used the lighter to set a signal fire, or so she said. By the time the fire was out, more than 730 square miles had been reduced to ashes.

The ground was also perfectly dry. January in the High Country used to mean snow. The mountain snowpack melted in the spring and filled the reservoirs for Phoenix's water supply. But we were getting less snow, had been for several years. I could only lose friends in Arizona by starting a conversation about climate change. Even Peralta didn't believe it was real.

Amid the grotesqueries, freak shows, and fears, however, the Mogollon Rim still kept watch.

Newcomers had to learn to pronounce it correctly, MUG-EE-on, like they learned Gila was HEE-la and the iconic cactus was a Sa-WAR-oh. Or they didn't learn.

The escarpment dropped as much as four thousand feet straight down from the Colorado Plateau. From here, in the late afternoon light, the Kaibab limestone gleamed alabaster. Above it, clouds were moving in.

Seeing it again, inhaling the tart smell of the pines, reminded me of my Boy Scout days. Camp Geronimo was north of here, at the foot of the Rim. My troop, which met at the Luke-Greenway American Legion Post near downtown, went there every summer. After dinner by the campfire, the scoutmasters would tell us stories of the Mogollon Monster, Arizona's version of Bigfoot. Then they would lead us on night hikes. Even with our flashlights, it was the blackest dark I had ever experienced.

All grown up now, I settled for an early dinner at Wendy's and then pulled into a deserted section of the enormous lot of the Walmart Supercenter to consolidate my load. Far fewer people lived here through the winter.

Stepping out, I slid on my leather jacket. The temperature was at least thirty degrees cooler than in Phoenix. I used the key fob to pop the trunk of the Lexus. The inside was immaculate, but sure enough two white athletic socks sat in the spare tire compartment. I lifted them out with effort, holding the bottom to keep the contents from fraying the threads of the cuff ribbing. They were heavy as hell. Back in the car, I indulged in feeling though the fabric. The contents indeed felt rough. Then I unzipped the duffel and hefted them inside, careful not to let the contents scratch the guns.

Yesterday, I had driven to the Beatitudes on Glendale Avenue. It was a large assisted-living center not far from where Susan's Diner once stood, one of our cop hangouts. Inside, it seemed clean and well kept. I showed my star and they led me to a room.

Mrs. Pennington's room.

The woman inside was so frail it looked as if she might shatter from the slightest breeze. If old age was a shipwreck, as Charles de Gaulle said, then she was clinging to the last fragment of timber. And this was before I walked in.

Kate Vare was thorough, but no one had bothered to tell Matt Pennington's mother that he was dead at age forty-five. I had done the next-of-kin notifications before but somehow this was harder. I thought about what Cartwright had said. I'm getting too old for this, too.

"He was a good boy, my Matt," she said over and over. I agreed with her. Now that I knew the information Lindsey had hacked about his undercover work, I should have said it with more conviction. What a hell to outlive your only child.

I didn't ask for much: only if she had a key to her cabin in Payson. She did. I took it and promised to return it. I already knew of the cabin's existence and location from a helpful clerk at the Gila County courthouse.

Now I studied my map. I was a map nerd, had been since discovering Grandfather's subscription to *National Geographic*, back when each issue contained one. So I could have entered the address into the advanced GPS device in the Lexus. But no, I would use the paper map. I was a dinosaur.

Before driving away, I rechecked the rounds in my Colt Python and slid a Ka-Bar combat knife on my belt. I loaded a carbine and shotgun from the duffle and made sure my Maglite batteries were good.

Be prepared.

With the little light left, I drove west-northwest out of town. The many cheaply built newer houses slowly fell away as the road turned to gravel and the pines enveloped me. Off to the left side, the east fork of the Verde River ran as a narrow stream.

The Pennington cabin emerged off to my right. Trees and underbrush nearly concealed the house and the nearest neighbor was a quarter of a mile east. It was a modest A-frame, probably from the 1960s. The downstairs had a log facing and two simple windows on either side of a door with a porch in front. The windows were draped. Above, the beams and rafters looked hand-hewn.

No lights were visible. A junker car was parked in the dirt beside the house. Orville Grainer's vehicle, I assumed. I drove on to an intersection with a dirt Forest Service road, turned around and waited fifteen minutes. I used the Steiner binoculars to study the road and forest. No one was behind me.

I crept back to the A-frame and pulled in behind the old car, very conscious of the breathing making my chest rise and fall.

Outside, the air was colder and clouds were overhead. It was nearly dark, a sensation exaggerated by the four-story-tall trees. I hefted out the heavy duffle and pulled out the Colt Python, then walked to the front door. Why not? My feet crunched over pine needles and pinecones, then went up to the porch reached by three steps.

The door was solid wood with a peephole. You never stand directly in front of a door. That's a good way to get shot. So I stood beside it, remembering another time and another door. My great-grandmother had ESP. That was the family story, at least. When she dreamed of flowing water in a river, someone she loved was going to die.

I couldn't claim such a gift, but when I was a young deputy I was the first officer to respond to an unknown trouble call. I had approached a darkened house with a peephole door and my Python drawn. The door had been opened three inches and beyond was only darkness. But something, some small voice inside me, had said, *Don't open that door*. So I didn't. It turned out a man with a shotgun had murdered his family and had been sitting on the sofa with the weapon pointed at the door.

And I heard that same voice this time.

But I ignored it, stood to the side, knelt down on my haunches to make myself less of a target, and knocked.

"It's open!" Peralta's voice.

No need for the key after all.

I turned the knob, hearing the rhythmic purr of water tumbling over slick rocks in the river across the road, and stepped inside.

Chapter Forty-two

"What took you so long?"

I only heard his voice in front of me. The room was black. I lowered the duffel bag to the floor and closed the door.

"You asshole," I said. "I could have been here a long time ago but you said I had the wrong number and hung up. When you called back, you wouldn't talk to Cartwright, either."

"I meant the drive up here," he said mildly, all innocence. "I can get from downtown Phoenix to Payson in an hour. I assume Sharon told you why we had to wait."

"She did."

"Do you think I'm a diamond thief, Mapstone?"

I slid the Python into its holster. "No."

"Well, crap. I did my best."

"Everybody else seems to believe you are."

"That's good. What about the woman?"

I told him she had shot and nearly killed Lindsey.

He cursed. He actually apologized, a rarity. If he hadn't, I might have strangled him.

He said, "I was trying to keep you both safe."

"Right. But you were nervous enough that you left me the message on the dictaphone."

My eyes adjusted enough to see him sitting in an armchair facing the door. He had several days of stubble growing out on his face but otherwise looked good. In front of him was a steamer trunk coffee table. Three straight-back chairs were arrayed in the room. Behind him was the kitchen. Up above was a railing for the sleeping loft.

"No electricity?" I asked.

"It's on. Better to keep things dark. Pham roped me in on this case. The plan was for me to check into a motel on Black Canyon and wait for Pennington. He would contact the Russians and we would have a meet to exchange the diamonds for cash. If everything went well, that would be when the bad-apple agent would show himself and Pham's people could move in and bag them all. But it seemed like there were a dozen ways it would blow up in our faces."

"When did it happen?"

"The moment that woman tried to ambush me in the parking garage. I got rid of the tracker in my boot. Then I made up my own Plan B. Get out of town and wait."

"For?"

"For you to find Pennington."

I shook my head. "You took a hell of a chance. What if I hadn't found your note in Flagstaff?"

"Then Sharon would have found a way to tell you," he said. "Anyway, I knew you couldn't resist the trains. Look, if I had told you about this ahead of time, you not only would have been in danger, but you couldn't have stopped yourself from immediately jumping supersonic. I needed to slow you down, but keep you going."

"You're a devious man."

He smiled. "Tell me I'm wrong about you. This is why I texted you so you wouldn't ask questions at the outset."

"That was the first thing that seemed suspicious," I said.

"I'm not an analog, Mapstone. This is also why I dropped Pennington's name but no other information. If everything went well, I'd be back in the office before you could find him. If it didn't, he'd know how to contact me, who was clean, who was dirty and we could find a way out. Only he and I knew about this cabin. But he never showed up."

"He's dead. The woman killed him." I filled in some details about Amy Russell.

He was silent for a long time. I found a wooden chair and sat.

"Well, if the world didn't suck, we'd all fall off," he said. "Do you have the rough?"

"In the bag. Why was the weapons compartment empty in your truck? That bugged Horace Mann."

"Good. I cleaned it out and transferred the stuff to Orville's car. Guns, food, beer, and cigars. All the essentials."

"I did a check of the Danger Room. Nothing was missing."

"I brought guns from home," he said, "Anyway, I made this place as secure as I could. Only one way in or out. Solid walls unless you're upstairs and they start shooting through the glass. Do you trust Pham?"

I thought about it and answered yes. "He was tracking you with a drone on Friday. They screwed up in not realizing it couldn't pass over Sky Harbor airspace. That's how he lost contact. Then you disappeared. I believe him. I think Ed believes him."

"How is he?"

"He's fine. Pissed that you shot him."

"He'll get over it. We needed to protect his cover at all costs."

He stood and walked to the bag, unzipped it and pulled out the socks. He hefted them in his big hands and shook his head.

"So do you have Plan C?"

I said, "Only the hope that I was followed by the bad guys."

He nodded and pulled an M-4 carbine with an optic sight and laser from the bag. I had already put a magazine in. He locked and loaded a round into the chamber and handed the rifle to me. Next he passed over two extra magazines. I put them in my pockets.

"If you're right, it won't be long," he said.

I was about to say something when a high-pitched tone sounded.

"Motion detector," he said. "I set up a couple outside. Get over there on the stairs. Take the duffle. Move."

I scrambled four steps up to a landing, turned, and took another four. It put me in total darkness with an unobstructed view of the living room. By the time I had taken up the position, Peralta was sitting back in the armchair with a blanket over his lap.

Four raps came on the door.

Once again, Peralta said two words. "It's open!"

I thought about the flash bang grenade in Cartwright's RV. If that was about to be thrown into the room, we were screwed. If an FBI tactical team followed with orders to shoot on sight, we were double screwed.

Instead, a large silhouette stepped inside.

He said, "Don't move an eyelash."

It was Horace Mann. He stepped in three paces and stopped, a semiautomatic pistol trained on Peralta. I silently switched the safety off the M-4 and took dead aim at Mann's head. Nobody was going to use body armor against me again.

Peralta said, "I don't think we've been introduced."

This would be the time for Horace Mann as good guy to produce his credentials and identify himself.

Instead, he said, "Where's Mapstone?"

"I had to kill him," Peralta said.

"You're one cold-blooded dude, Peralta." Mann used his left hand to swing the door closed. The latch snapped shut.

"Body's in the kitchen if you want to see."

"I'll stay right here," he said. "I believe you have something that belongs to me."

The athletic socks were two feet to his left.

Peralta said, "That something belongs to the FBI."

"Nobody knows who those stones belong to," Mann said. "That's the beauty of it. The rough was shipped FedEx from Vancouver to Seattle, concealed with some student rock collections. It was an accident they were ever discovered. The package came apart and Customs got curious. The diamonds were turned over to the Seattle field office, their investigation went nowhere, and they ended up in evidence."

"Where you took them."

Mann hesitated.

"That's how it went down," Peralta said. "Otherwise, you'd be here with a SWAT team and a dozen agents."

"It was easy as hell to spend ten thousand on a tech at the evidence center to look the other way while I took the diamonds and substituted junk. Then sprinkle some bread crumbs to throw suspicion on another agent. I was surprised they discovered it missing, but by that time it was with the Russians and headed to Phoenix."

"Why didn't you just take them?"

"And do what?" He looked like he wanted to spit. "Cut glass? The Russians had the means to move them here. They already owed me."

"Not a fifty-fifty split?"

Mann grinned grimly. "Not even close. But they had a fence here who could turn the rough into real money."

"Offshore account?" Peralta asked. "Or will you piss it away on your gambling habit? I'm surprised the Bureau didn't know about that."

Mann licked his lips. He was starting to get rattled. "It will be a nice supplement to my pension. Officially, the rough will never be recovered. When we find your and Mapstone's bodies, I'll theorize that one of the cartels got to you first and took the diamonds. I can't fix everything for the Bureau. I can finish out my career as SAC in Phoenix and spend half my time on the golf course. Maybe play some poker, too, asshole. Losing the diamonds has been a huge embarrassment. The Bureau will want to move on."

"Where are your agents?"

"Working," Mann said. "It's my day off. Figured I'd follow your boy and he'd lead me to you. Where are they?"

Peralta didn't answer. The room pulsed with the gravitational pulls of two big men. Mann scanned the room, ignored the socks.

"Why did you kill Mapstone?" he said. "I thought he was your friend."

Peralta shrugged. "He brought me the rough. That's all I needed."

In the dim light, I could see the confusion course through the veins on Mann's high forehead.

"What are you talking about?"

"I handed off the diamonds back in Phoenix," Peralta said. "Did you think I was going to keep them on me? That would have made it too easy for you. You're playing in the big leagues now."

"I'm here now." He stepped closer. Now he was about five feet from Peralta. He kept the gun on him.

Peralta said, "They're on the floor beside you, in those socks."

Mann quickly glanced to his left then refocused on Peralta. Five long seconds passed and he couldn't resist. He backed up to the wall and knelt down, feeling through the fabric of the socks with his left hand. He lifted one and gave an ugly smile.

"That's sweet. All that money inside a three-dollar pair of socks." He stood. "I sure don't like it that I can't see your hands."

Peralta didn't answer.

"I said, I don't like it that I can't see your hands." His tone was commanding.

"My hands are cold," Peralta said. "What makes you think you're going to get away with this?"

Mann moved forward again, gun at Peralta's middle.

"What makes me think I'm going to get away with it? I have so far."

"What about the Mountie?"

Mann looked confused.

"Those are the Mountie's stones," Peralta said. "She still wants them. Made me a promise to kill everybody I loved until I turned them over. Probably willing to kill the ones I dislike, too. She's not willing to move on."

He cursed under his breath. "I don't know what the hell you're talking about but I'd say the Mountie's out of luck. And so are you. You're a fugitive and if I shoot you where you sit, nobody's going to ask questions." His voice turned to a shout. "Now show me your hands!"

The blanket fell away and Peralta had his .40 caliber Glock trained on Mann.

"Now, hold on there," Mann said. "I'm a federal agent."

"You admitted to stealing fifteen million in diamonds," Peralta said. "You can't have it both ways."

Mann's eyes widened and he knew he was caught.

"Yes," Peralta said. "Everything you said has been recorded. Thank God for stupid criminals."

I could have taken him down right then but I waited.

"We could reach an understanding." Mann tried to soften his tone. "Half and half. I let you go. Clear your name. Blame the cartel."

"Tall order."

"I can make it happen." Mann's voice was no longer steady. "My fence is the best. He can set you up with a nice nest egg."

"He's dead."

Mann's gray pallor intensified.

"You killed him, too?"

"The girl did."

He opened his mouth and closed it without making a sound.

"So," Peralta said, "we have this multi-ethnic standoff and the only way to end it is for you to slowly put your weapon on the floor, back away, and put your hands behind your head."

There was another way and I saw Mann's gun arm start to tense.

I lit him with the laser. A red dot appeared on his forehead.

I said, "You'll be dead before you can squeeze that trigger."

When he had set the gun on the floor, he said, "What are you going to do now? I don't see any help on the way. You're both civilians. You can't hold me or arrest me. And I don't think you have the balls to shoot an unarmed FBI agent. So I'm walking out that door."

"That would be a big mistake." Peralta was up and roughly pushing him to the floor, handcuffing him. His face was pointed in the direction of the socks, which he continued to eye with lust.

"You're both nothing but civilians! This is kidnapping!"

I walked down the stairs, cradling the M-4.

"That's actually not true," I said. "Thanks to your friend Chris Melton, I'm a Maricopa County deputy sheriff with statewide powers of arrest."

Peralta glanced at me curiously.

I smiled and read Mann his rights.

Chapter Forty-three

We placed Mann in the seat of one of the straight-back chairs. He had stopped talking. That "anything you say can be used against you" part can have that effect. Peralta called Eric Pham.

Maybe twenty minutes passed before the knock at the door.

I looked at Peralta. "What about your motion detectors?"

He didn't answer. He already had his Glock out.

The house was still dark. I moved to the window to the right of the door and carefully pulled back the drape.

"It's alright." I moved to the door. "It's Cartwright."

He was somebody who could identify and bypass motion detectors.

I was at the door and turning the knob when Peralta said, "Don't…"

But it was too late.

Ed Cartwright stood before me with a gun in my face.

Behind him it was snowing.

"Get that expression off your face, David," he said. "You look like a six-year-old whose kitten just died."

I hardened my eyes and made my dry mouth form words. "What are you doing, Ed? Put the gun down."

"Step away from the door," he said.

I didn't move.

His sling was gone. His appearance was barely controlled fury.

I felt Peralta next to me.

Cartwright spoke through clenched teeth. "Put your gun down, Mike."

Peralta calmly drawled, "You know that's not going to happen, Ed. What the hell are you doing?"

Cartwright kept his weapon up, the barrel straight at my chest.

It finally fell together. Here was the "other" from Eric Pham's white board. I said, "It was you who called Sharon to the hospital when Lindsey was shot. Did you send the woman who did it?"

"Of course not, David. I was doing you a favor, sending Sharon to help you."

I didn't feel grateful. "Then you called me when I was in Pennington's office. It was you, wanting to set up a meet with him. You must have thought Pennington would know how to contact Peralta. I should have realized it later, the way you changed your voice when Peralta called me back, when we were standing in the parking lot. The 'Apache Mortgage' shit."

"You're a little slow, son."

"You were in on this with Mann."

"No. This was my play. All I had to do was watch the Bureau get tangled up with itself. Overthink and overplan. Try to blame this poor Grayson woman who pissed off her supervisors. But from the first time he talked to me, when I was in the hospital after the shooting at the mall, I knew he was the crook."

My hands felt heavy and useless at my side. "What does that make you? You're a lawman, Ed. You've served your entire life with honor."

"You were misinformed," he said. "The FBI made me into a renegade. The piece-of-shit disgraced Indian. They profited from making me into that man. Now it's my turn."

"It's only fifteen million, before you fence it! That makes no sense." I was arguing personal finance with an armed man, probably not in the best mood.

"It's enough," he said.

Peralta spoke in a calm cadence, "Step away, Mapstone. Ed, lower your weapon or I'll kill you where you stand. You know I'll do it."

He said, "And I'll kill your boy. If that's the way you decide to play it."

Peralta spoke with icy calm. "We go way back, Ed. Don't make me do this."

"Don't make me shoot him," Cartwright said, indicating me. His finger was inside the trigger guard, on the trigger. My insides were turbulent with dread. I forced it down.

Cartwright kept his eyes on me "You did a good job of disappearing, Mike. Pham doesn't have a clue where you are. But David did a better job of finding you. Now I'll take those stones."

"He's going to kill us all!" Mann's voice came behind me.

"Nobody's going to die," Cartwright said. "Mann, you're a disgrace. Me, I've got obligations that matter. The diamonds are a means to an end."

My fear fell away and an icy calm descended. I can't explain exactly why.

"The fucking diamonds," I said. "There's got to be another way."

"No." His eyes were black behind the heavy lids.

"They're right here," I said. I slowly stooped and picked up the socks, then stood and held one in each hand. "The rough is inside these."

He briefly studied them. "Step away from the door, David!"

I stepped aside.

Suddenly somebody spat behind Cartwright. That was the sound, at least. His eyes registered surprise and then the pupils went wide as he fell forward, the front of his shirt filling with blood, and he crashed face-first into the floor.

Amy Russell stood at the bottom of the porch steps, another H&K semiautomatic in her hands. She was dressed in black, the only color being her pale face and the halo of strawberry blond hair in a tight bun.

"Down!" I yelled as I dropped the diamonds. I heard a crash as Mann forced his chair to tilt and fall. My holster snapped as I pulled out the Python and went prone on the floor beside Cartwright. Another spit and a bullet sped over my head, fracturing the wall behind me.

I fired. The big Colt made its explosive sound. Peralta shot at the same time, three quick concussions.

I looked into the snow and she was gone.

Chapter Forty-four

Peralta yelled for me to stay put but I was already crossing the porch in two long strides and leaping down the wooden steps, looking for a body on the ground.

She was gone.

A dark shape disrupted the blackness ahead, moving across road.

My ears still ringing from the gunshots, I was already moving, taking one tree, then another, for cover. But no shots came. Snowflakes hit my face and melted.

The road, in my memory from daylight, was a good thirty feet wide. I ducked behind the nearest pine, but only for a few seconds before I advanced in an infantryman's crouch, adrenalin bearing me forward. The gravel crunched under my boots, then the surface turned to dirt and I dropped and rolled across the broken ground. It was the right move. I heard a snap behind me as a bullet meant for my head hit a tree branch. I saw the muted flash of her suppressor and fired at it.

As the echo of the Python subsided, I didn't hear any moaning of a wounded woman. So I propelled myself ahead with elbows, forearms, and knees, crawling across pine needles and hard-packed dirt. I carefully held aside a branch so it wouldn't make noise and shimmied to a fallen tree trunk. I hoped that I wasn't lying on a nest of hibernating rattlesnakes. For all I knew, the Mogollon Monster was beside me.

Another shot went over my head. How could she be ranging me in this darkness? I hadn't seen a night-sight on her pistol and she didn't have a backpack that might be holding one. Yet I had only seen her for a second. The one constant about Amy Russell and me was that I underestimated her.

Then I saw the white cloud of frozen air coming out of my mouth. I stifled a curse and made myself breathe through my nose. That lessened the mist. I stayed behind the log and slowed my breathing with difficulty.

There was a real monster in the woods. To defeat her, I had four rounds left in the revolver and two Speedloaders in my belt. I didn't have night-vision goggles. I didn't have the Maglite. I had no gloves and my hands were getting numb with the cold. This would have to do.

"Amy!"

Silence.

"Amy Russell!"

"Come get me!" Her voice sounded maybe twenty yards away and all the Southern was gone from her accent.

I looked toward her and saw nothing but empty night. I could make out six feet ahead, no more. It was the blackest darkness I had ever seen. If it weren't for the sound of the river and the snow hitting me like icy leaves, I might as well have been in the bottom of a well.

For all I knew, she was trying to circle back to the cabin. That would have been the smart move. But I stood and descended a rocky slope. Then my feet gave way and I slid ten feet, too loud, and landed at the edge of running water.

No shots came.

The river was about ten feet across here, maybe a little wider. I couldn't see that far. From memory, I knew a person could walk easily across. Unless it was flooding, this branch of the upper Verde was little more than a creek here.

"How's wifey, Doctor Mapstone?"

She was to my right, probably across the river. I called, "She's going to be fine."

"That's too bad."

I called, "Nobody else has to get hurt."

"You know that's not true."

Was she closer, or was I imagining it? Must keep moving. It was my only chance against someone with her training. So I made my legs rise and I surged forward, splashing across the Verde bent low, both hands on the Python. I nearly lost my balance on the small, smooth rocks in the streambed. Across and up a modest slope, a big ponderosa awaited me. I fell behind it and swept my perimeter with the gun barrel.

"I know all about you, Amy…"

"You don't know anything!" She was angry now. And closer.

The snow wasn't sticking to the ground yet, but it swirled in front of my face. I stared into the night, trying to detect texture and folds and movement in the blackness.

"How can all this bring back your husband and your daughter? I know what happened to them in Calgary. I know what you did to Chaos for revenge. Did cutting the throats of his children bring back your daughter?"

After a long pause, "I didn't expect it to."

"Your family wouldn't want this, Amy." I ratcheted my voice down to a conversational tone, tried to keep it steady. "When does it stop?"

"When I get my stones." Conversational tone. I heard undergrowth snapping to my left.

I said, "That's not going to happen."

I smelled Chanel Number Five. A pinecone crunched six feet away. Out of the gloom, I could see she was crouched, aiming at me with a combat grip.

Her face was flushed and her breathing came hard from the run, fog shooting out into the night. She nearly whispered, "You can't save me. You can't redeem what happened. You can't even save yourself."

I had the Python dead on her, both sights lined up.

"No," I said. "It ends right now."

"The world is evil, Mapstone," she said. "You can't stop it. You can't even make a stand against it. I played by your rules and I couldn't stop it. So either kill me or put your gun on the ground and walk back to the cabin with me behind you. Simple choice. No time."

The Python was steady. So was my breathing.

In the next nanosecond, as she opened her mouth, I took a breath, let it out slowly, and pulled, letting the smooth action of the Colt do the rest.

A boom, a long flash of red and yellow, and the echo of the explosion ruptured the night.

Chapter Forty-five

"You don't get out that easy."

I spoke the words as I searched her thoroughly. Her knife and backup gun went in my waistband. She stared at me, half disoriented, half furious, but she was in no condition to argue.

I carried her back across the river, across the road to the A-frame, looking like the bride and groom from hell. She was too traumatized to do a saddleback carry. Fortunately, she was light.

Peralta was crouched behind a tree with the carbine.

"You son of a bitch." He saw what I had done. "Now every civilian and reporter is going to think we can shoot the gun out of a bad guy's hand and never employ lethal force."

"Shut up and wrap what's left of her hand," I commanded. "She's lost a lot of blood already."

Surprisingly, he complied.

She was barely conscious. Her black clothing was white with snowflakes. Her right hand looked like a piece of meatloaf. I pushed her to him and ran into the cabin.

It was as I had left it. Mann was on the floor with the tipped-over chair, still securely handcuffed, staring with hate. Cartwright was lying face down in an expanding pool of red.

I carefully rolled him to his side, then onto his back.

"Tried to warn you," he gasped. His breathing was coming short and shallow.

"Don't talk."

He squinted at me as he always did and licked his lips.

"I served…"

"Don't talk," I said. "Save your strength. We're going to get you to a hospital."

He gave a quick shake of the head. "Too late."

I undid his coat and shirt. Both were wet with blood. The exit wound looked eight inches in diameter and had shattered his breastbone.

"My grandbaby…I did this for her. I was sending almost all my paycheck but it wasn't enough. You tell her I served…"

"You can tell her yourself," I said. "Help's on the way."

"No," he said. "Not this time. I was shot bad in 'Nam. They evac'd me. Hot zone. Medic got shot through the head. It's a fucked up world."

"Ed, stop talking. Focus on your breathing."

I took his hand and he tried to pull it back. Then he clasped mine, hard. His grip was painful. He stared at me and struggled to get the words out.

"I served…with honor."

Then his eyes were staring at nothing.

I pounded the floor with my fist and cursed. My eyes were wet but it was only the melted snowflakes. I whispered, "Yes, you did."

Chapter Forty-six

A week later, Peralta and I walked into the Sandra Day O'Connor United States Courthouse. It was safe for him to be on the sidewalks of downtown again. The day after the events in Payson, the U.S. Attorney had called a press conference to announce that forty people had been arrested in six states, an elaborate conspiracy to exchange diamonds for drugs, and a cast of bad guys in the Russian mafia and Mexican cartels.

Critical details about the FBI evidence were lacking but the television cameras were there to show Mike Peralta as a hero. His robbery had been staged. He was one of the good guys. As if any of you bastards had ever doubted it. They put me on the dais, too. And somehow Chris Melton joined the crowd.

The federal courthouse was a big glass box downtown, designed by a New York starchitect and totally unsuited for Phoenix. The jagged ornamental roof provided no shade and from the inside it looked like the ceiling of a hangar at a third-rate airport. The sun easily penetrated. In the summer, the immense atrium was almost unbearable because of the heat. The starchitect somehow thought it would be a good idea not to air-condition the space.

The result was bugs under a magnifying glass aimed at the sun.

To complete the blunder, the building was entirely surrounded by concrete surfaces, no shade trees, no grass. A special uniform had to be designed for the U.S. Marshals working here so they didn't faint from heat exhaustion.

Fortunately today it was January and raining outside. We were here to testify before the federal grand jury.

After we passed through security, I saw Eric Pham coming down the staircase and quickly walking toward us.

"Hi, guys." He sounded odd and positioned himself to block us rather than escort us upstairs.

"There's been a change." He held up a hand. "Now don't go ballistic, Mike."

Peralta grunted. "Get to it, Eric."

"Well, there's no way to tell you except to come out and say it. The U.S. Attorney has decided to drop the charges against Horace Mann and not seek an indictment."

"Are you people out of your minds?" This came from me, loud enough that a marshal started walking our way. Pham held out a hand and the man returned to his security perch.

"I know this can be dispiriting and appear unseemly from where you stand…"

"Cut the shit, Eric," Peralta said.

"This went all the way to the Attorney General. I did what I could. We all did. But the consensus was that it was better to make Mann take early retirement."

I reminded Pham that he was going to kill us in Payson and that he had confessed to stealing the diamonds.

"The DOJ isn't sure this would be admissible…"

Peralta jabbed his finger at Pham and cursed. It involved a complaint about being anally raped with no lubricant but he used far more colorful language. He went on, "I used to be the sheriff here and I was working this case under the direction of the FBI. Mapstone is a sworn deputy. Tell me how this is inadmissible?"

"There are national security considerations."

"Oh, bullshit."

"Real shit!" Pham did some finger-jabbing, too. "You don't know how those diamonds came to be taken from evidence control. It was a much more elaborate operation than picking them up and walking out. Computer systems were compromised. Tactics were compromised. Operational procedures…"

I interrupted. "It sounds like a massive ass-covering procedure to me. The Bureau doesn't want to be embarrassed again. You don't want to take the stand before a federal judge and explain how the FBI lost fifteen million in diamonds and how one of your senior agents was wrapped up with the Russians."

Pham stuffed his hands in his pockets. "It's not my call. Anyway, Mann claims he had arrived to rescue you when the asset followed him, handcuffed him, and was about to kill you when the Russell woman shot him."

"He's lying," Peralta said. "Mapstone and I told you what happened."

"You told me the asset arrived as your backup after Mapstone had arrested Mann."

"Say his name!" I shouted it before pulling my voice down. Once again, the Marshals almost intervened. "Say his name, goddamn it. He deserves at least that. He was in the FBI when you were in high school."

He glowered at me but gave in. "Special Agent Edward Cartwright, Thunder Seeker."

"Has his family been notified?"

Pham nodded. "He has a daughter in Southern California. She has a two-year-old, a special needs child. Money troubles. Very tragic."

I looked at Peralta, then back at Pham. "And the daughter is going to get survivor's benefits, right? And Ed gets a military funeral with full honors."

"Of course, of course."

I stared at Pham, wanting to demand that he be as diligent about making that happen as he was in making the scandal of Horace Mann go away. It wouldn't do any good.

Peralta finally spoke. "So the public will never know what really happened." He didn't phrase it as a question.

"You don't even know everything that happened," Pham said. He sighed. "Neither do I."

Peralta absently played with his tie. "So are you letting Amy Russell out, too?"

"Of course not," Pham said. "She'll be tried in the murder of the…Agent Cartwright. We're pretty sure we can make that happen…"

"Pretty sure?" It was impossible to keep the contempt out of my voice.

"The State Department is involved, too. She's wanted on theft charges in Canada. Based on what you said, the Calgary police might reopen the death of the biker and his family. But we're confident that we will be able to keep her here if the death penalty is taken off the table."

"What about Lindsey?"

"This is a federal case. It takes precedence. It involves the killing of an FBI agent and the likely killing of the DEA agent, Pennington. We can put her away for life. If the state tried her, the charge would only be attempted murder." He shook his head and returned his gaze to me. "Why on earth did she do this?"

"I was hoping you could tell me," I said. "We didn't have time for a lengthy conversation out in the woods. Her gun was on me. I shot first."

"Goddamned lucky," Peralta muttered.

"I'm a good shot."

Pham shrugged. "She told us that she wanted the diamonds to finance a secure new life in the United States. Or in a country without an extradition treaty with Canada if her theft was detected. We found a counterfeit U.S. passport—best quality— driver's license, and credit cards under the name Amy Morris. She keeps talking about wanting options. That's the word she uses, 'options.' The rich have them and the rest of us don't. Some of her testimony may be of a classified nature, so…"

"I'm not rich and I didn't kill people stealing diamonds."

"You may never get a good answer, Doctor Mapstone," he said. "Our psychologists theorize that she snapped when her family was murdered. Not that we're going to let her use an insanity defense. Her methods show she was sane enough, knew right from wrong…"

"She wore Chanel Number Five."

"What?"

"Expansive tastes," I said. "Maybe she was never Amy Do-Right."

"Well, when we sort this out…"

Peralta cut him off. "Whatever. I know you tried, Eric. Don't let her get away. Let's go, Mapstone."

I felt his hand cup my elbow and steer us back toward the entrance.

"So are you going to run for sheriff again next election?" This came from a marshal. She was female, young, Anglo, and more than a little starstruck.

"I doubt it," Peralta said. "Arizona's got some changing to do before I have a chance."

It was sad but true.

That afternoon, the rain departed and the remaining clouds made for one of those breathtaking sunsets that seem from another planet. I was on my way back to see Lindsey but had to pull into a parking lot and gape. As I took in the vivid pallet of colors, the White Tanks revealed themselves to the west, a dark tear against the horizon.

And I knew the job wasn't finished.

Chapter Forty-seven

I called the meeting for three p.m. at my office in the old courthouse. It gave me a chance to prepare the contents of my briefcase and do a little interior decorating.

Even so, Diane and Zephyr Whitehouse arrived ten minutes early. Diane was wearing a black pantsuit with tasteful diamond stud earrings. Zephyr had on jeans torn at the knees, a low-cut pink top, and vivid red lipstick, all probably to irritate her mother.

I invited them to sit down. Even though Zephyr was taller than Diane, the resemblance was clear, especially in the large, lovely eyes and the perfect noses. I thought about the photos I had seen of Lindsey's mother, Linda, as a young woman. They were almost identical. Robin didn't look like either of them.

"What's this about, David?" Diane sounded almost as familiar with me as she had been in the closet, or that was her act.

"David will tell us, Diane." Zephyr gave a wide smile.

"I need a few minutes," I said. "One more person will be coming."

Neither spoke for a long time.

Finally, Zephyr asked about the large black-and-white photo I had hung behind me, next to the portrait of Chris Melton.

"That's Carl Hayden when he was Maricopa County sheriff," I said. "He went on to become one of the longest-serving senators in American history. After JFK was assassinated, Hayden was second in line for the presidency. He spent his career fighting to ensure the Central Arizona Project. But he started out as sheriff. In 1910, he formed a posse to run down some train robbers. The 'Beardless Boy Bandits.' Usually, he didn't carry a gun."

Diane stifled a look of boredom. Zephyr winked at me. I didn't care if they were interested. I was interested. This photo had hung in my office for years when I worked for Peralta. Now, with Hayden in Stetson, straight serious mouth, and expressive dark eyes looking down, I felt reassured.

The women turned when two knocks came on the pebbled glass. Chris Melton walked in. He was actually wearing a suit.

"Sorry I'm late," he said. "Damned federal racial profiling case. Had to testify. It's all trumped up by the media."

He looked around, found no place to sit, and leaned against the wall.

"Who's that?" His eyes quickly found his competition on the wall behind me. I told a shorter version of the lesson I had given to the Whitehouse women.

Melton said, "Of course."

He had no idea who Carl Hayden was.

I said, "I asked you to come here today to discuss what I've found concerning the wallet that Mrs. Whitehouse discovered in her husband's closet."

Melton shot me an icy glance. *Why are you surprising me?*

Zephyr said, "This is very sexy. Like one of those Masterpiece Mysteries on PBS. But that might make us potential suspects!"

"Settle down, dear," her mother said. "And call me Diane, David. You know that."

Zephyr ran her hand in front of her face, turning her amused look into one of mock seriousness.

Several files were laid out on the desk. Screw the paperless office.

I laid down a photo of the wallet.

"This is it. It's been logged in as evidence so the photo will have to do. When Diane found it, she was curious enough to do some research. She said she discovered it went with a man who died in 1982. At that point, she contacted the sheriff."

I opened another folder and started laying out photos of men, some quite explicit.

"When I interviewed Diane, she showed me where the wallet was found. These are some of the photos that were also in the drawer…"

Diane turned toward Melton. "Chris, I didn't think these were relevant."

I continued. "I thought they might be, so I also placed the originals in evidence. These are copies."

"And they say size doesn't matter." Zephyr eyed the photographs and clicked her tongue against the roof of her mouth, smiled, and fiddled with the factory torn fabric of her jeans.

Melton folded his arms. "How is this relevant, David?"

"Among these photos was a smaller snapshot," I said, placing another picture on the desk. "This is the young man who died, Tom Frazier."

"He has clothes on," Zephyr said.

I nodded. "That's one curiosity. Another is that the snapshot is torn in half. Someone else was in this photo, but that part was discarded. Then there's the problem that none of these other photographs fit."

Diane started to twirl her hair but put her hands back in her lap. "What do you mean?"

"Every other photo can be found on the Internet, from gay porn sites to Flickr. They could have been downloaded and turned into physical photographs, even aged to look as if they had been sitting in that closet for decades. So if Elliott Whitehouse was gay or bisexual, and these were meant to be keepsakes from former lovers, it doesn't fit."

"Mother!" Zephyr stood, angry enough to dispense with using her mom's given name. "Daddy wasn't gay! He hated gay people. How could you have said such a thing?"

I held out a hand and lowered it. Zephyr sat.

"I never said any such thing," Diane said.

"You did imply it," I said. "Your husband wasn't interested in sex. He always had very handsome male assistants. 'Real hunks,' in your words. I'll be happy to read the report I wrote of our discussion to refresh your memory."

"I think it's very tragic he had to live a double life," she said.

"This is such bullshit!" Zephyr said.

"Let's set that aside for now," I said. "As I investigated this case, I did run across a woman named Stephanie Webb. She told me that she had a ten-year love affair with your husband, Diane. It went right up to the time of his death. In fact, when he had his fatal heart attack, he was at her condo in Scottsdale. She told me you forbade her to attend his funeral. She also told me she had found no evidence of him being interested in men. Quite the contrary…"

"You motherfucker!" Diane rose out of her chair and looked about ready to climb over the desk. She had dropped the mask of Arcadia gentility with ease. Melton put a restraining hand on her shoulder.

He said, "Is there a point here, Deputy?"

I was relieved we were beyond the forced casual first names. "I didn't ask for this case, Sheriff. In fact, you brought me into it under false pretenses, but that's another conversation. Diane started this by bringing you the wallet. As it turns out, that's a good thing."

"My private life is none of your goddamned business!" Her shout echoed into the high ceiling. Zephyr lost her tan.

"As a matter of fact, it is." I let that sink in for a few seconds. She stared at me, then looked down. "I was the deputy who found Tom Frazier's remains in 1982."

Diane's sharp intake of breath was noticeable.

I continued, "He was in the desert at the foot of the White Tank Mountains. That area was completely isolated back then. The death was ruled a suicide. The medical examiner found a fatal dose of heroin in his system. And that's where the case sat until you found this wallet."

"I don't understand." She attempted a laugh, about as droll as a Gila monster. "I was only trying to help. What on earth does this have to do with us?"

"I kept trying to figure that out myself," I said. "You see, the problem is that there was no drug paraphernalia found at the scene. Not in the desert and not in his car. We performed a grid search that day of the area between where the car was parked and where the body was found. No needle, no spoon, nothing. When I found the body, I followed his tracks through the desert. I assumed he was alone. But the soil was hard and it hadn't rained. So another person might have been with him. Someone petite who wouldn't leave obvious footprints."

"Who was Tom Frazier?" This came from Zephyr, in a small and tentative voice.

"He was about your age," I said. "An EMT who worked on the ambulance. He wanted to go to college." I pushed forward another folder. "These are interviews I did with six of his colleagues. Facebook has a page for Phoenix EMS veterans. It's an amazing resource. I was able to find people who actually knew Tom."

"What are you getting at, David?" Diane had regained her poise. "I think we've been very patient. I have things to do. If there's something you want to tell us about Elliott, we can find a way to handle it."

"Good," I said. "Tom was an excellent medic. Skilled, good under pressure, never missed a day of work. That isn't the behavior of an addict. In fact, they told me he wouldn't even smoke pot. Put all this together and we have a suspicious death at the least, a homicide more likely. That's why Sheriff Melton had me make this into a murder book."

I let those words settle over the room before continuing.

"Tom was also straight. He was awkward with women. Who wasn't at that age? He had an affair with a nurse who was ten years older. She broke it off. He was really hurt. You can read the statements here." I tapped the folder.

Diane looked at me, then at Melton. "So are we done? I don't really understand the point but I appreciate David's diligence in this, Chris. Really, I do."

She hastily stood. "Come on, Zephyr."

"I'm not done."

I might as well have pulled out the Colt Python and fired it. All the color drained from Diane's face. She slowly lowered herself into the chair.

"Two people told me that Tom had started dating a girl his age. He had met her on a call. She overdosed on heroin and he helped save her life. After she got out of the hospital, he started seeing her. Seems as if he wanted to help birds with broken wings. That's how his partner put it. The girl's name was Diane."

"What are you...?" Her face was a model of incredulity. "Chris, this has really gone far enough."

I watched his eyes as he did the calculus. She was a big campaign donor. Did he have enough of a lawman in him to let me finish?

He said, "You two can go. Deputy Mapstone and I will be in touch if there's anything further." He said it in the tone of a servant dishing out afternoon tea.

Diane stood and clutched her Barney's handbag close. Zephyr didn't.

She said, "What are you saving, David?"

"I'm saying that I found a booking photo of your mother from 1981. She was arrested for possession of heroin but the charges were dropped. It was a small amount. I showed this photo to three of Tom Frazier's former colleagues and they are willing to testify that Diane was his girlfriend. They described her as hot, impulsive, beautiful, but couldn't kick the brown sugar. They said Tom was crazy about her. He'd do anything for her. They identified her from the booking photo. The photo of you, Diane."

"I..." She made herself stop and pursed her lips.

After a minute of silence, I pushed Tom's photo toward her.

"He must have meant something to you, Diane, to have kept that wallet all these years. You were in that snapshot with Tom, weren't you, Diane?"

"We're leaving, Zephyr." Diane patted Melton on the shoulder. "Thank you, Chris."

Melton tried to lean in and scoop up the files but Zephyr stopped him.

"I want to know!"

I said, "Ask your mother what happened that night in the desert. Did they go out there to make love, and she talked him into trying the heroin, only she botched the dose? Or was it something more sinister? Maybe he was breaking up with you, Diane, and this was revenge."

"Is this true, Mother?" Zephyr's eyes were wide with anger.

"You can't prove anything," Diane said.

"If I could prove it at this point, I'd be reading you your rights. But it doesn't look good. It must have been an awful thing to watch him die out there."

Her large eyes filled with tears and they dropped heavily down her face. She made no effort to wipe them away.

"It's up to the sheriff to continue this investigation," I said. "I've always felt we owed it to the dead to make sure justice is done. Maybe he sees things differently."

He glared at me and undid his top shirt button, pulling aside his tie.

I looked at him. "Zephyr came to me a few days ago with copies of checks her brother wrote to county officials. We used to call them bribes back when Mike Peralta was sheriff."

"Diane told me to bring those," she said. "Anyway, Chip is an ass."

"I didn't get it," I said. "But I drink with lawyer friends at Durant's and I learned that there's a huge fight over Elliott Whitehouse's estate. He left money to Zephyr, her brothers, and his former wife. He left nothing to Diane. Not a dime. She's been fighting it in probate for a year."

Zephyr said, "I didn't know any of this..."

I gathered up the files. Then I brought them down between my hands with a hard smack, using the top of the desk to make them a neat stack. I slid a thick rubber band around them.

"If the sheriff got a subpoena, he might find that your father's will has a morals clause. I don't have any special knowledge here. Only questions. If Whitehouse were such a homophobe, would being a closeted gay breach the clause? Homicide certainly would. Elliott being officially implicated in the death of Tom Frazier, by no less than the Sheriff's Office historian who worked for Mike Peralta. That would have been a neat package. What if that morals clause could be invoked to invalidate the will? That might give Diane a shot at the entire…"

"You son of a bitch." Her voice was a whisper. "I was a good wife to him, all those years. All those slaps and punches he gave me when he was drinking."

I shrugged and stood, gently lifted my portrait of Carl Hayden from the wall, and pulled out my badge case.

I looked at Melton.

"This is yours." I set the badge on top of the files. "And those are yours, too."

I zinged a black flash drive at him. His eyes widened but he caught it.

"Paperless office," I said, and walked out.

"Mapstone, wait…"

I ignored Melton.

Instead, one more time, I took in the lovely hallway. I would so miss this place. But the price for being here was too high.

Footsteps, running behind me.

"David." Zephyr fell in with me. "I am so sorry. I had no idea."

"I might be wrong," I said.

She put her arm around me and we walked, descending the wrought-iron staircase with its Spanish tile and ending up outside the building, before the Swilling fountain. The water bubbled and sang, rather like the east fork of the Verde in snow.

We stopped and faced each other.

"What should I do?" she asked, eyes exquisite and wounded and her mouth tilted toward mine.

I bent toward her and cupped her face with my hands. "Grow up."

Epilogue

Lindsey is home now.

She spent more than three weeks in the hospital, fighting like a tiger to walk around the nurses' station, go through in-patient physical therapy, and address all the difficult and messy stuff that people never think about. The docs and nurses sanitize it with jargon. Lindsey is a lady entitled to her privacy.

It is mid-February now. I always thought this was the sweetest month in Phoenix. Soon we'll smell the citrus blossoms.

Lindsey sits outside while I work as her surrogate gardener. She's not quite physically ready to be digging in the dirt. So it is up to me to plant the tomatoes and herbs, go to Whitfill's for petunias and geraniums that will go in the sun and impatiens to fill the shady beds.

So I dig and plant, the timeless alluvial soil of the ancient river valley precious in my hands. My love watches and instructs.

Lindsey is back to her familiar long pageboy. She had her hair washed and cut the afternoon she was released from Mister Joe's. Even once she was moved out of the ICU, the showers and haircuts offered by the hospital left much to be desired.

I take her to physical therapy twice a week. She works hard and gets stronger every day. It is amazing seeing the ways the body can heal itself. We are now able to walk to the end of the block and back without her using a cane. She is the bravest person I have ever known.

She can't sleep on her stomach. Doctor's orders. That had always been her favorite sleeping position.

The scars on her chest are healing nicely. She is much more conscious of them than I am. To me, she has never looked lovelier.

Her next goal is to get completely off pain meds so she can enjoy a martini. Next week, she promises.

Mike and Sharon visit every few days. Lindsey appreciates their kindness and I…well, for me it's complicated. I have known and cared about them almost my entire adult life, long before I met Lindsey. But the lies told this time and their consequences ruptured something between us. We are finding our way back.

The office is closed. The private detective trade will have to wait awhile. In the meantime, we have given depositions about what happened in Payson. Amy Russell will be tried in federal court for the murder of Cartwright.

Melton has disappeared from my life. I have read nothing about Diane Whitehouse. For all I know, she will prevail in the fight for the estate, and Melton will keep his donor. At the least he can avoid humiliation by not pressing the case I began, the one he foolishly passed my way.

The one we failed was Tom Frazier. I think of him often and all the years I was allowed to live, years denied to him by what happened in the desert that long-ago night. I feel guilty when I look at the mountains to the west. As a historian, I can provoke memory. Absolution and benediction are beyond my means. So, apparently, is justice. I could try to take the case to the state attorney general, but he's a friend and political ally of Melton. This is Arizona, at least for now.

I made plenty of promises during those dreadful days, about a different future for us if only Lindsey would survive. There would be time to talk about all this.

In the meantime, she has gone offline. No computer, no news, no Facebook or Twitter. I took over a table for literary magazines and book reviews. In paper. She devours them and calls it the Sanity Table.

I follow the diminishing news enough to know that Phoenix is wracked with insanity. Chris Melton is more popular than ever. The state is a national punch line.

Soon summer, ghastly summer will come. The toffs will be gone to their houses in the San Juan Islands and the California coast. Zephyr Whitehouse will be in Palo Alto. Only the monsoon might bring the rest of us relief. But the storms don't come into the city anymore.

That's not quite true. Now, if they do penetrate the heat island of the concrete desert, the result is often violent microbursts. The dust storms come as they always have. They've been discovered by the national media and dubbed "haboobs." Great visuals. But less and less rain. Lindsey and I have given up on television.

She has not spoken again about her out-of-body experience after the shooting. I have not asked.

The day they released her from the hospital, I got on my knees and asked her to marry me again. Then I slipped her rings back on. It's only a diamond solitaire. But it is enough.

Every day we have, every night I hear her breathing next to me, is enough.

Paying My Debts

Cal Lash has lived a remarkable American adventure. Part of it involves being a Phoenix Police patrolman, sergeant, and detective, as well as a private investigator and diamond courier. I am grateful for his patience in answering my many questions. The same goes for Ellie Strang, R.N., who was most helpful on the medical front.

Help also came from David R. Foster, a deputy Maricopa County Attorney, and Lt. Rob Settembre of the Phoenix Police.

I am indebted to my friend Tom Zoellner for his book, *The Heartless Stone: A Journey Through The World of Diamonds, Deceit and Desire*. The title says it all, except that this is the best piece of journalism on the subject.

As always, blame me for any errors, inconsistencies, and deliberate changes in procedures or descriptions.

Barbara Peters, my editor at the Poisoned Pen Press, is rightly considered the finest editor working in the mystery field. I've been blessed to have her guidance through most of the Mapstone novels. I'm also grateful to Robert Rosenwald, president of the Poisoned Pen Press, and an excellent staff including Suzan Baroni, Beth Deveny, Diane DiBiase, Annette Rogers, and Pete Zrioka. They make this a gem among America's independent publishing houses.

To receive a free catalog of Poisoned Pen Press titles, please provide your name and address through one of the following ways:

Phone: 1-800-421-3976
Facsimile: 1-480-949-1707
Email: info@poisonedpenpress.com
Website: www.poisonedpenpress.com

Poisoned Pen Press
6962 E. First Ave. Ste 103
Scottsdale, AZ 85251

C. S. LEWIS

by Amy Van Zee

ABDO
Publishing Company

Essential Critiques

How to Analyze the Works of

C. S. LEWIS

by Amy Van Zee

Content Consultant: Andrew Lazo, MA
Special Programs Coordinator and Faculty Liaison, C. S. Lewis Foundation

Credits

Published by ABDO Publishing Company, PO Box 398166, Minneapolis, MN 55439. Copyright © 2013 by Abdo Consulting Group, Inc. International copyrights reserved in all countries. No part of this book may be reproduced in any form without written permission from the publisher. The Essential Library™ is a trademark and logo of ABDO Publishing Company.

Printed in the United States of America,
North Mankato, Minnesota
042012
092012

♻ THIS BOOK CONTAINS AT LEAST 10% RECYCLED MATERIALS.

Editor: Lauren Coss
Series Designer: Marie Tupy

Library of Congress Cataloging-in-Publication Data
Van Zee, Amy.
  How to analyze the works of C. S. Lewis / Amy Van Zee.
     p. cm. -- (Essential critiques)
  Includes bibliographical references.
  ISBN 978-1-61783-455-4
  1. Lewis, C. S. (Clive Staples), 1898-1963--Juvenile literature. 2. Authors, English--20th century--Biography--Juvenile literature. I. Title.
  PR6023.E926Z919 2012
  823'.912--dc23
                                        2012007215

Table of Contents

1

Introduction to Critiques

What Is Critical Theory?

What do you usually do when you read a book?
You probably absorb the specific language style of
the book. You learn about the characters as they are
developed through thoughts, dialogue, and other
interactions. You may like or dislike a character
more than others. You might be drawn in by the plot
of the book, eager to find out what happens at the
end. Yet these are only a few of many possible ways
of understanding and appreciating a book. What
if you are interested in delving more deeply? You
might want to learn more about the author and how
his or her personal background is reflected in the
book. Or you might want to examine what the book
says about society—how it depicts the roles of

women and minorities, for example. If so, you have
entered the realm of critical theory.

Critical theory helps you learn how various
works of art, literature, music, theater, film, and
other endeavors either support or challenge the way
society behaves. Critical theory is the evaluation
and interpretation of a work using different
philosophies, or schools of thought. Critical theory
can be used to understand all types of cultural
productions.

There are many different critical theories. If you
are analyzing literature, each theory asks you to
look at the work from a different perspective. Some
theories address social issues, while others focus on
the writer's life or the time period in which the book

was written or set. For example, the critical theory that asks how an author's life affected the work is called biographical criticism. Other common schools of criticism include historical criticism, feminist criticism, psychological criticism, and New Criticism, which examines a work solely within the context of the work itself.

What Is the Purpose of Critical Theory?

Critical theory can open your mind to new ways of thinking. It can help you evaluate a book from a new perspective, directing your attention to issues and messages you may not otherwise recognize in a work. For example, applying feminist criticism to a book may make you aware of female stereotypes perpetuated in the work. Applying a critical theory to a book helps you learn about the person who created it or the society that enjoyed it. You can also explore how the work is perceived by current cultures.

How Do You Apply Critical Theory?

You conduct a critique when you use a critical theory to examine and question a work. The theory you choose is a lens through which you can view the work, or a springboard for asking questions about the work. Applying a critical theory helps you think critically about the work. You are free to question the work and make an assertion about it. If you choose to examine a book using biographical theory, for example, you want to know how the author's personal background or education inspired or shaped the work. You could explore why the author was drawn to the story. For instance, are there any parallels between a particular character's life and the author's life?

Forming a Thesis

Ask your question and find answers in the work or other related materials. Then you can create a thesis. The thesis is the key point in your critique. It is your argument about the work based on the tenets, or beliefs, of the theory you are using. For example, if you are using biographical theory to ask how the author's life inspired the work, your thesis could be worded as follows: Writer Teng Xiong, raised in refugee camps in

> ### How to Make a Thesis Statement
>
> In a critique, a thesis statement typically appears at the end of the introductory paragraph. It is usually only one sentence long and states the author's main idea.

Southeast Asia, drew upon her experiences to write the novel *No Home for Me*.

Providing Evidence

Once you have formed a thesis, you must provide evidence to support it. Evidence might take the form of examples and quotations from the work itself—such as dialogue from a character. Articles about the book or personal interviews with the author might also support your ideas. You may wish to address what other critics have written about the work. Quotes from these individuals may help support your claim. If you find any quotes or examples that contradict your thesis, you will need to create an argument against them. For instance: Many critics have pointed to the protagonist of *No Home for Me* as a powerless victim of circumstances. However, in the chapter "My Destiny," she is clearly depicted as someone who seeks to shape her own future.

How to Support
a Thesis Statement

A critique should include several arguments. Arguments support a thesis claim. An argument is one or two sentences long and is supported by evidence from the work being discussed.

Organize the arguments into paragraphs. These paragraphs make up the body of the critique.

In This Book

In this book, you will read summaries of famous works by writer C. S. Lewis, each followed by a critique. Each critique will use one theory and apply it to one work. Critical thinking sections will give you a chance to consider other theses and questions about the work. Did you agree with the author's application of the theory? What other questions are raised by the thesis and its arguments? You can also find out what other critics think about each particular book. Then, in the You Critique It section in the final pages of this book, you will have an opportunity to create your own critique.

Look for the Guides

Throughout the chapters that analyze the works, thesis statements have been highlighted. The box next to the thesis helps explain what questions are being raised about the work. Supporting arguments have been underlined. The boxes next to the arguments help explain how these points support the thesis. Look for these guides throughout each critique.

C. S. Lewis is one of the most widely read writers and philosophers of the twentieth century.

2

A Closer Look at C. S. Lewis

Clive Staples Lewis was born in Belfast, Northern Ireland, on November 29, 1898. His father, Albert, was passionate and emotional. His mother, Flora, was logical and calm. Both were well educated and loved to read. When Clive was four years old, he declared he wished to be called "Jacksie," and he came to be known as "Jack" to those close to him. Jack and his older brother, Warren, were raised in a scenic part of Northern Ireland near the sea and with views of nearby ridges and hills. The boys explored their house, read, and wrote stories together. Jack's stories featured knights and animals in human clothing. He sometimes added his own illustrations. Although the brothers were close, their mother's death from cancer on August 23, 1908, brought them even closer. Albert was devastated. That year,

Jack joined his brother at a boarding school in England.

During his school years, Jack changed schools numerous times. His school years were not always pleasant. While he found happiness in learning, he struggled in math and was sometimes bullied by his schoolmates. At one school, Jack witnessed violence at the hand of a schoolmaster. He eventually received schooling from a private tutor. He learned German, Italian, and French. And he discovered a love of Norse mythology and wrote his own poetry. Jack proved to be a voracious reader. He read fairy tales and the works of H. G. Wells, Virgil, Homer, Euripides, Sophocles, the Brontë sisters, Jane Austen, Charles Dickens, and many other authors. Jack used his spare money to purchase books for his own library.

Growing up, Jack went to church, where he heard Christian teachings and learned to pray, but religion was not interesting to him. When he was 13 years old, Jack "ceased to be a Christian."[1] He became interested in the occult and grew pessimistic about life. Through his readings, he explored other religions and was intrigued by the preternatural. Soon, Jack declared himself an atheist.

World War I

In late 1916, Lewis took his entrance examination for the University of Oxford and was accepted at Oxford's University College in Oxford, England. But World War I had broken out in Europe in 1914, and Lewis would soon join the fight. He arrived at Oxford in the spring of 1917 and began training in the Officer's Training Corps. As a second lieutenant in the infantry, he was sent to the trenches in France in November 1917. The war ended in November 1918, and he returned to Oxford the following January. In March 1919, Lewis's first book, *Spirits in Bondage*, was printed. It is a collection of poems mainly centering on the tension between good and evil. The book received some strong reviews, but it was not popular and sold poorly.

While training for the war, Lewis had befriended Edward "Paddy" Moore, along with Paddy's sister and mother. Paddy did not survive the war, but Lewis became very attached to Mrs. Moore and her young daughter, Maureen. Mrs. Moore, who was separated from her husband, became something of a mother figure to Lewis. He spent a great deal of time with the Moores and soon came to live with them near Oxford. They lived in several rented homes, and money was often tight.

By 1923, Lewis had three degrees from Oxford in Greek and Latin texts, classical philosophy, and English language and literature. In May 1924, Lewis took a temporary tutoring and lecturing position at Oxford. In October, he began teaching philosophy and English at Magdalen College, which was one of the many colleges making up the Oxford system. On September 20, 1926, he published *Dymer*, a long poem that was intensely personal for Lewis. The poem did not sell well. On September 24, 1929, Lewis's father died.

Conversion to Christianity

As a teenager, Lewis had abandoned his Christian upbringing and declared himself an atheist. However, in the late 1910s and early 1920s, Lewis began reading the writings of Christian authors such as G. K. Chesterton and George MacDonald and liked their work. As both a student and a teacher at Oxford, Lewis held many discussions about Christianity with peers and colleagues he respected. As a result, he began to accept the existence of God. When a cynical and atheistic colleague told Lewis he believed there was strong evidence the Gospels had really happened, Lewis was shaken and researched the evidence himself. And he began attending church.

On September 22, 1931, on the way to a zoo, Lewis converted to Christianity. As he famously wrote in his spiritual autobiography, *Surprised by Joy*: "When we set out I did not believe that Jesus Christ is the Son of God, and when we reached the zoo I did."[2]

Life at the Kilns, More Writing, and the Inklings

Lewis, Warren, and Mrs. Moore collectively purchased a property known as the Kilns in 1930. The property was three miles (4.8 km) from Oxford. It needed updating, but the eight acres (3.2 ha) held a house, a lake, and woods.

In the 1930s, Lewis began meeting informally with a group of other academics and friends to read, discuss, and criticize literature and each other's writings. The group included author J. R. R. Tolkien, who would become well known as the author of *The Lord of the Rings*. Called the Inklings, the group often met in Lewis's rooms at Magdalen College.

Lewis also began regularly publishing books, many of which were overtly Christian. *The*

Pilgrim's Regress, published in May 1933, tells the story of Lewis's conversion through allegory. *The Allegory of Love*, a work of literary criticism, was published on May 21, 1936, and helped establish Lewis as an important scholar in his field of literature. *The Problem of Pain*, published in October 1940, was an immediate success. Taking a different route, Lewis wrote 31 entries, which were published weekly, in the *Guardian* newspaper from May to November 1941. The writings were well received and compiled into an enormously successful book titled *The Screwtape Letters* in February 1942.

By this time, Europe was consumed with World War II (1939–1945). The residents of the Kilns hosted young children who had been evacuated out of large cities. In August 1941, Lewis began giving radio talks discussing morality and other Christian topics. He continued his radio broadcasts through April 1944. These broadcast talks were published in a number of volumes and eventually compiled into the book *Mere Christianity* in 1952.

Even though his writings and his speeches were popular, Lewis received criticism—often from his colleagues—for openly sharing his religious beliefs. Others criticized him for publishing outside his field of English literature. Lewis began to feel attacked by anti-Christian sentiment, especially at Oxford. Nevertheless, he continued publishing books with Christian themes. But some of his most well-recognized writings were still to come.

While hosting children at his home during World War II, Lewis became concerned with their lack of imagination, which had always been a large part of his own life. Lewis set to work writing a children's book, *The Lion, the Witch and the Wardrobe*, which he completed in 1949 and published in 1950. It was the first of seven books making up The Chronicles of Narnia. Lewis continued publishing one book a year in the series for the next six years. *Prince Caspian* was published in 1951; *The Voyage of the* Dawn Treader was published in 1952; *The Silver Chair* was published in 1953. The seventh and final book, *The Last Battle*, was published in 1956. Some critics disliked the books, believing they were too Christian, but they were very popular with children.

The Later Years

Life at the Kilns was often not easy. Lewis worried about Warren, a lifelong alcoholic, and

Mrs. Moore, whose health was failing. She died on January 12, 1951. Lewis's workload was very demanding and he, too, was showing signs of ill health. In 1954, he took a prestigious teaching job at the University of Cambridge in Cambridge, England, and he continued writing. His spiritual autobiography, *Surprised by Joy*, was published in 1955. But there was still one more surprise in store for Lewis.

In 1950, Lewis began a relationship with Joy Davidman, a divorced mother of two young boys. Lewis's books had been a large influence in her conversion to Christianity, so she wrote him a letter from America. Davidman and Lewis met for the first time in 1952. Davidman eventually moved with her two young boys from the United States to be near Lewis. But in 1956, her permit to stay in England was set to expire unless she married an English citizen. Additionally, Davidman was suffering from pain that was diagnosed as cancer. In 1956, Lewis, a lifelong bachelor, married Davidman, first in a registry office and later in a religious ceremony in 1957.

Everyone expected Davidman to die soon after the marriage. But her cancer went into remission,

The story of Davidman and Lewis's relationship is portrayed in the play *Shadowlands*, which was made into a movie starring Anthony Hopkins as Lewis and Debra Winger as Davidman.

and the two enjoyed more than three years of happy marriage. After Davidman's death on July 11, 1960, Lewis published *A Grief Observed* in 1961, an intensely personal account of his dealing with his wife's death. Lewis spent more time with friends and writing letters. By 1961, his health began seriously deteriorating, and in July 1963, he suffered a heart attack and fell into a coma. Although he recovered, his body was weak, and Lewis died shortly after on November 22, 1963. He left an undeniable impact on literature and religion, and his work lives on around the world to this day.

In 2005, a film adaptation of *The Lion, the Witch and the Wardrobe* was released as the first installment in the film series The Chronicles of Narnia.

3

An Overview of
The Lion, the Witch and the Wardrobe

The Lion, the Witch and the Wardrobe begins
when the Pevensie siblings Peter, Susan, Edmund,
and Lucy are sent out of London to the country
house of an old professor to escape air raids during
World War II. One rainy day, the children are
exploring the large old house and come across a
room containing an old wardrobe. Lucy opens the
wardrobe and discovers it is filled with fur coats.
As she moves farther inside the wardrobe, she finds
herself surrounded by trees and walking on snow.
She continues to a nearby lamppost, where she
meets a Faun named Mr. Tumnus. The startled Faun
asks Lucy if she is a "Daughter of Eve" and invites
her for tea.[1] On the way to his cave, Mr. Tumnus
informs Lucy she is in the land of Narnia.

During tea, Mr. Tumnus tells Lucy tales of dwarfs, nymphs, and stags and then begins playing a small flute. Mr. Tumnus reveals that the White Witch, who rules Narnia and makes it "always winter but never Christmas," gave orders that anyone who meets a human must catch him or her for the Witch.[2] Mr. Tumnus agrees to escort Lucy back to the lamppost to get away safely. Lucy finds her way back to the wardrobe and back into the Professor's house.

Edmund Travels to Narnia

When Lucy finds Peter, Susan, and Edmund, she is surprised that despite being in Narnia for hours, no time has passed in their world. She tells the others where she has been. But when they go to the wardrobe, the back of it is solid, and her siblings do not believe her story. Edmund especially teases Lucy.

A few days later, while playing hide-and-seek, Edmund follows Lucy into the wardrobe and finds himself alone in Narnia. He meets the White Witch, who woos him with a hot drink and enchantingly addictive turkish delight, a type of English sweet. Once she finds out he is a human, she urges him to return to Narnia with his siblings and bring them to her castle, telling Edmund she will give him more turkish delight and will make him a king. On his way back to the wardrobe, Edmund meets Lucy, who has been eating lunch with Mr. Tumnus.

When Lucy and Edmund return to the house, Edmund refuses to confirm her story and pretends they were just playing. Soon after this, the four children find themselves hiding from the housekeeper in the wardrobe. This time, it leads them all into Narnia together. Everyone realizes Edmund had been lying about being there before, and Peter reprimands him.

Trouble in Narnia

Lucy leads the group to Mr. Tumnus's cave, but when they get there, they see it has been ransacked. A note tells them Mr. Tumnus was arrested and is awaiting trial for harboring a human in disloyalty to the queen.

The four children soon meet Mr. Beaver, who informs them that "Aslan is on the move."[3] The children do not know what this means, but they follow Mr. Beaver to his dam, where they meet Mrs. Beaver. The group enjoys a hearty meal together before Mr. Beaver tells them about Aslan, a lion who is the true king. An old rhyme tells that when Aslan returns, winter and evil will be gone. The group intends to meet Aslan at the Stone Table the next day. But soon, they notice Edmund is missing. He has gone to the White Witch.

Edmund travels to the Witch's castle alone. In her courtyard, he sees many creatures that have been turned into stone. When Edmund meets the Witch, he tells her he has brought his siblings into Narnia and that the Beavers spoke of Aslan's return. The White Witch is troubled by the news about Aslan and prepares to leave her castle.

The Thaw Begins

Peter, Susan, Lucy, Mr. Beaver, and Mrs. Beaver hastily set out to the Stone Table. On their way, they meet Father Christmas, who has been kept out of Narnia by the White Witch but has returned now that Aslan is near. Father Christmas gives a shield and a sword to Peter. To Susan, he gives a bow and arrows and a magical horn that will summon help. To Lucy, he gives a dagger and a diamond vial containing a magical liquid that will heal any wound.

Traveling with the White Witch to the Stone Table, Edmund finds she has not honored her promises to him. Now she is openly hostile to Edmund, and he walks with his hands bound as they travel through the forest. As they travel, Edmund notices the snow melting.

Peter, Susan, Lucy, and the Beavers also notice the warming weather as they travel to the Stone Table. Once there, they meet Aslan the lion, who is accompanied by centaurs, a unicorn, and many other creatures. Aslan greets the group and learns Edmund has joined the White Witch. Aslan shows Peter the castle of Cair Paravel where he will be High King. At that moment, they hear Susan's horn and find a wolf that serves the Witch about to attack her. Peter draws his sword and kills the beast. Aslan sends his creatures after a second wolf to follow it to the Witch and Edmund.

Edmund Rescued

The wolf returns to the Witch to tell her of Aslan's return to the Stone Table. She commands the wolf to summon all her loyal creatures to prepare for a fight. The White Witch prepares to kill Edmund, but Aslan's creatures rescue him and bring him to the Stone Table. After talking with Aslan, Edmund apologizes to his siblings.

The Witch comes to speak with Aslan. She reminds him of Deep Magic, which says that as a traitor, Edmund belongs to her, and blood must be spilled or Narnia will be ruined. After a private discussion with the Witch, Aslan announces the Witch has removed her claim on Edmund's life. Aslan's army moves their camp to a nearby river.

Death Defeated

That night, Lucy and Susan follow Aslan as he quietly leaves the camp. He goes to the Stone Table, where the Witch and her followers are waiting for him. Lucy and Susan hide as the Witch's allies bind, shave, torture, and mock the passive Aslan. On the Stone Table, the Witch kills Aslan with a magical knife. The Witch's army sets out for battle with Aslan's forces.

Heartbroken, Lucy and Susan creep up to Aslan's dead body and untie his muzzle. They notice little mice nibbling away at the cords binding his body. The girls leave the Stone Table for a short while and then hear a large crack. When they return, the Stone Table is broken, and Aslan's body is gone.

In disbelief, the two girls look around until they hear Aslan's voice and see him alive. He tells them, "though the Witch knew the Deep Magic, there is a magic deeper still."[4] When an innocent victim dies in the place of a guilty traitor, the Stone Table will crack and death will begin working backward.

The Witch's End

Aslan, Lucy, and Susan travel to the Witch's castle, where Aslan breathes on the stone statues to bring them back to life. Now with a considerable army of creatures, the group hurries to join the fight between the White Witch's army and the rest of Aslan's army, including Peter and Edmund. Aslan kills the Witch, and his army defeats hers. Lucy uses her magical liquid to heal the wounded.

They all travel to the castle of Cair Paravel, where Peter, Susan, Edmund, and Lucy are crowned as kings and queens. They rule for many years, driving out the rest of the Witch's followers and making fair laws. One day, as they hunt a stag, they find themselves at the old lamppost, among the fur coats, and back in the wardrobe. It is the very same day they had entered. When they tell the Professor about their journey, he hints the four siblings will soon return to Narnia—but not by the same route.

Essential Critiques

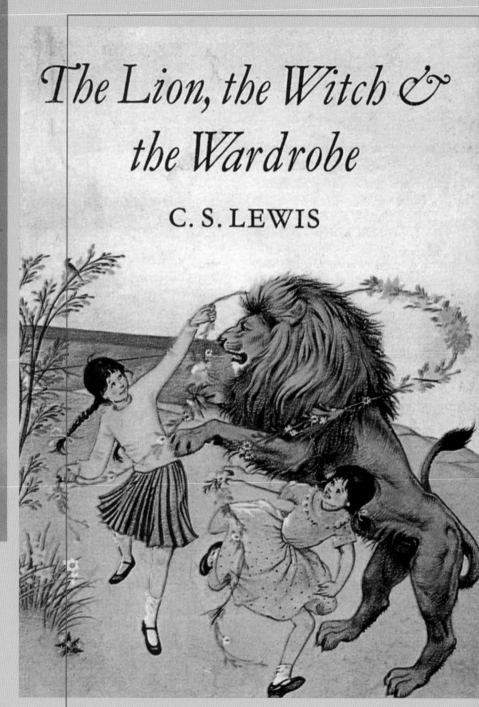

The Lion, the Witch & the Wardrobe

C. S. LEWIS

Susan and Lucy are overjoyed when they learn Aslan
has come back to life.

How to Apply Archetypal Criticism to *The Lion, the Witch and the Wardrobe*

What Is Archetypal Criticism?

Archetypal criticism, which is sometimes called myth theory, deals with recurring themes, patterns, or character types that emerge in literature. It is based on the ideas of psychologist Carl Jung, who studied the influence of the unconscious.

Jung put forth the idea of the collective unconscious, which he believed to be a part of a person's unconscious mind that is common to all people. Unlike a person's unique unconscious, which is influenced by personal experiences, the collective unconscious is inherited and ancestral. It allows humans to react to and relate to common experiences in uniform ways. According to Jung, archetypes are part of the collective unconscious, for these themes, patterns, or characters are universal throughout history.

Common character archetypes include the trickster, the antihero, the Christ figure, and the powerful woman. Examples of common structural archetypes include stories about creation, floods, hero quests, and the underworld. Studying archetypes can help identify themes and patterns in literature and relate seemingly different works of literature to each other. Identifying these underlying themes can give a reader insight into common elements of the human experience and hidden structures that guide the text and the reader.

Applying Archetypal Criticism to *The Lion, the Witch and the Wardrobe*

The archetype of the dying god can be found in many world religions, mythology, and cultures, including Jesus Christ of Christianity. Through Aslan, Lewis explores the archetype of the dying god, but Aslan is an archetype of the dying god who bears characteristics similar to Jesus Christ and highlights themes specific to the Christian faith.

Thesis Statement

The last sentence of the first paragraph is the thesis statement: "Through Aslan, Lewis explores the archetype of the dying god, but Aslan is an archetype of the dying god who bears characteristics similar to Jesus Christ and highlights themes specific to the Christian faith." This essay compares and contrasts Aslan to other myths of dying gods, but it ultimately aligns Aslan with the biblical Jesus.

<u>As a god figure who is killed, Aslan is similar to the dying gods of other world mythologies.</u> In discussing the dying gods in his essay "Myth Became Fact," Lewis specifically mentions Balder and Osiris. According to Norse mythology, Loki, a mischievous god, tricks another god into killing Balder. Although an attempt is made to rescue Balder, Balder's death is final, and he remains in the underworld. In ancient Egyptian mythology, the god Osiris represented fertility and was associated with the Nile River. As a pharaoh, Osiris was killed by another jealous god and was restored by the goddess Isis to become the god of the afterlife. In most versions of the story, Osiris did not actually rise from the dead, and like Balder, he remained in the underworld.

In *The Lion, the Witch and the Wardrobe*, Aslan's story contains elements similar to the stories of Balder and Osiris. Mr. Beaver describes Aslan as "the son of the great Emperor-beyond-the-Sea" and "the King of Beasts."[1] He maintains an elevated position above the other talking beasts in Narnia,

> **Argument One**
>
> The first argument states: "As a god figure who is killed, Aslan is similar to the dying gods of other world mythologies." The author is describing other world myths about dying gods and shows how Aslan fits into this universal archetype.

who on the whole revere, trust, and love him. While the White Witch is not on the same level as Aslan, her powers are strong enough to imprison Narnia in perpetual winter. Therefore, similar to the stories of Balder and Osiris, Aslan is a god figure who is killed by another powerful figure who functions as a peer.

Unlike Balder and Osiris, Aslan is fully raised from the dead and returns completely to his previous form. After their deaths, Balder and Osiris remain in the underworld. In Balder's story, despite an attempt to rescue him, he is not restored to his life as it was before his death. And even though Osiris is restored, his new life is very different from his former one—he is no longer a pharaoh and dwells in a new realm. But Aslan's restoration is full. The story contains no trip to the underworld, and physically, Aslan is completely resurrected. Even though the Witch's minions cut off his mane, when Aslan is resurrected, his mane has grown back. Soon after Aslan returns to life, he leaps and plays with Susan and Lucy and roars so loudly that "all

Argument Two

The second argument states: "Unlike Balder and Osiris, Aslan is fully raised from the dead and returns completely to his previous form." The author is now contrasting Aslan's story with the two example myths to set up the third argument.

the trees in front of him [bent] before the blast of his roaring as grass bends in a meadow before the wind."[2] In addition to his full physical restoration, Aslan's death is unique from other dying gods of myth because it is voluntary. He willingly gives himself as a sacrifice to save the life of the traitor Edmund. Conversely, Osiris and Balder are killed against their wills, either through trickery or murder.

Lewis's representation of Aslan closely aligns with the Christian story of Jesus Christ, and Aslan fulfills the archetype of the Christ figure. In the Bible, the Gospels record Jesus's death as both voluntary and sacrificial. Aslan's death is similarly so. He takes Edmund's place, willingly allowing the White Witch to torment and kill him to save Edmund. Furthermore, Jesus is represented in the Bible as being eternal. The Gospel of John describes Jesus as existing "in the beginning," long before being born on Earth.[3]

Ultimately, Aslan beats the White Witch through his knowledge of magic that is older than the magic

> **Argument Three**
> The third argument states: "Lewis's representation of Aslan closely aligns with the Christian story of Jesus Christ, and Aslan fulfills the archetype of the Christ figure." This argument supports the author's thesis, in which she states Aslan is an archetypal dying god, but here she argues he fits into a more specific archetype as well.

she knows. Aslan says, "Her knowledge goes back only to the dawn of time. But if she could have looked a little further back, into the stillness and the darkness before Time dawned, she would have read there a different incantation."[4] It is implied that Aslan knows this magic because, like Jesus, he was there in the beginning before the moment of creation.

Conclusion
The last paragraph is the conclusion to the essay. The author has finished her arguments and restates the thesis statement.

While Lewis's story aligns with many myths regarding the archetypal dying god, it delves further into specifically Christian themes. For centuries, humans had told stories of dying gods, and Aslan bears some of the characteristics common to these stories. In its relation to other myths about dying gods, Lewis believed Christianity is a myth that became fact.

Thinking Critically about *The Lion, the Witch and the Wardrobe*

Now it is your turn to assess the critique. Consider these questions:

1. The thesis argues that Aslan is an archetype of the dying god and that this archetype is used to emphasize Christian themes. Do you agree with this archetype, or do you see other archetypes that might fit better? What are they?

2. What other similarities or differences exist between the stories of Balder, Osiris, and Aslan? How can these similarities or differences be used to support the thesis? Could they be used to argue against it? How?

3. Do you think this conclusion effectively summarizes the thesis statement and the arguments? Why or why not? How could it be improved?

Other Approaches

This essay is just one way to analyze *The Lion, the Witch and the Wardrobe* using archetypal theory, but there are many other ways to analyze the book. One method might look at ways in which the archetype of the femme fatale, or powerful woman, is represented in the book. Another method might compare and contrast Edmund with the Judas archetype.

The White Witch as the Powerful Woman

Another familiar archetype is that of the femme fatale. This woman is so beautiful and bewitching that she ensnares men and often causes their ruin. The White Witch is certainly powerful and commanding. Physically, she is tall and intimidating, but attractive nonetheless. When Edmund first sees her in her sleigh, although her face is "proud and cold and stern," it is also described as "a beautiful face."[5]

A thesis statement for an essay exploring the White Witch as a femme fatale might be: As a powerful, beautiful woman, the White Witch proves to be a femme fatale when her charms and enchantments contribute to the moral decline of Edmund.

Edmund as Judas

Although Edmund eventually repents his betrayal of his siblings in *The Lion, the Witch and the Wardrobe*, he still bears some resemblance to the biblical Judas. A thesis statement for an essay comparing Edmund to the Judas archetype might be: Edmund's selfish betrayal of Aslan, his siblings, and the whole of Narnia is Judas-like, yet his repentance underscores the book's themes of forgiveness, redemption, and reconciliation. Arguments might include the evidence that Judas betrayed Christ for pieces of silver and Edmund betrayed Narnia for pieces of turkish delight.

Prince Caspian is living in a very different Narnia from that of *The Lion, the Witch and the Wardrobe.*

5

An Overview of
Prince Caspian

A year after their first adventure in Narnia,
Peter, Susan, Edmund, and Lucy find themselves
magically transported from a railway station to a
forested island. They happen upon an apple orchard
and a deserted, overgrown stone castle. Slowly,
the four children realize the castle is Cair Paravel.
Although only a year has passed since their last
visit, centuries seem to have passed in Narnia.
The children find the gifts given to them by Father
Christmas: Lucy's vial of magical healing liquid,
Susan's bow and arrows, and Peter's shield and
sword. Susan's magical horn is missing.

The next morning, the siblings see a small boat
floating near them. In it, two soldiers are preparing
to drown a Dwarf. Susan quickly fires an arrow
at the first soldier, and the second soldier retreats.

When the Dwarf, Trumpkin, is rescued, he tells the children about Prince Caspian.

Caspian's Story

Prince Caspian is an orphan raised by his uncle King Miraz in a castle in the middle of Narnia. Caspian loves his nurse, who tells him wonderful stories about Narnia in the old days when animals could talk. Aslan the lion came, and the Kings and Queens Peter, Susan, Edmund, and Lucy reigned after defeating the White Witch. When Miraz finds out the nurse has been telling Caspian these stories, he sends her away and hires a tutor named Doctor Cornelius for Caspian.

Through his lessons with Doctor Cornelius, Caspian learns he and his ancestors are not native Narnians, but Telmarines from a faraway country. Doctor Cornelius explains how, after the High Kings and Queens departed Narnia, Prince Caspian's ancestor, Caspian the First, fought against the talking beasts, nymphs, Dwarfs, Fauns, and other creatures of Narnia and sent them away. Miraz does not want young Caspian to learn this history. Doctor Cornelius reveals himself to be half-Dwarf, half-human, and he urges Caspian to attempt to restore the creatures of Old Narnia when he becomes King.

Over the next few years, Caspian learns much more about Old Narnia from Doctor Cornelius. One night, Doctor Cornelius wakes Caspian and urgently prepares the young man to leave for a long journey. That night, a son had been born to Miraz and his Queen. Now Caspian's life is in danger because Miraz has a male heir to the throne. Doctor Cornelius tells Caspian he is the true King of Narnia and that Miraz murdered Caspian's father years ago and took the throne unlawfully. Doctor Cornelius gives Caspian a purse of gold and Susan's magical horn.

Caspian Meets the Old Narnians

Caspian sets out immediately, but during his frantic ride through the woods, he is knocked from his horse. He wakes up in a cave and meets Trufflehunter, a talking Badger. Also in the cave are Nikabrik, a Black Dwarf, and Trumpkin, who is a Red Dwarf. Nikabrik wants to kill Caspian because he is a Telmarine, the enemy of Old Narnians, but the other two favor keeping Caspian alive. When Caspian tells them his story, the three are surprised to find stories of Old Narnians are still told among humans. Trufflehunter is eager to call Caspian the King of Narnia, but the Dwarfs doubt all humans.

In the following days, Trufflehunter and the
Dwarfs take Caspian to meet more talking creatures,
including Bears, Squirrels, Centaurs, Fauns, the
valiant Mouse Reepicheep, and Red and Black
Dwarfs. Everyone agrees to hold a midnight council
to decide what to do.

When all the Old Narnians have gathered and the
council is about to begin, Doctor Cornelius appears
to tell them Miraz is on his way. Doctor Cornelius
suggests they travel to Aslan's How, a large mound in
a wooded area near the sea, for Telmarines are fearful
of forests and the ocean. The How is where the
Stone Table stood in the children's first adventure.
Now the mound has been built over it and has been
hollowed out with tunnels and underground rooms.

Soon after they arrive, Miraz's armies begin to
engage Caspian's army of Old Narnians in battle.
Caspian's friends advise him to use Susan's horn in
the hope it will bring the great Kings and Queens of
old or Aslan to help them. Trumpkin is sent to Cair
Paravel to meet any help that might arrive there.

Help Arrives

The story shifts back to the four children as
they listen to Trumpkin tell about Caspian's need

for help. After proving to him they have skill for battle, the five set off to meet Caspian's army at Aslan's How. They soon get lost, but once they decide which way to go, Lucy sees Aslan beckoning them in the opposite direction. Everyone but Lucy and Edmund vote not to follow Aslan, and Lucy is crushed.

After an ambush by Miraz's sentries, the five travelers retreat to safety and set up camp for the night. Lucy wakes from a deep sleep to find the trees dancing and someone calling her name. It is Aslan. He instructs Lucy to wake the others and make them follow him, even though they cannot see him. Edmund trusts her, and he helps her convince everyone else. They follow Aslan to Caspian's camp, and by the time they get there, everyone can see Aslan.

Old Narnians Fight the Telmarines

When they arrive, Aslan instructs Peter, Edmund, and Trumpkin to go to Caspian's aid. Inside Aslan's How, Peter, Edmund, and Trumpkin overhear Caspian, Nikabrik, Trufflehunter, and Doctor Cornelius discussing the desperate situation. They believe no help has come from blowing

Susan's horn. Nikabrik reveals his plan to summon the White Witch and has brought a Hag and a Wer-Wolf to help him, but Caspian refuses. Peter, Edmund, and Trumpkin rush in just as a fight begins. At the end, Nikabrik, the Hag, and the Wer-Wolf are killed. Peter and Edmund introduce themselves to Prince Caspian. They all decide Peter will challenge Miraz to one-on-one combat to determine the true King of Narnia: Caspian or Miraz. Two of Miraz's power-hungry lords manipulate him into accepting.

The fight between Peter and Miraz goes back and forth, with both taking hits. Before the fight is over, Miraz's lords charge into the fight and summon the rest of the Telmarines to open battle against the Old Narnians. Miraz's own lords kill him. But the Telmarines retreat when they see the walking trees, which Aslan has awakened, storming toward them. The Telmarines turn back to cross the Bridge of Beruna, but Aslan, along with Lucy, Susan, and the rest of the group, has destroyed the bridge.

As the battle dies down, the Old Narnians gather to greet Aslan. He crowns Caspian King of Narnia under Peter the High King. Lucy heals the wounded

Reepicheep. After locking up the Telmarines, the Old Narnians enjoy a massive feast and a bonfire. The next day, Aslan sends Peter, Susan, Edmund, and Lucy back to their world, telling Peter and Susan that only Edmund and Lucy will come back to Narnia again. The four Pevensie children find themselves back at the railway station.

Edmund and the other Pevensie children fight Miraz's forces on behalf of Caspian and the Old Narnians.

The Dwarf Trumpkin is one of the Old Narnians oppressed by Miraz's rule.

How to Apply Marxist Criticism to *Prince Caspian*

What Is Marxist Criticism?

Karl Marx, who lived from 1818 to 1883, studied the struggle for economic power within nineteenth-century European society. He believed economic competition, or the struggle for access and control of resources, guided all human action. In 1848, Marx published *The Communist Manifesto*, which criticizes capitalism and predicts the rise of the working class.

In Marxist terms, *bourgeoisie* refers to the upper classes that have control of resources, and *proletariat* refers to the lower classes that have little control and often perform manual labor. Marx believed the upper classes tend to use repressive ideologies to keep the lower classes from rising up against their oppressors. For example, the ideology of the American dream might be seen as a repressive ideology. By putting forth the idea that hard work will always be rewarded by success, the upper classes can instill competition within the lower classes and keep them working on behalf of those who own economic resources. Marxist critics often look for ways in which classes are represented in a work and analyze these representations.

Applying Marxist Criticism to *Prince Caspian*

The Narnia that Peter, Susan, Edmund, and Lucy return to differs greatly from the Narnia they left. Hundreds of years have passed, and the days when the Pevensie siblings ruled Narnia justly as the High Kings and High Queens are long gone. In this new Narnia, class systems have risen and resulted in outright war between Miraz's Telmarines and Caspian's Old Narnians. The events in *Prince Caspian* illustrate the Marxist theory that within a society, the lower class will drive out the ruling class through the overturning of a repressive ideology.

Thesis Statement

The last sentence of the first paragraph is the thesis statement. It states: "The events in *Prince Caspian* illustrate the Marxist theory that within a society, the lower class will drive out the ruling class through the overturning of a repressive ideology." The author will argue that the class system within the story represents Marxist concepts.

The Telmarines are usurpers—
they are not native Narnians, but
they have assumed the role of
Narnia's aristocracy, or upper
class, through force and cruelty.
Doctor Cornelius tells Caspian
Narnia's real history and describes
true Narnia as a country of
magical creatures. This is the way
Narnia was when Peter, Susan,
Edmund, and Lucy ruled, which
was called the "Golden Age."[1] Presently, Narnia is an
unhappy place with high taxes and a cruel and violent
leader. Miraz is ruthless and power hungry. He
murders his brother to get to the throne and intends
to murder Caspian. Although the Old Narnians still
dwell in the land, they are forced
to live hidden, secretive lives with
limited freedom.

To keep their power over the
Old Narnians, the Telmarines
promote a repressive ideology
that outrightly suppresses
knowledge. Specifically, the
book notes Miraz's attempts

> **Argument One**
> The first argument states: "The
> Telmarines are usurpers—they
> are not native Narnians, but
> they have assumed the role
> of Narnia's aristocracy, or
> upper class, through force and
> cruelty." This argument sets up
> the Telmarines as the upper
> class that rules forcefully over
> the Old Narnians, who make
> up the lower class.

> **Argument Two**
> The second argument states:
> "To keep their power over the
> Old Narnians, the Telmarines
> promote a repressive
> ideology that outrightly
> suppresses knowledge."
> This argument explains how
> the book demonstrates the
> Marxist concept of repressive
> ideologies.

at preventing his subjects from learning the true history of Narnia. Miraz removes Caspian's nurse when he learns she is teaching him about Old Narnia. Doctor Cornelius tells Caspian,

> *It is you Telmarines who silenced the beasts and the trees and the fountains, and who killed and drove away the Dwarfs and Fauns, and are now trying to cover up even the memory of them. The King does not allow them to be spoken of.*[2]

A school scene describes a history lesson in Miraz's Narnia as "duller than the truest history you ever read and less true than the most exciting adventure story."[3] Furthermore, the Telmarines create stories to instill fear of the sea, for they know Aslan comes from a land beyond the sea, and they do not want Aslan to be known by their people. Similarly, Telmarines fear the forests, where the powerful tree spirits lived when Old Narnia thrived. The leaders make up stories about ghosts living in these woods to keep their subjects away from the forests.

Hope in Aslan becomes a new ideology the Old Narnians

Argument Three

Argument three states: "Hope in Aslan becomes a new ideology the Old Narnians can unite behind to overturn the repressive ideology of the Telmarines." The author focuses on the idea of Aslan as a unifying force.

can unite behind to overturn the repressive ideology of the Telmarines. Among the Old Narnians and those who favor them, siding with Aslan is the key to their success. Even though he is an Old Narnian, the Black Dwarf Nikabrik is killed when he sides with the White Witch and dark magic. Throughout the story, the Red Dwarf Trumpkin is skeptical about "magical lions" and other beliefs about Old Narnia.[4] But when he finally sees Aslan with his own eyes, he becomes Aslan's friend and contributes to the victory over Nikabrik and his

Caspian, *left*, and the Old Narnians revolt against Miraz, *right*, and his aristocratic and oppressive rule.

dark allies. Finally, once Caspian is taught the true knowledge of Narnia, he is freed from the ideology placed upon him by his own people. He escapes from the castle—the only place he has known—and slowly befriends the Old Narnians. He becomes their recognized leader through his hope in Aslan and love of Old Narnia.

Conclusion

The last paragraph is the conclusion of the essay. It restates the thesis and the arguments, highlighting the Marxist concepts present in the story.

While *Prince Caspian* contains themes of bravery, obedience, and teamwork, it is also full of Marxist concepts. The class struggles in the story highlight the role of repressive ideologies in a society. But the story offers a glimmer of hope. The book shows that by binding together with a common belief, the lower classes can unite to overturn a negative ideology and ultimately free themselves from its confines.

Thinking Critically about *Prince Caspian*

Now it is your turn to assess the critique. Consider these questions:

1. The author argues that the overturning of a repressive ideology was the key to the Old Narnians' victory. Do you agree that this is the reason for their victory? Why or why not?

2. The arguments discuss the people and creatures living in Narnia when Peter, Susan, Edmund, and Lucy arrive. How do the children fit into the story? Do they align with one of the classes, or are they in a separate category? Can you think of any ways in which their actions could support the thesis or argue against it? What are they?

3. Does the conclusion effectively summarize the thesis and arguments? Does the essay leave you thinking differently about class structures in your own society? If so, in what ways?

Other Approaches

This essay demonstrates one way to analyze *Prince Caspian* using Marxist criticism. However, even within Marxist criticism, there are a number of ways to approach a given book. Another Marxist critique of *Prince Caspian* might look at classes within the Old Narnians. A different approach might explore the concept of rugged individualism.

Classism among the Dwarfs

In the story, Doctor Cornelius the half-Dwarf faces discrimination from full-blooded Dwarfs, who do not accept him as one of their own. Nikabrik calls Doctor Cornelius "a renegade Dwarf" and a "half-and-halfer" before threatening to kill him.[5]

A thesis statement for an essay analyzing classism among the Dwarfs might state: The full-blooded Dwarfs' treatment of Doctor Cornelius shows that even the lower classes tend to dominate those below them.

Narnians and Rugged Individualism

In American society, the concept of rugged individualism goes along with the ideology of the American dream. When people in the lower classes internalize the concept of rugged individualism, they become focused on their own rise through the class system. In some ways, the actions of the Old Narnians represent an overturning of this concept.

An essay that analyzes these ideas might state: By working as a united group, the Old Narnians defy the concept of rugged individualism and prove that true change comes through group action. One example is Nikabrik, who strays from the group to come up with his own plan for victory and is eventually killed.

The majority of the third book in The Chronicles of Narnia takes place aboard the *Dawn Treader*.

An Overview of *The Voyage of the* Dawn Treader

The narrator introduces Eustace Clarence Scrubb, who is cousin to the four Pevensie children. He is a selfish, rotten boy who loves books about drains and grain elevators. Edmund and Lucy are staying with Eustace and his parents while their own parents are traveling. One day, Edmund, Lucy, and Eustace notice a picture on the wall of a ship sailing on the sea is coming to life. They find themselves drawn into the picture and flailing in the ocean. Caspian rescues the children and brings them aboard the ship. There, Lucy and Edmund are reunited with Reepicheep.

The Voyage Begins

The children learn Caspian is sailing east to find seven lost lords who were friends of his father's.

Furthermore, Reepicheep tells them he intends to sail as far east as possible in hopes of finding Aslan's country. They take a tour of the ship, the *Dawn Treader*. The reader then hears from a sullen Eustace firsthand as he begins a diary and complains about almost everything.

At the Lone Islands, Caspian, Reepicheep, Lucy, Edmund, and Eustace get off the ship to walk and explore. Slave traders soon capture the group. Caspian is bought first and learns his new master is Lord Bern, one of the seven lost lords. Lord Bern joins with Caspian to help him reunite with those onboard the *Dawn Treader*, overthrow the unfit governor of the Lone Islands, and put an end to the slave trade. Eventually, Caspian is reunited with his friends. The crew of the *Dawn Treader* replenishes their supplies, and the ship continues east.

Eustace's Transformation

Not long after departing, the group endures a terrible storm at sea. Eustace continues complaining in his journal, which explains the ship's mast has been destroyed and many of the rations have been swept overboard. The crew eventually spots an island, and they travel ashore to repair the ship, find food, and collect freshwater. Eustace sneaks away from the group.

Eustace soon comes across a dying dragon. He takes shelter in the dragon's cave and finds the dragon's store of treasure. After putting on a golden bracelet and taking some diamonds, he falls asleep. When he wakes, he is horrified to discover he has turned into a dragon. He begins to feel ashamed and lonely and regrets acting so poorly to his friends. Meanwhile, Caspian and the rest of the group look for Eustace. They soon come into contact with the dragon and realize it is Eustace transformed. They also learn that Lord Octesian, one of the seven lords, probably died on the island.

As a dragon, Eustace becomes helpful by finding food for the group and uprooting a pine tree to use for a new mast. Early one morning, Edmund awakes to find Eustace back in human form. Eustace explains that the previous night, a lion had appeared and told him to follow him to the top of a mountain. There, the lion transformed him back into a boy. Edmund tells Eustace the lion was Aslan. Eustace apologizes for his poor behavior, which improves as the group continues its journey east.

More Adventures

At the next island, the group comes across the sword and mail shirt of one of the missing seven lords. They discover a lake that turns objects into gold. Edmund and Caspian are momentarily tempted to selfishness by the discovery, but when Aslan appears, they come to their senses and move on.

As they explore the next island, Lucy falls behind and hears voices plotting to attack the group, but she sees nobody. Lucy warns Caspian and the others that they face invisible enemies. The enemies want Lucy to read a spell to make them visible again, which they say can only be recited by a little girl or the Magician in the house whom they fear.

The next morning, Lucy finds the book and starts paging through the spells. She is tempted by a spell that will make her beautiful, but Aslan appears on the page to warn her. Although Lucy skips that spell, she utters a spell to eavesdrop on her schoolmates. She hears one of her friends saying something bad about her. She finally finds the spell to make things visible. When she utters it, she hears footsteps and turns to find Aslan, who was also invisible until she read the spell. He takes Lucy to meet the Magician, Coriakin, before disappearing.

Coriakin tells Lucy about the invisible enemies, called Duffers, who are now visible. The Magician also tells them how years ago, four of the lost lords passed the island. The *Dawn Treader* continues east in search of the last four lords.

Eustace as a dragon, shown with Reepicheep, is embarrassed by his sullen attitude and poor behavior earlier in the adventure.

The Journey Ends

The ship enters a black mist. Everyone wants to turn back, but Reepicheep urges them onward. They soon hear a voice and take aboard a wild man who warns them to turn away from this place, for in it, terrible dreams come true. As they turn back, each person hears nightmarish sounds, and they fear they are lost. When Lucy asks Aslan for help, he comes in albatross form to lead them back toward the light. The man they rescue is Lord Rhoop of Narnia, one of the lost lords.

Their surroundings become increasingly beautiful as they sail east and land on another island. They come across a long banquet table spread with a tremendous feast. At one end, sit three men in an enchanted sleep. They are the three remaining lords. Everyone returns to the ship except Reepicheep, Caspian, Edmund, Lucy, and Eustace, who stay at the table overnight.

After falling asleep, the group awakes when a beautiful young woman approaches the table. She tells them how the three lords fell into the sleep and invites them to eat the food at the table, which is placed there by Aslan's will. Then the travelers meet her father, Ramandu, a retired star. Ramandu tells the travelers that, in order to break the enchanted sleep over the three lords, they must travel to World's End, but leave one person behind once they get there. Lord Rhoop is put into a dreamless sleep with the other three lords to recuperate while the *Dawn Treader* sails into the east.

As the group continues, the sun becomes larger and brighter. The water becomes shallower, and the *Dawn Treader* can sail no farther. Caspian intends to go on to World's End, but the crew talks him out of it. Aslan tells him Edmund, Lucy, and Eustace must sail with Reepicheep. The four depart from the *Dawn Treader*, which turns and sails back west.

Edmund, Lucy, Eustace, and Reepicheep sail on in a smaller boat and see a glimpse into Aslan's country. When their boat runs aground, Reepicheep alone travels on to Aslan's country, and the children turn and walk south. They meet a talking lamb, who has cooked them a fish breakfast. The lamb turns into Aslan. He tells Lucy and Edmund they will not return to Narnia. Then he sends all three children back to their own world. The *Dawn Treader* makes it back to Ramandu's island, and Caspian marries Ramandu's daughter. Back in his own world, Eustace begins to be a much better boy.

Even though she should know better, Lucy is tempted by vanity to read a spell that will make her beautiful.

How to Apply Reader-Response Criticism to *The Voyage of the* Dawn Treader

No. 2

What Is Reader-Response Criticism?

Reader-response criticism embodies a great variety of theories about how a reader interacts with a text. The school of thought asserts that when analyzing a text, the role of the reader cannot be ignored. According to author Lois Tyson, "reader-response theory . . . maintains that what a text is cannot be separated from what it does."[1] Reader-response critics argue that when readers interact with a text, they actively create meaning. Some types of reader-response criticism focus on the process of reading itself. Others analyze the reactions readers experience while interacting with a text. Some types of reader-response theory consider what examples of texts within a story might say about the experience of reading.

Applying Reader-Response Criticism to
The Voyage of the Dawn Treader

As the crew of the *Dawn Treader* lands at each island and sails the open sea, the characters face obstacles, learn lessons, and make friends. The episodes create a reader-guiding structure that combines with a number of positive and negative experiences with stories, books, myths, and journals to guide the reader to an important principle. The encounters with texts in *The Voyage of the* Dawn Treader, and the characters' responses to these encounters, illustrate to the reader the importance of not only reading well but also reading properly.

One example of this is Eustace Scrubb. Eustace is described as having read "none of the right books," and this leads him into trouble in Narnia.[2] When the reader first meets Eustace, it is clear the types of books he reads set him apart

---

Thesis Statement

This essay analyzes the examples of texts within the book to highlight its themes. The thesis states: "The encounters with texts in *The Voyage of the* Dawn Treader, and the characters' responses to these encounters, illustrate to the reader the importance of not only reading well but also reading properly."

Argument One

The author has started to support her thesis by discussing Eustace. The first argument is: "Eustace is described as having read 'none of the right books,' and this leads him into trouble in Narnia."[3]

---

from Edmund and Lucy. Eustace reads about drains and likes books with pictures of grain elevators. Eustace has not read any books that challenged his imagination or forced him to step outside the world of science. He does not know what a dragon is, much less the lore surrounding dragons. He believes in information over imagination. It is this lack of imagination that causes Eustace to be transformed into a dragon.

Additionally, Eustace's journal, a text within the text, offers a narrow, ignorant view of the circumstances because of his limited comprehension. This information about Eustace causes the reader to feel disgusted at his ignorance. The narrator contributes to this reaction as the reader witnesses Eustace's transformation into a dragon. Contrasting the reader with Eustace, the narrator says, "Most of us know what we should expect to find in a dragon's lair, but, as I said before, Eustace had read only the wrong books."[4]

In contrast to Eustace, Lucy, Edmund, Reepicheep, and Caspian are guided well

> **Argument Two**
>
> The second argument is: "In contrast to Eustace, Lucy, Edmund, Reepicheep, and Caspian are guided well by their knowledge of fairy tales and myths." The author gives examples of the characters referencing different myths and stories.

Left to right:
Caspian, Edmund,
and Lucy all use
their knowledge
of books and
fairy tales to
aid them in their
adventure.

by their knowledge of fairy tales and myths. Lucy references the story of Androcles and the lion when she encounters the dragon. By seeing a potential parallel between the story and real life, Lucy is led to compassion and helps the group recognize the dragon as Eustace. Reepicheep mentions the myth of "Fortune's Wheel" when he attempts to comfort the dragon Eustace by reciting the stories of bad luck changed to good fortune. He turns out to be correct. On one island, Edmund's knowledge of detective stories helps the group understand how a Narnian lord died—and aids them in avoiding danger themselves. Even Caspian references a fairy tale, "Sleeping Beauty," when suggesting how to wake the sleeping lords.

This knowledge of fairy tales and mythology helps the characters relate well to each other and make wise decisions about how to act because they have learned from what they have read. These anecdotes make the reader feel satisfied about the characters' well-rounded reading and application of such knowledge. It is as if their knowledge of myth, legend, and fairy tales will ensure their success.

One final experience of a text within the book gives further substance to the reader's response. When we witness Lucy reading the Magician's Book of spells, we are disappointed by her selfish reading of the text. This guides our experience as we see the dangers of reading a text with a limited or selfish view. Lucy, who has proven herself to be wise and levelheaded, is lured by the book's promises of beauty and knowledge. She is determined to read a spell to make herself beautiful until

Argument Three

The third argument is: "When we witness Lucy reading the Magician's Book of spells, we are disappointed by her selfish reading of the text. This guides our experience as we see the dangers of reading a text with a limited or selfish view." This argument takes into account what the example of Lucy does to the reader.

Aslan appears on the page to warn her. But Lucy does not learn from this and recites a spell to learn what a good friend, Marjorie, really thinks of her.

Later, Aslan tells Lucy the consequence of her actions is she will never be able to forget what Marjorie said, even though the friend does love her. We feel disappointed that although Lucy has read the right kind of books, her selfishness has caused her to read them the wrong way. She has been drawn in by vanity. This experience reinforces the theme that it is important to read good books, but we must read them properly and with an open mind.

In *An Experiment in Criticism*, Lewis wrote, "in reading great literature I become a thousand men and yet remain myself. Like the night sky in the Greek poem, I see with a myriad eyes, but it is still I who see."[5] In *The Voyage of the* Dawn Treader, the characters embody this very thought. They see the world through the eyes of others, of those whose stories they have read, yet still remain unique individuals. This combination of experiences helps them successfully navigate the waters ahead.

Conclusion
The last paragraph is the conclusion of the essay. This conclusion wraps up the arguments with a quote from Lewis, stating his opinion about reading well.

Thinking Critically about *The Voyage of the Dawn Treader*

Now it is your turn to assess the critique. Consider these questions:

1. The thesis statement asserts the importance of both reading well and reading properly. Is this idea adequately supported by the arguments? Why or why not?

2. The arguments of this essay assert that the reader experiences disgust at Eustace's ignorance and pleasure at the characters' knowledge of applicable stories. Do you think a reader might respond differently to the examples of Eustace, Reepicheep, Edmund, Lucy, and Caspian? If so, what might those reactions be?

3. Sometimes, a conclusion will introduce a new thought related to the theme of the essay. Do you think the quote from Lewis is an effective way to do this? Why or why not? How does the quote relate to reader-response criticism and this essay?

Other Approaches

This critique is only one way to approach *The Voyage of the* Dawn Treader using reader-response criticism. There are many other ways to analyze the text using this method. One might focus on the effects on the reader of the Dark Island and its vague descriptions. Another might further analyze Lucy's interaction with the Magician's Book.

The Dark Island

One method of reader-response criticism focuses on places where descriptions in the text might be missing or incomplete. These portions of text invite the reader to participate in the text by actively filling in what is not explicitly there. In *The Voyage of the* Dawn Treader, the description of the Dark Island is scant. The ship enters a vague, cold darkness. Soon, everyone on board hears his or her own version of nightmarish sounds.

A thesis statement for an essay exploring a reader's response to this scene might be: The vague descriptions of the nightmarish island provoke a psychological uneasiness and underscore the universal fear of uncertainty.

Lucy and the Book

Reader-response critiques often perform an in-depth analysis of one short section of a long book. In looking at Lucy's encounter with the magical book on Coriakin's island, an essay could analyze the text describing her desire to say the beauty spell. When she reads the spell, she sees herself elevated above Susan, and she knows her beauty would be so powerful it would harm others.

A thesis statement for an essay analyzing this scene could be: As a consistently compassionate character, Lucy's vanity suggests the certain weakness of humanity in the face of temptation.

Lewis was an avid reader and an imaginative man, and he believed an active imagination was important for young readers.

An Overview of
The Silver Chair

At his school, Experiment House, Eustace Scrubb
finds his classmate Jill Pole crying behind the gym.
She has been bullied, and he consoles her by telling
her about how he once visited another world. Jill
and Eustace begin asking Aslan to bring them to
the other world when the bullies interrupt them and
begin chasing them. As they try to hide, Jill and
Eustace find a door. When they go through it, they
know they are no longer in England.

The two classmates walk through a forest and
come to the edge of a very steep cliff. Eager to
show Eustace she is not afraid, Jill ventures near
the edge. When Eustace tries to pull her back, she
shakes him off. He loses his balance and falls over
the edge. Nearby, Jill sees a Lion blowing Eustace
up and far away. Then the Lion disappears.

Jill meets the Lion again, who tells her that her task will be difficult because her showing off led to Eustace's fall. The current King of Narnia, who is old, has no heir because his only son was lost years ago. But the Prince is still alive, and Jill must find him or die trying. The Lion gives Jill four signs to follow. First, Eustace must immediately greet the old friend he meets when he arrives in Narnia. Second, they must travel to the ruined giant city, and third, they must find the writing in the city's ruins and do what it says. Finally, they will be able to identify the Prince because he will ask them to do something in the name of Aslan. The Lion urges her to recite the signs often and follow them completely. Then the Lion blows her down and west into Narnia where she meets up with Eustace.

The First Sign Missed

Jill and Eustace have landed near a large castle where a ship waits to set sail. They observe a very old King and a well-dressed old Dwarf. Jill quickly tells Eustace about Aslan's first sign, but he does not recognize any of the people or creatures at the castle. The King gives a speech, boards the ship, and sets off.

Next, Eustace and Jill meet the Owl Glimfeather, who informs them the King they saw was Caspian. The Owl takes them to the old Dwarf, Trumpkin, who invites them into the castle of Cair Paravel. Jill tells Eustace about the four signs, and they realize they have missed the first sign by not speaking to Caspian. Later, Glimfeather takes them both to a Parliament of Owls to decide how to find the lost Prince. Jill and Eustace learn many men have died looking for the Prince.

The Owls explain that ten years earlier, the Queen was bitten by a green snake, and she died. For weeks after her death, Caspian's son, Prince Rilian, searched the country for the snake to take revenge. One day he went out and never returned. Next, the Owls take Jill and Eustace to meet Puddleglum. He is a Marsh-wiggle, a long, thin creature with webbed hands and feet and a pessimistic manner. The three set out on foot to find the ancient giant city.

In the Land of Giants

The trio encounters a few giants before coming to a wide gorge. As they cross a bridge, they see two humans on horseback coming toward them. One is a silent, helmeted knight dressed fully in black.

The other is a beautiful woman in a green dress. Jill tells the woman they seek the ancient giant city. The woman suggests they stop at the city of Harfang, where gentle giants reside. The giants will welcome them if they mention her, the Lady of the Green Kirtle. Puddleglum does not want to visit Harfang, believing it is not part of Aslan's plan. But Jill and Eustace convince him to travel there with them.

They spot Harfang from afar and spend the next day crossing rough land in a terrible snowstorm to get there. They climb up strange ledges and banks. Puddleglum reminds Jill about the signs, but she is so set on getting to the warm castle that she snaps at him and ignores his protests. When they arrive, they tell a giant of the Lady's greeting, and he brings them in.

That night, Jill dreams Aslan is in her room. He asks her to repeat the signs, but she cannot remember them. He takes her to the window, and she sees the words "UNDER ME" written in the sky. The next morning, Jill, Puddleglum, and Eustace realize all the strange things they climbed over during the snowstorm are the remains of an ancient giant city. They see the words "UNDER ME" written on the pavement. They decide to leave the giants and find a way to look under the city.

The Deep Realm

The three learn the giants intend to cook and eat them. While the giants sleep in the afternoon, Jill, Eustace, and Puddleglum escape through a kitchen door. The giants chase them, but the three travelers crawl into a crevice and block the entrance. After poking around in the darkness, they slide down a rocky slope and meet an army of Earthmen, who take them through many tunnels and caves to meet the Queen of Underland. They cross an underground lake and come to a large city with a castle.

In the castle, the Earthmen tell Jill, Eustace, and Puddleglum the Queen is away, but they meet a young human. He identifies himself as the Knight they met on the bridge, and he praises the Lady of the Green Kirtle, who is Queen of Underland. He feeds his guests and tells them his story, though he acts strangely. The young man does not remember his life before the Lady brought him to Underland. Every night, he suffers a violent fit and turns into a great serpent. He is always bound in a chair before this happens, but afterward, he does not remember anything that occurred. The Lady intends to overtake the land above and make him king. While Puddleglum, Jill, and Eustace protest at the injustice of this plan, the man does nothing but praise the Queen. But soon, he becomes serious, for he feels the hour of his transformation is coming.

Puddleglum, Jill, and Eustace stay with the Knight, who is bound to a silver chair. He makes them promise that no matter what he says, they will not release him. The Knight begins moaning and speaking clearly of his memories. He declares now he is in his right mind, and every other moment of the day he is bound by the Lady's enchantments. He begs them to release him so he can take his revenge. The three travelers are determined not to, but then he asks in the name of Aslan. The three remember the fourth sign and, after some hesitation and argument, decide to set him free.

Underland Overturned

The man first destroys the silver chair. Then he reveals he is Prince Rilian. The Lady returns and finds him freed. The Lady enchants the group and attempts to convince them all their memories of Narnia and lands above are dreams. But when Puddleglum stamps out her enchanted fire, they begin to think clearly again. The Lady turns into a giant green snake, which Puddleglum, Eustace, and Rilian kill. Rilian declares his mother avenged.

The four soon realize the Lady has enchanted
Underland to fall to pieces after her death, so they
flee on two horses. The four follow a path and find
themselves below Narnia, where a group of Fauns,
Dwarfs, and animals help dig them out. Rilian
travels back to Cair Paravel to be reunited with his
father. Jill and Eustace say good-bye to Puddleglum
and travel to Cair Paravel in time to see Caspian's
ship return, but the King is very ill. He and Rilian
embrace before the King dies. Aslan appears and
brings Jill and Eustace back to the place where their
adventure began. There, they see the dead Caspian
in a streambed. By Aslan's blood, Caspian is made
youthful again and awakes to reunite with Aslan
and Eustace. Caspian declares he would like to see
Jill and Eustace's world, and Aslan consents to send
him back with them for a few minutes. When they
arrive at Experiment House, the bullies see Eustace,
Jill, Caspian, and Aslan's back and run away.
Things change for the better at school, and Jill and
Eustace remain friends. In Narnia, Rilian buries his
father and rules a happy land.

Lewis, shown at Magdalen College in 1946, crafted *The Silver Chair* to reflect the changing values and culture of the time he was writing.

How to Apply Historical Criticism to *The Silver Chair*

What Is Historical Criticism?

Historical criticism is a method of analyzing a piece of literature by taking into account the historical context of when it was written. A critic using historical criticism studies elements of the author's life, the culture in which the author lived, and the historical events occurring when the work was being written. Then the critic looks for ways in which the work relates to these elements, or how these elements can be used to understand the text and its themes.

Historical criticism is similar to biographical criticism and cultural criticism because it takes into account forces outside the text, such as the author's life, in analyzing the work. These methods differ from critical theories that study the work only, such as New Criticism.

Applying Historical Criticism to *The Silver Chair*

In the 1930s and early 1940s, Lewis published numerous books on theology and Christian themes. While many of these books received positive feedback from the public, Lewis began receiving criticism from his colleagues for his Christian viewpoints and moralistic teaching. One Lewis biographer wrote, "Skepticism, tolerance, and even indifference were commonly thought to be the proper attitude toward Christianity."[1] In this social climate, Lewis began writing his Chronicles of Narnia. *The Silver Chair* is a reaction against the religious skepticism and changing academic philosophies of the post-World War II era.

A shift in popular philosophy in the late 1940s may have cemented Lewis's decision to move away from straight Christian apologetics and into more subtle Christian symbolism, as seen in *The*

Thesis Statement

The thesis states: *"The Silver Chair* is a reaction against the religious skepticism and changing academic philosophies of the post-World War II era." This essay analyzes the events in Lewis's life around the time he wrote the book.

Argument One

The first argument states: "A shift in popular philosophy in the late 1940s may have cemented Lewis's decision to move away from straight Christian apologetics and into more subtle Christian symbolism, as seen in *The Silver Chair*." The author discusses the philosophical shifts taking place in the 1940s, when Lewis was writing.

Silver Chair. At Oxford, Lewis became president of the Socratic Club in 1942. The group was a place for open debate between atheists, agnostics, religious skeptics, and Christians. At a meeting of the club in 1948, Catholic philosopher Elizabeth Anscombe engaged Lewis in a debate on naturalism and religion and criticized a chapter in his book _Miracles_. Lewis feared he lost the debate. To him, it was a "humiliating experience" and some believe it shook him deeply as he saw firsthand that popular philosophies were changing to embrace a general skepticism about objective religious or moral truths.[2] Lewis did not publish any more directly apologetic works, but he was not finished writing on Christian topics.

Eustace and Jill's school, Experiment House, is a satire of postwar England's educational philosophies seeking to impart modern ideas and throw out any moral absolutes. Experiment House is described as a coeducational school run by people with "mixed" minds who have "the idea that boys and girls should

> **Argument Two**
> The second argument states: "Eustace and Jill's school, Experiment House, is a satire of postwar England's educational philosophies seeking to impart modern ideas and throw out any moral absolutes." The author compares Experiment House to schools in England after World War II.

The bullying common at British schools in the 1950s and when Lewis was a child is reflected in Jill and Eustace's school, Experiment House.

be allowed to do what they liked."[3] Therefore, because boys and girls like power and control, a system of student bullying dominates the school, which both Jill and Eustace have experienced firsthand.

Instead of intervening to help the bullied students, the head of the school treats them as "interesting psychological cases."[4] Because of these "curious methods of teaching," students do not learn much about the basic subjects or how to behave morally.[5] Instead, students who bully others learn that bullying is acceptable in society. The victims of bullying learn how to avoid the bullies or tolerate suffering. As a child, Lewis himself was bullied. This depiction parallels Lewis's negative view of the progressive education of English schools.

As far as religion is concerned, Eustace is ignorant of the Bible because "Bibles were not encouraged at Experiment House."[6] When Jill and Eustace get to Narnia, they are confused by a biblical reference because "people at Experiment House haven't heard of Adam and Eve."[7] Experiment House is portrayed as a place where chaos reigns and old systems of educational philosophy, which focused on being a moral person and the consequences of bad behavior, have been thrown out to the detriment of all.

Within Narnia, Aslan's four signs represent Lewis's own belief in the guiding power of reason and truth. When Aslan gives Jill the four signs, he urges her to remember them at all costs, for they will guide her on her quest for Rilian. She must recite them to herself over and over and

> **Argument Three**
> The third argument analyzes the signs given by Aslan. The argument states: "Within Narnia, Aslan's four signs represent Lewis's own belief in the guiding power of reason and truth."

follow them no matter what. Aslan urges Jill to "remember the signs and believe the signs. Nothing else matters."[8]

She and Eustace miss the first sign because he does not recognize the aged Caspian, but the missing of the second and third signs are due to Jill's neglecting to recite the signs to herself. She forgets them and becomes consumed with thoughts of tangible things, such as warm beds and hot baths in Harfang. She even tells Puddleglum to "bother the signs."[9] Jill has forgotten her guiding principles—her absolutes. She loses her way and puts herself and others in the path of dangerous giants. The popular philosophies at the time Lewis was writing *The Silver Chair* denied any scientific, moral, or religious truth. The strong emphasis Lewis places on the four signs, as well as the consequences of them being ignored, could be seen as a reflection of his own conviction in guiding principles.

The Lady of the Green Kirtle represents the voice of philosophies that deny moral and religious absolutes. Aboveground, the Lady is

---

Argument Four

The last argument analyzes the character of the Lady of the Green Kirtle. The argument states: "The Lady of the Green Kirtle represents the voice of philosophies that deny moral and religious absolutes."

beautiful in appearance and manner. She entices Jill and Eustace to visit Harfang, blinding them to the signs and muddling their minds. After the encounter with her, Jill and Eustace "never talked about Aslan, or even the lost Prince" because they are thinking only of the physical comforts of Harfang.[10]

Once underground, the Lady reveals her true nature. When she discovers Rilian is freed from her enchantments, she attempts to enslave them all. Her magical instrument and enchanted fire have the effect of clouding her captives' thoughts as she attempts to convince them that their memories of Narnia are dreams. She mocks their description of the sun, declaring it would be impossible for such a thing to hang in the sky. She denies Aslan's existence and declares her world is the real world. She eventually succeeds in making all four say aloud that there is no sun before Puddleglum stamps out the fire and ends her control over their minds. The Lady's attempt to enchant her captives into believing their true memories are false is a representation of the influence of the popular philosophies skeptical toward Christianity on a culture formerly more accepting of the religion.

Conclusion

The last paragraph is the conclusion of the essay. It partially restates the thesis and summarizes the arguments. The conclusion also takes the thesis a step further with the idea that the book illustrates Lewis's stance on the importance of absolute truth.

In the years prior to the publication of *The Silver Chair*, Lewis faced criticisms of his belief system and apologetic efforts. While he no longer wrote apologetic books, he continued to publish books reacting against the prevailing voices of his culture. *The Silver Chair* indicates Lewis's stance on the importance of absolute truth amidst a sea of philosophies that would disagree.

Thinking Critically about *The Silver Chair*

Now it is your turn to assess the critique. Consider these questions:

1. The thesis states the book is a reaction against philosophies and attitudes that were common at the time it was written. Do you agree or disagree? Explain.

2. The first argument helps give context for what was happening in Lewis's life in the years prior to the publication of *The Silver Chair*. Do you think this argument is necessary? Would the essay make sense without it? Why or why not?

3. Does the conclusion effectively restate the thesis and summarize the arguments? Why or why not?

Other Approaches

This essay is just one of many ways to explore *The Silver Chair* using historical criticism. Remember that historical critics study the personal, political, social, and economic events that occurred around the time a story was written. Then the critic analyzes how these relate to the author or the story. Other ways to analyze *The Silver Chair* might focus on imagination among the children of Lewis's day or the nation of England after World War II.

Lewis and a Culture Lacking Imagination

When Lewis hosted children at his home during World War II, he noted their lack of imagination. *The Silver Chair*, which contains talking beasts, giants, and otherworldly creatures, nonetheless takes place in a world that is very real to Jill and Eustace.

A thesis statement for an essay exploring these ideas might be: Lewis wrote *The Silver Chair* as a morality tale that stresses the importance of imagination to a culture that did not value it.

Puddleglum as Encourager

Characterized as serious and pessimistic, Puddleglum seems unlikely to be an encouraging character. But some literary critics believe the character of Puddleglum represents faith and constancy. This steadfastness could be seen as representative of the nation of England during the time Lewis was writing. The years from 1939 to 1945, during which England was engaged in World War II, were tumultuous, yet the English united to fight and win the war.

A thesis statement for an essay connecting these ideas might be: In his faithfulness and constancy, Puddleglum stands as a reflection of and an encouragement to the English people after the devastation of World War II.

You Critique It

Now that you have learned about different critical theories and how to apply them to literature, are you ready to perform your own critique? You have read that this type of evaluation can help you look at literature in a new way and make you pay attention to certain issues you may not have otherwise recognized. So, why not use one of the critical theories profiled in this book to consider a fresh take on your favorite book?

First, choose a theory and the book you want to analyze. Remember that the theory is a springboard for asking questions about the work.

Next, write a specific question that relates to the theory you have selected. Then you can form your thesis, which should provide the answer to that question. Your thesis is the most important part of your critique and offers an argument about the work based on the tenets, or beliefs, of the theory you are applying. Recall that the thesis statement typically appears at the very end of the introductory paragraph of your essay. It is usually only one sentence long.

After you have written your thesis, find evidence to back it up. Good places to start are in the work itself or in journals or articles that discuss what other people have said about it. Since you are critiquing a book, you may also want to read about the author's life so you can get a sense of what factors may have affected the creative process. This can be especially useful if working within historical, biographical, or psychological criticism.

Depending on which theory you are applying, you can often find evidence in the book's language, plot, or character development. You should also explore parts of the book that seem to disprove your thesis and create an argument against them. As you do this, you might want to address what other critics have written about the book. Their quotes may help support your claim.

Before you start analyzing a work, think about the different arguments made in this book. Reflect on how evidence supporting the thesis was presented. Did you find that some of the techniques used to back up the arguments were more convincing than others? Try these methods as you prove your thesis in your own critique.

When you are finished writing your critique, read it over carefully. Is your thesis statement understandable? Do the supporting arguments flow logically, with the topic of each paragraph clearly stated? Can you add any information that would present your readers with a stronger argument in favor of your thesis? Were you able to use quotes from the book, as well as from other critics, to enhance your ideas?

Did you see the work in a new light?

Timeline

1898 Clive Staples Lewis is born in Belfast, Northern Ireland, on November 29.

1916 Lewis takes his entrance examination for the University of Oxford. He is accepted at University College in Oxford, England.

1917 On November 29, Lewis arrives in the French trenches to fight in World War I.

1931 On September 22, Lewis converts to Christianity.

1930 Lewis moves into the Kilns, which he purchases with his brother and Mrs. Moore.

1933 In May, *The Pilgrim's Regress* is published.

1940 *The Problem of Pain* is published in October.

1941–1944 Lewis gives radio talks that discuss morality and other Christian and philosophical topics.

1942 A collection of entries for the *Guardian* newspaper are compiled into *The Screwtape Letters*, which is published in February to extraordinary success.

1919 Lewis returns to Oxford in January; in March, his first book, *Spirits in Bondage*, is published.

1924 In October, Lewis begins teaching at Oxford, then at Magdalen College.

1950 *The Lion, the Witch and the Wardrobe* is published. It is the first book in The Chronicles of Narnia.

1952 Lewis's radio recordings are compiled into the book *Mere Christianity*; Lewis meets Joy Davidman, whom he has exchanged letters with since 1950.

1955 Lewis's spiritual autobiography, *Surprised by Joy*, is published.

1956 Lewis marries Davidman.

1960 Davidman dies in July.

1961 Lewis publishes *A Grief Observed*.

1963 Lewis suffers from a heart attack and falls into a coma in July; he dies on November 22.

Glossary

agnostic
> A person who does not believe in the existence or nonexistence of God, but who believes such things are unknowable.

apologetics
> A branch of theology that deals with the defense of Christianity.

archetype
> A recurring plot, character, or theme in literature.

atheist
> A person who does not believe in the existence of God or gods.

bourgeoisie
> In Marxist terms, the highest, or ruling, class that has control of resources in a society.

capitalism
> An economic system in which goods are privately owned and the government intervenes little in trade.

collective unconscious
> According to Carl Jung, a part of a person's unconscious mind that is common to all people.

cynical
> Distrustful.

Faun
> A mythical creature that is half human and half goat.

myriad
> A great number.

occult

Practices and beliefs regarding the supernatural.

pessimistic

Negative.

preternatural

Something abnormal or outside the laws of nature.

proletariat

In Marxist terms, the lowest class, who have little access to resources and often perform manual labor.

repressive ideology

A belief system imposed by the upper classes on the lower classes to keep them from rising up against the upper class.

Bibliography of Works and Criticism

Important Works

Spirits in Bondage, 1919

Dymer, 1926

The Pilgrim's Regress, 1933

The Allegory of Love, 1936

The Problem of Pain, 1940

The Screwtape Letters, 1942

Perelandra, 1943

The Abolition of Man, 1943

That Hideous Strength, 1945

Miracles, 1947

The Lion, the Witch and the Wardrobe, 1950

Prince Caspian, 1951

The Voyage of the Dawn Treader, 1952

Mere Christianity, 1952

The Silver Chair, 1953

The Horse and His Boy, 1954

The Magician's Nephew, 1955

Surprised by Joy, 1955

The Last Battle, 1956

Till We Have Faces, 1956

A Grief Observed, 1961

An Experiment in Criticism, 1961

Critical Discussions

MacSwain, Robert, and Michael Ward, eds. *The Cambridge Companion to C. S. Lewis*. New York: Cambridge UP, 2010. Print.

Rogers, Jonathan. *The World According to Narnia: Christian Meaning in C. S. Lewis's Beloved Chronicles*. New York: Warner Faith, 2005. Print.

Ward, Michael. *Planet Narnia: The Seven Heavens in the Imagination of C. S. Lewis*. New York: Oxford UP, 2008. Print.

Resources

Selected Bibliography

Green, Roger Lancelyn, and Walter Hooper. *C. S. Lewis: A Biography*. New York: Harcourt, 1974. Print.

Lewis, C. S. *On Stories, and Other Essays on Literature*. New York: Harcourt, 1982. Print.

Lewis, C. S. *Surprised by Joy: The Shape of My Early Life*. New York: Harcourt, 1956. Print.

Sayer, George. *Jack: A Life of C. S. Lewis*. Wheaton, IL: Crossway, 1994. Print.

Further Readings

Dorsett, Lyle W., and Marjorie Lamp Mead, eds. *C. S. Lewis: Letters to Children*. London: Collins, 1985. Print.

Ford, Paul F. *Companion to Narnia: A Complete Guide to the Magical World of C. S. Lewis*. New York: Harper, 2005. Print.

Howard, Thomas. *Narnia and Beyond: A Guide to the Fiction of C. S. Lewis*. San Francisco: Ignatius, 2006. Print.

Lynn, Steven. *Texts and Contexts: Writing about Literature with Critical Theory*. Boston: Longman, 2011. Print.

Web Links

To learn more about critiquing the works of
C. S. Lewis, visit ABDO Publishing Company online
at **www.abdopublishing.com**. Web sites about the works
of C. S. Lewis are featured on our Book Links page.
These links are routinely monitored and updated
to provide the most current information available.

For More Information

Marion E. Wade Center

351 East Lincoln Avenue, Wheaton IL, 60187

630-752-5908

www.wheaton.edu/wadecenter

The Wade Center maintains a collection of materials from
several British authors, including C. S. Lewis. Artifacts
include Lewis's childhood wardrobe, letters, the original
map of Narnia, and books from Lewis's own library.

The New York C. S. Lewis Society

84-23, 77th Avenue, Glendale, NY 11385-7706

www.nycslsociety.com/index.html

Founded in 1969, this group holds monthly meetings to
discuss Lewis and his writings.

Source Notes

Chapter 1. Introduction to Critiques
None.

Chapter 2. A Closer Look at C. S. Lewis

1. C. S. Lewis. *Surprised by Joy: The Shape of My Early Life*. New York: Harcourt, 1956. Print. 58.

2. Ibid. 237.

Chapter 3. An Overview of *The Lion, the Witch and the Wardrobe*

1. C. S. Lewis. *The Lion, the Witch and the Wardrobe*. New York: Harper, 1994. Print. 11.

2. Ibid. 19.

3. Ibid. 67.

4. Ibid. 150.

Chapter 4. How to Apply Archetypal Criticism to *The Lion, the Witch and the Wardrobe*

1. C. S. Lewis. *The Lion, the Witch and the Wardrobe*. New York: Harper, 1994. Print. 79.

2. Ibid. 164.

3. The Holy Bible, English Standard Version. John 1:1. Wheaton, IL: Crossway Bibles, 2001.

4. C. S. Lewis. *The Lion, the Witch and the Wardrobe*. New York: Harper, 1994. Print. 163.

5. Ibid. 31.

Chapter 5. An Overview of *Prince Caspian*

None.

Source Notes Continued

Chapter 6. How to Apply Marxist Criticism to *Prince Caspian*

1. C. S. Lewis. *Prince Caspian: The Return to Narnia*. New York: Harper, 1994. Print. 54.

2. Ibid. 51.

3. Ibid. 199.

4. Ibid. 148.

5. Ibid. 88.

Chapter 7. An Overview of *The Voyage of the* Dawn Treader

None.

Chapter 8. How to Apply Reader-Response Criticism to *The Voyage of the* Dawn Treader

1. Lois Tyson. *Critical Theory Today: A User-Friendly Guide*. New York: Garland, 1999. Print. 154.

2. C. S. Lewis. *The Voyage of the* Dawn Treader. New York: Harper, 1994. 84.

3. Ibid. 84.

4. Ibid. 87.

5. Ibid. 141.

Chapter 9. An Overview of *The Silver Chair*

None.

Chapter 10. How to Apply Historical Criticism to *The Silver Chair*

1. George Sayer. *Jack: A Life of C. S. Lewis.* Wheaton, IL: Crossway, 1994. Print. 285.

2. Ibid. 308.

3. C. S. Lewis. *The Silver Chair*. New York: Harper, 1994. Print. 3.

4. Ibid. 3.

5. Ibid. 3–4.

6. Ibid. 7.

7. Ibid. 42.

8. Ibid. 27.

9. Ibid. 101.

10. Ibid. 92.

Index

About the Author

Amy Van Zee is an editor and writer who lives near Minneapolis, Minnesota. She has an English degree from the University of Minnesota and has contributed to dozens of educational books.

Photo Credits

John Chillingworth/Picture Post/Getty Images, cover, 3; Everett Collection, 12, 98; Keith Hamshere/Savoy Pictures/ Photofest, 21; Walt Disney/Everett Collection, 22; Advertising Archive/Everett Collection, 30; Walt Disney/Everett Collection, 40, 47, 48, 53; Twentieth Century Fox Film Corp./ Everett Collection, 58, 63, 70; Phil Bray/Fox-Walden/Everett Collection, 66; John Chillingworth/Getty Images, 76; Hans Wild/Time & Life Pictures/Getty Images, 84, 99; Maurice Ambler/Picture Post/Getty Images, 88